COLD AS
ICE

RACHEL JONAS & NIKKI THORNE

RACHEL
JONAS

&

NIKKI
THORNE

SAVAGE KINGS OF
Bradwyn
U

CONTENTS

COPYRIGHTS

Published September, 2023

WRITTEN AS RACHEL JONAS

THE LOST ROYALS SAGA
The Genesis of Evangeline
Dark Side of the Moon
Heart of the Dragon
Season of the Wolf
Fate of the Fallen

DRAGON FIRE ACADEMY
First Term
Second Term
Third Term

THE VAMPIRE'S MARK
Dark Reign
Hell Storm
Cold Heir
Crimson Mist

**WRITTEN AS RACHEL JONAS
& NIKKI THORNE**

KINGS OF CYPRESS POINTE
Golden Boys
Never his Girl
Forever Golden
#Pretty Boy D
#Mr. Silver
#SexyBeast

SAVAGE KINGS OF BRADWYN U
Break the Girl
Cold As Ice

DESCRIPTION

I swore I'd never fall for an enemy, but now... I've fallen for them all.

The Savages are ruthless on ice and downright coldhearted in every other way. They once promised to ruin me—and came incredibly close to succeeding—but our hearts have aligned, and my secrets are theirs, too.

Tragedy has again darkened my world, leaving me afraid of my own shadow. I swear there's danger lurking around every corner. Still, these four have vowed to protect me at all costs.
Whoever did this is about to learn a valuable lesson.

The only thing worse than messing with a Savage... is messing with their girl.

Warning: This book is dark and twisted, but keep in mind that it's a work of fiction. Nothing between these pages reflects the authors' views, nor does it imply that they condone any of the situations or actions you'll read within the series.

Authors' Note/Trigger Warning: This book was written purely for your entertainment. Be advised, this series contains the following scenarios and themes that may not be suitable for all readers: *violence, drug use, dubious consent, knife play, stalking, mention of various forms of abuse, reference to off-page sexual assault, reference to off-page suicide, and kidnapping.*

This list is in no way exhaustive, so please read responsibly and at your own risk.

For all inquiries, please contact:
author.racheljonas@gmail.com or visit www.racheljonasauthor.com

Thank you for your purchase! I would love to get your feedback once you've finished the book! Please leave a review and let others know what you thought of
COLD AS ICE
https://amzn.to/3PhNxGr

You can stay up to date on new releases and sales by joining my **Facebook Group.**
https://www.facebook.com/groups/141633853243521

DEDICATION

This one's for the unapologetically loud, fierce, magnetic girl I met in 8th grade, who taught me that curves aren't a curse but a blessing.

That year, I learned to love myself and never stopped.

Chapter 1

Tate

"Is everything okay?"

The groggy voice on the other end of the line incites guilt. He was asleep. Of course, he was. It's almost midnight and there's no clearer sign of desperation than when someone calls their therapist this late.

I hate thinking of myself in that light—weak, desperate, lacking control.

"Hello, Tate? Are you still there?"

I've reached the front door of The Den when Dr. Owens' voice comes through my phone. This place was my home for years, a sanctuary I shared with my brothers. But now? I can't even bring myself to step foot inside. Not yet. All because I'm pretty sure Stevie's in there, hanging out with the guys, like the shit we got into this weekend was normal.

Like it didn't shine light on how broken and depraved we all are. At the thought of her—my live and in-the-flesh reminder of what a dick I am—I feel this soul-crushing weight on my chest, knowing I haven't sorted out what my next move will be.

Avoidance? Pretending I'm indifferent toward her, like it never even happened? Or will it really not matter what I decide because… she's got this tight fucking hold on me, this ability to control my thoughts, my actions.

If I'm honest, it's been that way since the moment I laid eyes on her months ago. While we sat seated at the same table as her mother and my father, discussing their wedding plans and ideas for family vacations.

"Tate?"

"I—yes. I'm here," I finally answer, dropping down onto the porch steps.

"How can I help? You don't sound like yourself. Did something happen?"

Dr. Owens' questions have me weighing my words, honestly thinking I should just end the call before I make a complete ass of myself. Then again, I called him for a reason.

"I messed up." A sigh leaves me as scenes from the last twenty-four hours flash in my head—Stevie with *me*, Stevie with the *others*.

Everything.

I lower my head, grip my hair, still unable to wrap my head around it—the things we did to her. The things she *let* us do to her. The way I enjoyed it.

Stop. She's off limits for a million different reasons. That can't happen again.

Even if you really, really want it to.

"Okay," Dr. Owens says. "Messed up how? Whatever it is, I'm sure we can work through it."

The way he says it makes things sound so simple. Meanwhile, this situation is anything but that. My eyes fall shut as I feel Stevie's breath against my lips, her hands warming the back of my neck, serving as a reminder of why I've dialed him in the middle of the night.

"It's been six months," I finally speak up, staring blankly across the lawn while I get it all out. "I've stuck to my guns. No close calls. No slipups. Not until last night," I add with a deep breath.

"Based on past conversations, I take it this means you were recently intimate with someone?" Dr. Owens asks.

I nod like he's here in the flesh. "Something like that."

He's quiet, maybe processing. It doesn't really matter that what happened between me and Stevie wasn't actual sex. That's just a technicality. The point is that I was weak enough that I would have let it go as far as *she* would have.

In a heartbeat.

No questions asked.

"If you're comfortable talking about it, I'd like to hear how this came about."

I gather my thoughts, aware of Stevie still being with me. Like a ghost, haunting me now that we've given in, now that the memory of her taste and the feel of her live rent-free inside my head. Dr. Owens has made it clear on many occasions that he doesn't see how completely abstaining from sex will benefit me, but he might understand if I stopped holding back, if I told him how bad things had truly become.

I vowed to change, vowed to leave the past behind. A past that includes having shared my bed—the backseat of my car, brick walls in random alleys, and public bathrooms—with countless women whose names I never remember. A past that also occasionally included dodging pissed off boyfriends or husbands I didn't know were in the picture.

Once at gunpoint, might I add.

At the end of the day, I just got tired. Of *everything*—the drama, the emptiness, using sex as a Band-Aid for the shit that's *really* wrong with me.

"Tate?"

The sound of Dr. Owens' voice brings me back to the present, and I recall him waiting on a response.

"Some friends and I went away this weekend, and I was with a girl last night, but… she wasn't just any girl."

"Okay," he says, sounding a bit more coherent now than when I first dialed him. "Was she one of these friends you mentioned?"

The question is hard to answer. "No, not a friend."

He hesitates. "Okay, is she an ex? A co-worker maybe?"

I feel like literal shit, thinking my answer before it finally leaves my mouth.

"She's… my stepsister. Well, she will be in the coming months," I admit.

The silence that follows doesn't surprise me. I get it. This isn't at all the answer he expected.

"Hm, I—okay," he says lightheartedly, a tactic he employs to dispel any thoughts that he might be passing judgment. "Let's unpack that. Is there a concern that your... *encounter* will complicate things? Any concern that this could affect your parents in some way if they were to find out?"

"Yes. All of this."

He clears his throat. "Okay, well, I think it's important to look at the facts. There isn't anything particularly unhealthy or wrong here, per se. As long as you and *any* partner you choose feels safe and these acts are mutually consensual, it's my opinion that you're free to do what you please, Tate. You're young and responsible. So, as far as I'm concerned, who you choose to be intimate with is no one else's business."

I hear him, *have* heard him for months now. He isn't a fan of the guilt I carry for having been such an asshole in the past, but it's deeper than that. I've chosen this because sex was becoming a crutch, an excuse to ignore trauma and shit from the past.

The end result?

It all became so... fucking... empty.

I was empty.

Dr. Owens speaks again, but I tune him out, not needing to be coddled or excused for my behavior. Deep down, before I even dialed him, I knew what the solution would be, so I make a snap decision to end the call and man up, preparing to do what I feel in my gut is right.

"Thank you for your time. Sorry I disturbed you," I cut in, interrupting him midsentence before hanging up.

His opinion is valuable to me, but in this instance, fuck his professional analysis and whatever other bullshit he was just rambling about. There's only one solution.

When it comes to Stevie, I have to keep my distance, pack all the emotion and sexual tension neatly inside a box, and pretend we never let that shit out in the first place. It's the only solution. Otherwise, things will get incredibly complicated, potentially jeopardizing our parents' happiness, and that can't happen. It has to be this way.

Has to be.

She'll understand. Outside of family situations, outside of whatever help I can offer where sorting out her sister's assault is concerned, I won't get close. Not again.

Standing from the porch, I decide to head inside to give my newfound sense of resolve a test run. Mentally, I'm preparing to feign indifference when I lay eyes on Stevie, but I lose my train of thought when my hand slips from the knob as someone snatches it open from the other side.

The look of frustration in Micah's eyes, the distress in Ash's brow, and the tension in Vince's shoulders can only mean one thing. Something's gone terribly wrong. It confirms as much when all three storm past like I'm not even there, hyper-focused on getting to Ash's truck as they trudge down the sidewalk. And that's when I take note of something.

She's not with them.

"What happened? Where's Stevie?"

Damn. Not even five minutes into my resolution and I'm already faltering, seeking her out.

There's no break in Micah's stride as he tosses a response over his shoulder.

"Not with us," he answers. "And she's not picking up her phone either. If you want answers, you'll have to ride."

None of them slow their pace, so it looks like I'm going wherever *they* are, with their sense of worry proving to be contagious. There's a sick feeling in my gut, though, and I'm reminded of my recent vow to keep my distance from the one girl capable of making me break my own damn rules. But joining them tonight doesn't have to mean I'm going back on my word. It *can't.* I'm still committed to not getting wrapped up in whatever she has going on with my brothers.

So, I'll join them tonight, make sure she's safe, but after that? I'm stepping back. As far back as humanly possible.

Because if I don't, if I fail to contain the flame that ignited the night we met, I can honestly say there's no guarantee this won't turn into a wildfire.

Unpredictable.

Consuming.

Destructive.

And for fuck's sake, nobody wants that.

Chapter 2

Micah

All at once, the doors of the truck slam shut. Then, the engine revs. Knowing how Ash drives even when there *isn't* an emergency, I know to brace myself now that there is. As expected, he takes off, going from zero to eighty in what feels like no time at all, but I'm all for it. We all feel the pressing need to haul ass.

My gut could be wrong. Bird could be perfectly fine. Only, deep down, something tells me we need to get to her as quickly as possible.

She wouldn't just ghost us. Before, I would've said this out of arrogance, claiming that she knows better. But now, with how things have changed, it's more than that. While her connection to us is still something I don't fully understand, I'm done denying it. Yes, she gives us shit, goes out of her way to remind us that we don't own her, but she wouldn't do this.

Not knowing we'd be waiting around to hear how things went.

Everyone's silent. I take it to mean they're focused on not thinking the worst, focused on figuring this shit out, focused on having her back with us.

Out of habit, I check the app again and, as expected, nothing's changed. Bird's icon shows that she's still where she was when I looked a few minutes ago. Still where she was when I looked *an hour* ago.

"Tell me everything you know about this Tory chick." I turn to gaze out the window while waiting for Tate to answer.

He sighs and, with his height, his knee nudges the back of my seat when he shifts. "I've known her family through her father for years. She's a good kid—straight A's, competitive chess player, swim team, in church every week with the rest of her family. Doesn't give her parents any trouble from what I've seen."

"And how's she connected to all this shit with Stevie's sister?"

"From my understanding, she and Mel were good friends, and they were together the night of the assault."

"Got her number?" I ask.

"She's a kid. Why the fuck would I have her number?" Tate shoots back. "I told Stevie to look her up on social media."

"What about her father?"

Tate sighs. "Yes, I have his number, but I'd rather not involve him until we know there's a good reason."

"Bird's missing. Isn't that reason enough?" I snap, feeling heat creep up the back of my neck.

It's always like this. Tate's older and has had our back through some pretty ugly shit, but he doesn't know how to turn off the fucking rationale and just... be in the moment. And right now, in *this* moment, we don't need Analytical Tate.

We need Get-Shit-Done Tate.

I know he's still in there. Having a fucking W-9 on file with the university shouldn't change that.

I feel his eyes burning a hole through the back of my head, but I'm not really in the mood to give a shit about anyone's feelings. I've got my own emotions to keep in check right now, as my head fills with unwanted images from a past I wish I could erase from memory. Images of an innocent girl I failed all those years ago.

And I can't let that happen again.

Ever.

"Speed up."

Ash responds to my words by pressing down on the pedal, moving the needle on the speedometer to ninety.

"How do we know she's missing?" Tate asks, and I fight to quench the flare of annoyance that has my fists clenching. I'm not in the mood to reiterate this shit, but I did promise him answers, so...

"I used an app, synced my phone to hers, and the last forty-fuck-ing-times I checked it, she's been in the same place. Somewhere across town."

Tate doesn't speak, which usually means his wheels are turning, trying to make sense of the bits and pieces I've given. It's not his fault he's lost. He came in on the tail end of things, missing the part where I, along with Ash and Vince, happily did all the twisted shit we could think of to Bird. And in an effort to be as efficient in that endeavor as possible, we needed to know her whereabouts at all times.

When we left the cabin this morning, I was *this* close to untethering her phone from mine. But for some reason, I couldn't do it. And when she didn't bring it up, I decided it could wait.

Now, as it's become our sole lifeline to her, I'm grateful for that decision.

"We should've just taken her ourselves," Vince grumbles from the backseat. I toss a look over my shoulder toward him as he stares out the window, his jaw flexing in frustration.

I don't disagree but keep my thoughts to myself as I face forward again.

"Is it possible she just went somewhere to think?" Tate asks, and I grip the handle above the door when Ash takes a sharp right. "I mean, shit, for all we know things didn't go well today. Maybe Tory brought out things Stevie didn't want to hear, and she just doesn't feel like talking, doesn't want to be found."

"Yeah, well, she doesn't have that option," Ash chimes in. "We shut the world out, but not each other. That's how this works."

He leaves it at that, but even having said so little, it's clear he sees Bird like I do, like Vince does. And hell, maybe even like Tate's hard-to-read ass does. But what I think Ash is trying to say is... Bird's one of us now. Through and through.

19

We might be a little fucked up in the head, but we're loyal. Maybe to a fault. And the way I see it, regardless of whatever bullshit came first... that loyalty extends to Bird, too.

We licked her, she's ours.

Those are the fucking rules.

If something's happened to her tonight, if someone's laid so much as a *finger* on her... they're dead.

It's fucking inevitable.

The truck slows at the curb and Ash barely has it in park when Vince and I hop out. I stare up the side of all 4 stories of aged brick, the pattern occasionally interrupted by graffiti and broken windows. It's an old warehouse or manufacturing building, but there's no question it's deserted.

Ignoring the warning signs blaring inside my head, I rush in with reckless abandon, crossing the threshold into the dark space beyond it. Three sets of footsteps trail me, and no one's saying a word. I'm positive we're all thinking the same thing.

Why the fuck did Bird's phone lead us here?

"No way this is the place," Vince says under his breath, peering up as we all take in the state of this shithole. Moonlight filters in through dirty windows and spaces of the walls where the cinderblocks have crumbled and fallen away.

"Should we split up?"

"Two go up, two stay on this floor to look around," I shoot back, answering Ash's question.

"No, first we need to try calling again. If she *is* here, or at least if her phone is, we might be able to hear it." Tate finishes, then dials while the rest of us wait, damn-near vibrating with anticipation, wondering what the fuck is going on.

"We shouldn't have let her go alone." I step toward a window, peering down to the alley while I acknowledge how this could've all been avoided. The feel of Ash's hand on my shoulder doesn't bring even an ounce of comfort, but I'm sure he means well.

It's true, though. We should've been with her, or at least tailed her if she didn't want us getting in the way, because who even knows what the hell is really going on with all this shit? It's entirely possible that what happened to her sister was just a small piece of a much bigger picture, and we let our girl walk right into the lion's den.

Alone.

"Shit."

The sound of my voice has Vince eying me when I begin to pace.

"Ok, it should be ringing," Tate whispers, and we're so silent I don't think anyone's even breathing. I listen, then I listen harder. Then, when the ringing stops and Stevie's voicemail kicks on, I've never felt more defeated in my fucking life.

"Try again," Ash demands, and without hesitation, Tate dials.

This time, I close my eyes, counting down the seconds until I lose my shit and start demolishing walls with my bare fists, but like an answered prayer, the faint undertones of a song begin to float in from some unknown space. It's so quiet we missed it the first time, but I know I'm not insane.

"This way!"

I don't wait for the others or even consider the endless list of safety hazards. All I can think about—all *any* of us are thinking about —is her.

We're swift, we're reckless, all bounding toward the same sound. It's unclear whether I'm feeling more relieved or terrified as we get closer, unsure what we'll find when we get there, but I have to keep pushing. Have to get to her.

"Over there!"

Vince points as he runs toward a dark figure lying in a heap in the corner beside a glowing phone screen. The song finally stops, and I swear my fucking heart does, too. That image hits me again. The one that plagued me the entire car ride over. And despite being determined to help Bird, the others rush forward, and I... hesitate.

I *fucking* hesitate.

The long, dreadful hand of fear grips my throat, squeezing like a vice.

And now, as I stand so close to Bird, not knowing whether she's alive or dead, I'm frozen.

Vince, Ash, and Tate crouch down beside her. It's Ash who aims his phone's flashlight, illuminating the streaks of sticky blood that poured out of her nose before drying on her face and the cement floor. Debris crunches beneath my feet when I take a step, but not in the right direction. Instead of going *to* her, I've moved back. Seeing her like this—the side of one eye swollen, bruised jaw—it feels like too much.

"She's breathing, but we have to get her to a hospital. *Fast.*" Tate's already going for his phone again. My immediate guess is that he intends to call 9-1-1, which Vince seems to realize, too.

"No, fuck that. We're not waiting. We'll carry her to the truck and take her ourselves," he reasons.

"And if she has internal injuries?" Tate shoots back. "Lifting her will do more harm than good."

Vince takes a breath, and I can see he's starting to get pissed.

"In the time it would take an ambulance to get to us, in the time it would take us to even figure out where the fuck this place even *is*, we could make it to the hospital and back twice. Look where we are," he adds. "The cops don't exactly rush to this side of town."

Tate's quiet, clearly wanting to argue his point, but he seems to see Vince's point, too.

"Fuck it. Let's just do it," Tate concedes, and before he even finishes speaking, Vince has already slipped one arm beneath Bird's back, and the other beneath her knees. He has her in the air the next second and her head slumps against his chest, her arm limp at her side. He's quick about getting her out of here, and Ash uses his flashlight to make sure the pathway is clear.

And me?

I feel fucking useless. Completely. All because I can't stand the sight of her like this, can't stand the idea of this happening on our watch.

But there's one thing I *am* good for, and that's figuring out who's responsible. And when I do—because I *will* figure this shit out—I intend to make it hurt.

"Get her to the hospital. I'll call to check in soon."

Ash calls after me as I brush past, headed for the alley. "What? Where the fuck are you going?"

"Someone may have seen something, and we need all the answers we can get."

They're already hurling more questions, which means my response went in one ear and out the other. But I ignore them because I've got a one-track mind.

Whoever did this, whoever thought they could hurt one of us and just… walk away… I'll see to it that they regret this day for the rest of their fucking life.

Chapter 3

Tate

No mother likes getting a call like the one I just made to Val in the middle of the night. But especially not a mother who's already lost *one* daughter to tragedy. The panic in her voice, the dread as I explained what we found when we got to the warehouse, it's practically palpable.

When she and Dad arrive at the hospital, the look on Val's face has my heart sinking, going out to her as I try to imagine what must be going through her head right now.

"Thank God you were there when your friends got the call." Her voice quivers as she rushes toward me, then brings me into a hug.

She's just recited the lie I told her a while ago. The one that seemed necessary because the truth—that the guys were tracking Stevie's phone—would've raised red flags. I had to think quick, come up with a more fitting explanation. So, as far as Val knows, Stevie and I have mutual friends I happened to be hanging with when she reached out to them for help.

"It was honestly all them. They acted quickly when they sensed something was wrong," I explain. "I just happened to be in the right place at the right time."

"Either way… thank you," she sniffles. "Thank you for calling me, for going after her." She pulls away, swiping tears with the back of her hand. "I need to see my girl."

Dad puts his arm around her shoulders, bringing her to his side.

"I know you're anxious, but the doctor isn't allowing anyone back just yet."

Her eyes widen at my response. "But I'm her mother. I can't just sit here and—"

"I'm sure the staff has everything under control," Dad softly interjects, stroking Val's arm. "They're taking excellent care of her. Trust me."

Val holds his gaze a moment, and the defiance in her eyes eventually melts, giving way to reason.

"The doctor promised he'd have updates soon," I add, hoping to bring her a bit more peace while she waits.

She blinks, the look on her face deepening as she shakes her head. "I reached out to Stevie tonight, but she never returned my text. I should've known something was wrong. I should've sensed it," she rambles, lowering her gaze to the floor.

"You couldn't have done anything more, Honey," Dad says, squeezing Val tighter. "Half the time, I don't hear back from *this* one until the next day, so it's understandable that you'd assume Stevie just didn't have a moment to respond."

He smiles at Val warmly when she peers up, meeting his gaze, but tears fill her eyes again.

"Yeah, maybe," she says just above a whisper. "But this time, it *did* mean something. It meant my little girl was in trouble."

An image hits me. One of Stevie lying on the cold cement, breathing, but otherwise not with us. It's hard to accept that we still don't know the extent of her injuries, still don't know how or why this happened, but all we can do at this point is wait.

I glance toward the guys when Val's sadness becomes too heavy. They're on the other side of the waiting room. Vince with one foot propped on a chair, tightly clutching his phone, and I imagine he's just tried Micah again. Ash with his fingers interlocked across his torso, his head resting on the back of his seat while staring blankly at the ceiling.

They're worried. Not just about Stevie, but also Micah. I know because I feel it, too. The pull to fix it all, to speed up Stevie's recovery, to find Micah and remind him that he isn't alone like he tends to think. We tried to center him before he went off the rails. Ash took off after him while Vince and I secured Stevie in the truck, but it was pointless. When Micah Locke doesn't want to be found, when he wants to be left in the shadows, he doesn't come out until he's good and damn ready.

We all saw that look on his face when he first laid eyes on Stevie tonight. It took me a bit to figure out that it ran deeper than his concern for her, but then it clicked. Seeing her like that—on the ground, helpless, bleeding—it triggered him.

"Are those the guys?"

Val's question has me facing her again. Her eyes are on Vince and Ash, tension in her brow.

"Yeah," I answer.

"They stayed?"

I nod. "They insisted on being here when she wakes up."

Val fidgets with her necklace as she observes them. "Stevie never mentioned having new friends. Which one did she call?"

The question catches me off guard, but I'm quick on my feet, naming the one I think would cause Val the least amount of worry.

"Uh… Vince."

Not having the gages and tattoos Ash sports, Vince is the safe option from a parents' perspective. Plus, he's admittedly the most stable of the *three*, which Micah and Ash have admitted, *themselves*, so I don't feel guilty for thinking it.

"Which one is Vince?"

"Dark sweats, baseball cap," I say, pointing.

She nods and falls silent. Then, her eyes don't leave Vince as she asks, "Are he and Stevie… together?"

It's such a complicated question. Especially seeing as how I don't know how to classify the connection between Stevie and them, no more than I can define the one between she and *I*. So, an answer just sort of falls out of my mouth.

"I think they've been seeing each other, but I'm not sure how serious things are yet."

Val arches a brow, blinking her red rimmed eyes. "Serious enough that she'd call *him* when she's in trouble before calling *me*."

Shit. I didn't even think of that.

Instead of putting my foot deeper in my mouth, I decide now's a good time to just shut the fuck up.

"I should go talk to him," Val decides. "Maybe he knows what Stevie was doing on that side of town. Maybe she said something during the call that might be useful."

As soon as she finishes speaking, she's already starting toward Vince, and there's no time to think of a diversion.

"Hi," she says, her voice quiet and strained with emotion. She manages a faint smile, though. "I'm Stevie's mom, Val."

Vince peers up from his phone, looking a bit startled. My guess is he's never done this before, met the parent of a girl he's interested in.

"Uh...hi," he forces out, extending his hand when Val does the same.

"Tate explained that Stevie reached out to you tonight," she adds, motioning toward me. As soon as she's focused on Vince again, I widen my eyes, hoping he gets the hint to go along with it.

"Uh... yes, she did," he answers, sitting straighter in his seat.

"Well, I'm curious what she might've said. Was there anything that can maybe clue us in on why this happened? Or who might've done this?"

Her voice breaks when she asks, then she covers her mouth as her eyes well with tears.

"No, ma'am. She didn't tell me anything. I'm sorry," Vince says, and Val's eyes slam shut.

"It's just... I—"

Dad has his arms around her before she can finish.

"Honey, the police are here and would like to have a word with you."

My father's words have me glancing toward the door where two officers stand, waiting. Val spots them, too, then nods as Dad pulls her off to the side to gather herself first.

I lower into a seat near the guys and let out a breath. The mood in this place is heavy and waiting idly by, hoping for the doctors to give us *something* is pure hell.

"Dude, what the fuck? You told her Stevie called me?" Vince asks through gritted teeth.

"I did, but admittedly didn't think that all the way through."

"Fucking perfect. Now they'll want to talk to *me* when they're done with her mom," he adds, gesturing toward the cops.

"Relax. Just tell them you got the call, and Stevie shared her location so you could find her. Once she wakes up, we'll fill her in, and she'll go along with it."

"Fuck," he growls, making it clear he's not exactly happy with the route I've taken, but what's done is done.

"Still no word from Micah?" I ask.

Ash shakes his head. "Nope. Nothing. I've called, I've texted, and he's ignored all of it."

"Shit. We can't leave him out there all night. You know how he gets when he's in his head."

They're quiet, probably recalling the same incident I just did. The one that made his father aware of just how dark his son can go while also bonding them with a secret. The one that first landed him in therapy, and then a group home when his dad realized he needed more dedicated help.

"This has been one incredibly fucked up night," Vince concludes with a sigh, and I couldn't agree with him more.

It's fucked.

We're fucked.

And there isn't shit we can do to fix any of it.

Micah

. . .

My hands are shaking. So bad I shove them in my pockets as the bus comes to a stop, and I rush off before anyone even has the chance to stand. I've looked everywhere and didn't find anyone or *anything* suspicious. The few people still out this late are either high, drunk, or think I'm up to no good and refuse to answer my questions.

Which means I'm no further ahead than I was when we found Bird lying in that filthy fucking building.

I trudge down the sidewalk and ignore the buzzing in my pocket. There's no need to guess who it is. The guys have been blowing my phone up every fifteen minutes with calls and texts.

I'm fine.

They need to focus on Bird.

The scenery on this side of town is much different than the atmosphere I just drove in from. And the presence of navy and white signage on the buildings, and now the frat and sorority houses, has adrenaline driving me forward despite being exhausted.

I take out my phone, but it isn't to return Vince, Ash, or Tate's calls. It's to dial one asshole in particular I think might be behind what happened tonight. And I don't give a fuck that it's late. His ass better answer and come outside, or I'm letting myself in.

It rings three times, then a gravelly voice answers. "You've gotta be shitting me."

"Outside. You've got sixty seconds, or I'm kicking your fucking door down," I warn him, counting down in my head as I hang up.

I stare up at the dark windows of the house, pacing while I wait for Whitlock to meet my demands, and right around the fifty-second mark, he stumbles down from the porch in plaid pajama pants and a dark tee, raking his fingers over his scalp.

"This better be good," he growls, meeting my gaze.

But before I can even think of how to react, my hands are moving, gripping his collar in my fists, driving him into the base of a pillar as our eyes lock.

"Just admit that you did it, you ignorant fuck!"

29

He chuffs a laugh, and I slam him against the plaster again. "What the hell are you talking about?"

"Admit that you left her in that fucking abandoned building for dead!"

Whitlock laughs louder this time, and I lose my shit, slamming my fist into his nose.

"Fuck," he groans, getting his arms beneath mine to shove me back. Mirroring my size and height, he moves me easily. "What the hell are you talking about?" he repeats.

"Stevie, you son of a bitch! Tell me where you were tonight. In detail."

He swipes a trickle of blood from his nose, then glares. "You're still crying about that same bitch?" he asks. "I've never known you to fuck the same girl more than once, so what's so special about this one?"

I swing on him, and he dodges it, but he isn't expecting me to sweep his feet out from underneath him, so as he stares up at me from the grass, we both know I have the upper hand. The porch light comes on and a handful of his boys file out onto the porch.

"Tell them to stand down or I swear to God I'll break your fucking neck."

Whitlock's stare is intense, defiance in his eyes, but he knows I'm just psychotic enough to keep my word.

"It's cool," he calls out, halting the footsteps that just thundered down the stairs.

"Last time I mentioned her, you thought *she* was a *he*, so what the hell changed? Why is it that, all of a sudden, you know who she is?"

"What changed is that I did a little research," he shrugs. "Seemed smart to figure out who'd gotten under your skin bad enough that you called to give *me* shit about it. Besides, the enemy of my enemy is my friend, right? Only... I'm guessing she's *not* exactly your enemy anymore?" he asks, trying to read me. Smirking, he adds a vague, "Interesting."

That sick smirk is back, and I lift his collar, slamming him down to the grass again, but he isn't fazed now that he knows he's getting to me.

"Tell me what you fucking did to her!"

"What would she think if she knew the truth about you?" he asks, ignoring me. His words sink in, and I feel my expression go slack. "What would she do if she found out you're such a fuck up your own *father* couldn't bear to look at you, so he sent your ass away?"

I feel my grip loosen on his shirt and I'm slipping, going back in time. Back to when I was a lost, fucked up kid who didn't know up from down, and no one in my life had any clue what to do with me. Unfortunately, me and Whitlock's paths have been entangled for just that long, so he had a bird's eye view of just how shitty things were.

"We both know your ass should've been locked up in some backwoods nuthouse and left to rot, but the thing is, no one even cared enough to try and fix you."

For a moment, I forget we're not alone, because all that exists are his words, swirling inside my head as they awaken thoughts I haven't let get to me in a very long time.

But... there they are, latching on, biting into my flesh, burrowing their way under my skin like some kind of nightmare parasite.

Whitlock's bullshit doesn't usually get to me, but I'm raw tonight, filled with unfamiliar emotions I'm not sure how to manage.

When I stand, his eyes are glued to mine, and I hate that the fight's drained out of me. This asshole deserves every hit, every broken bone, every ounce of blood that would leave his body. But something's wrong. I'm not myself.

"Bring your ass back here again, and I swear to you, you'll be hauled off in a cop car or a hearse. Your call," Leo adds, brushing grass off his shirt when he gets to his feet.

Unshed tension flares in my shoulders as I square them and walk away. There's unfinished business between us, but then again, there always has been and probably always will be.

I may have drawn blood tonight, but he got inside my head, and at the moment... I'm not entirely sure which is worse.

Chapter 4

Stevie

"Mom?"

The world spins and the space around me slowly fades in from the void. A faint, and yet consistent beep to my right is disorienting, and a light tug in my arm makes me feel like I'm tethered to something.

The fog in my head begins to clear, and I recall the last images I saw before everything went dark for a final time.

First, the bag over my head, an arm around my neck. Then, I awakened in some foreign place—cold, water dripping from a pipe somewhere close to where I'd been placed on the cement.

Then... pain.

A solid fist to my face, a boot to my ribs. Then more of the same. Over and over and over again. In actuality, it may have only lasted a few seconds, but it felt like it went on forever. The memory of it has me anxious to sit up, desperate to protect myself.

"Whoa. Hey, it's okay, Stevie. I have you."

Those words are softly spoken off to my left when I gasp, just as a warm hand slips into mine. I turn toward the sound of it with a start, disoriented when there's a familiar face beside me.

Tate smiles a little, but it's weary, like he's not quite sure what to make of my reaction to *him*, to waking up here.

Cool air fills my lungs, a steady flow from a tube just beneath my nose. And now the beeping begins to make sense, as does the tug of an IV in my arm.

This is a hospital.

"I… How… I need my mom."

"Relax, you're safe. She just ran out for coffee with my dad. They've been up all night. We *all* have," he adds, and I'm too out of it to analyze what that means.

"How am I… *here?*"

My hand squeezes in his and he smirks a little. "Micah. Being the persistent stalker that he is, when you didn't answer his calls or texts, he tracked your phone. Then, we came and found you."

I blink, breathing deep. "All of you?"

"Yeah, all of us."

He nods and there's a softness to his eyes at first, but the longer I stare into them, it fades. Just as that *look* retreats, his grip on my hand loosens, too. Only enough to barely notice.

"I'm glad you're awake," he says. "Val will be over the moon when she sees your eyes are finally open."

"How long was I out?"

"We got you here around midnight, and it's nearly noon."

The jump in time is a bit confusing, but this whole experience has been that. I push off on the mattress with my free hand, attempting to reposition myself, but a sharp pain in my side has me crying out.

"Shit!"

"Take it easy," he says, bracing his hands against my shoulders, holding me in place.

"What the fuck is wrong with me?" The heat of a tear streaks down my cheek when the pain doesn't readily subside but lingers instead.

"The doc says you're pretty banged up. Concussion, lots of bruising, but nothing's broken."

I can hardly catch my breath as my head falls back against the pillow.

"Here, you should drink something."

He brings a straw to my lips, and I don't realize how thirsty I am until I begin to sip, nearly draining the entire cup. Tate sets it aside, and I still feel his gaze.

"How can I make you more comfortable?"

I hear him but don't answer. Instead, my eyes fall closed as it all sinks in—how something so terrible could happen right outside my door, how I have no idea who to trust and who to fear, how this ball of tension in my gut is probably stuck with me for life.

"Hey, hey, hey… no, don't cry. You're safe."

Tate's soft words go in one ear and out the other, because how can he know that? How can I *ever* truly be safe when whoever did this is still out there?

Heat from his arms encircles my shoulders, then my cheek warms against his chest when I let my weight settle against him.

"We're not leaving you. Everyone's here to make sure nothing else happens."

I swipe at a tear, trying to believe that protecting me is even possible, but I'm not so sure anymore. My sense of security was already rocked when my sister was assaulted, now it's stuck in my head that bad things seem to keep happening *to* and *around* me. Like I'm a magnet for it or something.

"Knock, knock."

Startled, I lean away from Tate's chest but I'm still in his arms. But even that small, abrupt motion proves to have been a bad idea. The pain hits again. It's not quite as sharp as before, but still hurts like a bitch.

I glance toward the door as Maddox walks in. He's clutching a vase filled with flowers in one hand and shoves his cell into the pocket of his jeans with the other.

"Hey," he says, his voice quieter than usual, taking it all in—the tubes, the machines.

"Hey," I echo. My voice is raspy as I fight to keep the tears in. "I'm glad you're here."

Before speaking, Maddox scans Tate with a look, and I don't miss how his gaze seems to linger where Tate's arm is still draped around me for support.

"How'd you know I was here?" I ask.

Maddox's eyes finally leave Tate and lock with mine again. "Uh, your mom. She reached out this morning and said it might do you some good if I stopped by. Although, at the time, you hadn't woken up yet."

I shrug. "Yeah, it's only been a few minutes and I'm pretty disoriented. But at least I'm alive, right?"

I laugh at the dark comment, but I'm fully aware that it isn't funny. When one corner of Maddox's mouth turns up with a weak grin, I'm guessing he doesn't think so either.

His stare settles on Tate again, and I realize they haven't met. "Tate this is Maddox, best friend extraordinaire. Maddox, this is Tate. You've met Rob, but this is his son."

The tension in Maddox's brow eases up ever so slightly, and he's terribly transparent. Discovering that Tate isn't just some random guy, but actually my stepbrother-to-be, seems to set Maddox's mind at ease.

Little does he know...

"Pleasure," Maddox greets him.

"Likewise," Tate shoots back, then his eyes are on me again. "I'll give you two some privacy. Will you be okay?"

He asks the question, then flashes a fleeting look toward Maddox.

"Yeah, all good."

He doesn't move as soon as I finish answering, and I feel him wanting to stay.

"I'll be right down the hall in the waiting room. Send a nurse if you need me."

I nod and his arm slips from around my shoulders, then he's gone, leaving Maddox and I alone in the silence. He stalks over, seemingly unsure how close he's allowed to get.

"You can sit. You won't break me," I tease, wincing when I shift beneath the thin blanket to make room for him on the edge of the bed.

He lowers and I'm aware of how strained things have been between us lately. And yet, here he is, showing up in my hour of need.

"Those for me or a part of your outfit?" I joke, pointing at the flowers he's clutching.

"Oh, shit. I almost forgot I had them." A dim smile touches his lips as he leans toward the small table beside my bed and sets the roses on top of it.

"They're beautiful. Thank you."

He shrugs. "Didn't feel right coming emptyhanded. How are you?"

He peers up and meets my gaze, and I don't miss the concern behind his eyes.

"Well, you know. About as good as one might expect after getting their ass kicked by an angry stranger."

He shakes his head. "I hope they find whoever this motherfucker is."

"Me, too," I add, although *his* reason likely has more to do with revenge. Whereas *my* desire to have this sick fuck in custody is that I'd like to have my peace of mind restored. And also, so I can possibly sleep again.

One day.

Maybe.

"When I um… when your mom explained everything and got to the part about how you were found, she said those guys brought you here. The ones you've been hanging around."

I feel the tension in my brow when I frown, having no recollection of that whatsoever. I don't even remember being coherent before now.

"I… maybe," I stammer. "Everything's such a blur, I honestly don't know *what* happened."

Maddox nods and if I had to guess, he has questions. Questions he'd love to ask, but likely knows now is neither the time nor the place. So, he lets it go.

For now, anyway.

"Well, I'm just glad you're safe," he says, and I'd like to leave it at that.

"Enough about me, I need a distraction. Tell me about you. Anything new?"

He shrugs and is about to speak, but before a single syllable leaves his mouth, the doorway darkens, and in files Ash, Vince, and Micah. Maddox's eyes are locked on them, watching as the three stand near the wall, out of the way, but with the way they command a room, they may as well be taking up every inch of space.

I get the sense that having them here makes Maddox feel crowded out, and it's confirmed when he breathes deep, then faces me again.

"I should go. Call me later. When you're *not* under surveillance," he adds under his breath, unable to hide the hint of annoyance that creeps in.

I want to tell him to stay, want to tell him he's as welcome here as anyone else, but with the fierce expressions of the Savages, I'm not so sure that's even true.

"Thank you for coming."

He nods in response, then stands from the edge of my bed. On his way out, he does that macho thing guys do, where they silently size one another up, and then he's gone.

I take note of how, before the guys' eyes flit to mine, they zero in on the flowers beside me. Yes, they're possessive and territorial and all the other red-flag traits you can think of, but they're more than that, which was more than evident this weekend. I haven't forgotten about our time together, but *that* memory has admittedly been over-shadowed by recent events.

"Good to see you're awake," Ash says, and I smile a little, already feeling fatigue settling in again.

"It's good to *be* awake."

They come closer, but I note how Micah—the one who naturally stands front and center in most cases—lags behind a bit. I feel my brow twitch when I question what's up with him, but with things so off balance and weird right now, who knows what's really behind it.

"I hear I have you three to thank for getting me here. Guess I owe you one," I tease, noting how much quieter my voice has gotten from even a moment ago.

"One of the good things about being in with us is that we don't keep score," Vince smirks. "We're just glad we were able to find you."

His words trigger a thought. "Someone said I called you? I don't even remember that."

"Yeah, that's because it's a lie," Vince laughs. "Tate had to think fast when talking to your mom. I'm pretty sure she would've been suspicious if he'd told her the truth, that we have a tracker on your phone."

He's probably right about that.

"So, when the cops come in to talk to you, just go along with it," he adds, and I nod, agreeing.

My gaze settles on Micah again, and while I've definitely got my own shit to worry about, I'm also concerned about *him*. But he seems to notice me reading him, and before I can dig deeper, he's wearing his mask again—confident, collected, together.

"You guys stayed the whole night?" I ask, giving up when I realize he intends to ice me out.

"Most of us did." These are the first words Micah's spoken, and I arch a brow. "I was out for a while, searching the area where we found you."

"And?"

He shakes his head when I ask. "I didn't find anything. And no one saw anything unusual."

That wasn't the response I hoped for. If we don't have answers, or even a *lead,* that means whoever did this is still out there. Still capable of coming back.

"I'm sure the police will get things sorted," I lie, secretly fearing this will be just like Mel's case.

Forever a mystery. Forever a nightmare.

"Do you… remember anything?" Micah asks, a gentleness to his tone I'm not familiar with.

Shaking my head, I sigh. "Only being taken, being... *beaten,* but... I didn't see or hear anything helpful."

They're quiet, likely just as frustrated with the vagueness of that answer as I am.

"And was there anything notable about meeting with Tory yesterday? Any chance she had something to do with this?"

I picture Tory's face, the innocence I sensed behind her eyes, the genuine affection I believe she felt toward my sister. I shake my head. "No, I don't think so."

"And she was alone?" Micah adds.

"She... no. Her brothers tagged along."

Frowning, he grumbles one word. "Why?"

I shrug. "No clue. They sat at a nearby table, not so close that they were listening, but they were definitely keeping an eye on her. But I got the sense that they only wanted to know she was safe. I can't blame them honestly. Considering."

The guys are quiet, and they share a look. There aren't words exchanged between them, but as close as they are, that isn't necessary. With a mere glance, they've just communicated all they needed to say.

I rack my brain for more details, *anything* that might be helpful, but there's nothing. And on top of that, I'm exhausted. Like I didn't just sleep for twelve hours.

When I yawn, Ash moves closer, placing the back of his hand on my forehead. "You're warm. Have they checked your temp since you got up?"

A laugh slips out. Can't help it. With all his piercings and tattoos, I hadn't pegged him for the nurturing type.

"No, Dad, they haven't," I tease.

He smiles back, cocking his head a little. "I like it, but... don't you mean Daddy?" he whispers, arching his brow with the question.

"What the fuck is wrong with you?" Vince sighs, pushing Ash aside.

"Relax. I made her laugh, didn't I?"

Vince glares, clearly not buying into Ash's rationale. "Let's just focus on getting her better. Preferably *without* you being a fucking horny asshole for once."

Ash shrugs and I'm honestly grateful for the moment, the unexpected lightheartedness, being able to laugh and not think about the bad stuff. Surprisingly, Micah smiles, too, and it's nice to see they're still pretty much the same. Even *after* the closeness and uncertainty the weekend first brought with it, and then… everything else.

This feels familiar. Normal.

I need this.

I need… *them.*

Vince hovers over me, gentle when he lightly squeezes me with a hug. "Get some rest. We'll be in the waiting room."

My fingers splay across his back, feeling his warmth through his t-shirt. I feel my eyes beginning to sting again, and at the risk of sounding like the needy girl I've never been, I make a request.

"Will you guys at least stay until I fall asleep?"

He leans away, and I can't help but feel like he knows there's something deeper behind my request. So, when he nods, locking me in with his green stare, there's a sense of trust I don't extend to people very often.

"Just sleep. We'll stay," he promises.

As two settle into chairs and one on the edge of my bed, it surprises me that there isn't even a sliver of doubt in my mind that he means it.

I can drift knowing they'll protect me, because these boys—twisted and dark as they may be…

They're with me.

Stevie

"Hang on! Big bump," Mom warns as the vase of flowers from Maddox shifts between my feet where it's been placed on the floor. I squeeze the pillow meant to make my ride home easier, but so far, I'm not impressed.

The point is to give me a heads up in enough time to hug said pillow to stabilize my ribs *before* things get rough, but my mother can't seem to get the timing right.

"Sorry, Sweetie. Almost there."

One can only hope.

Things get quiet, and I glance down at my phone where it's clutched in my hand. I've wanted to reach out to Micah all day but hadn't gotten up the nerve yet. I know I didn't imagine how different he's been. He's quiet, withdrawn, and just generally distant. But... I haven't decided if hearing from me would be appreciated or an annoyance.

Honestly, with how little he's had to say, I'm leaning toward the latter.

I dial anyway, because if there's anything I took away from my sister's passing, it's that you should never stop checking in on people you care about. Even if it's uncomfortable, even if you imagine them seeing it's you on the line and completely ignoring it.

By the third ring, I'm pretty sure he won't pick up. Then, when I'm connected to his voicemail, I'm certain of it.

A sigh leaves me, but going unanswered could mean anything—he wasn't near his phone, he was on another call, he was busy. It doesn't have to mean he's intentionally ghosting me.

Only, my brain seems to want me to lean in that direction.

"Doing okay back there, kiddo?" Rob asks from the passenger seat, pulling me from my thoughts.

"Well, if Mom can maybe miss *one* pothole, I'll be fine."

They both laugh, but meanwhile, I'm wondering why they thought that was a joke.

"Looking forward to sleeping in a real bed tonight?" Mom asks. "It's been three days since you've gotten fresh air."

I gaze out the window while I think, not wanting to tell her the truth—that I was beginning to feel safe there. But out here, in the real world, it feels like there's potential danger everywhere.

"Yeah. Sure," I say with a fake smile, just in case she's watching from the rearview mirror.

There's a moment of silence, and I stupidly think the conversation has ended.

"So, I didn't want to bother you while you were in the hospital, but when were you going to tell me about Vince?"

My stomach twists hearing her ask. "What about him?"

She flashes a smile toward Rob, then eyes me from over her shoulder. "Relax. Tate already told us you and Vince have been, you know, hanging out. But even if he *hadn't* said anything, I would've guessed *something* was up. Vince and his crew stuck around the entire time you were hospitalized."

My heart's racing, but I play it cool. "What did Tate tell you, exactly?"

She shrugs. "Just that you're seeing Vince and that he thinks you two are pretty serious. But from what I gather, he and Tate are also pretty good friends, so he must be a decent guy."

I'm silent. *Dead* silent. Because I don't have a clue what to say to that. My mother and I don't discuss guys or my dating life. And if I'm being honest, I'm pretty comfortable with things staying just like they are.

"Shit, I've scared you off," Mom teases with a laugh. "Fine. We can drop it."

Thank God.

"Anyway, we've got Tate's old room set up for you, and I'm making your favorite dinner. Won't that be nice?"

"Mm hm." I sigh, nodding as we ride, grateful for the change of subject. But if I know my mother, this won't be the last I hear of it.

We pass the convenience store Mel was obsessed with for an entire six months straight. It was their nachos. She had to have them every day, so as soon as I got my license, I became her designated nacho-run driver. A smile crosses my face remembering how *hers* used to light up the moment we'd pull into the parking lot.

Mom weaves us through traffic, eventually making it to Rob's side of town, and I'm grateful she's not taking me back to the old house. Sure, Rob's place will feel unfamiliar, but *that* I can deal with. Unlike having memories of my sister awaiting me around every corner.

We take a few more turns, stop at a couple lights, then ease into the driveway. I wince and squeeze the pillow as Mom puts the car in park, and I'm grateful to be stationary once again.

"Ok, so we're gonna get you settled, then Rob's running me to the grocery store to pick up the last few things I'll need for dinner. We'll grab your prescriptions while we're out, too. Think you'll be okay on your own for half an hour or so?"

My eyes flit to her, and I hate that my pulse races. I've been on my own for two years now and all of a sudden, the idea of being alone scares the living shit out of me.

"Sure. Sounds fine," I lie, faking yet another smile as I reach for the door handle.

"Slow down. Let me help," Rob offers, then climbs out of the car. He opens my door and takes my hand, letting me use his balance to steady myself, instead of risking doing more harm than good by pulling me.

Eventually, I'm on my feet and shuffling toward the front door. Mom unlocks it and steps aside to let me in. I was here not too long ago, but definitely made a less-than-stellar exit when an argument with Tate resulted in me taking Mom's keys and making my own way home. But the past is the past, right? I can only guess that's true, seeing as how I've been invited to stay until I fully recover.

"We've done quite a few new things to the house since you were last here," Rob says. "We're renovating one of the bedrooms, so you'll be in Tate's old room. Your mom already brought some of your things over and put them away, so you don't have to worry about it."

I peer up at him. "My things?"

"Oh, I thought I told you," Mom says. "We stopped by your room and packed clothes, your laptop, your books, and things for school. I just wanted you to have whatever you'll need to be comfortable here. And your housemates were so sweet and accommodating. Especially that one. Honey, what was her name?"

Rob mulls it over a moment, then answers. "Delia? Delilah?"

"Dahlia," mom cuts in, snapping her fingers when Rob jogs her memory.

But there's no fucking way my mother just called that bitch sweet.

No fucking way.

"They wanted us to tell you they're praying for your speedy recovery and they hope to hear from you soon."

I roll my eyes. As if those sluts actually pray. But I hold my tongue, gritting my teeth to restrain the tirade threatening to spew from my mouth like flames.

"Sure. Thank you," is all I can force out when my jaw tenses.

"Here, let's get you upstairs, then we'll head out." With that, my mother's arm loops around my waist despite me insisting I can just use the rail.

My phone sounds off and Rob pauses. "Need us to wait while you get that?"

I glance down, half expecting to see Micah's name on the screen.

But when I realize I was wrong to assume, I shove it back into my pocket.

"Nope, it's an unknown caller, and I don't answer those."

Mom grips me tighter, then we finish climbing, making it up and into Tate's old room.

I glance around and it's an interesting space—posters of singers and actresses I'm guessing he thought were hot back in high school. And there are, of course, a fair amount of hockey trophies and plaques all over. A plaid bedspread is neatly folded across the bottom of a fresh blue sheet that matches the paint almost perfectly.

"I dragged a spare hamper in last night, so just let me know when it's full and I'll get your things all washed up."

I smile, lifting an eyebrow when she offers. "Mom, you haven't done my laundry since I was twelve. Seriously?"

She shrugs, aimlessly twisting her necklace. "Well, you need me," she says, "and don't tell anyone, but I think I'm looking forward to taking care of you again."

I roll my eyes. "Okay. Fine. Whatever floats your boat."

She steps into the room, only long enough to kiss my forehead, and then she steps back out into the hallway. "Oh, need anything while we're out?" she asks, popping her head inside again.

"Nope, all good." As soon as I answer, I think of something. "Wait… if they have purple hair dye, can you grab me a couple bottles? I'm ready for a change."

She flashes a curious smile, and then nods. "You've got it."

I listen as she and Rob descend the steps, and my heart sinks when I hear the front door slam shut. There was once a time when I loved a bit of solitude, but now, I'm already counting down the time it'll take them to return.

I check my phone again. No missed calls other than the one from an unknown caller, so I set it aside.

Still no Micah.

To kill time, I dig through my things Mom unpacked in the drawers until I find a pair of shorts and a t-shirt. I head out to the hallway bathroom and lock the door behind myself, deciding now would be an excellent time to sneak in a shower without my mother asking if I need help. So, I turn the water as high as I can stand it and hop in, making quick work of soaping up what I can reach of my body before giving up from fatigue.

I hardly towel myself off because it feels like extra work. So, I replace the waterproof bandage covering the brand on my hip—courtesy of the guys—then slip into comfy clothes before taking a long, hard listen out in the hallway. And once the silence assures me no one's gotten in while I showered, I step out and into the bedroom.

A sigh leaves me when I slowly take a seat on the edge of the bed, staring out the window as a bird lands on a thin branch. This space isn't anything like mine, and I feel out of place, or rather *displaced*.

Homeless.

Not that my old spot was all that great, but it was home. Kind of, anyway. But now, I know I can't go back. Not with Dahlia and her gaggle of bitches there. Kicking her ass was definitely worth it, but needing to find a new place to live is the downside.

I imagine how fake they must've been while Mom and Rob were there, pretending to be perfect fucking angels. Meanwhile, they were probably glad to see my things being hauled out. And if I'm being honest, it's crossed my mind that... maybe Dahlia had something to do with all this. I mean, I gave her plenty of reason to target me after The Hunt, considering we fought. So, who's to say this wasn't her doing?

I consider it, but the messed up part about all of this is that it could've literally been anyone. Anyone I pissed off recently, anyone who didn't like me digging into what happened to my sister.

Anyone.

Which leads me to my next thought. That I'm not entirely sure I want to live on my own, or even in a house filled with strangers and constant traffic. I never considered myself a fragile girl, but... right now... I kind of feel that way.

But where does that leave me? Living with my mother again? Giving up the independence I embraced in the not-so-distant past? Listening to Mom and Rob screw at night?

"Eww. Fucking disgusting." Shaking my head, I try to rid my mind of the thought.

"Do you always talk to yourself?"

"Holy shit!" When I spin toward the sound of the voice, my ribs throb. However, pain is a secondary concern as my head wars between fight or flight. My heart's racing double-time, only slowing once my eyes finally settle on Tate.

He drops his shoulder against the doorframe. "Shit, I'm sorry. I didn't mean to scare you."

"No, it's fine. I just… my nerves are a little shot is all."

From the looks of things, he regrets not being more sensitive to that, but I don't really want to think about my trauma right now. He makes that easy when he takes slow steps into the room, settling beside the window and the fading sunlight glints in his dark eyes.

I draw in a breath and linger on a memory, feeling the faint ghosting of his hands on my skin, his jaw rhythmic against my inner thighs as he tastes me, then his solid flesh throbbing between my lips. Blinking, I clear my throat and force my thoughts to focus on today, instead of the recent past.

"So, what brings you by?" I ask, smiling a little.

"I'm meeting my dad. We're purchasing a new rental and need to go over some details first."

My smile wants to slip, but I keep it intact when it becomes clear he's not here for *me*. "Oh. Well, you just missed him."

Tate nods and I'm hit with a newly familiar feeling. I first noticed it at the hospital when he seemed to regret taking my hand that first day. I noticed it when he didn't visit or even text after that. And now, as he seems to be pretending we *didn't* just hook up this past weekend.

Few things make a girl feel more gross and used than being blown off by a guy who's just seen her naked.

Yeah.

Fun.

As if things aren't already awkward enough, he's silent as he glances around his old room again.

"Are you… settling in okay?" he asks.

"Yep, and I'll be all set as soon as I locate your porn stash," I tease, but he looks damn-near embarrassed.

Like the mere mention of anything regarding sex is a total turn-off now. My gut twists and I'm tempted to just leave well enough alone, but it simply isn't in my nature. So, I just come right out and ask.

"Are we... good?"

Seemingly surprised by my forthrightness, Tate blinks, and then looks away. "Of course, we are."

His answer doesn't match his body language, or the distance I've felt from him.

"You sure about that? Because if I'm being honest, that... kind of feels like a lie."

He has this look on his face, like he'd rather be anywhere but here, talking about anything but this. Eventually, he finds it in himself to meet my gaze, and I brace for it, whatever his response will be.

"It's just that... I've been thinking."

Deep breath, Stevie. "Ok, I'm listening."

His back settles against the wall, his gaze lowers to the floor, and then he's just silent.

Being as patient as possible, I arch a brow when he releases a sharp exhale.

"You know what? I shouldn't have brought this up. You're not well. It can wait."

He pushes off from the wall, intent on leaving, but *fuck that*! "You can't just walk out without finishing."

"You have enough to deal with without me rambling about shit that doesn't even matter."

"Shit that doesn't matter?" Those words hit me square in the heart, reading between the lines.

He sighs, seemingly annoyed. "You know what I mean."

"How about you let me decide what I can and can't handle," I scoff. "I'm an adult and—"

I attempt to stand, needing him to realize I'm not some frail child whose feelings he needs to tiptoe around, but my ribs don't allow it.

"Shit!" I wince.

Tate moves toward me at lightning speed, concern in his eyes as he grips my waist and scoots me back into place. I barely have to put any effort into it because he's strong like the others, making me feel practically weightless.

"You have to take it easy," he says, but I hardly hear him because he's so close. And he smells like citrus-scented shampoo and cologne.

His eyes lock with mine, and while I'm still sharply aware of my frustration, I'm also forced to admit that everything I feel toward him isn't all bad.

But instead of lingering in my space, instead of taking advantage of the closeness, and the moment alone, Tate backs off. As he steals his warmth and that scent away in a rush, he also confirms so many fears that plagued my thoughts. Before this moment, I clung to a hope that it was all in my head, my imagination. Only, now, as a chill fills Tate's expression, I know I was right to worry.

"I—we—we'll talk," he says, retreating completely.

My lips part to protest, to tell him how shitty it is to start a heavy conversation with no intention of finishing it, but I never get the chance. Mom and Rob bound into the house, laughing and acting like teenagers in love, and the opportunity is gone.

I hold Tate's gaze, but he's already on his way out of the room. And now, on top of everything else, I'm left to wonder what the hell he *didn't* say, and how pissed I'll be when he finally says it.

Just fucking great.

Chapter 6

Vince

"Locke, tighten up that release. Set your body *before* the puck comes at you," Coach yells toward Micah, shifting his gaze to Ash next, as he runs the same drill. "Nice, Blaine. That's what I'm looking for."

It's on me next, so I skate up, find the seam between Fletcher and Enzo, then slice the puck through and into the net.

"Killing it, Ricci. Excellent pace," Coach says.

I'm skating out of the way when a loud crack gets everyone's attention. Micah's stick ricochets off the wall where he's just tossed it and he's headed off the ice. I can't see his face but sense his rage. It hasn't left him since that night, when we found Bird and something in *him* broke seeing *her* broken.

"Shit."

I'm moving fast as practice ends behind me, knowing it's imperative that I get to Micah before the locker room fills and he explodes on the first innocent victim his path crosses. Tate must be thinking the same thing because he's coming down from the stands, headed in the same direction.

The ground changes beneath my blades from ice to rubber just as Micah bursts through the door to the locker room. Tate crosses in front of me and shoots me a confused look, but I honestly don't know what's going on either. Makes it tough to keep up when Micah barely speaks to *anyone* these days.

"What the fuck happened?" Ash asks when he reaches us, and my only response is a shrug.

The sound of our blades against the floor echoes in the broad space, bouncing off the hard surfaces and high ceilings. It's a familiar sound and this place usually feels like a second home, but at the moment, nothing feels quite right. This team is like a family, and these three are my brothers, but... Micah's been drifting lately, shutting us out.

"Talk to us," Tate says with a sigh, crossing both arms over his chest.

Micah peers up but doesn't lift his head, glaring at us like he's snapped and doesn't even know who we are.

"I'm fine."

"Yeah, right," Ash scoffs. "You're one of our sharpest players. You don't mess up simple shit like you just did out there. You're too good for this to be about skill, which means the problem's in your head. That won't change until you—"

"Back... the fuck... off," Micah grumbles, holding Ash's stare as he undoes his skates, then stands to remove his gear. The other players file in, breaking the silence, but our corner of the room is still quiet and tense as hell. We stand there, watching as Micah tosses shit around, then slams his locker shut.

"I'll be at the truck," he says, hiking his duffle bag up his shoulder before pushing between me and Tate to get to the exit.

Concerned, Ash looks to me.

I lower onto the bench and start on my laces, trying to convince myself Micah isn't already too far gone for us to reach him. But he's spiraling. Fast.

"Was this the kind of entertainment you were expecting when you popped in?" Ash asks, removing his gear as he glances toward Tate.

Tate's brow tenses as he leans against the row of lockers, his eyes trained on the floor. "I see not much has changed since last time I saw him."

"He's actually worse," Ash corrects. "Hardly speaks, spends most of his time in his room, and his game is slipping. You saw him out there tonight."

"I came in late, but from what I saw… yeah… that wasn't Micah. When's the first game?"

"Right before Halloween," I answer with a sigh, noting how that's likely not enough time for him to get his shit together, but that's honestly a secondary issue. The bigger problem being his failing mental state.

Yeah, I like to win, and I like that we kick ass on the ice, but I prefer having my friend intact.

"What brought you out tonight anyway?" Ash asks, pulling on a pair of sweats.

Tate shrugs. "Just out for a drive to clear my head, then I saw the arena lights on and figured you guys were practicing late, so…"

"…you came home," Ash says with a smirk.

Tate nods. "Yeah, I guess you could say that."

I grab my bag, then remember my phone at the top of my locker and shove it into my pocket. "You hear from Bird today?"

Tate doesn't answer right away, so I glance toward him just as he takes a breath. "Yeah. I stopped over to talk business with my dad and chatted with her for a bit."

"She good?"

He nods. "Seems like it."

I stand there, waiting for him to elaborate, but he never does. So, my guess is that he's being vague on purpose.

I check the time. "Shit, it's getting late. I need to get home."

I told my followers I'd be live tonight and need to shower before getting online.

"Yeah, I need to take off, too. I've got papers to grade," Tate says. "But do me a favor and text if anything changes with him."

Ash nods, knowing he means Micah. "Will do."

Ash and I part ways with Tate at the exit, and head toward the truck. Micah made it clear he wants to be left alone, but that's not how we do things. We stick together because that's how it's always been.

Because that's what families do.

Micah

Why the fuck am I even here?

It's late, I'm exhausted, and I hopped on the bus instead of into Ash's truck when practice ended.

All because there's only one place I want to be, one person I can think of who might be able to take this shitty feeling away. And look at me, I can't even bring myself to go to the fucking door and knock.

Whitlock's words echo in my head. I've relived them daily, feel them rough against my insides like the fingers of my inner demons clawing their way to the surface. I combat them with the arsenal of defensive thoughts I've armed myself with over the years, but they're louder, bigger, stronger, and defeat sets in quickly.

So, instead of going inside, instead of telling Bird that I just... that I fucking need her right now... I stand here. Lurking across the street in the shadows because I don't have the balls to face her, no more than I've had it in me to return her calls. Not after all the shit we did to her, not after I couldn't even look at her as she lay there, needing me.

As if the universe is in on the joke, too, I look down when my phone goes off and it's my father. I hit ignore, then peer up at Bird's open window just as she passes in front of it.

I should call. I should at least tell her I'm sorry and that I know I'm a piece of shit.

But my eyes slam shut when I hear Whitlock's words again.

I'm a fucking failure. A twisted asshole no one's ever cared enough about to fix.

And just like that, I lose my nerve. I spotted a bar a few blocks away when the bus passed it—a little hole in the wall that probably has shitty beer. But I don't really fucking care at this point. Whatever will get me wasted, whatever will help me forget who I am for the night... I'll take it.

Chapter 7

Stevie

Someone's out there.

My steps halt at the window, then I do a double-take. A thought forces its way into my head as I peer out into the darkness, and I hate what I'm considering, but…

Maybe that was him—the one who came out of nowhere that night. The one who hurt me. The one who shattered what little peace of mind I had left.

Stevie… stop. You're safe.

For now, anyway.

I shut off the light, then approach the window for another peek. Slowly this time, staying low so I won't be easily seen above the sill. I'm startled to realize I *hadn't* imagined it. There's definitely someone out there. A guy—sporting jeans and a dark hoodie pulled over his head—is nearly at the corner now. He doesn't look back, but it dawns on me how ridiculous I'm being. Yes, there will be people out and about at night and, no, they're not all out to get me. I can't go my whole life thinking everyone who passes my window is a villain.

I lower onto the mattress, being careful not to aggravate my ribs, then I slowly swing my legs up and lie back. One reason my imagination is so active is because it's been a long, boring-ass day. Other than talking with Maddox for a bit, I haven't heard from anyone. They're all busy, living their lives like I should be doing.

My earlier conversation with Tate also showed me that there's a line in the sand where I didn't realize one existed. And it crosses right between me and the guys. I'd stupidly thought we'd gotten closer. I thought letting them in, letting them be the ones to share such a vulnerable moment, meant something to *them* like it meant something to *me*. But I should've known better. And as if to emphasize that, my hip stings where the brand they burned into my skin continues to heal.

"You're a fucking idiot."

I breathe those words to myself, then look at the facts. Tate all but said there's nothing between us this afternoon, Micah's been distant as hell, and I haven't heard from Ash or Vince all day. Not that anyone's obligated to reach out or shower me with texts or phone calls, but... shit.

A girl could really use that right now.

But wait a fucking minute. Why am I taking all the blame for the confusion? If they don't care, why were they all at the hospital when I woke up? Why was at least one of them there at any given time of day to report to the others how I was doing? They *fed* this illusion.

But, at the end of the day, all that matters really is that I was wrong, I guess.

About them.

About *us*.

Wincing, I turn onto my side just as my phone dings. Speak of the fucking devil.

Vince: Hey, you up?

Stevie: Yeah.

I breathe deep, hoping he felt the chill in my response.

Vince: Need anything? Sorry for asking so late. Practice ran long today.

I stare at my phone, narrowing my eyes as I question whether he has an angle or if this is genuine.

Stevie: I'm good. Thanks.

Vince: Feeling okay?
Stevie: Just sore. And tired.
Vince: Glad to finally be out of the hospital?
Stevie: Fuck. Yes.

A smile leaves me after hitting *'send'*, and I imagine him doing the same. Okay, so maybe I'm not so mad at him.

Vince: Had any visitors?
Stevie: Nope. Well, Tate. Kind of.

I know my wording probably raised a red flag in his mind, but that wasn't intended. It's simply the truth. Tate was in fact here, but... just not to see me. Then, what little conversation I did manage to pull out of him only made me wish we hadn't talked at all.

Stevie: How'd practice go?

Hopefully a change of subject will keep him from overthinking what I said before.

Vince: Same shit different day. You should come sometime. When you're feeling up to it.
Stevie: What? And scare off all your beloved puck bunnies? I would never dream of it.

Another smile leaves me as I settle deeper into the mattress, trying to picture him, what he's doing right now.

Stevie: You could always stop by in the meantime. I mean, if you wanted to.

I rush to add that last part, hoping it makes me sound a little less clingy. But then, when he takes longer than before to respond, I wish I hadn't extended the offer.

Vince: I don't really do parents, but... it's you, so... maybe.

Without looking him in the eyes, it's hard to tell if he means it, hard to tell if he'll actually step out of his comfort zone. Then there's the whole *'it's you'* bit that's incredibly confusing. So, I move on.

Stevie: Sure. It's whatever.
Vince: Get some rest. I'll be up if you can't sleep. If you need to talk, or if you need to not *talk, I'm good with either.*

I tilt my head and arch a brow, re-reading his response.

Stevie: Careful, Mr. Ricci, that was almost romantic.

RACHEL JONAS & NIKKI THORNE

Vince: Shit. Total accident. Happens sometimes.

A loud laugh leaves me, then I cover my mouth, knowing Mom and Rob probably heard.

Stevie: Ok, I'm turning in. Night.

He doesn't respond, and I assume he won't, but then my phone sounds off again. It's Vince. Only, it isn't a text notification.

He's going live soon.

My heart speeds up. I've always loved watching him, but now it's different. Because I *know* him.

He sends another message.

Vince: How tired are you really?

Stevie: Why?

He takes a few seconds to respond, so I lower my phone and reach for the bottle of water Mom brought up a couple hours ago. I sip and start replacing the cap when my phone sounds off again.

Vince: Because I want you online. When I come, I need to know you're watching, need to know you're touching yourself.

I'm aware of my audible, uneven breaths as my lungs inflate again. I glance toward the door to make sure it's locked, then back down at my phone.

Stevie: Getting on now...

I settle beneath the covers and fire up my laptop where I left it on the nightstand. Vince's setup is familiar—dark background, the camera pointed at an empty chair. I don't have toys because Mom didn't rummage through that particular drawer in my bedroom—thank God—but I can manage without them.

A shadow darkens one side of the screen, then there he is—in all his chiseled, athletic glory. He's shirtless like always, but tonight, he's wearing a towel instead of sweats. It's rolled and tucked at his taut waist, a hint of his muscular thigh showing where the fabric parts. He lowers onto the seat and the camera is just low enough that those of us tuning in are blessed with a clear visual of his... equipment. We can't see it all, but enough that I'm able to imagine the rest.

I study him, wondering how I missed all the clues before, but he does make it difficult to pin down his identity. His facial features are always just hidden enough in the shadow of his cap, thanks to a clever lighting arrangement. Then I glance at his scar, remembering the feel of the soft, puffy ridge of skin when he brought my fingertips to it that night, wanting me to know him.

The sound of the chat firing up usually prompts me to turn it off, but not tonight. Tonight, I want to watch, want to know what his fans are thinking. A feeling fills me. It's one of pure satisfaction, knowing they're all going crazy for a guy they can only fantasize about. Meanwhile, I've touched him in the flesh.

Anonymous: ($20 tip pledged) "What I'd give to be that fucking towel right now."

I smile, slipping a hand underneath my shirt, cupping my breast. My nipple pebbles against my palm and I'm living on the memory of his touch, pretending my hands are his.

Anonymous: ($35 tip pledged) "Can I just say that you're beautiful? I don't think men hear that enough."

Anonymous: ($25 tip pledged) "When's the show start? I'm hard and need to finish before my wife gets home."

I smile, reading the comments.

Anonymous: ($10 tip pledged) "Any update on you letting us watch your first time?"

This time, it's Vince who smiles, and I wish I could see his whole face. I'm curious when he reaches for his phone, and a few seconds later, he's in the chat.

Host: "I've seen all the requests and... I'm considering it."

My heart flutters, my brow arches. There are too many thoughts going through my head to list them all.

Anonymous: ($60 tip pledged) "Holy shit! Seriously?"

Host: "Provided that my intended is interested."

Anonymous: ($50 tip pledged) "Question: Are you taking applications?"

I see Vince's chest move when he laughs again.

Host: "No. Sorry."

Anonymous: ($55 tip pledged) "Give us this girl's phone number, *address, email... everything. We'll bug the shit out of her until she agrees."*

Anonymous: ($35 tip pledged) "Is there seriously a girl walking this earth who'd have to think about whether she wants your dick inside her? I'm confused."

Anonymous: ($35 tip pledged) "My thoughts exactly. I swear my pussy parts like the red sea whenever this man's notifications come through. No way this girl will turn you down."

Anonymous: ($15 tip pledged): "Ask her now!"

Host: "You think I should?"

Anonymous: ($20 tip pledged) "Yes!"

Anonymous: ($15 tip pledged) "Is that even a question?"

Anonymous: ($20 tip pledged) "Do it!"

Anonymous: ($10 tip pledged) "One sec. Let me turn up my ringer so I don't miss your call... Ok, I'm ready."

Host: "I'll give it a shot."

Host: "Bird... what do you say. Will you do me the honor?"

My entire body buzzes when he addresses me directly. Like, what the actual fuck? I'm frozen, staring at the screen as the cursor blinks in the chat box.

Anonymous: ($30 tip pledged) "Wait a fucking minute. She's HERE?"

Anonymous: ($15 tip pledged) "Aww... What a cute nickname! I wanna be someone's Bird :("

Anonymous: ($50 tip pledged) "Lucky bitch."

My fingers hover over the buttons, and then... they're moving over the keys.

VIP Member: "I'll... Maybe?"

My gut twists. I wanted to say yes, wanted to be firm on this, but couldn't bring myself to do it. Not on a whim, with so little time to think things through. I've made the mistake of giving myself to a Savage before and look where that got me—waiting for a phone call, or even a fucking carrier pigeon, *something* that lets me know it meant something to him.

Meant *anything* to him.

Host: "Fair enough. We'll talk."

Anonymous: ($75 tip pledged) "Did she just sideline him? What kind of alternate universe shit is this?"

Anonymous: ($10 tip pledged) "She's a VIP member? What even is that? Is one of the perks that we're allowed to fuck you? If so, sign me up..."

From what I can tell, Vince isn't too rattled by my response. So, maybe he gets it. He sets his phone aside and relaxes deeper into his seat, parting his legs so we have a better view. He leaves the towel secured around his waist and his cock is hardening, slowly rising toward the ceiling. Given the conversation, it takes me a moment to get into it this time, but I eventually get out of my head and touch myself through my underwear, thinking about Vince's proposal. Tonight, I went from feeling somewhat iced out by the guys, to now considering the possibility that I'll be Vince's first.

I know I played coy in my response, but I'm turned the fuck on just at the thought of it. I follow his hand when he reaches between his legs, slathering a gratuitous amount of oil down his dick. He takes it into his fist and begins stroking himself. My clit awakens when I tease it, imagining myself opening up for him, letting him in to experience my body for the first time.

To experience *anyone's* body for the first time.

My teeth sink into my lip as I get even more turned on at the thought of how good I can make him feel. At the thought of how good he can make *me* feel.

My fingers tease my lower lips, and my pussy is so slippery, wet with anticipation for what could be.

I can't take my eyes off the screen as Vince's breathing quickens and he parts his knees more, using his free hand to massage his sac. Tweaking my nipple harder, I push two fingers deep inside, remembering how it felt being filled with something other than a toy, remembering the sweet ache of taking someone's cock, stretching my pussy in ways I'm now admittedly addicted to. If I could relive that feeling every day, if I could feel that good always, I would in a heartbeat.

And now, it's possible I'll have that again.

With Vince.

I imagine it, my pussy gripping him as he comes inside me and the thought of it is my undoing. In no time at all, I'm soaking my fingers as my eyes slam shut. My body tenses, but not even the sharp pain in my ribs can overshadow the pleasure. It's too intense, too sweet.

"Fuck," Vince grunts, and I focus on him as the last traces of an orgasm pulse through my core, and I stare in awe as he erupts, splashing cum all over his stomach, his towel, and down the back of his hand.

The sound of his deep breathing, and the squelching of cum and oil in his palm flow through my speakers as I continue to touch myself. The urgency to get myself off has come and gone, but I watch him, staring at his huge, sated cock releasing remnants from the tip. And despite my reservations, there's only one thought ringing inside my head.

I fucking want him.

And I'm not sure I'll be able to deny myself such a tempting opportunity.

Chapter 8

Stevie

"Shit."

"You okay?"

I sigh before answering Maddox, resting against the headboard as the room spins.

"I'm fine. I guess gaming and having a concussion don't pair so well together." I set the controller aside and accept defeat.

"We can try again later," he says.

"Maybe. But my guess is it'll just happen again." I chew my lip in frustration having just had my one source of entertainment taken away.

The phone vibrates, and I glance down at the text.

Ellen: Hey! Just checking in and letting you know I'm around if you need anything.

What the fuck?

I stare at the message, knowing she meant well, but it's a little awkward that I've spoken to this girl a whopping *one time*, and that was several months ago. It was the beginning of summer, actually. She took me on a tour around campus when I first enrolled. We exchanged numbers at the end of the day, but I honestly never expected to hear from her again.

But this random check-in lets me know there's talk going around campus, and God only knows what colorful spin people have put on the story.

Fun.

"I'll call you later. Don't you have a class to get to anyway?" I ask Maddox through the headset, shooting Ellen a quick *'Thank you'* text before setting the phone aside.

"Yeah, but I can stop by after if you want. You know, if you're bored or something."

"Ok. I'll text."

"Cool. Later."

I remove the headset and shut the game down. It feels like I've been stuck in this room my entire life. Meanwhile, it's only been five days.

Five long, boring days.

The aroma from Mom's cooking just began to waft upstairs, so I assume I have a bit until she bursts in with a tray of food. My eyes flit to the two boxes of hair dye on the dresser and it seems like a great way to kill time while I wait.

With a small groan when my torso tightens, I stand and grab the boxes, then head to the bathroom. A quick search lands me a couple dark towels that won't get ruined by the color, and I luck up on a few clips and a tint brush nestled deep in one of the drawers. After removing my t-shirt, I slip on the gloves from the box, then prepare the dye.

Things start off well, but about halfway through it becomes a bit of a struggle. What started out as a slight throb in my side, now has me afraid to lift my arms to finish. I manage to get the second bottle worked in, but I'm more than aware of having bitten off more than I can chew. Like, big time.

Mom offered to help last night and I'm thinking I should've taken her up on that.

The doorbell rings, and I vaguely hear footsteps downstairs, trailing from the kitchen, past the steps, headed toward the front door. I stare at myself in the mirror and evaluate. I've got two options. I can power through, slowly of course, rinsing the color out myself. Or I can accept that I'm nowhere near being one-hundred percent yet, and call Mom in to finish.

That seems like the better choice when I attempt to lift my arm again, only to quickly lower it as the ache in my side takes my breath away. Which means my body has just decided *for* me.

Beg Mom for help it is.

I groan and I'm even more frustrated than before. I just wanted to do something for myself, wanted to feel at least *somewhat* independent, but I guess that's still a ways off.

"Damn it!" The whispered words only convey an ounce of my annoyance. First, I couldn't game. Now, I can't do this on my own either.

Fucking perfect.

A knock at the door has me nearly dropping the tint brush when it startles me. "Come in."

Mom peeks her head around the door, wearing a smile at first, but then she sees the state I'm in, notices my hair.

"You must've felt my desperation all the way downstairs," I joke. "Wanna help?"

She gives this sympathetic look that makes me feel like even more of a loser than I already did.

"Honey, I would, but I'm in the middle of cooking," she says. "Besides, your friend is here."

"I told Maddox I'd let him know if—"

"No, not Maddox," she interrupts with a whisper. "*Vince's* friend. The one with the gauges and all the tattoos."

Her description paints a clear image of who she's talking about.

Ash.

My eyes widen as I stare at her in the mirror's reflection. I have mixed emotions. Embarrassment because I'm a total fucking mess right now, and there's even excitement. But I'm also not surprised by the undertone of sadness that puts a damper on all the other emotions. It's triggered by a simple fact.

I've now had both Vince *and* Ash check on me, and yet... not a single peep from Micah.

"Want me to ask him to come back later?"

Mom's question has me abandoning thoughts of the one who seems to have forgotten I'm alive, and I shift my focus back to Ash. I consider it, letting her turn him away.

"No, send him up," I say, and Mom looks me over, concern present in her eyes.

Likely not because I'm unwell, but rather because I currently look like ten miles of bad road.

"But, honey, your hair," she whispers again, as if I've forgotten.

"I'll figure something out. Just tell him to hang out in Tate's room until I'm done."

She eyes me with this *'Are you sure about that?'* look, and then I lock the door behind her once she's gone. I hear her speaking to Ash when she makes it back down, then there's the sound of heavy footsteps as he climbs the stairs. After that, Tate's door opens just before his bed creaks beneath Ash's weight, and I've given myself about five minutes to figure this out.

The only thing worse than being in pain is being in a *hurry* when you're in pain. I grunt through it when I turn on the shower, and then again while trying to maneuver one arm out of my sports bra. But it doesn't take long to realize I've reached my limit. Heat sears through my ribs, catching me off guard, and I fall against the wall for support.

"Shit!"

My head drops back as I wait in agony for the pain to subside, staring at the ceiling, wondering how the hell I'm supposed to make this work. The sound of Mom trying the door, and then pounding on it, only makes me *more* frustrated.

"You already said you don't have time to help, so please, just... let me figure this out," I sigh.

"You screamed. Let me in."

My eyes pop open. The deep voice on the other side of the door is definitely *not* my mother's. I scramble, touching the clips in my hair like there's more I can do to make myself presentable, but I accept that that's not really possible. So, when Ash knocks for a second time, I give the lock a slow twist and then open it.

I'm halfway hidden behind the door, eyeing him in silence—crisp white t-shirt, ripped jeans, brightly colored art that draws attention to the definition in his arms. Broad shoulders fill the doorway, his height reaching almost to the top of the frame. I don't miss that look of concern on his face or how his chest heaves with each deep breath he takes.

"You yelled," he says, looking me over. "What happened?"

My face heats with embarrassment.

"I'm good. I, um… I'm going for a new look and… things aren't quite going my way," I add with a faint smile.

He looks me over, as if only now realizing there's purple goop slathered in my hair. I guess he was so worried at first that he didn't even notice. But now that he does, now that he *sees* me, I feel awkward and unattractive.

Like a complete trainwreck.

Especially when his gaze lowers to my torso and he frowns. It isn't until I glance down, too, that I remember what I'm wearing—an old pair of basketball shorts and a sports bra. I find myself wishing the towel around my neck were longer, long enough to cover more of me.

Long enough to *hide* me.

"Look what they fucking did to you," Ash whispers.

It takes a moment, but then I realize *that's* what he was staring at. The bruises. It's an old habit to think people only view my body in judgment, but it's never like that with them. I should've known better.

Ash steps into the room, touching my waist as he looks me over. He's seen the marks on my face, but this is the first he's seen of my other injury—the boot-sized, purple splotch on my side that feels as bad as it looks.

The urge to cover myself is back. Only, it has nothing to do with thinking my stomach isn't flat enough or my boobs aren't perky enough. I want to hide because the idea of being pitied makes me uncomfortable.

Makes me feel twice as fragile. Twice as broken.

"It's um... it's actually getting a little better," I say, hoping to draw Ash's attention back to my face. It works. He meets my gaze, probably seeing I'm not really as okay as I want everyone to think I am. But he doesn't point it out. He lets me keep this one thing to myself, lets me live this lie that keeps me going.

And that's when I remember the lines of puffy skin all over his body, the untold stories behind them. If anyone understands this—the mental toll an ordeal like mine can take on someone—it's him. He's lived through worse.

Much worse, I imagine.

When he lifts my chin with his finger, whatever thought I just had begins to float away. And all it takes is the smile slowly curving his lips. It's soft, and warm, and... it settles me.

So much that words leave my mouth without me meaning to say them. "I'm glad you're here."

My heart flutters inside my chest with the confession. The words are true, yes, but I'm not this way with them—soft, vulnerable, open. When I blink and clear my throat, wishing I could take back those words, Ash's smile grows.

"Where else would I fucking be?" he rasps.

My stomach flutters, and I try to hide how he gets to me. "I don't know. Practice maybe?"

He shrugs. "Vince is covering for me. We flipped for who got to come see you today. I won, so... here I am."

He won.

Those words sit with me. The realization that he skipped out on something I know to be important to him, just to be with me. And not to mention that it seems Vince wanted to be here just as badly. With how we started off, I wouldn't have thought any of this was possible, but I'm not even sure what the rules are anymore.

I swear, his stare is hypnotic—deep blue irises filled with unleashed emotion. Maybe more than I've seen in anyone else. But then I'm abruptly cut off from their depth when his lids lower. He leans in, kissing me, letting his lips linger against mine. Just long enough that it leaves me dizzy when we separate.

"Let me help with your hair," he suggests, so smoothly it's almost a whisper. It actually isn't until I hear these words that my eyes open.

I laugh a little, arching a brow as I imagine it. "*You...* want to help with my hair? Do you even know what you're doing?"

He shrugs. "I know *enough*. I went through a phase in junior high where I colored mine practically every month."

Squinting, I look him over. "If I say yes, promise me I'll get to see pics documenting this phase you speak of."

He laughs and does this sexy eye roll as he nods. "If that'll make you happy, then, yes. I'll dig out the yearbook next time you're over."

I smile but bite my lip to keep it small. "Deal. And... thank you."

He nods once, locking the door behind him. "All you had to do was ask. All you *ever* have to do is ask."

My heart skips a beat, and there's only a small, fleeting thought about what my mom will think when she comes up to find Tate's room empty, and the bathroom light on.

Without a second thought about where to start, Ash nods toward the shower where the water I left running pelts the floor of the tub.

"Take everything off and hop in," he says casually, but the command gives me pause. Old hangups and insecurities are never far out of reach, so they rush at me with a vengeance when I reach for my waistband. But then I remember something important.

Ash isn't my father. He's only ever made me feel sexy and beautiful, and the fact that he's here—visiting simply because he was concerned, wanted to see me—says so much.

So, before I can overthink it, I push the shorts down and step out of them. Then, I manage to wriggle one arm out of my bra before Ash notices I'm struggling and helps with the other side. And once I'm naked, he scans me with this look. It's equal parts carnality and heat. It's just enough to let me know he doesn't hate what he sees.

I wasn't in this for a confidence boost, but damn. I'm eating this shit up.

"Slow," he warns. The next thing I feel are warm hands against my waist, holding me steady as I step into the tub and underneath the shower.

"Thank you."

"Does the showerhead detach?"

I nod, glancing up at it when he asks.

"Good. Sit," he says. "You'll be more comfortable."

He steps away, and I lower to the bottom of the tub without help, although I definitely could've used it. But I was too busy watching him take off his shirt to notice the pain. I stare shamelessly as he tosses his tee to the counter, then removes the silver rings from his fingers before starting this way again. The sight of him has me blinking to catch every detail through the water droplets gathering on my lashes. I accept that I could literally stare at him—this living, breathing work of art—all day, every day, and would never get tired.

He reaches for the showerhead, aims the sprayer inside the tub, then kneels.

"Are you able to lean back?"

I test my balance before giving an answer, carefully bracing myself on the heels of my palms, tilting my head toward the ceiling.

"Yeah, I think I'm good."

I relax a bit, feeling the rush of tepid water streaming down my skin as Ash's fingers move into my hair. He's gentle. Surprisingly so. There's an edge to him, a roughness I didn't realize he could turn on and off, but it's apparent now.

"You saved me," I say with a smile. "I wasn't sure I'd be able to finish on my own. My ribs hurt like a bitch."

"Good," he says, earning the sharp look I aim his way as he smiles. "Maybe next time you'll remember that shit and ask for help *before* you do something reckless."

He's scolded me in a sweet, playful way, but I don't question for a second whether he's being sincere. He pauses and his fingertips leave my scalp. I glance over and catch him working his shoulder a bit.

"You do that a lot. Old hockey injury?"

I smile and my eyes close again. But when he doesn't answer right away, I realize I might've guessed wrong. Nervous I've opened my big mouth and stuck my foot right in it, my eyes dart toward him. And the look I find there says he'd rather talk about something else.

70

Anything else.

"Shit. I'm sorry. You don't have to—"

"No, it's cool," he cuts in. "My, uh… my grandfather was a world-class asshole. His heart was hard, but his fist? That shit was even harder."

Ash chuffs a quiet laugh, but it's a dark sound, filled with nothing but sadness.

"That old man made a sport out of finding new ways to beat my ass as a kid. I mean, I'll be the first to admit I wasn't easy to raise, but… no one deserves what I went through."

My eyes fall closed, and his fingers continue to work through my hair.

"You asked about my shoulder, though," he says quietly. "I got suspended from school in seventh grade. There was this dick named Johnny who'd mess with me almost every day about my clothes. I was wearing shit from thrift stores before it was considered cool, I guess," he adds with a laugh. "He caught me on the wrong day, at the wrong time, and… I kicked his ass. The principal called the house and, as you can imagine, my grandfather wasn't too happy about it. So, when we got home, he slammed the door, and stormed off to his room. There wasn't a doubt in my mind he was going for his belt. So, I did what any kid would do, living with a mean son of a bitch like that. I hid."

He pauses, and I can see it all so clear—Ash as a frightened little kid, making the same mistakes we've *all* made as kids, but paying a hefty price for it. I've always seen his pain. He wears it on his sleeve, holds it in his eyes, but hearing him explain the horrors he experienced as a child paint him in a new light. One where it's not so farfetched that he's a little bit darker than most on the inside.

"What happened?" I ask softly.

He breathes deep. Not sounding annoyed, but more so like the trauma of it still lives rent-free inside his head.

"There was this old, rickety treehouse out back. It was my uncle's from when he was a kid. I hardly played in it because the thing was a deathtrap, but that night, *anything* seemed safer than facing my grandfather," he shares. "I hid up there for about ten minutes before he found me. And when he *did* find me, I got it twice as bad for making him hunt me down. So, to show me how bad I fucked up, he didn't think I needed the ladder. He... *pushed* me."

My heart lurches. My throat tightens. And it takes a moment to realize that the stinging in my eyes is from unshed tears.

"Landed right on my shoulder," Ash recalls. "It was nothing short of a miracle that I didn't break something, but I definitely did damage. Every now and then, it wakes up, reminding me of that day. Reminding me why I look forward to dancing on that asshole's grave in the near future."

I fill in the blanks myself. I'm guessing no one thought enough to have the shoulder x-rayed or properly cared for by a doctor. I'm guessing no one even thought to ice it or even offer Ash something to ease the pain while he tried to rest that night. Then, I imagine him crying himself to sleep, wishing things were different, wishing he was loved. Protected. But instead, he was alone. And it was the worst *kind* of loneliness. The kind inflicted by negligent relatives who didn't give a shit.

"They say what doesn't kill you only makes you stronger, right?" he says, and I hear him making light of this, but I see through the façade. I see through it because I've tried casting up the same wall in the past.

"That's what they say," I answer. "But sometimes, what doesn't kill you only makes you wish it had."

He's quiet, mulling over my words as he smooths a hand down my hair, pushing more of the excess color from it.

"Damn, Bird. That's kind of fucked up," he says with a quiet laugh.

"Kind of fucked up, but also kind of true."

A dull ache in my side makes those words more real, thinking about the attack. Thinking about my sister. It all got to be too much for her, and then, one day, she just... let it all go.

The pain.

The hurt.

The burden.

"I thought I had it bad with *my* dad, but that was nothing compared to what you dealt with."

"Nah. Shit parenting is just that. Shit parenting. No matter how you cut it," he reasons. "It all leaves us with scars. Including the kind you can't see."

When he says this, I remember the textured feel of his skin beneath my fingertips.

"Now it's your turn. What's *your* damage?"

"Well, the short version? My dad was a verbally and emotionally abusive piece of shit," I answer, shifting a little when my hands start to fall asleep. "I was never small enough or pretty enough to meet his standard. And unfortunately, I didn't wake up and stop *trying* to meet it until I was about fourteen or fifteen. By then, the damage had been done. His thoughts became *my* thoughts, and I stopped thinking I was enough, too."

Ash is quiet and without being able to lay eyes on him, I can't get a clear read on what he's thinking.

But then, I don't have to guess anymore. Because he grips my chin, turns my face toward his, and kisses me. His fingers slide down to my neck, adding the slightest bit of pressure. And then *more* pressure when he squeezes my throat. His mouth leaves mine and I eventually have the presence of mind to open my eyes. He's staring into me and there's an air of frustration that seems misplaced at first, but when he speaks, I get it.

"Fuck whatever lies people have told you about who and what you are. You're perfect. Every fucking inch of you. Understood?"

I hear his words loud and clear, but I also feel them. All the way down in my bones. He knows this when I nod. Instead of backing off now that he's made his point, he leans in until his mouth connects with mine again. His taste on my lips has my tongue seeking his, wanting to be closer.

At the feel of his hand cupping my breast, I inhale deep through my nose and my chest fills with air. The rough pad of his thumb brushes over my nipple and I'm at his mercy. Water drips from my hand and down the back of his neck when I grip it, holding him captive.

"Open your legs for me," he breathes.

Without hesitation, my knees part. Just like he commanded. He interrupts the kiss to switch the showerhead to the opposite hand, angling the stream of water perfectly between my legs. Then, his free hand moves into my hair, lightly tugging until my head tilts back, exposing my neck as his mouth presses to my throat.

A steady stream of water rushes over my clit, just powerful enough that I'm breathing deep and ragged. And the feel of Ash's tongue—slick and warm—gliding over my racing pulse makes my stomach swirl. There's an explosion looming in my core and I'm already anticipating it.

"I need to make you come," he whispers. "Will you let me do that for you?"

The depth of his voice reverberates against my throat, and with very little thought, I nod.

"Good," he croons, licking the side of my neck before placing a gentle bite just below my ear. And much to my disappointment, he angles the showerhead away, toward my thigh while asking a question. "Think you can keep quiet?"

I feel him smile against my skin, and I swear if I weren't already sitting, I'd be in a puddle at his feet. It's possible he already knows this, already *senses* it, but I'll do whatever he wants.

Whenever he wants it.

"Can you keep quiet?" he repeats, his tone low and gravelly.

I nod again, desperation making it hard to breathe. "Yes. Probably," I add, correcting myself.

He smiles against my throat again, slowly moving a heated kiss to my mouth. I'm only certain he's accepted my response when the stream of water shifts back to where I craved it, awakening my clit once more.

He sinks his tongue into my mouth, and I open for him, drawing him in deep. What started as a gentle hum of pleasure at the base of my stomach becomes a full-on wailing siren the next instant. A whimper leaves me, filling Ash's mouth as his hold on my hair tightens. I yield to him. Bending to his will.

Coming on his command.

My body continues to quiver, even once he's lowered the showerhead and released my hair. But I still have his lips. He's never kissed me like this before—slow and deep. He's never quite as brash as Micah, but definitely not gentle.

Definitely not soft.

He kisses my bottom lip, then my chin, then pulls away, leaving me in a daze as he comes close to whisper.

"A little louder than I'd hoped, but I'll take it," he teases, mocking how the volume of my voice rose a bit as I finished.

He stands, and I stalk him with my eyes, watching as he approaches the open linen closet and takes out two more of the dark towels I scored earlier. Wanting to feel independent I brace the edge of the tub and attempt to stand, but Ash rushes over when it becomes a struggle.

"Still haven't gotten the message," he grumbles, securing his arms around my waist as he lifts me with such ease I feel like a child.

"*What* message?"

He grabs the towels from where he's placed them on the counter.

"The message is that you don't have to do everything alone," he says, wrapping one towel around my body and the other around my damp hair. "You have *us* now," he adds, staring me right in the eyes.

In the very recent past, the three wanted nothing from me but to be an instrument for their pain, to bleed *their* hurt from *my* veins. All so they wouldn't have to feel it anymore. Or maybe just for the sake of having someone suffer with them. But the night all our emotions came tumbling out—physically and then with words when a night of heat and lust transitioned into something more—their intentions became a blur.

Ash looks me over and then smirks. "I don't do shit like this for just anyone, Bird," he explains, and I find myself dissecting those words, their deeper meaning.

I'm quiet, hearing his statement swirl inside my thoughts for several seconds, trying not to jump to conclusions. But when I lock both arms across my chest, holding Ash's gaze, there's no denying that I'm on the defense.

"What's *that* supposed to mean?"

He smirks, then winks at me. "It means you're one of the lucky ones."

A quiet laugh leaves him when he's done, but nothing's funny. Not even a little. He scans me with a look, maybe noticing I'm suddenly tense, and only now does he seem to read the room and realize we're not on the same page.

"Relax. It's a joke," he says, and then reaches to take my waist, but I brush his hand away.

When that smile finally leaves, I can gather that he realizes I'm not laughing with him.

"Shit, I was kidding. I only meant that we don't show up for other people the way we show up for you."

"And do you also burn and humiliate other people like you've done to me?"

He holds my gaze and his brow knits together, a shocked smirk on his lips. "What the fuck is even happening right now?"

I don't answer. Instead, I'm trying to convince myself he didn't just allude to the fact that he thinks I should be grateful his ass is standing here. Grateful one of the gods stepped down from his throne to assist a lowly mortal. Yes, they were at the hospital. Yes, Ash is here now, but... does he honestly think that's enough to make me forget all the other shit? Enough to convince me to just fall in line?

No.

Fuck that.

Inevitably, my thoughts shift to Micah, shift to the fact that I've called him three times since being released from the hospital, and... nothing. There's a bitter taste in my mouth at the thought of it. At the thought of what he let me give him, and then how he's been a complete asshole since. Proving that Ash was wrong.

I *don't* have them.

I'm still only certain I have the one person I've always had.

Me.

Ash's finger catches my chin, forcing me to meet his gaze again when my head and eyes lower to the floor.

"Tell me you believe me, believe that we only want to be here for you," he says, but his commanding tone doesn't work this time. Because actions speak louder than words.

"I believe you mean well," is all I say, and his mouth opens to scold me for not readily taking his word, but we're interrupted by a knock at the door.

"Sweetheart? You okay in there?"

My eyes widen, my heart races. Ash is completely still.

Did she hear his voice?

"Um... y-yeah. All good. I'll be out in a sec."

I peer up at Ash and he's expressionless as he glances toward the door. I can read him even though he's silent, can see the tension in his broad shoulders, which tells me he's upset with how our conversation just shifted. And because I know him and the others to be a relentless bunch, I know this isn't over.

"Okay. Just letting you know dinner's done," Mom adds. "Do you think your friend would want to eat with us? I can knock on the door and ask him."

"No! I'll... I'll invite him when I get out." Her offer has adrenaline pumping through my veins as I envision my mother going into Tate's old bedroom, finding it empty. She'd jump to the only logical conclusion from there—that Ash is, in fact, in the bathroom with me committing any number of unholy acts.

He stares down on me, seemingly closer than before, but he hasn't moved. My eyes land on his heaving chest, and I want to touch him, feel his heat beneath my palms, but a swift reminder of our argument stops me.

Mom's quiet on the other side of the threshold. *Too* quiet.

"Sure," she finally says. "Rob just got in and you know he's always starving come dinner time, so... you guys just meet us down there once you're done, okay?"

Relieved that this ordeal is nearly over, I nod. "Okay. Be there in a few."

She hesitates, but I eventually hear her steps retreat. And thank God she doesn't open Tate's door. A sigh of relief leaves me, and I take a step, planning to go out into the hallway while the coast is clear, but ash's light grip on my arm halts me.

I peer up, noting the sternness in his eyes when our gazes lock. And before he even speaks, I feel his frustration, his discontentment with how we ended things.

"Do you even believe a word I said?" he asks, low and even, lacking desperation. I get the impression he just wants to know where we stand.

My chest rises and falls when I take a breath, deciding I've earned the right to be direct with him. And the others too, for that matter.

"I'll just say actions speak louder than words," I answer. "If you want me to believe you, if you want me to trust that you're not just blowing smoke up my ass, show me. I think I deserve that."

He stares, unmoving, and I wonder if I actually got through to him.

"Show you?" he scoffs. "What do you think I'm trying to do? Why the fuck do you think I'm here?"

His tone is clipped, hinting at his growing frustration. But I'm frustrated, too. And rightly so.

"I think you're here because you're used to the bare minimum being enough. I think you're here because I haven't voiced how bad the shit you three did has fucked with my head. So, consider this me giving you notice, I guess."

He draws in a deep breath to curb his anger. "Okay, I think we agree the joke was bad, and my timing is shit, but we've been with you every step of the way since your injury," he points out. "You're saying that doesn't mean shit to you?"

"This isn't about the joke," I snap. "This is about how much I've put up with, and how the weekend we spent together might've clouded everyone's judgement. But contrary to what you guys might think, I'm not just some... *thing* you can set down and pick up whenever the fuck you want to."

"No one thinks that."

My brow arches when he says that with such certainty. "No? Then, tell me, Ash. Where the fuck is Micah?"

Ash holds my gaze, but falls quiet. "He's working through some shit. We're giving him room to get his head together, sort things out."

"Sort things out," I scoff. "Seems there's a lot of that going around these days."

"What are you talking about?"

I'm silent, thinking of a very recent conversation I *almost* had with Tate. A conversation I can probably play out on my own, which involves him giving me some bullshit reason why he chased me for *months,* only to leave me with regret for ever having let my guard down with him.

I almost say it. Almost tell Ash everything, but I don't.

"Just... leave it alone."

At the risk of seeming ungrateful for his help, I walk to the door, then head to Tate's room without another word. Ash stands alone in the bathroom. For so long, I was the one feeling insecure, but it's time *they* feel that shit, wondering if there's room for them in my heart.

Wondering if they've fucked up too bad to hold on to me.

And while I don't know that I realized this before now, all things considered... I'm not totally sure they haven't.

Chapter 9

Stevie

Light glows dimly through my eyelids, and last night feels like a dream.

Only, not the good kind.

I can hear the conversation with Ash replaying in my head. I can feel the conflict that coursed through my veins—one side of me very much wanting to pretend things are perfect, and the other remembering all the bad shit, seeing how half of them hardly even acknowledge my existence.

It's crossed my mind that I might be judging them as a unit instead of as individuals, but at this point, it's hard to see the forest for the trees. Hard to tell if they aren't all one and the same.

"Hungry?" Mom asks, letting herself into my room without knocking. "Rise and shine!"

Was she always this fucking perky in the morning?

I'm still groggy, and last night feels like it's bleeding into today, all the emotion that hung over my head while I tried to sleep still plaguing me. Ash left after we talked. There was no family dinner, no small talk. Instead, I spent the night alone, holed up in this bedroom, asking myself if *I'm* the asshole.

Was I too hard on him?

Did I take out my frustration on him simply because he was the one who showed up?

Am I in my feelings and being bitchier than usual?

I hate that I have these questions in my head, but what I hate even more is that he and I are now officially on the outs, too.

He was sweet to me yesterday, caring, helping, but did he think that would be enough? Showing up for me *once* after all the shit they did? And after how I've been ghosted since leaving the hospital? I'm still wounded for fuck's sake. The brand on my hip might be the only *physical* scar they left, but the emotional ones are abundant, so I think I'm allowed to feel a bit resistant. It was bad enough that I so easily bent to his will, but when it came to talk of trust and understanding, I had to draw the line. Had to let him know I'm not some dumb, desperate girl who'll accept whatever bullshit they toss her way.

"Look at your hair!" Mom beams. "It turned out great!"

I rub my eyes and want to ask her to save the conversation until sometime after nine, but I imagine that would seem rude.

"Thanks."

She's moving around my room. I hear her but can't quite see clearly yet. A drawer opens and closes, and I realize she's putting my laundry away, which is still taking some getting used to.

"Made you breakfast," she announces. "Eggs, toast, and bacon. I set it right on your nightstand. But first, take a look out the window."

I manage to open one eye and toss her a look. She's staring with this huge-ass grin on her face that makes me a little skeptical. But she doesn't say more and I'm incredibly curious what the big deal is.

So, I drag myself out from under the covers and brace my hands against the sill while I peer down—a neighbor walking her dog, random cars parked along the curb, a newspaper lying in the driveway.

"I give. What am I looking for?"

Mom sighs and sets the laundry basket down. "If it were a snake, it would've bitten you," she teases, taking the sides of my head in her hands, and then angling my gaze down to the large oak tree by the sidewalk. And just in front of it, there's a navy-blue car parked at the curb.

"Okay, so… we have company. Who is it?" I ask, aware of sounding like a major smart-ass.

Smiling, she rolls her eyes. "No, Stevie. We don't have company. But what we *do* have… is a new car. Well, *you* have a new car."

My brow gathers when I question what she's saying.

"Rob and I talked, and we decided that we don't want you on that bike anymore. With what's happened, it's just too dangerous for you to be riding that thing around in the middle of the night."

I look at her, then back down at the car. "I don't really know what to say, Mom. I—thank you."

She responds with a hug, tight around my neck.

"All I want is to keep you safe. And I'm sorry if you didn't always feel that."

My eyes fall closed with those words, feeling their hidden meaning. It's no secret that we've bumped heads over the years. Mainly because of her lack of action where my father's verbal and emotional abuse are concerned. Had it been physical abuse, there's no doubt in my mind she would've stepped in, protected me, but sometimes I think it was easy for her to pretend like his teasing and jabs *'weren't a big deal'*.

Only, they *were* a big deal.

Even if only to me.

The thought makes my arms loosen around her as the all too familiar sting of bitterness sneaks in, reminding me why I've kept her at arm's length for years now. When we separate, she seems to notice the change in my mood and looks away, a smile barely present on her lips now.

"Anyway, we just thought you should have it. And don't even *think* about trying to pay us back. This is our gift to you," she adds.

I glance out the window again. "Thank you. I really appreciate it."

"The key is hanging on the hook beside the front door," she says, and then goes back to the dresser where she folds the last two t-shirts in the basket. "Was… everything okay last night?"

I meet her gaze, but when I don't respond to the vague question, she elaborates.

"Your friend... Ash, is it?"

I nod, letting her know she's right. However, I don't particularly want to go wherever this conversation is headed. I know what she saw that has her questioning me this morning—Ash likely unable to hide his frustration as he left, ignoring Mom's dinner invite, me never coming down to join her and Rob at the table.

To her, I'm sure it looked like a fight.

And... I suppose it was.

"He left so abruptly," she says. "And he seemed upset. I just—"

"All good, Mom. Nothing to worry about." I drop back down onto the bed where I reach for a piece of bacon.

She closes the open drawers, pretending her wheels aren't still turning, but when she meets my gaze, I know better.

"It's just that... aren't you involved with his friend, Vince? Doesn't he mind you and Ash spending time alone together?" she asks. "It just seems... I don't know... a bit risky."

I sigh discreetly, remembering that she does in fact believe Vince and I are exclusive, which I suppose is better than her knowing the truth. Her poor heart couldn't handle the truth.

"He's fine with it," I say, going along with the lie as I force a smile. "I didn't eat because the medication sometimes makes me nauseated. And Ash *was* upset, but not with me. He got a call from someone who needed to borrow money and took off to handle it. That's all," I lie again, knowing good and well the one Ash was frustrated with was, in fact, me. But hopefully this explanation kills any chance of there being follow-up questions.

Hopefully.

Her eyes linger on me a bit, heavy on the skepticism, then she shrugs. "Just thought I'd check in. And if the medication isn't sitting well with you, maybe we should have the doctor—"

"It's fine," I cut in. "Doesn't happen all the time."

She stares, clearly concerned, but she's used to my stubbornness. "Whatever, it's your body, and I can't force you into anything, so..."

RACHEL JONAS & NIKKI THORNE

Looking a bit defeated, she lowers her gaze to the floor, but I get the sense there's more coming.

"Anyway, I'm sure I just shot myself in the foot by prying," she says with a nervous smile, "but Rob and I have been discussing more than just buying you a car. We've been thinking it might be good for you, for *all* of us, if you stayed here for a while."

I'm quiet, wading through the hundreds of thoughts her offer just awakened.

"You're an adult, so we'd treat you as such, but... I'd sleep better knowing you're safe, knowing you're under the roof with people who care about you and want what's best for you," she adds, and that's when I notice the tears in her eyes.

I can't imagine being her right now, living with having lost one daughter, knowing she could've easily lost another. So, I get why she'd want to keep me close, but it's more complicated than that.

We're more complicated than that.

"I'm sure you'll have to give this some thought. You've been on your own for a while, so I know it might not be an easy decision to make. But I just need you to know that staying here is an option. Actually, we'd love to have you, so..."

Her words hit me hard. I don't miss their vulnerability, the courage it took to say them. Especially considering our history.

But... it's that history that gives me pause, prevents me from leaping into her arms with an immediate *'yes'*. Because this side of her—the self-aware, self-reflective, sensitive side of her—it's all new to me, something she tapped into after I left and moved on.

Something she tapped into after I needed her most.

So, while this arrangement seems ideal, I have reservations. And I owe it to myself to address those reservations.

"I appreciate this. Seriously, you and Rob have been my saving grace," I admit, lowering my gaze as I muster up the courage to say more. "But I don't know if this is what's best, Mom."

When I peer up, her eyes are already locked on me, filled with so many different emotions—sadness, shock, confusion.

"Okay, well, let's talk about it," she offers, coming to rest on the edge of the bed. "Tell me what you're concerned about, and we'll work through it."

I hold her gaze, needing to see her eyes when I ask a question. The question that's been lingering in my head for days now. The one that, depending on how she answers, will make or break this decision.

"Mom, I need to know why you texted me the night I... the night I was..." My words trail off when my mind flashes back to the attack, but I pull it together quickly. "You said that we needed to talk, and I need to know why. What were you going to tell me?"

I watch her, study the way her pulse races at the base of her throat despite the rest of her appearing to be unbothered by the question. She swallows deeply, then snaps out of the brief spell of shock that momentarily gripped her. And, as expected, she puts on that fake smile, the one she dons to hide all her secrets.

"Is that seriously what's gotten under your skin?" she asks with a laugh. "Honestly, sweetheart, I don't even remember, so it must not have been important. Something about the wedding maybe? We do have the cake tasting coming up, so maybe that was it?" she adds with a dumfounded shrug.

And... there it is.

The lie.

One of many reasons it's almost impossible to fully trust her. Do I know she'd do anything she could to protect me? Yes, of course, she would. But do I also know her to do what's necessary to cover her own ass, keep up this façade of perfection she thinks people buy into?

Abso-fucking-lutely.

She smiles, patting my leg as she stands, thinking things are resolved. My gaze follows her, and she has no idea what's going through my head right now—that living here long-term isn't even an option until she finally, *finally,* owns up to the truth.

Whatever it is.

And just like that, she's headed toward the door. No further explanation. No bother asking if there was more I wanted to discuss. She's just... leaving.

"Oh, and speaking of the cake testing, I want you there," she says with that killer smile that's gotten her out of so much shit in her life, but it isn't enough to wriggle out of this.

When I don't answer, she arches a brow.

"I'll text you the date as soon as I have a second to glance at my calendar, but can I count on you?"

My heart races with her question. My stomach churns, and I fight the urge to show my cards. But I know better. These things are best flown under the radar when it comes to her.

"Sure," I say with a smile, being just as deceptive as the one who birthed me. She's satisfied, thinking we're done with this, but as soon as she turns her back...

"Mom, who's Dusty?"

Her steps halt, her body goes still, and she's silent. I stare, watching as movement in her shoulders gives away that she's breathing deeper. However, when she composes herself, and turns to meet my gaze, you'd never guess anything is amiss.

She does that dismissive shrug again, flashes a smile, and lies straight through her perfect teeth.

"I have no idea, Sweetheart. Be back to check on you in a few, though. Gotta get the roast in the slow cooker. Did I mention that Tate's joining us for dinner?"

I smile again, then she leaves. She's gone, and I'm fucking stunned. By the ease with which those words left her mouth when she very clearly *does* know who Dusty is. If she didn't, she wouldn't have faltered. That moment of hesitation said so much without her saying a single word.

But I know my mother. She'll block me from whatever she has to hide at every turn, so I've got a new plan. One that will allow me to completely leave her out of the equation, but it means asking the one person for help I swore I'd never turn to again.

My father.

I can only hope that, when all is said and done, whatever insight he's able to give will be worth reopening old wounds.

Because if I'm honest, I'm not sure I have it in me to stitch myself closed again.

Chapter 10

Tate

Our waitress approaches the table, a pitcher of beer in hand. She sets it down, and I thank her—not just for bringing our order, but also for breaking up some of the tension.

I've been sitting with these two for less than five minutes and, already, I regret asking them to meet me here. After all, it's their father I've built up a rapport with, not them.

But alas, here I am, playing my role, digging to see what I can find out from Tory's brothers.

The moment I heard they accompanied her the evening she met with Stevie, I knew something was up. It's not every day you hear of the daughter of simple people—a college professor and a freelance sign-language interpreter—needing bodyguards.

I fill my mug, then glance up at Nolan and Zach from across the table, having run out of small talk by this point. Which means it's time to get into why we're *really* here.

"Again, I appreciate you guys for coming."

Zach nods. "No problem. Anything we can do to help."

"Not sure if you know this, but the meetup between Tory and Stevie was my idea," I share.

"To be frank, we're not really sure where *any* of this shit is coming from, but what we *do* know, is that we're committed to protecting our sister," Nolan speaks up, and the hard glare set in his eyes is proof that whatever promise he's made to Tory or himself, he intends to keep it.

Confused, I nod, buying myself a bit of time. "And I respect that. Completely," I add. "But... can I ask what you're protecting her *from?*"

That question lingers in the air for a bit, then the brothers share a loaded look. As if to ask whether they should say more or leave things where they are. It isn't until Nolan meets my gaze again that I have hope they'll continue.

"A girl visited the house. The day of Mel's funeral. She wanted to speak with Tory," he adds.

I feel my brow tense. "About what?"

They do that thing again, where they glance toward one another before answering. This time, it's Zach who speaks up.

"The chick was drunk or high or, hell, maybe she was both," he scoffs. "Scared the shit out of Tory."

I'm on the literal edge of my seat. "What did she want?"

"She got in Tory's face, demanding to know if Mel met up with anyone that night, or if it seemed like she was being followed. Then, when Tory mentioned that someone named Stevie wanted to meet up, we invited ourselves just to make sure things were on the up and up."

I've got a million questions.

"Chances are you don't know the answer to this, but any idea if Tory disclosed this info to Stevie?"

"Actually, she mentioned beforehand that she wouldn't bring it up," Nolan explains. "Apparently, the girl who showed up at our door is someone Tory knows."

"Knows *of*," Zach corrects. "From what Tory said, the girl's kind of a troublemaker, known for being a world-class fuck-up."

My eyes lower to the table, knowing the confusion and frustration *I* feel only having a piece of the picture is just a fraction of what Stevie's going through.

"When Tory brought up Mel's sister, we honestly told her to just… let this shit go, but she was adamant about helping Stevie find closure. Mel was a good friend to her, and I think that went both ways," Zach adds. "Our sister doesn't know anything. Only that this Mel girl took off on her that night, then stopped talking to Tory completely afterward. Next thing we know, we heard she'd taken her own life, and we were left to help Tory make sense of it all."

"But the fucked up thing about it is, there *is* no making sense of shit like this. It's just a tragedy from every angle, any way you spin it," Nolan concludes, and it feels like that—a conclusion.

A closed door.

"Shit, it's getting late. We should take off," Zach says after glancing down at his watch.

"Right, of course. I'm actually running a bit late for dinner myself, but I appreciate you both meeting with me, for helping me understand a little better."

Nolan nods and he grips my hand when we stand from the table. "Anything we can do to help. Let us cover our half of the bill," he offers, but before he has the chance to take out his wallet, I stop him.

"No, you did me a favor coming here tonight. Beers are on me."

He holds my gaze a moment, then nods. "If there's anything else we can do, you know how to reach us."

I thank them both again, then watch them make their exit. I drop cash on the table and leave a moment later, feeling more confused now than I did before.

And now I feel torn, between my gut telling me to bring Stevie up to speed and wanting to protect her. She's been through a lot, and not just this past week. Maybe Tory was right to withhold this information. Maybe this thing with Mel can *never* be solved, and Stevie would be better off just letting it go.

Letting it all go.

I make it to my car and climb in, but don't start the engine. Because I'm hit with a thought that changes things. The man who robbed and killed my mother was never found, and it eats at me every day. So, who the hell am I to stand in someone else's way of having the closure I wish I'd been afforded?

And it's with this thought that I pull out into the street, headed in the direction of the one girl I can't seem to get out of my head.

Regrettably.

I'll have to talk to her in private—something I hoped to avoid—and then distance myself right after. But... she needs this. Even if it doesn't answer all her questions, even if it isn't the smoking gun, it matters.

So, by default... it matters to me, too.

Chapter 11

Stevie

I haven't said a single word to my mother since this morning, and don't plan to unless we're discussing Dusty's identity. Yet, the woman hasn't shut up since we sat down at the table. She's talked all through dinner, only getting responses from Rob and Tate, and now, I get the impression she intends to talk through dessert as well.

Just fucking great.

"Okay, Tate. Since *Stevie* won't tell us much about Vince, how would *you* like to tell us about your friend?"

My teeth grit when she brings him up. How ironic that she wants to know every single detail of my life, unfiltered, but I can't get a single ounce of truth out of her?

I don't meet anyone's gaze as I fork a small bite of German chocolate cake into my mouth.

"Well, I… I'm not really sure where you want me to start," Tate says, clearing his throat right after. "Vince is a good student, he's on the hockey team—a starter, actually—and he's… crazy about your daughter."

I peer up at him then, wondering why he'd say that. Is he just laying it on thick or is that something Vince actually told him himself?

It hits me that I'm doing it again, living in this fantasy world where me and the guys are more than what we are, more than what they've *shown* me they are. So, I bring myself back down to earth and take Tate's words for exactly that.

Words.

"He's the total package then," Mom says.

Rob laughs and arches a brow. "Val, do I need to worry that you'll leave me for this guy?"

I glance up just as Mom playfully arches a brow, too, like she's considering it before a laugh breaks free.

"I'm kidding, but it does seem like my girl's found a good one," she says. "The way he and his friends all stuck by her side at the hospital. I mean, granted, they were mostly hanging out in the waiting room, but they were there, and... it mattered. It mattered to *me,* as a mother, that they're all so protective, so loyal."

I nearly scoff out loud but relieve some of the frustration brought on by her manifesto with a deep sigh.

Loyal.

They're so loyal I haven't heard back from Micah once.

"Anyway, I'm sure they'll be looking out for you when I can't, since you *insist* on going back to school and work so soon," she complains.

"Really? *How* soon?" Rob asks.

"Monday."

Without looking up, I see Tate's head shift when Mom answers the question, and I'm guessing he's curious how that'll work out, seeing as how I'm not fully healed. Inside *or* out. But I can't sit here, putting my life on hold, waiting for some perfect moment to get back out there.

"Shit, speaking of Monday," Rob says, "we have until then to respond to the offer."

I peer up again, staring at my mother, although she's very obviously avoiding eye contact with me.

"The buyer's agent wants to move things along quickly and—"

"Buyer's agent? Someone's already interested in the house?"

My voice cracks when I ask, and I hate it. Hate that it hints at the emotions bubbling inside me.

"Honey... you knew it was on the market," Mom says, softening her voice. "We need to get it sold before the wedding, so..."

She trails off there, and I process the finality of it. No, the new owners haven't closed just yet, but it's coming.

That house—the last place I shared memories with my sister—is gone.

Unshed tears sting my eyes, and everyone's silent, focused on me, which I hate. When I push back from the table and Mom stands next, I motion for her to stay where she is.

"I'm fine, I just... I need to be alone."

Before she can protest, and before the pools in my eyes overflow, I make as smooth an exit as possible. But then I hear the words, "I'll talk to her," spoken behind me.

I roll my eyes as Tate's footsteps approach, catching up to me when I make it out onto the porch, but not before I'm able to grab my keys from the hook beside the door. He doesn't speak until we're down the walkway a few yards. I'm guessing he only waits because he'd like to avoid his dad spotting us on the security camera mounted near the door.

Heat from his long fingers encircles my arm, jerking me back with a light tug, but it's enough to irritate me and grate the last nerve I have left tonight. When I whirl toward him, rage blooms in my chest. I don't want to *look* at him, much less *talk* to him. Judging by the bewildered look on his face, I imagine he has zero clue why that might be.

We haven't talked in days. Like so many others in my life right now, he's been distant and hasn't been very forthcoming with... well, *anything* lately. Our last conversation ended abruptly when he decided I needed to heal more before he spoke his piece. Which lets me know he didn't have anything good to say. And because I'm a pretty smart girl, I'm fairly certain I know how that conversation was going to go.

He'd say something about our emotions running high that night and how we *both* let things go too far. And he'd conveniently leave out the part about him trying his best to get my attention months before that night even seemed like a possibility. Then, he'd dumb the entire encounter down to a mistake, something we shouldn't have done and can never happen again.

Simple.

And while I definitely haven't shed any tears over him, I'm also not in the mood to pretend it didn't mean anything. I'm woman enough to admit that I like him. Or... *liked* him, have since the day we met, before all my bullshit logic and detective work convinced me he was a bad guy. But now that he got what he wanted from me—one wild and dirty night that will forever remain an unspoken secret between us—he wants nothing to do with me.

How fucking typical.

He's staring, and I hate it. He knows these tears aren't for him, but the mere idea of being vulnerable around him doesn't sit right with me.

"What do you want?" I hiss, resenting the familiarity in his touch as he continues holding my arm. I want to forget it, forget that the feel of his hands on me ever incited any feeling but anger.

"Where are you going?"

Sniffling, my brow knits together. "What's it matter? It's not like you actually care anyway."

"That's not fair."

"No, what's not fucking fair is—"

I catch myself, stop the words before I say too much. He doesn't deserve to know I still think about how we left things.

"Listen, I know you're upset about the house, and I know I'm probably the last person you want to hear from, but we need to talk."

"We—" I stop, letting a dark laugh slip as I brush moisture from my cheeks. His hand finally falls away, and I could technically walk off now, but I don't. "Whatever you need to say, it'll have to wait. There's something I have to do."

"It's important, Stevie."

His expression is firm, unyielding. I take a step back, lifting my eyes toward the sky when I breathe deep.

"You don't get to do this."

"Do what? I—"

"You don't get to control this. You don't get to decide that *now* is the time you're ready to talk and just expect me to put everything on hold and listen. It doesn't work like that."

I walk away, but then I think of more that needs to be said, and double back, only to find that he was trailing me anyway.

"And do you have any idea how fucked up it is that you pursued *me,* screwed around with the rest of us that night, and now you can hardly even look me in the eyes?" I scoff, thinking about the pure fucking audacity. "I get it. I'm not like the tall, skinny, perfect bitches you probably have falling at your feet, but—"

"Are you fucking insane?" His expression shifts from desperation to anger in the blink of an eye.

"I'm not some inanimate... *thing*, Tate. Some toy you can pick up and put down whenever you fucking feel like it! I'm real. I'm a real person, with real feelings, so the only thing I have to say to you is, *go fuck yourself!*" I yell, and when I storm off this time, I have no intention of turning back.

"Stevie, you're not hearing me," he says, keeping his voice low as a couple pass by, taking their dog for an evening stroll. "You don't understand."

"I understand enough," are my final thoughts on the matter, climbing into my car, cranking the engine for the first time since Mom and Rob brought it home. I adjust the seat and fiddle with the lights, taking longer than it would normally because my hands are shaking.

"You're making a huge mistake," he says through the closed window, but I ignore him, having said all I intend to say to him tonight.

There's another asshole I need to deal with. One who lives across town and probably wants to see me about as little as I want to see *his* mean ass.

I take off so quickly my tires screech at the end of the driveway, and I only glance back in the rearview mirror once. Tate's watching, of course, both hands tucked inside his pockets.

He looks frustrated, but I don't care. Fuck him. My default setting lately has been *frustrated*. And as I watch his silhouette fade in the distance, I realize it's true what they say.

Misery absolutely does love company.

Chapter 12

Stevie

I've only made this drive one other time. And afterward, I swore I'd never make it again.

Yet here I am.

My father's house is nestled deep in the woods, off the grid so he can't be bothered. Maybe this proves that he not only hates *me,* but people in general.

I kill the headlights long before I reach the house, thinking it'd be best not to tip him off to my arrival before I'm ready for him to know I'm here. So, I park as straight as I can, considering it's pitch black out here.

The engine goes quiet, but I don't get out right away. Instead, I sit behind the wheel, trying to convince myself that I'm doing the right thing, that this is the right move. But the thing is, I generally don't know the answer to those questions until after it's done.

So, here goes nothing.

Leaves crunch beneath my feet as I make my way toward the door. Briefly, my thoughts shift back to Tate, back to the argument, but I push it aside.

One problem at a time. That's all I have room to deal with.

I take a deep breath, then lift my hand to knock, only hesitating a moment before my fist makes contact with the door. The dog barks, announcing my arrival on the off chance that my father didn't hear me. Then, I breathe. I wait. Then I'm *holding* my breath when I hear footsteps.

Just... get in and get out. No need to linger.

I shake out my hands a bit, only now remembering the slight bruise still visible beside my eye, but it's too late to cover it with makeup. So, it is what it is.

The lock disengages, then the knob twists, and I peer up in total shock because... this isn't my dad. Instead, I'm staring into the eyes of a man who's been many things to my family over the years—my father's best friend, family, a protector.

A villain.

Frank.

My father's demon dog, Duke, stands dutifully at Frank's side, growling as a smile curves Frank's thin lips. I'd forgotten how tall he is. How *foreboding* he is.

I give him a onceover and he does the same, clearly not expecting it to be *me* on the other side of the threshold.

Not much has changed with him, besides there being a smidge more gray in his dark hair than the last time I saw him. Which, if I recall correctly, was inside a courtroom. Otherwise, he's still a giant with the most intimidating stonefaced glare I've ever seen. Comes with the territory of being a cop, though, I guess. And speaking of being a cop, he's still wearing his dark blue t-shirt with the symbol for the local police department embossed on the pocket over his heart.

A basketball game plays loud in the background, and judging by the nearly-empty bottle of beer in his hand, I can guess that I've interrupted.

"Well, shit. Look who it is," he slurs, and I realize something else.

Frank is very much drunk.

"What are *you* doing here?" I ask, because the last I knew, he and dad weren't even on speaking terms. Then again, I haven't made it a point to keep up with the status of their friendship after the shitshow that went down between our families. So, there's also that.

"Damn. Hello to you, too, sweetheart" he says in his usual gruff tone, hints of his New Jersey accent bleeding through despite having left his hometown decades ago. He pushes the rickety screen door open, then steps aside. "You coming in?"

I peer inside, noting that the only light seems to be coming from the television screen, then I glance back down at the beer bottle in his hand.

"Is... my dad around?"

Frank shrugs. "Nope. He's out of town on business. Asked me to water his plants and check in on Duke," he says, widening the door a little more. "We could use the company, though."

Instinct tells me this isn't a good idea. Paranoia tells me to go back to my car and take my ass home. But curiosity? Curiosity has me taking a step in the wrong direction, and wincing when Frank latches the door behind me.

I've never been further than the porch, so I find myself glancing around like I've just stepped inside a museum, ogling a collection of DVDs and CDs lining a cheap bookcase beside the entertainment center. Next, my eye is drawn to a single picture in a frame. There's not really any need to turn it for a better look. I'm already certain whose image I'll find there.

Sure enough, smiling back at me is my sister, Mel. Seeing how she's been memorialized in his home, seeing that hers is the face he'd rather see when it comes to his two daughters, doesn't breed resentment toward her. She couldn't change that she was his favorite, and she never leaned into the idea of it. Hell, she actually hated how differently he treated us. Which is why it's only hatred for *him* I feel flaring up right now.

"Sit," Frank says, and when I turn, he gestures to the old couch beneath the window. "I'd offer you a beer, but I'm pretty sure you're not legal yet. Or am I wrong about that?" he teases, flashing a blatant look toward my breasts when he does.

Sick fuck.

"Anyway, how's life treating you these days?" he asks with a disinterested sigh, finally angling his gaze toward the TV as I lower onto the sofa.

"Life's... life, I guess," I answer, eyeballing Duke when he comes close to sniff me.

There's a long pause before I realize Frank's watching me again—eyebrows raised, smirk on his lips.

"Aren't you going to ask how *I've* been?" he jokes.

I look him over. "Doesn't look like much has changed, guess I didn't feel the need."

At first, he just stares, then cracks a smile. "Smart-ass."

I don't argue with him. He isn't wrong.

"You... also forgot to ask about Nora," he slips in, and that's when I go from being mildly annoyed to the edges of my vision turning red.

"I didn't forget about her. I just didn't care."

This time, I get the feeling my answer isn't quite as cute to him as last time, because he hasn't blinked in about ten seconds. When he eventually looks away, his eyes are fixed on the TV like before as he sips his drink.

"Well, either way, she's fine. At least, I *think* she is. She's on her second stint in rehab and the facility we got her into limits communication," he adds, despite me having made it incredibly clear that I couldn't give two shits about his niece and her big-ass mouth. Seeing as how she's the reason I'm currently on probation, walking on eggshells.

Nora was a couple years behind me in high school, when she actually attended, that is. That bitch couldn't be *paid* to stay out of trouble. I only tolerated her because Frank and Dad were so close. Which, unfortunately, meant Nora was around a lot once Frank got custody of her.

This didn't change me and Mel's dislike for her, though. I swear, bad things followed that girl everywhere she went.

"I know you probably think I'm pissed at you for what you did," Frank slurs, "but I wouldn't hold a grudge about that. Not with what you were going through back then. I get it."

My gaze lowers to my hands, remembering how deep I was drowning in grief in the beginning. It was like someone had turned off the light inside my head and all I could see was darkness.

Everywhere.

And it was during that dark period that Nora and I had our run-in. One that resulted in me wearing handcuffs, spending days inside a courtroom, and my father temporarily being on the outs with his best friend.

Buzzing in my pocket pulls me from my thoughts and I'm hesitant to even check my phone. I have a sinking feeling it's either my mother or Tate and, at the moment, I don't really want to hear from either one of them. But I'm clearly a glutton for punishment tonight, letting curiosity lead me over yet another cliff.

Tate: Listen, I'm sorry, but we need to talk. Tonight.

I roll my eyes and shove my phone inside my pocket again, wishing I'd been strong enough to ignore it like my gut told me to.

"But you know what?" Frank speaks up, his eyelids dipping as he starts to doze. "I think you and Nora can clear the air one day. I have hope," he adds with a weak laugh. "If two polar opposites like her and Mel can become as close as they were, there's hope for you two yet. Watch."

My head whips in his direction, tension in my brow as I question him. "What did you just say?"

He groans and his eyes are completely closed now. This fucker *would* choose now to pass out drunk, when I need him to explain what the hell he just meant by that.

My sister would've *never* been close to a loser bitch like Nora. Ever.

"Frank!"

Yelling doesn't even rouse him, so I stand and walk to the armchair where his head has just slumped into the crook of his shoulder.

"Frank!" I shout again, but he's completely out of it.

Meanwhile, I'm losing my shit because... did I even know my sister? Was my head so deep in the sand that I missed *everything?*

101

Drinking? Drugs? A boyfriend no one seems to know about? Seeing the school counselor? Hanging out with fucking Nora?

My head is reeling, and I can't be here. I can't stand here in the home of a man I hate, staring at *another* man I hate, questioning every fucking thing.

I just… can't.

The screen slams behind me, and I don't bother closing the door, nor do I bother checking the dozens of text messages that have my phone going crazy right now.

I drive home in silence—no radio, just my thoughts. And they're darker than usual, bleeding with despair and anger.

Why the fuck does this keep happening to me?

It's like the universe wants me to know how badly I failed her, how little I knew her. I've asked myself if I could've done more, but… how could I when it seems I didn't even *know* my sister?

Surprisingly, my mother isn't pacing by the door when I let myself in. I close the door quietly, being sure to double-lock it before heading upstairs. All I want is to go to sleep, hit reset on this day, then pretend none of this ever happened.

It's wishful thinking, I know, but it's my only comfort.

I don't bother turning on the light when I make it to the bedroom. I peel off my socks and jeans, then lie on top of the comforter, staring at the wall. My head's reeling, going over thoughts about Frank and Nora, Mom and Tate, and just… everything.

With any luck, I'll doze eventually, but just as that inkling of hope seems possible, a hand covers my mouth, my eyes stretch wide, and two words whispered against my ear have my heart pounding out of my chest.

"Don't. Scream."

Stevie

It only takes half a moment to realize that the one holding me against his chest is Tate. His scent gives him away—expensive cologne that would otherwise make him impossible to resist.

But not tonight.

Not anymore.

"What the fuck are you doing?" I whisper, glaring at him when I finally break free, rolling to the other side of the bed.

Tate's eyes are locked on me as he stands from beside the mattress, holding both hands out as if to remind me he isn't a threat.

"How did you even get in here?"

"I climbed in through the window. It doesn't lock," he explains. "I didn't want to risk waking my dad and Val, so I let myself in."

"You didn't want to wake them, but you were more than willing to risk giving me a heart attack. Thank you for that," I add, clutching my chest before going back to my original question. "What the fuck are you doing here?"

Tate blinks slowly as his hands lower to his sides. "We need to talk."

I roll my eyes. "And I already told you, I'm not interested in hearing it, so if you wouldn't mind letting yourself out however you got in, that'd be great."

With that, I turn onto my side, giving him my back, praying he does as I've asked.

But, of course, he doesn't.

"I know you think it's about... us, but it isn't that," he says.

The admission has me of two minds. On one hand, my interest is piqued, wondering what *else* we could possibly have to discuss. And on the other hand, I'm a little wounded that the status of our... whatever it is... isn't the reason he's been hunting me down all night.

No, I didn't want to talk to him, but I suppose I also didn't want to be a nonfactor.

"It's about Tory," he says, and I'm listening more closely now. "I met with her brothers today. It's been bugging me that they were with her the night you two met. I needed to know why."

I finally turn, facing him. "And?"

"According to them, they had reason to believe Tory might be in danger."

I don't understand. "In danger... *why*?"

He takes a breath, maybe realizing he finally has my attention. "A girl stopped by their house the day of your sister's funeral. They said she was high on something, irate, questioning Tory about whether she and Mel had met up with anyone that night, or if she maybe noticed they were being followed. But the guys didn't have a name. All they knew was that the girl seemed problematic, so they went on the defensive."

My brow tenses, and I start connecting the dots. "I know who she was."

"You do?"

I nod. "Maybe. I went to my dad's tonight."

Tate's quiet. I'm not sure how much he knows about my father and I, but his silence means he's maybe gotten an overview from Mom. Enough to know there's not much of a relationship there, and that what's left is one-hundred percent toxic.

"He's out of town, but his friend was crashing there. Long story short, I found out that his niece, Nora, had apparently gotten pretty close with Mel. Based on what you just said, I can't imagine anyone else it would've been."

Tate paces a little, but stops when the floor creaks. I'm guessing to avoid waking our parents. "But why would she go to Tory with those questions? Something's not adding up."

"*Nothing's* adding up," I scoff, turning onto my back, focusing on the ceiling.

In my peripheral vision, I notice Tate's eyes on me, scanning me in nothing but underwear and one of my favorite t-shirts. I would've covered up if I'd known he'd be here, but that's kind of hard to do when someone sneaks into your window.

Which reminds me.

"Thanks for the info, but... you should go now."

He meets my gaze when I face him again. "While I'm here, we should—"

"Go," I assert, feeling my breathing become uneven as a familiar rage sets in.

However, his feet don't move, and if I stood any chance of over-powering him, I'd toss him out myself.

"Stevie, you've got the wrong idea," he says and... fuck me, I don't shut him down. Mostly, it's mental exhaustion, but also maybe a bit that I need to close this door once and for all. And maybe, just maybe, hearing him say it—that we were never a thing, that we'll never *be* anything—will be the kick in the ass I need to accept it.

So, I let him talk.

He breathes deep, shoves both hands into the pockets of his sweats, then leans against the wall.

"You're wrong," he sighs. "You said something today. Something incredibly fucked up, and then you didn't even give me a chance to correct you."

I roll my eyes but opt to stay silent.

"Do you really think I pulled away because I'm not attracted to you?" he asks.

A breath leaves me. "It's not such a farfetched idea, is it?" I shoot back.

We're at a standoff, neither one wanting to bend on their stance, but then he blurts out the last words I expect to hear tonight.

"For fuck's sake, Stevie, I'm in therapy."

I'm quiet when he finishes, but *this* time, the silence is because I don't quite know what to say.

"I've been celibate for six months. Haven't touched a woman in any way that's not platonic. Not until you," he adds gravely.

I follow his silhouette as he moves this way from the other side of the room, lowering onto the edge of the bed where he leans forward, holding his head.

"Why?"

His shoulders heave when he breathes deep. "I'd been sort of... reckless," he says. "It got to the point that I was with so many different women, I developed this fear. I got it in my head that if I kept up this way, if I continued to let sex just be this casual *thing*, the day would come that I'd want it to mean something, I'd want it to be special, and I wouldn't feel anything but the physical part. *Couldn't* feel anything but that."

It crosses my mind that he could totally be feeding me bullshit right now, but I think I've gotten pretty good at reading people. Which is why I don't question his sincerity for more than a few seconds. He's got no reason to lie to me, nothing to gain.

"So, I went and got tested for every possible thing you can think of, thanked my lucky stars for a clean bill of health, then just... *stopped*. All of it—dating, fucking, all of it," he repeats, and I don't miss the emotion that riddles his voice.

"And, shit, before I met you, I'd hardly even been tempted to break my rule. And now... you're all I fucking think about."

He doesn't sound the least bit happy about this. In fact, he sounds tortured, like he's punishing himself for what he feels and I'm paying the price right alongside him.

"If you had this rule, this *plan*, why flirt with me in the first place? Why put yourself in that position?"

He scoffs, and I wait for an answer. "I just... I couldn't stop myself. And it's only like that with you."

That's it. Plain and simple, I guess.

My gut twists in this weird way. In a way it hasn't with him for a while because of the anger and bitterness I'd built up toward him. But now, hearing what I believe to be his truth, my mind has changed about him.

Again.

He shifts and the bed moves with him. Our eyes lock. I can see him clearly now, even through the darkness, and there's so much going on within him I feel the struggle, the inner torment.

But then, right when I think he'll take my initial advice and go straight out the window... he kisses me.

Rough and deep, filled with all the tension and desire we've bottled up this past week. I'm tempted to let it go on, but something inside won't allow it. Tate realizes this, too, when I place both hands on his chest and force him back, putting distance between us.

"No," I say quietly. "I can't do the wishy-washy bullshit. I'm no good at the hot and cold thing guys do sometimes."

He stares at me, or rather *into* me, and my gaze falls to his lips when they part, taking in every single word.

"Stevie," he breathes, "I don't think I could stay away from you even if I tried."

Heat creeps up my legs, then between them, reaching my core as an all too familiar ache takes hold of me. I expect Tate to take advantage of my apparent weakness, but he doesn't.

Feet planted on the floor, he leans over the bed, hovering over me as his mouth brushes against mine. "You aren't worried?" he asks.

"Why would I be worried?"

He exhales and the heat of his breath flows into me. I want to swallow him whole. All of him. When I can't stand that we're not touching more than this, I reach around, slipping both hands underneath his t-shirt. He's warm and smooth where my palms flatten over the rigid muscle I find there.

"Worried about what?" I ask again, seeming to remind him that he'd just asked a question.

He smiles, lowering his gaze to my lips. "That we could get caught? That we could ruin things for our parents?"

I study him, with only an inch of space between his face and mine, breathing in the hint of cologne still lingering on his skin before I'm able to give an answer.

"A little," I admit, "but that just means we can't get caught."

I pull him to me, and he smiles against my lips, pressing a kiss to them.

"Besides… it's just sex, right?"

My words seep into his mouth before our kiss resumes. I'm mostly teasing, but also trying to see where his head might be. The comment got his attention, though, and he pauses, staring down on me with this depth in his eyes that I wasn't expecting.

"I think we both know good and fucking well there's more to us than that," he admits.

And there it is.

His answer.

The truth.

Finally.

The tip of his tongue nudges my lip. Then, he licks it. Slow. Soft. In just the right way, causing my legs to squeeze tight at the realization that he isn't between them yet. I pull his shirt up his back and he leans away to let me remove it completely. He steps out of his shoes, then he's right back on me, sliding on top to settle between my legs, his cock hard and impatient where it presses against my panties. His tongue is in my mouth, pushing deep, and it feels like I'll suffocate if he isn't inside me soon. He seems to sense the urgency in my touch, because he backs away, resting on his shins as I draw my knees higher. I don't blink as I watch him lower the waistband of his sweats just enough to reach inside them and pull out his dick.

My lip aches with how I bite it, wanting him so badly I think I might literally go insane. I go for my waistband, planning to remove my panties, but Tate has other plans. I stare when he reaches between my legs and takes the inner hem of my underwear, tugging them aside, exposing my pussy. He presses forward, aligning with my slit before hovering over me again, his tip resting between my lower lips, teasing the ever-loving shit out of me.

I've wanted him for so long, even when I intentionally filled my heart with only hatred for him. There was a connection between us that I hated, but now... I need that shit. It's like a drug to me. The thought of him pulling away this week killed me, and now that he's back, now that we're so close to giving in, I can't stand that he's making me wait.

"I want you inside me," I whisper against his lips, but he's hesitant, likely for the reason he already brought up.

Our parents.

Maybe he needs a little push. Maybe he needs someone to remind him that they don't matter right now, because it's just us. So, I free his tongue just long enough to tell him what's on my mind.

"Fuck. Me."

Tension builds in his back where I cling to him, and then, slowly, his hips push forward and my eyes roll back at the feel of him entering, filling me like I've wanted him to do for so long.

His deep, labored breaths send me into a daze, lifting my hips to meet his thrusts blow for blow. I turn my face into his bicep, fearing I might forget what's at stake and moan or scream too loudly.

A breath of air puffs into my ear, and then I feel Tate's lips against the rim of it. "Tell me to stop," he begs, pumping his hips faster, sinking deeper into me as my pussy opens, welcoming him in.

He lets out this delicious, deep groan into my ear, and I love that shit, love knowing how good I feel to him.

"Stevie, we shouldn't be doing this," he says, genuine conviction in his tone, but... he keeps pushing into me, and I keep letting him.

He's right, though. Soon, my mother will have his father's last name. No one would understand our complex relationship, no one would accept it, but... I can't stop any more than he can.

It's too good, this feeling too powerful.

"Just this once," I whisper back. "Then, never again."

His lips crash down against the side of my neck, and I squeeze him tighter, feeling the rhythmic roll and thrust of the muscle covering his back like armor as I hold him.

"Just this once," he echoes, and it's like those words, the acknowledgement of this being the one and only time we'll fuck, take the guilt away.

He powers into me, eyeing my tits as they bounce freely beneath my tee, without the restriction of a bra, and I love the way he looks at me.

"You're so... fucking... sexy," he breathes, and my pussy grips him tighter, and that feeling is back. The deep, intense, tingling I've only felt once before. I know what's coming and I'm ready.

Tate seems to notice I'm breathing harder, squeezing him tighter, and his eyes lower to mine.

"Fuck, yes," he rasps, craning his neck down to kiss me. "I've wanted to make you come for so fucking long."

He sounds so relieved to be inside me, and the thought of him secretly wanting me, and fighting it, is my undoing. My back arches into him, pushing my chest flush against his. Then, with my legs locked tight around his taut waist, I grant his wish, coming for him, soaking his dick as my core pulses and throbs around him.

"You're a fucking drug, you know that?" he asks, not really expecting an answer.

My orgasm peaks and then lingers with me, making me grip him tighter.

"Let me come inside you," he groans, taking my tongue again once I nod, giving him permission.

His mouth locks to mine and everything but his hips goes still. He pistons into me a few more times, then thrusts so hard his pelvis audibly connects with my thighs, and I feel him—the pressure building as his liquid heat pumps into me, an endless stream surging from his body to mine, and I take it all.

His body stills, and I realize we're panting in sync. Excess cum streams down my ass because he filled me to the brink, soaking the sheet beneath me. But my focus is elsewhere, on him as we kiss. It's slow and passionate as his cock softens inside me.

I made him a promise. That this would be the one and only time we'd do this, the one and only time we'd give in. But the longer we cling to one another, the more apparent it becomes that it *isn't* just about sex, and the less I think only having him once is possible.

From my point of view, we're stuck. Or better yet, addicted.

And if I'm being honest—and reckless—I can't think of a better drug of choice.

Chapter 14

Stevie

I return from the bathroom, and he's still here. Before, I would've convinced myself that he'd slip out the window while I was gone, but tonight, the thought honestly never even crossed my mind.

He surprises me, proving to be more complex than I ever could've imagined in my wildest dreams, but I welcome it. Actually, the idea of peeling back his layers, discovering what else is underneath, excites me a little.

I approach the bed, noticing that he's changed the sheets, because they've gone from blue to white. But I also notice something else. Tate's sweats and boxers are now in a heap near the foot of the bed, which means he removed them while I was gone, and he's naked beneath the covers.

My brow lifts when I smirk at him, but don't ask questions. Instead, I follow his lead and pull off my t-shirt, the clean panties I'd slipped into, then join him under the blanket naked.

Smooth, warm skin meets mine when his solid arms engulf me, making me feel safe and small. His hips inch forward and his dick presses against my ass. He's not hard, but for some reason, that makes this moment better. Because it means this isn't about that, isn't about him trying to squeeze in another quick round before the night ends.

He just wants me close.

My cheek settles against his arm where it rests beneath my head. His other hand starts at my thigh, then moves to my waist, until it finally settles on my breast. He squeezes.

"I've got a confession."

I smile a little. "What's that?"

"I'm fucking obsessed with your body." The words spoken softly into my ear go straight to my head.

"I'm good with that." My smile grows when he laughs.

"You're healing pretty quickly," he says, and I realize it's getting easier to talk about the attack.

"I'm in a lot less pain, that's for sure."

"Good. I hated seeing you like that, knowing there wasn't anything I could do to make it better."

When he finishes, he retraces his original path, back down my waist, but this time, he stops when his hand brushes over the bandage on my hip.

"This one's from The Hunt, right?" he asks, and I'm reminded of the lie I told him. It'd be easy to keep it up, but I feel too close to him now.

Too close to lie.

"That's... not exactly true."

He's silent behind me, and I know I'll have to weigh my words. The guys are his friends, yes, but I've seen him pissed at them before. I'm not really going for that. Am I still angry that they took things this far? Fuck, yeah, I am, but... things have changed since then.

When that happened, they didn't know about my sister, didn't know I wasn't against them. So, despite wanting to choke them all with my bare hands at the moment, I don't want to be the cause of a rift between them and Tate.

His lips brush against my shoulder, then he kisses me there.

"What really happened?"

I take a deep breath. "It was... part of the hazing."

113

His hand, where he'd been gently stroking my skin a moment ago, goes still. In fact, his chest isn't moving anymore either, as if he's stopped breathing, too.

"What the fuck did they do to you?" he growls, and before I can stop him, he pulls the cover back. I manage to place my hands over the bandage seconds before he gets to it, and I meet his gaze. I've never seen him like this—enraged, feral.

While I'd probably love this if his anger were directed elsewhere, I seriously don't want to cause trouble.

"Let me see it, Stevie," he demands, but I don't budge.

"That isn't necessary."

His brow knits together. "Isn't necessary? They fucking injured you and you're protecting those assholes?"

It's on the tip of my tongue to explain to him the same points I just used to rationalize it to *myself*, but I know how it would sound.

Like I'm some lovesick, brainwashed damsel in distress, but that couldn't be further from the truth.

I *know* what they did to me was fucked up. Hence the reason I flipped on Ash the other day—soft and yielding at first, until I realized he thought it'd be that easy to get back on my good side.

But the last thing I need is Tate thinking I'm some stupid, defenseless girl who can't hold her own. That's not me. Not now, not ever.

He realizes I'm not going to budge and backs off, settling on his elbow while I gather my thoughts, sorting out the best way to tell him. But there really *is* no way to say it other than to just... *say it.*

"It's a brand. *The* brand. *Your...* brand," I clarify.

He does that thing again, where he's completely silent, hard to read.

"They fucking... I'm gonna kill them," he says in this matter-of-fact tone that's honestly a little disturbing. But when he pushes the cover down his torso and turns to leave the bed, I realize he isn't kidding about going after them.

"No," I say a little louder than I mean to, gripping his wrist to stop him.

He meets my gaze, confusion in his eyes.

I breathe deep, knowing I'll have to say more if I'm going to convince him not to act.

"It's done," I say. "It's over with and I'm not even mad anymore."

"But shouldn't you be?"

I push my hair back, searching for the right words. "Under normal circumstances, yes. If *they* or *I* were normal, yes, but... I'm not holding a grudge. It happened, I raged, and cussed them out, and now we've moved past it."

Tate studies me, and I let him read me, let him see I'm not hiding anything, not harboring ill feelings or fear. I'm an open book for him.

My hand lands on his and that look on his face softens.

"I don't need you to fight my battles," I tell him, and he eventually nods, accepting this.

Without me having to ask, he settles into bed again, covering us both with the comforter. He's quiet and still a bit unsettled, but I trust that what I've shared won't leave this room.

"Have you even heard from them?" he asks, and I swallow deep, going over it all in my head.

"Vince and Ash, yes. They check in, and Ash stopped over the other day, but... not Micah. Not even once."

I try to hide how the reality of it stings, but I do a pretty shit job of that. Because it *does* hurt.

Pretty fucking bad, actually.

I half expect Tate to get angry, threatening to have it out with Micah when he sees him again, but when he responds, his tone is softer than before. Like, in this instance, he doesn't think Micah's just being an ass.

"Micah's got... a lot going on," Tate shares. "He goes through these phases where he goes deep within himself, inside his head. Too deep for anyone to reach him. So, when it happens, we have to just... *wait*. Eventually, he'll resurface, but it has to be in his own time."

I hear him. Loud and clear. But I'm not sure this explanation changes things.

"We *all* go through shit," I point out, "but that doesn't mean we get to just disappear, Tate."

"I don't disagree with you, but you deserve to know the truth and, whether we like it or not, this is Micah's truth," he adds. "The guy's head is pretty fucked up and, sometimes, it's a little harder for him to hide that than usual. I think this is just one of those times."

I consider it, asking myself if I'm just being a bitch about it all, but my gut isn't saying that. Not now, anyway. But I do feel like, when it comes to Ash, I was *definitely* the asshole. First chance I get, once I believe he's cooled off, that is, I'll apologize.

He's owed that.

I chewed him out simply because he showed up when, honestly, that's all I've wanted from *any* of them. Just be here for me while my life's crazy.

"Shit!" Tate whispers that word just as a thud in our parents' room makes my heart beat twice as fast.

Shit is right.

Tate is out of the bed in zero seconds flat, naked, collecting his things as another sound from the other side of the wall startles me.

"You've gotta hurry!" I climb out of bed, wrapping myself in the sheet as I give the floor a onceover to make sure he isn't leaving anything. It'd suck to be so focused on getting him out that his boxers are still lying at the foot of the bed.

He grabs a pair of sweats from the top shelf of the closet—a pile of clothes he left behind when he moved out. Then, he rushes to slip his t-shirt over his head, already making his way to the window. I'm right behind him, shoving his shoes against his chest. He tosses one leg over the sill, and then his crazy ass stops.

"What are you doing? They'll catch you," I whisper, unable to stop my smile.

"I just..." he pauses, realizing he either *can't* or doesn't *need* to explain why he's lingering, then grips the back of my neck to bring me to him.

He kisses me. Like we're not on the verge of tipping off our parents that we're up to something, and I fucking love it—the urgency of it, the passion.

"Go," I say against his lips.

"Fuck. Okay." The steps in the hallway grow louder. "I'll call you."

After making this promise, he steps out onto the roof with his things tucked beneath his arm, slides off the edge on his stomach, using only the raw power in his arms to hold him up, then he shimmies down the pillar onto the porch. He's gone from my line of sight for a moment, then when I have eyes on him again, he's wearing shoes. The extent of his athleticism becomes even more apparent as he sprints down the sidewalk, then around the corner to wherever he parked.

I'm breathless and can't seem to stop smiling as I glance over my shoulder toward the sound of approaching footsteps. I don't move when either Mom or Rob tries the knob, then breathe a sigh of relief when they eventually walk away.

It was an incredibly close call, but if I'm honest, it was completely worth it.

I take a step toward the bed when a set of taillights catch my eye. I hadn't noticed them before, maybe because they were partially hidden behind a tree. But I don't blink, only losing sight of them when they disappear down the street.

I know I'm overthinking it, know I'm probably making something out of nothing, but I can blame the recent attack on this heightened sense of paranoia.

It's probably just a neighbor.

This is what I tell myself in order to tear my gaze away from the window and climb back into bed.

Silently, of course.

I'm still on a high, so I force my eyes closed. It's the only way I stand a chance of getting any sleep. But the moment my lids lower, they open, because the conversation with Frank is on my mind again.

Especially now that I know Nora visited Tory after Mel's funeral.

I need to talk to her, but according to Frank, that isn't possible. The facility won't allow it. But I can feel it in my gut that she knows something, or at least *her* questions will possibly align with some of mine, which, in the very least, proves I'm not crazy.

My phone vibrates on the nightstand, stealing my focus. I'm smiling before I even have it in hand, and by the time I answer, I'm grinning like a lovestruck teenager.

"Damn, you miss me already?" I expect Tate to laugh or have some sort of a smart-ass comeback, but... silence.

I pull the phone away from my ear and glance at the screen, only now realizing his number didn't come up.

Because *no* number came up.

It's an unknown caller.

"Hello?" I call out quietly, but the moment I speak into the receiver, the call drops.

I still have the phone to my ear, feeling a chill inch its way down my spine. My first thought is of the mysterious vehicle that just pulled off, but then I stop myself.

There's no proof one has anything to do with the other.

I've made the mistake of seeing connections where there were none before. And not only did I waste precious time, I nearly drove myself crazy holding on to what I *thought* was a clue.

That was just some random person's taillights.

This was just a random call.

There's nothing more to it.

Chapter 15

Stevie

There are whispers and there are certainly gawkers. Yet, amidst all the unwanted attention and chatter, not one person bothers asking if I'm okay as I walk from my car to the quad.

They've speculated, they've gossiped, they're hungry for details. But as far as there being any actual concern for me, I wouldn't hold my breath.

I just keep telling myself this will all die down soon. Well, eventually.

Because of all the extra eyes on me, I've mostly walked with mine glued to the sidewalk. Which accounts for why I didn't notice an incredibly sexy guy, covered in tattoos seated on the steps of the building I'm headed into. He's surrounded by books, and there's a notebook propped on his knee, pen in hand. His hair looks like he just rolled out of bed, but in a good way, and the dark-framed glasses he only seems to wear when he studies make me want to attack him right where he sits.

Ash peers up and our eyes lock. He clearly didn't notice I was coming either, so there's a brief moment of awkward silence.

"Shit, I didn't realize how late it'd gotten," he says, which strikes me as curious.

"You've... been here a while?"

He nods, pushing a hand through the mess of dark hair on his crown. "About an hour," he says. "I don't have classes today, so... I'm on Bird watch."

The corner of his mouth curves when he finishes.

"Bird watch?"

"It's a term I've coined," he grins. "We know today's your first day getting back to things, so we figured you'd need some company."

I translate the word *company* to mean *babysitting*.

I arch a brow when I can't help but to smile at the gesture. "All day?"

"All day," he clarifies. "And for however long you need us."

My heart flutters and the sensation spreads to my stomach. Butterflies. Ashton Blaine just gave me fucking butterflies.

"I—that's really sweet."

He shrugs like it's nothing, then does this thing where his eyes flash to the ground for a moment before meeting my gaze again. It almost makes him appear boyish, innocent.

"Listen, the other day, I—"

"Don't even worry about it," he cuts in, but I need to finish.

"No, I owe you an apology. I was a bitch to you and all you did was show up for me. You didn't deserve that," I admit. "I was in my feelings about... other things, and I took it out on you because you were there. And I'm a bit of a coward, so if you hadn't shown up today, I'm not even sure when I would've called to say all of this, so... I'm sorry for that, too."

When my lips stop moving, he's already smiling. And when he sets his notebook aside and stands, towering over me even when he comes down off the steps, my heart does that thing again. His hand moves into my hair, warming the side of my neck when he cups it, and I lose my train of thought.

"You don't have to apologize. I should've stayed and, hell, fought things out with you if I had to."

I smile again. "Even though I was being a bitch?"

He laughs at that, nodding. "Even though you were being a bitch."

He barely finishes his sentence and I'm on the tips of my toes, stretching up to reach his mouth. The hand not gripping my neck takes my waist, and I cling to him, kissing him like we're not surrounded by about a hundred others. But who fucking cares. Let them look.

I lower onto my heels again, still unable to tear my eyes away from his.

"Get to class," he says. "I'll be here when you get back."

Wishing I could stay here, just like this, I nod and force myself to leave him. There's the stupidest grin on my face as I walk the hallway, and it's still there when I open the door to the lecture hall. And as if I'm not already in a giddy mood—when I *should* be dreading being back in this place—I meet Tate's gaze. He removes a folder from his bag and sets it on the corner of Professor Lange's desk at the front of the lecture hall. Then, he shoots me this knowing smile, a silent acknowledgement of what we did.

A silent nod to the fact that we fucked despite knowing we really, *really* shouldn't have.

I flashback to that night, remembering how he made me come for him, remembering how my heart raced at the mere thought of getting caught together. All of a sudden, my face feels unusually warm and it's official.

These boys are going to be the death of me.

Exhaling to gather myself, I take a seat and *try* to focus. It works. Well, kind of. I manage to take notes and catch most of Professor Lange's lecture, but I'm understandably distracted. Especially when Tate takes the floor to elaborate on the lesson. My eyes are glued to him, hanging on every word that leaves his mouth. He's so poised and intelligent, which is why no one would ever guess what we've been up to.

Class ends, and I gather my things, glancing toward Tate, noting that I have his attention despite the three students surrounding him.

He smiles politely, answers their questions, but I know who he's really focused on.

Me.

"Ms. Heron?"

I turn, glancing back as soon as I hike my bag up on my shoulder. "Yes?"

Tate fights a smile. "I'll be finished up here in a moment. Can you stick around? We need to discuss your makeup assignments," he lies. I've already been contacted by the university. There *are* no makeup assignments.

"Sure," I smile, and hang out off to the side while he finishes his conversation. The students walk off, chatting amongst themselves as they climb the steps, then the large doors latch behind them.

It's just us here now, Tate and me.

My steps are slow when I approach him, holding my breath as he slips both hands inside his pockets, smiling just enough to make me want to reach out and grab him. But I don't, for fear of scaring him off. This is his place of business, after all.

However, the moment I'm within arm's reach, Tate surprises me, his fingers hooking into my belt loops, and he draws me closer. Without so much as a greeting, his mouth is on mine and I'm at a loss for words.

He struck me as the type who scared easily, the type who resists the urge to break rules, but it's becoming apparent I was wrong about that. The other night, I voiced my concerns about him being hot and cold, and it seems I got through. Because this... *this*... is definitely hot.

His hips press into me, and I feel him, hardening inside his slacks as we toe a very, very fine line. He pecks my lips one last time before ending the kiss, but he keeps me close, staring down into my eyes as he speaks.

"I'm sorry for doing this here, but... I couldn't help myself," he admits. "I haven't been able to think about anything but kissing your lips since I left that night."

Having him finally be so transparent with his feelings is dizzying.

"That's the only part of me you've thought about?" I tease, lowering my eyes to his chest before meeting his gaze again.

He leans in, feathering his lips across mine, then trails them to my ear. "It should go without saying that I'm fucking crazy about the rest of you, too."

I turn my head until I catch his mouth and he squeezes me, pulling me closer. It crosses my mind that Professor Lange could easily pop back in if he left something behind, or a student could come back, and maybe it's this sense of being hyper aware of our surroundings that has me pulling away.

"We shouldn't," I breathe touching my lips, putting a foot of space between us.

"You weren't saying that the other night," he teases, smirking as he takes a step this way. But the moment he does, my fear proves valid.

We both straighten our expressions and our posture when the door unlatches, the sound echoing through the lecture hall. My eyes dart to the exit, expecting to see Professor Lange, but who I'm *not* expecting... is Rob.

When I steal a glance at Tate, he's confused, which means this wasn't a scheduled visit. He covers his surprise well, though.

"Hey, didn't realize I'd see you today."

Rob smiles. "Yeah, I remembered I forgot to get your signature on a few documents. I'm headed over to Ed's office now to get things squared away with the loan, so..."

It dawns on me that I haven't spoken yet. "Hey, Rob."

I probably sound a little too chipper, but I've never been good at shit like this, sneaking around.

He meets my gaze and smiles, but it's a weird smile. Like, he's got shit on his mind or something.

"Hey," he says back. He's polite, but I think I'm right. There's definitely something up.

His eyes flit to Tate again. "Aside from needing the signatures, mind if I have a quick word with you before I go?"

Tate's brow tenses again when he nods. "Of course." He turns to me again. "I'll get those notes printed out for you this week."

"Sure. Sounds good." I smile and nod, going along with the farce. "See ya, Rob."

He responds by flashing another tight smile, and I see myself out. Whatever they need to discuss feels heavy, and I can honestly say I want no parts of it.

Tate

We move to the desk, and I study my father as he pulls documents out of his folder, marked with stickers where I need to sign.

"These are the only two I need you to look over." He's reaching into his pocket for a pen before realizing I've already taken one off the desk. He chuffs a quiet, awkward laugh. I know him pretty well and, yeah, something's definitely not right. I put my name down on the line, and the official reason for his visit is taken care of, but there's more.

"You wanted to talk to me about something? Is it about the deal?"

After asking, I meet his gaze for a fraction of a second, but he looks away, glancing down at the papers he's organizing in the folder instead of making eye contact.

"No, it's not about the deal," he clarifies. "I... there's..."

After stammering a moment, he finally looks me in the eyes, and I don't miss that uncomfortable look on his face.

"Son, I... there was something on the camera. Footage from the other night. Footage of you. Climbing up to your old bedroom. Climbing up to... *Stevie's* bedroom."

I didn't understand at first, but then when he explains further, it hits me. Hard and fast, like a huge ton of bricks falling right on my fucking head.

124

Shit.

"Now, listen, I'm not accusing you of anything, and I don't want to make a big deal of this. Hell, for all I know your visit was completely innocent and I'm connecting the wrong dots, but that's why I'm here. To ask you face-to-face, man-to-man. Is... there something going on that I should know about? Something I need to get ahead of before Val finds out?"

And there it is, the whole reason I tried to fight the pull toward Stevie. The last thing either of us wants is to cause a rift between our parents and seeing that worried look in my father's eyes right now only confirms that we were right.

This thing between us, this unavoidable attraction, has the potential to cause irreparable damage. But the problem with all of this is simple.

I can't fucking stop.

With her, I have no control, no willpower whatsoever, and I have no plans to stay away.

My lack of a response seems to trigger my father, because he releases a heavy sigh, shoving both hands into his pockets.

"And she's dating your friend. For fuck's sake, Tate. I didn't raise you to be that kind of guy," he adds in a quieter tone, as if there's someone else who might be listening.

I can't even look him in the eyes, which I'm sure only makes me look even *more* guilty. Although, I don't know if it's possible to look more guilty than sneaking into my stepsister's room in the middle of the night, then not coming back down until over an hour later.

"I know, it's just... it's not like that," I lie. "Stevie and I texted earlier that day and planned to meet up. It was about school stuff. Things got pushed back when she got upset after dinner, but she still wanted to hang out and get help catching up on some of what she's missed being off this past week."

Dad studies me, maybe trying to decide whether or not he can believe the words that just left my mouth.

"Then why not use the front door? Why not get together at a more decent hour?" he asks, clearly wanting me to lift this burden from him. He doesn't *want* to believe Stevie and I were up to no good, and I don't blame him. I wouldn't want that image in my head either if I were him.

"It was a stupid plan, I guess. But she was just... really upset and needed to vent. So, I figured I could kill two birds with one stone—help her study *and* cheer her up. I was just trying to make her feel better."

Those words leave my mouth and a memory flashes into my head. A memory of Stevie moaning while her pussy clenched around my dick. While she breathed against my shoulder to keep quiet. While she took my cum.

I blink hard and leave my eyes closed a couple seconds to rid my mind of the image.

"That was it? There's nothing else to it?" he asks, tension in his brow while he watches me.

"No, there's nothing else."

He studies me a few seconds, then there's this look of pure relief that crosses his face.

"Oh, thank God," he sighs. "I thought I was going to have to keep this from Val, and that woman has this uncanny ability to know when I'm hiding something. And, being honest, she scares the living shit out of me," he adds with a laugh.

I laugh, too, with hopes of making this all more believable, but I'm so fucking tense it hurts.

He places a hand on my shoulder and there's pride in his eyes when he smiles this time.

"I'm sorry," he says. "I saw the footage and let my imagination run away with me. I should've known it was innocent. You're the best man I know. And I'm not just saying that because you're my son."

My gut twists in a knot hearing him speak so highly of me, knowing I just lied, knowing I am, in fact, guilty of what he's hinted at.

"I should get going. Ed's waiting on me, so..."

"Yeah, of course. We'll catch up later."

Dad smiles again and heads toward the door, clutching the folder at his side. I manage to keep up the fake expression until the door slams shut behind him, but the second it does, it feels like my heart's about to stop.

"Fuck!"

My fist slams the desk and the sound echoes through the lecture hall. I breathe deep, trying to re-center myself, but nothing's working. That was a close call. *Too* close. It crosses my mind to give Stevie a heads up, but then I realize that won't help anything. I successfully threw my dad off our scent, which means I'd only be causing her undue stress. So, this stays with me.

Well, sort of.

Without another thought about what to do next, I'm already dialing, pacing while I wait for an answer.

"Good morning! This is Rita with Dr. Owens' office. How can I help you?"

"Yes, good morning, Rita. Does Dr. Owens have any openings this afternoon?"

"Let me check that for you. Is this an emergency?" she asks, and I don't even have to think of my answer.

"It is. And the sooner he can see me... the better."

Chapter 16

Stevie

Ash kept his word.

He was with me all day, waiting after each of my classes. He walked me to grab lunch when I had a break, paid, then walked me to my car at the end of the day. I suspect he would've followed me to the rink, too, if he didn't have practice this afternoon.

If his goal was to make me feel even *guiltier* for how I behaved the other day, mission accomplished.

Ash is a lot of things—brash and unyielding at times, but I'm also realizing he's more than that.

He's kind, and sweet, and so loyal it's hard to even grasp the extent of it. And the best part is? I'm pretty sure I'm the only person who sees that sweet side.

Daydreaming about Ash, I toss a trash bag out the back door for Kip to take care of when he heads out to his truck. He's adamant about us girls not going out into the alley alone at night, and I'm grateful for it.

Being back to work has been pretty okay. If nothing else, it's given me a sense of normalcy. My co-workers know what happened to me, so once they got out their questions and words of condolence, that was the end of it. Kip made them swear I wouldn't have to keep hearing about it, so I didn't have to keep reliving my recent horror, which has made for a relatively peaceful shift.

Well, as peaceful as yelling at kids for running out onto the rink in their shoes, or teenagers for smoking and making out in the bathrooms can be.

"Ok, we're heading out," Kip announces. "Sure you don't want someone to wait around with you?"

I smile at his offer, seeing the kindness in his eyes. He's worried about me closing alone tonight, but I think I need to. It'll show me there's nothing to be afraid of, show me I can slowly take my life back.

"All good. I'll see you in a couple days."

His stare lingers on me a bit, but he eventually nods, saluting me as he walks toward the back. "Okay. Night, kiddo."

"Night," I call out after him, and then… it's just me.

Following my usual routine, I climb up into the DJ booth and turn on some music, but not as loud as usual because, okay maybe I am still a little paranoid. Hearing my surroundings would maybe keep that at bay.

I hit the center spotlight, grab the dust mop from where I leaned it against the rail, then I get to it.

There's always something nostalgic about the way my wheels move over the smooth, polished floor. Even the smell of this place is unique, bringing up childhood memories I cherish, knowing the innocence of those days is long gone. They're part of a past I'll likely mourn for a lifetime.

But at least I still have this—my sanctuary, my safe haven. This world that, once everyone's gone, exists only for me.

The song changes—*Nothing's Gonna Hurt You Baby,* by Cigarettes After Sex. A memory comes to mind and a slow smile curves my lips. Maddox and I danced to it at prom. While all the couples rocked slow to the rhythm, we flailed around wild and fast, making complete asses of ourselves out in the middle of the dancefloor. It was amazing, and one of those nights that lives rent-free inside my head, and probably always will.

I'm deep in thought, reliving the moment when the music cuts off mid-song.

This oddly warm sensation floods my body as my stomach drops. Sometimes the system gets wonky when I hook my phone up to it, so I decide not to freak out.

It's just one of those things, Stevie.

It happens.

I skate to the wall, leaning the dustmop against it when I decide to go fix the sound system, hooding my eyes from the spotlight, thinking I spot something.

Or... *someone.*

"Kip?"

I hate myself for acknowledging the mirage, knowing it's just my eyes playing tricks on me. Being here alone is just putting thoughts inside my head. There's no one else here and I'm—

My thoughts cut off when the music comes blaring through the speakers again, but ten times as loud as where I set it. My entire body shudders, and I regret thinking I was ready for this, regret thinking this was safe.

All of a sudden, it feels like I'm back at that night, back in that warehouse with the sound of dripping water in the distance, footsteps crunching over debris littered across the crumbling floor.

I close my eyes and tell myself I'm no longer there, in that place that brought so much pain and fear into my world. Yes, I *tell* myself this, but the truth is I'll *always* be there. Until whoever did this terrible thing to me is caught, and they're off the streets so I can have my life back.

The shadow I saw before is still there and I'm still scared shitless as the loud music only makes me that much more terrified. It embodies the fear, making me feel it all over, inside and out.

And then...fuck me... it moves.

The silhouette I told myself was only in my imagination.

"Shit!"

I skate as fast as I can toward the edge of the rink, but with my mind and heart racing a mile a minute, my feet get twisted, and I fall.

Hard.

Right on my side.

My ribs throb on contact, but I can't lie here. I have to move, have to get out of here.

I'm back on my feet the next instant, glancing toward the figure again, and I didn't imagine it. It's moving faster now, coming right for me. Using the toe of each foot, I push the skates off my feet, then run for the front door, slamming into the glass because I'm only now realizing it's locked. My hands shake as I twist the latch, holding my breath when I burst through, racing out into the darkness with only socks on my feet.

I glance back at the building to make sure I'm not being pursued, but when I face forward again, I slam into a solid, wall-like chest. Equally solid arms hold me in place, making it impossible to move, impossible to get away.

My first thought is that he caught me. Somehow, he circled around the building and cut me off before I could get to my car. Not that I could've gone anywhere anyway, seeing as how I left my keys inside along with everything else.

But when I scream and freakout, fighting off my attacker, a familiar voice makes me slow down, take in my surroundings.

"Stevie, whoa, hey. It's just me," Vince says, staring into my eyes until it settles in that I'm okay, that I'm safe. "What happened?" He glances toward the building.

"Someone's in there," I ramble in between sobs. "Everyone went home, I was doing the floors, and someone was fucking with the music, then they chased me out here."

I push both hands through my hair, feeling like I'm losing my shit as I glance back toward the building.

"Listen to me. I'm gonna put you in the truck. I need you to lock the doors," he instructs. "I'm going in to check things out."

"No! What if he's still in there?" I'm frantic, hysterical, but Vince

131

doesn't feed into it. Instead, he takes my face in both hands and locks in, making me focus only on him.

"Nothing's gonna happen to me," he promises. "I want you to lock the doors like I told you to, and if anyone approaches the truck, start the engine and drive off."

I hear him, but don't immediately comprehend. "You want me to leave you? I—"

"Drive. Off," he reiterates, still clutching my cheeks. "You can pull over and call the cops once you're safe, but I want you out of danger. Understood?"

I nod, grateful he even believes me. Because, hell, I'm not sure *I* believe me.

He opens the door, and I climb into the truck, accepting the keys when he hands them to me, and then I lock the door like I was told to do.

My eyes are glued to him in the rearview mirror as he heads to the back of the truck, takes out a baseball bat, then rounds the truck again to go into the rink.

I'm shaking all over, vibrating with fear and worry, hardly blinking as I watch the glass doors he just disappeared through. Only now do I have time to assess—noting how he's just put me, my *safety*, before his own. And even the fact that he's here says a whole hell of a lot.

He had practice tonight. He smelled like soap and shampoo, which means he showered and came right over, maybe after dropping the others at the house. *Bird watch* is what Ash called it. And here I was, thinking they were only keeping an eye on me while I was at school, but thank God, he's here.

I gasp when the few lights on inside the rink go dark, but the next second, I breathe a sigh of relief seeing Vince step outside, using the keys he must've found in my bag to lock up.

The driver's side door opens, and he climbs in beside me.

"Did you see anything?"

He meets my gaze and shakes his head. "No, but the back door was unlocked. Whoever it was must've gotten in that way."

I'm silent, noting he hasn't questioned *once* whether this is all in my head.

He hands me my belongings—my purse, my phone, my keys—then just sits there.

"I think you should stay with me tonight," he says. "I know you're an adult and can take care of yourself, but—"

"Okay."

His eyes narrow when I cut him off, answering so quickly I even surprise myself. But the truth of it is… I don't want to be alone tonight. Yes, Mom and Rob are home, but… I don't want to *sleep* alone. I'd probably lie awake, staring at the ceiling all night for fear of whoever that just was coming back.

Note to self: Ask Rob to fix the lock on that bedroom window.

Vince's eyes are still on me and I'm getting used to their intensity, how he reads me in silence, probably divulging all my secret feelings and emotions surrounding this. But I don't really care if he knows—that this all has my head pretty fucked up, that I live in a constant state of fear.

All the time.

He nods, and I imagine I'm right about him seeing it all. "Good," he says. "We'll sort out how to get your car tomorrow."

I draw a breath and settle deeper into the seat, wishing he'd get me out of here already. And just before I'm about to request that he do just that, he starts the engine and shifts into reverse.

I watch the building through the rearview mirror as we leave the lot, wondering how close I just came to history repeating itself. If Vince hadn't been here… there's no telling what might've happened.

And this is the reality that haunts me every day, the feeling that, whoever is after me, whoever wants to hurt me… they're always right on my heels.

Chapter 17

Stevie

Vince clutches the food we stopped off for in one hand, and he holds *me* with the other. His grip on my waist as we approach the steps of The Den is the reason I've almost forgotten that not even half an hour ago I was scared for my life.

While his touch, and the realization that he's so committed to protecting me, definitely helps, I'm still shaken.

We step inside the house and it's lively as usual. I realize my eyes are darting around from one room to the next, and it's because I'm looking for the others—Ash, Micah.

Ash, because I wouldn't pass through a room and not acknowledge him. Micah, because I hope to *avoid* him, actually. I don't see either, so I focus solely on Vince.

We walk through the manor, and he greets his frat brothers in passing—as we cross the foyer, as we walk the long hallway to the elevator. Then, once we're closed in, slowly climbing to the next floor, I get a glimpse of us in the reflection of the stainless steel.

He's... sexy as sin, which, duh, I already knew. But I don't hate the sight of us *together*. My gaze lowers, staring where his hand rests gently on my hip, like I'm his. I like what I see so much that I'm fixated, not realizing Vince is watching me right back.

He says nothing, but a slow, knowing smile curves his lips, stealing my breath.

Damn. Did I seriously tell him I'd have to *think* about filming together? I have no clue how I didn't cave, how I didn't give him a definite yes right on the spot. Now, the details of that night are officially stuck in my head, and I feel myself leaning toward my response being *'yes'*.

Yes, I'll steal what little innocence you have left.

Yes, I'll fuck you.

Just... yes.

The visual comes to an abrupt end when the doors part and we step off the elevator. Vince keeps conversations short with the guys we pass. His pace slows some, but he never stops moving. Eventually, I realize this is because of me, because he knows I'm still pretty frazzled from what happened at the rink.

Despite trying to keep Micah as far out of my thoughts as possible, that's not so easy when we pass by his bedroom door. There's no light, no sign of life, so for all I know he isn't even home.

Or... maybe he isn't *alone*. It kills me to consider it, but what's to stop him from moving on? Finding some other girl who doesn't have so much baggage?

Don't do this, Stevie. Don't make excuses for his shit behavior.

Reminding myself of this, I force Micah out of my head. If he's not thinking about me, I'm sure as shit not going to spend my night thinking about him.

I'm grateful for the silence when Vince shuts us into his space, leaving all the noise, all tonight's drama on the other side of the door. His room is neat, like always, so I don't worry if his covers are clean when I drop down on the edge of his bed. My eyes are glued to his back, watching as he removes his t-shirt, stripping down to the wife-beater tank underneath. The cut of his trim waist tapers toward his belt, and I can't help but imagine myself undoing it, removing those expensive-ass jeans.

My brow arches when I smile and, once again, I'm caught in the act when he seems to sense my eyes on him before glancing over his shoulder. I don't even bother pretending I don't love staring at him. Hell, any girl with eyes would agree.

"You're not hungry?" he asks, nodding toward the bag sitting beside me.

I shrug. "I'm still not quite settled enough to eat, I guess."

My admission brings this look to his eyes. It's sympathy, I think.

"That's why I suggested we stop at the deli," he says, moving around his room to straighten the few things left out of place. "I had sort of a nervous stomach as a kid, so I made myself a lot of sandwiches. That way, I'd eat what I could, set it aside, then eat again when I felt better. And... it used to help that lunch meat and bread were relatively cheap," he adds with a smile, but I don't smile back.

I'm stuck on the part about his life being so fucked up that he could hardly eat, could hardly relax enough to finish a meal in one sitting. Trying to imagine what could've been that bad, I feel a little stupid for thinking my problems are so big. Yeah, I've experienced some disturbing shit, but I have a feeling *those* things are nothing compared to what Vince has seen.

He glances at me when the bag rustles, and when he sees me removing my sandwich, he arches a brow.

"Shit, did I say the magic word or something?"

He smiles and I'm reminded that, physically, he's painfully perfect. I take a bite and nod, covering my mouth when I answer. "Yeah, something like that."

"I'll take it," he says, then comes to join me on the bed. He stretches out on the opposite side, one foot still planted on the floor. He's solid muscle, heavy, so I readjust my posture to balance myself.

I feel his eyes on me when I swallow. "Tonight was pretty scary. Are you okay?"

I don't answer right away, replaying the situation in my head. I know what I saw tonight, but... I'm honestly not so sure anymore. I'm not really sure I can trust even *myself* these days. I've gotten into this rut of functioning on very little sleep, coupled with having a very overactive imagination. I see shadows and danger where there is none, hear footsteps behind me when I'm in a room alone.

All of a sudden, my appetite's gone again, and I wrap up what's left of the sandwich. Then, I meet Vince's gaze before answering his question.

"Not really. But I like to think I will be one day."

He blinks, and I can't help but wonder what devastation those green eyes have seen that I feel so connected to him right now, feel so understood.

When my hand warms, I lower my eyes to where he's reached out for me. He squeezes.

"Well, you're here now. With me. And I won't let anything happen to you," he promises, and I nod, actually believing him.

I look away when my phone vibrates inside my bag. I stand and get to it one second before the unknown caller hangs up. I frown a bit. I've gotten several of these over the past week. At first, I didn't think much of it because telemarketers are *always* cold calling, but it's a little late for it to be that kind of call. And… maybe I should be paying closer attention, taking note of whether I'm getting the calls more than usual.

I reach to set my phone down again, but another call comes through before I get the chance. It's Mom this time. I'm still not quite over being lied to, so I decide to text instead of picking up.

Stevie: Don't worry. I'm safe.

Mom: Be home soon?

Stevie: No. I'll be out all night.

As expected, she takes a while to answer. I imagine her typing out responses, then promptly deleting them, trying to correctly word what she says next.

Mom: Where will you be?

Stevie: With Vince. Be back tomorrow.

She sends another text, but I've already stashed my phone in my pocket. When I lower back onto Vince's bed, I'm wondering how this will work tonight—having a sleepover with someone who, until very recently, was adverse to touch. He may want space between us, and

I'll respect that, but... it's just awkward. Not knowing how much space is enough. Or how much space is too much.

I turn to face him, and he arches a brow.

"Are you... coming to lay with me?" he says with a smile and this hopeful look I wasn't expecting.

I try not to let it show on my face that I'm shocked he wants this, but that's definitely my prevailing thought. Part of me imagined he'd offer me his bed and he'd take the futon underneath the window, but... no.

While I climb up to the top of the bed, he reaches to turn off the lamp, then stretches his arm across the pillow before I lie there. His bicep is solid and warm beneath my head, and I like the feel of him, like that his size makes me feel small and comforted. The scent of his shampoo or soap is stronger now that I'm directly on his skin, so close to his side that I could easily curl into him. I've definitely considered it, and I'd probably go for it if I weren't trying to respect his boundaries.

"Is your mom gonna freak out about you not coming home tonight?" he asks.

"That was actually her I just texted. She knows I'm with you, so... all good."

He laughs quietly and my body moves with his. "You told her you're staying here? With me?"

I shrug. "She was cool with it. Does your mom get weird about things like that?"

I yawn, waiting for him to answer, but when he doesn't right away, it dawns on me that I don't know anything *about* his mom. Maybe I shouldn't have said anything.

My lips part to tell him exactly that, but I'm interrupted by his deep timbre breaking the silence.

"She... isn't around," he says. "Hasn't been for years. And even when she was, she didn't exactly give a shit where I spent my nights."

His response is heavy, weighing on my heart as his picture becomes even clearer. I have questions, *so* many questions, but I wouldn't dare pry into his life like that—unearthing the skeletons he's probably spent years trying to bury.

"I had the honor of being born to a woman who loved heroin more than her son," he shares, but I didn't expect him to say so much.

I stay silent for fear of saying the wrong thing.

"Not to make excuses for her, but she had a shit life, too. Before me. After me," he adds. "So, part of me knows she did it trying to numb the pain, trying to feel free for however long the high lasted. But the other part of me wishes she'd paid attention."

He's silent after that, and I wonder what he means. I'm torn between still not wanting to pry and not wanting him to think I don't care. So, despite my better judgment, I speak.

"Was your dad around?"

He shakes his head. "Never met him. But from what I've heard, it's better that way."

"Your mom told you about him?"

"She did. And her memories didn't exactly paint a pretty picture of the guy. He's the one who got her addicted, convinced her to leave home when she was sixteen. Not that that home was the healthiest place for her to be *either*, but better than sleeping on the street, better than being strung out or raising a kid she didn't want."

He says that so casually it doesn't register at first, but then it does. And it sits heavy. Right in the center of my chest. I find myself wondering if it was her actions that conveyed this message to Vince or… words straight from his mother's mouth.

"Do you have any *good* memories of her?" I note how quiet my voice is when asking.

"Not one," he admits, and my heart breaks for him. "As far back as I can remember, I took care of myself. I took care of myself when I was sick, got myself out the door for school, did my homework alone, ate dinner alone. She'd be up and about sometimes, entertaining whatever guy she was fucking that week, but most of the time she'd spend her evenings getting drunk or high in her room."

He's quiet and his breathing is even. His ribs expand against my arm with each draw of air he takes in.

"That's... when it would happen."

Even without him explaining further, my heart picks up speed with those words, anticipating something dark connected to them.

"She had this friend, Maggie, who'd stop over a couple times a week. They'd get high together—Mom a lot higher—and then once she passed out... it would just be us. Me and Maggie."

Although he could mean *anything* by that, I know what he's saying, without saying it. I have the full picture now, a clear understanding of what he endured, what kind of nights he faced when his mom wasn't on guard, wasn't protecting her son.

"I'm sorry."

I'm not sure why I say it, but it feels right.

"I'm fine. I'm here. I've learned to let that be enough," he says back, but this doesn't stop my heart from breaking for him.

But when I turn, curling into his side like I've wanted to do since I joined him in bed, it all makes sense.

I feel his pain because we're connected, bound to each other in ways I never would've imagined possible when we first began. And as his heat becomes *my* heat, I know he feels it too.

"This is the safest I've felt in a long time. Who knows? I might actually sleep tonight."

"Peace of mind is highly underrated," he says, "and I'm sorry someone stole that from you."

I breathe him in, feeling his heartbeat against my palm. "I'm sorry someone took that from you, too." Closing my eyes, a tear slips down my cheek.

The bed shifts when Vince turns onto his side to face me, drawing me closer despite his trauma. He pushes his thumb across my mouth, then the next sensation against my lips is the feel of *his* crashing down on them. There's a reluctance about him that I've come to expect and understand, but it's not present now. When he grips my waist, then lets one hand slip down to my ass, he's not the same timid guy I first encountered. He touches me like he knows what I want, like he knows the space we share is always safe.

As his tongue breaches my lips, his hips press forward and he hardens against my thigh, squeezing me tighter, pulling me closer. And as I melt into him, I breathe a word into his mouth with zero context.

"Yes."

He smiles into the kiss. "Yes, what?"

"Yes, I'll do it. Yes, I'll record with you. Yes... I'll be your first."

He presses his hips toward me again, and I moan, feeling my need for him grow with every second that passes.

"Took you long enough," he teases, breathing the words over my lips before kissing me again.

His hand lowers to my thigh, and he lifts it, bringing it to his waist so we're even closer now.

"You said you've had trouble sleeping." He pauses and the depth of his voice rouses goosebumps on my skin. "Will you let me help with that?"

A breath hitches in my throat as I let his words sink in, as I wonder what exactly he has in mind. However, instead of asking questions, I simply nod against his forehead, deciding to trust whatever he has planned.

Now that I've given him permission, he kisses me again, but his hand leaves my thigh. My skin cools there and it's strange, missing his touch for the millisecond it takes for him to touch me again. This time, he lifts my shirt, moving to the waistband of my work shorts, slowly pushing his hand inside them, inside my panties, and then his fingers slip into my pussy.

I inhale deeply, then release a slow breath against his mouth.

"There?" he asks, teasing his fingers into my slit, making me crazy.

"Yes."

He moves in deeper, pushing into my core. "Or... *there?*"

My eyes clench tighter, and I can't even speak this time. I rock against his fingers, thrusting them deeper as the heel of his palm brushes against my clit. It's the perfect combination of friction and warmth, everything I didn't realize I needed. I move my hand to his shoulder, squeezing tight, keeping him close as I soak his fingers, fantasizing that it's his dick inside me instead. But this will do for now.

He churns his fingers in further, twisting them out, then plunging them in again. I'm losing my breath, feeling lightheaded as my pussy constricts around his fingers, as I start coming for him.

"I can't wait to feel you. I mean *really* feel you," he says, feeding the fantasy as I climb higher and higher, clawing my way toward a deliciously powerful peak. I'm dripping and Vince's deepening breaths nearly match my own as one final tremor ravishes me. My body quakes against his, and then seconds later, I go still.

He leaves his fingers buried inside me, and I ride them slowly, not wanting this feeling to leave because... damn, I want more. More of this, more of *him*.

He presses a slow kiss to my mouth. "Better?"

I nod, letting my head settle against his chest. "Better."

He chuffs a soft laugh, pulling his hand free from my panties before resting it on my hip. When he speaks again, I assume it'll be to tell me what he wants in return, but he's always full of surprises.

"We're throwing a party tomorrow night. I want you here and won't take no for an answer."

His eyes are fixed on me. I can see that even through the darkness.

"But tomorrow's a school night."

I can guess that's not the response he expected when he laughs again. "Okay... so, if I promise to pack you a lunch the morning after and make sure you get to the school bus on time, will you say yes?"

I smack his arm when he teases me, and then I give it some thought. It isn't lost on me that he's not always so open, so willing to say what he wants, and that matters to me. So, I nod.

"I promised to go to this cake testing thing with my mom in the afternoon, but... okay. Yeah, I'll be here."

He smiles. "Good."

A moment later, he leaves the bed to change out of his jeans and into sweats. Then, he loans me a t-shirt that barely hits my waist, so a sliver of skin shows where the shirt ends, and the waistband of my panties begins. But this is apparently how he wants me in his bed, seeing as how I wasn't offered pants.

We climb back into bed and underneath the covers. It's scary how natural this feels—his chest at my back, my feet pressed against his legs for warmth. I smile when his hand slinks up my waist and he palms my breast, only to leave it there while he relaxes.

A month ago, I would've thought this was too much for him, but as his breathing deepens and he drifts off, I'm now convinced it's just enough.

Chapter 18

Ash

"Pulling up now."

"Right behind you," Tate says back.

The line goes dead, and I look up to see his headlights in my rearview. Some shitty bar across town is the last place I expected my night to end, but here we fucking are.

I hop out of the truck and look this place over. Neon signs fastened to the roof and brick walls cast the entire parking lot in an ominous red glow, adding to the weird vibe this night has taken on.

Tate meets me beside the truck just as I slam the door and lock it. He looks about as exhausted as I am, which means he was probably *asleep* like I was before the call came in, a call from a teammate. Micah wanted to grab a drink, ended up having a few too many, and now he's fucked up. Bad from what I've been told. So, I called Tate—leaving Vince out of it since he's looking after Bird tonight—then rushed here as fast as I could.

"Ready?" Tate asks.

I nod, and then we start toward the door. Loud music penetrates the thick glass before we even reach it. When we open it and step inside, it's ten times as loud, piercing our eardrums. The exterior was deceiving. With all the noise, I expected the place to be packed out, but it's small, and the crowd is thin, making it easy to spot Micah and Bobby on the other side of the room.

"Thanks for coming, man. I didn't know who else to call," Bobby says.

"You did the right thing. Thank you," I add, noting the look of relief on Bobby's face as he relaxes, relieved that Micah's no longer his responsibility.

And speaking of Micah, I take note of the state he's in—slumped over on the table, beer still in hand. A royal fucking mess.

I pass a look toward Tate, and the concern in his eyes is valid.

I look to Bobby again. "Take off. We'll get him out of here."

Bobby nods as he stands, but I remember something else and slam a hand down on his shoulder.

"This stays between us."

He nods again, and I hold his gaze until I'm positive he feels the gravity of what I've just said. The last thing the team needs is to know one of our starters, a core asset, is currently losing his shit with our first game coming up.

Bobby tips his head with one last nod, but I stop him before he gets to the door. "Call for a ride. You shouldn't be behind the wheel tonight either."

He only now seems to acknowledge he's pretty tipsy himself. I mean, nothing like *Micah,* but enough that he doesn't need to be driving.

"You're right. I'm on it," he says, grabbing his phone from his pocket, and then he's gone.

Now, it's just me and Tate, and I'm honestly not even sure where to start.

"Should we just lift him? Carry him out? Try to wake him?"

Tate shoots me a look. "Waking him isn't really an option."

My eyes are on Micah again and Tate's right. He's completely gone.

I've never seen him like this. Yeah, we party, have a good time, but he's always able to maintain some level of control, stopping before he goes too far. So, this is new.

This is... *bad*.

"Take that arm, I'll grab him from this side," I say, crouching to get Micah's right arm over my shoulder. Tate does the same with his left, and we lift.

"Shit," Tate groans. "Why's he so fucking heavy?"

We manage to get him upright, and I'm dreading carrying him out to the truck, but what the fuck else are brothers for?

"Where the hell is Vince? A third set of hands would've been helpful."

"He texted earlier to say he has Bird, so I didn't bug him. We don't need her seeing this, and we sure as *shit* couldn't leave her at The Den without one of us being there."

Tate arches a brow, cocking his head when he agrees with that, but I think we both wish Vince had been here, too. Micah's size isn't so much the problem, but trying to keep a grip on him as we maneuver sucks ass.

But we make do, damn-near dragging him across the floor because he's one-hundred percent dead weight. We pivot sideways to get out the door, then finally make it out to the parking lot.

We pause and I pat my pocket for my keys, unlocking it so we can toss Micah into the backseat. We manage it, but it's nowhere near as smooth as I imagined it would be. But the important thing is he's with us and he's safe.

"I can't take him back to The Den like this. I can't let the others see how far gone he is."

Tate nods in agreement. "Bring him to my place. He can crash there for the night and get his shit together." He pauses, glancing at Micah when he stirs a bit. "What the hell are we supposed to do from here? He can't keep going like this."

I shrug, because I'm at a loss, too.

"I mean, I know he'd fucking hate us for it, but... should we get his dad involved?"

I imagine it, what a shitshow that would be, then I shake my head.

"No, if anything, calling Nate in would make things worse," I say, and I hate the next thought that comes to mind. Because as things stand, it's an impossibility. "He needs Bird."

Tate's eyes shift to me when I'm done, but I note that he doesn't disagree. Instead, when his gaze shifts back toward the road, one word sums it up.

"Fuck."

I zone out, watching the few cars still out at this hour, feeling stuck. Convincing Micah to tuck his tail between his legs and beg her forgiveness for being absent while she needs him, is about as likely as convincing *her* to listen to a fucking word he has to say right now.

"It'll take an act of God to get these two to talk again."

"A fucking miracle," Tate adds, then he shoots me a look. "You know how to pray?"

A laugh leaves me. I can't believe he even asked.

"Depends," I answer. "You got a fire extinguisher in your car? It'll be on you to put me out when I go up in flames."

He laughs, too, knowing I'm probably not overexaggerating. "Looks like we're stuck letting nature take its course, then. And with any luck, that'll be sooner rather than later."

I couldn't agree with him more, because looking at the state Micah's already in... I'm not sure how long we have until he completely self-destructs.

Chapter 19

Micah

Blinding light.

Deep, quiet laughter off to my right.

I can't pinpoint who the sound is coming from yet, because it still feels like I'm in a fever dream.

Or… more like a nightmare.

Yeah, that's more accurate. Seeing as how I kind of wish I was dead right now.

"You look like shit."

I manage to open one eye and see Tate staring down on me, wearing a dress shirt and tie, lidded cup in hand.

"And you look like an asshole hipster," I shoot back. "Let me guess. You're drinking a chai latte oat milk."

He laughs again, then tosses a towel at me.

"Actually, it's a green smoothie. Grabbed it on my way home from work. Yours is on the counter."

His words register slowly, but then they catch up. "Wait… you're not *leaving* for work?"

He arches a brow at me. "No, you slept the whole day away. So, drink your smoothie, shower, then get your ass to practice before Coach bitches you out the next time he sees you."

"What the fuck?" I whisper those words to myself, covering my face with both hands. Last night is a blur. Starting with the fact that I have no clue how I ended up here. The last thing I remember is grabbing drinks with Bobby, and then…

Damn, I guess that's it. I must've passed out not too long after we made it to the last bar.

"Mic, I… think we should talk."

I hear Tate but don't look at him. Mostly because I feel a lecture coming on.

"We both know I'm not perfect, so don't take this the wrong way. But, dude, you've gotta get your shit together. Sooner rather than later," he adds.

I let out a breath. This is the last thing I need right now. From him or anyone else.

"Listen, I appreciate you letting me crash here last night, but I'm fine. Okay, yeah, I drank a little too much, but if memory serves me correctly, I've scraped *all* your asses up off the floor a time or two."

"Maybe, but this is different."

"Why? Because it's me this time?" I scoff.

Tate sets his drink down on the coffee table, then lowers to the smaller sofa across from me. He gives me that dad look he gives whenever he chastises one of us.

"It's different because of everything else you have going on—the blowup at practice, closing yourself off," he says, and I feel what he'll say next before he says it. Because his eyes go soft on me. "And you haven't reached out to Stevie in a while."

"Here we fucking go."

"Yeah, here we fucking go. Because if *I* don't tell you you're screwing up, no one else will. Maybe they're all worried you'll detonate, but I don't give a fuck," he adds. "Be mad at me, have a temper tantrum, whatever you need to do, but I'll always tell you what you need to hear because I care. So, if that means pissing you off on occasion, sign me up."

I glare at him, wondering when he got to be so damn annoying, but also wondering what took him so long to call me on my shit. I knew it was coming, just didn't know when.

I look away, hearing *his* words at war with Whitlocks. One telling me I'm such a fuckup no one has ever bothered to fix me. And the other telling me that no matter how far I go off the rails, he'll always bring me back.

I breathe deep as anger settles, giving way to reason.

"I know I need to fix this shit. That isn't lost on me, but… fuck. I don't even think I know how anymore. Where would I even fucking start?"

"We've all gotten ourselves in bad spots before. And it's the same for everyone. You start at the beginning."

I hear him, and I know it's probably that simple, but it's hard to see my way through this one.

"I just… when I saw her lying there, when I thought she was…"

I fall short of finishing my statement, knowing I can't let the word *dead* roll off my tongue. Not when it comes to Bird.

"It took me back to when I was a kid," I admit. "All I could think about, all I could *see*, was my sister. And… it fucked with my head."

Tate's quiet, and I close my eyes, resenting the shit out of the tragic images that race through my mind. They're stuck there. Probably forever.

"We assumed as much," Tate says quietly. "What you went through was… unthinkable. But you can't ruin all the good things you have going for you *now,* because of what happened back then. You deserve happiness, Micah. And no one who loves you, no one who's *ever* loved you, would want you to sabotage that."

I'm quiet, thinking over what he says, owning that he's right about that sabotage part. It's my toxic trait, the thing I do to make sure I don't get too high, for fear of what will happen when I inevitably come back down.

"I'm glad you talked to me," he says, "but I think we both know who really needs to hear this."

I open my eyes and stare at the ceiling, wondering if Bird will even hear me out at this point. God only knows what she's thinking or what she thinks I've been doing all this time. The thought of her going through the recent shit she's faced without me has me feeling sick to my stomach, but Tate's right. It's time to gut up and face her.

Even if she punches me in mine when I try.

"Yeah," I say with a sigh. "I'll talk to her."

"If she's at the party tonight, that might be a good time to pull her aside, but… don't be all Micah about it."

I laugh, hearing him use my name in that way. "What the fuck is that supposed to mean?"

He shrugs. "Just… don't be a brute. She's fragile right now. Keep that in mind."

I've never been good with fragile things. Gentleness isn't one of my attributes, but it sounds like I'd better learn quickly. Because if all goes well, come tonight… I might be able to get my girl back.

Chapter 20

Stevie

"Ok, ladies. Here are your samples," Deb says with a smile, lowering a silver platter in front of me and Mom. On it, there's an array of tiny cups, each with a tiny piece of cake.

"We have bananas foster, peanut butter cup, chocolate and vanilla swirl, red velvet, key lime, and lemon," she adds.

Mom scans it all, her eyes widening. "Wow. I wasn't quite expecting this kind of a spread," she says, smiling. "At this rate, I won't be able to fit into my dress."

She and Deb share a laugh, and I'm trying to hide my frustration.

I've spoken very few words to my mother these past few days. Ever since I asked point blank about why my sister was so fascinated with Cypress Pointe. She lied right to my face, and now I'm expected to sit here and pretend everything's fine.

But I'm a woman of my word, and because I promised I'd show up… here I am.

Deb places gold spoons in front of Mom and me. "I'll leave you two to dig in. The pen and stationary are to jot down your selections once you decide. Enjoy!"

"Thank you," Mom says, practically glowing.

Once it's just the two of us, she hovers over the cups for a bit, then chooses the red velvet to start. I follow her lead, grab a cup, then taste a piece with my spoon.

"So..."

I glance at her from the corner of my eye, my suspicion growing. "So?"

She nudges me with her elbow, like I should already know what she's hinting at.

"Last night was interesting, was it not?"

My brow arches, and I set the key lime aside to give the peanut butter cup a try.

"Mom, please don't."

"What? I'm just saying, now I know you and Vince are, you know, *spend-the-night-together* close."

Her words draw the hardest eye roll from me that I've ever given. My only other response is a heavy sigh.

"We can talk about these things, can't we?" she asks. "I mean, you're twenty and you have a boyfriend now. A very *attractive* boyfriend, might I add," she says with another nudge. "You think I live under a rock? I know what goes on."

Oh, God, kill me now.

"I'm just saying, I'm cool with it," she adds.

"Well, since you're so *'cool with it'*, you may as well know I won't be home tonight, either. Vince invited me to a party, then I'll probably just crash with him again."

Mom doesn't speak right away, but I feel her eyes on me. She's giving me this creepy-ass look that I won't even acknowledge.

"You're really serious about this guy, aren't you?"

I don't give an answer, because... I've struggled with how to classify my relationship with *any* of the guys. I feel close to them, closer than friends, but... there's a bit of fear around considering them to be more than that.

They're loyal and fiercely protective, but it's all so difficult to define.

A smile curves my lips when I think of how I was met by Ash

again just this morning. It was barely six, but I needed to retrieve my car, then rush home to shower and change before class. So, when I left Vince's room, I found Ash waiting out on the front steps to take me back to the rink. We rode mostly in silence because he's not much of a morning person, but my fingers were laced with his the entire way. Then, before letting me out of his truck, he handed me two things—a knife and a can of pepper spray—and made me promise I'd never go anywhere without them.

"Ooh! I have an idea!"

Mom's outburst snaps me out of the daydream and nearly stops my heart.

"You and Vince should do a double-date with Rob and me!" she beams. "And who knows! Maybe Tate will bring someone along. I know you two have been getting closer lately, so it might be fun."

I nearly choke on my cake, but mask it by grabbing a napkin and coughing into it, wondering what she'd say if she knew I'd be both Tate's *and* Vince's first choice for a plus one.

She pats my back. "Here, drink some water."

I take her up on that, sipping as I fight back a smile, thinking of how preposterous her idea is.

"Thank you," I say, lowering the bottle.

"Of course. And just think about what I said. It'd be fun!"

No. It wouldn't. It'd be the opposite of fun.

My phone buzzes in my bag and it saves me, giving me an excuse to walk away and gather myself. I don't even know who's calling, but whoever it is, I'm grateful.

"Let me get this. Be right back," I announce, then head toward the door as my eyes lower to the screen.

There are a few people I wouldn't expect to be hearing from right now, but at the top of that list is my father.

I push through the door of the cake shop and out onto the sidewalk, feeling my heart race. There's a lump in my throat just at the thought of speaking to him, but I wanted this. In fact, I sought him out *for* this.

So, I take a breath, lean against the brick column beneath the awning, and answer.

"Hey."

"Hey," he echoes, sounding about as uninterested in talking to me as I'd normally be to talk to him. Only, *this* time, I'm hoping he holds the answer I seek.

"Frank said you came by," he says. "This about money?"

I frown, wondering why he'd even ask that. I've *never* asked him for a single dime.

"Is this... no. It's not about money."

"Oh," he says, relief heavy in his tone. "Then what'd you need that was so important you stopped by without calling first?"

I don't let his words get to me. I'm *used* to him being an asshole, so this is just more of the same. And since he clearly wants to get straight to the point, that's what I do. Besides, the sooner we get this over with the better.

"I need to ask you something, and I want you to be straight up with me."

"Works for me. Let's make this quick. I've got shit to do."

I hate this man. Like, literally *hate* him. And most of all, I hate his indifference toward me, his constant, blatant reminders that I don't matter, that I'm nothing in his eyes.

"Ok, cool. So, I came across something of Mel's and, long story short, I found out that she made a trip to Cypress Pointe shortly before she... well... shortly before she was gone." The words just kind of tumble out, but that's the only way I can manage it. "From what I know, she only made one stop while she was there. She was looking for someone and... I'd like to know if you know why."

There's silence on the other end and it's eerie, reminding me of my mother's reaction when I brought it up to *her*.

"I... need you to tell me who Dusty is."

My heart races and it feels like I might actually stop breathing. This could be it, the truth I've waited to hear for over a month now.

"Where's your mother?"

I frown. "Why does that even matter? Just tell me who he is, and we can be done with this."

"It matters because that's who you should be asking. Not me."

"Don't you think I already tried that? Do you honestly think you'd be the *first* person I'd come to for help?" I snap. "I went to Mom, and she gave me some bullshit lie to chew on, thinking I'd let this go, but no! Mel thought Dusty mattered enough that she got on a fucking bus and drove all that way to lay eyes on him, to know if he was real, and I need to know why. Why was he so important? Why did she need to see him before she..."

My voice trails off when tears spill over. A lady and her daughter on their way into an ice cream shop eye me with concern as they pass, so I don't speak again until they're gone.

"I need to know who he is. That's all," I say quietly, pleading for *someone* to finally give me a direct fucking answer.

Dad's quiet and it kills me. I can't keep doing this. Can't keep going in circles and coming up empty.

"Who do you *think* he is?" Dad asks. "What's your gut telling you?"

Frustrated, I sigh. The last thing I need right now is games and riddles, but because I need him to cooperate, I play along.

"I've gone over it a million times, looked at the situation from a million different angles, and the answer that keeps coming back to me, over and over again is that... maybe... he was her father," I admit. "Like, maybe Mom had some sort of onetime thing with him when you two were maybe on the outs and, I don't know, the result of it was Mel."

He chuffs a short laugh on the other end, and it kills me. That he could find something funny while I'm pouring my heart out, laying everything out on the table.

"Damn," he says. "You're not *too* far off."

It's like my tears dry up out of nowhere. I stand straighter, listening harder as a burst of adrenaline fills my veins.

"Your mom and Dusty *were* involved," he admits, and I'm

relieved to at least know I'm not crazy. "But the part you got wrong... is the timing."

I feel tension spread across my brow, wondering what that means.

"Your mom grew up in Cypress Pointe," he shares, revealing something I never knew.

From what I've gathered, her family back home was into some pretty deep, illegal shit. So, she wanted to separate from that, redefine herself, so she left for college and never looked back.

"So, he was a friend? Someone she knew as a kid?"

"I'm not really sure when they met or how long they knew each other, but what I *do* know is that she went home to settle some family business, said she didn't want me to go with her because she was embarrassed by how they lived, their lifestyle or something. Who the fuck knows, honestly. That part was probably just a load of bullshit, freeing her to lay up with *that* asshole the entire week she was away. But long story short, she went home, then she joined me back at school like nothing had changed, then the next thing I know, she tells me she's expecting."

My shoulders heave as the pieces begin to fall into place, what he's hinting at, but... I need to hear him say it. I need to hear the words.

"Tell me," I demand, forcing the words out because I'm breathless. "Tell me who Dusty is."

Dad's quiet again, and I'm honestly afraid he'll backtrack, repeating that I'll have to go to my mother for the answer, but... I'm wrong. Finally, someone puts me out of my fucking misery and a piece of the puzzle fits into place.

"He's your father, Stevie. Dusty is the man your mother cheated on me with, and the end result of that was... you."

And there it is.

My heart is on the ground, and then, so are my knees.

I lower the phone, not bothering to hang up because I can't even think right now. My mind is racing just as quickly as my pulse, so I hadn't even heard the door to the cake shop open, hadn't heard my mother's footsteps. But when she places her arm around my shoulders, I'm more than aware of her—her lies, her deceit.

"How could you do this to me?" I ask, my voice barely higher than a whisper. "How could you know all this time and not tell me?"

She searches my eyes, her mouth agape, but she doesn't speak.

I'm reeling, rewinding and replaying my entire life, seeing it all through a completely different lens now—the way my *'father'* treated me, looked at me like I was nothing to him. And now I know why.

Because I *am* nothing to him.

Nothing but a constant reminder of my mother's infidelity, his heartbreak.

"I know!" I scream. "You wouldn't tell me, but I figured it out. Dusty's my father and you were willing to take that shit to your grave."

Tears well in her eyes when I shove her back, not wanting her fucking hands on me.

"I deserved to know. I deserved to know that Dusty's my father, deserved to know that *this* is why your fucking husband treated me like shit my entire life," I sob. "How could you do this to me?"

"Stevie, I—"

"Don't fucking touch me!"

I stand, shrugging her hands off my shoulders when she tries to stop me from walking away, but I can't be here, can't look at her face knowing my entire life has been a lie.

She follows me into the cake shop, pleading as I gather my things into my bag, dropping my keys because my hands are quivering.

"Stevie, wait!"

I spin on my heels. Not because she's pleading, but because I have one last question.

"Mel figured it out, too, didn't she?"

My mother looks absolutely stunned. Like a deer caught in headlights, which gives me my answer.

"Did she confront you?" I ask next.

"Stevie, things are complicated and—"

"Did you make her cover for you? Did you make your fragile, vulnerable little girl keep your dirty little secret?" I hiss.

More tears well in her eyes, and I can't stand to even look at her. Can't stand to think of how that must've weighed on my sister on top of everything else she was dealing with.

"Wait!"

This time, I don't stop. I hear my mother's footsteps thundering behind me the entire way to my car. And when I slam the door in her face, she bangs her palms on my window as I shift into drive. My tires screech and she chases after me until I speed up, peeling out of the parking lot, feeling like a fucking orphan.

The man I've called dad my entire life hates me.

My mother's a liar.

And my *real* father might not even know I exist.

Chapter 21

Stevie

Light glows beneath the surface of the turquoise pool. I zone out, staring at the vivid color as Vince's arm settles behind my neck. I lean into his side, then my thigh warms when Ash's palm lands there and he squeezes. Right here, poolside with these two, is the most settled and relaxed I've been all day.

Especially seeing as how, this afternoon, I discovered that my mother is quite possibly the most deceptive, diabolical human being alive.

My head's been spinning all afternoon and evening, just at the thought of the man I met in the diner that day actually being my father. With how shitty my childhood was, it's impossible not to wonder what might've been different if I'd known him then, but I was never given the chance. Instead, Mom stuck by my tormentor to protect her own ass.

I wince when the word *bitch* pops into my head. It's harsh, but I'm so enraged right now I'm not certain I wouldn't call her that to her face if she were standing here. She'll never know what she might've cost me—time, a healthier relationship, having an actual father figure in my life—and that's the part that kills me most.

I'll never know.

I showed up here at The Den earlier with tears in my eyes, expecting to be grilled about what happened, but it didn't quite go like that. Maybe because they knew I'd spent the afternoon with my mother and that me being upset likely had everything to do with her, but Vince and Ash respected my silence.

I've sensed how in tune they've been with me lately, so once I assured them I wasn't in danger, wasn't in pain, they didn't press. I was allowed to keep to myself that my entire world—or what was left of it, anyway—had fallen apart this afternoon. The shitshow with my mother undid the final few threads holding it all together. I was, and *am*, too exhausted to even grasp the full scope of what that truly means. But the important part is that these two, by some strange twist of fate, seem to get me and have allowed me space to mourn.

While they prepped for the party, I rested in Ash's bed. He and Vince checked in from time-to-time, brought me food when I got hungry, and now that the party's begun, neither has left my side. The moment feels reminiscent of being babysat. Aside from the fact that they kept the bad thoughts at bay by kicking off the night by rolling a few joints.

More than a little high, my head's finally starting to clear, and I zone out listening to the music. Vince is on one side of the oversized lounger with his feet crossed beside mine. His arm's draped around my neck and shoulders, and his hand casually rests on my chest. Ash is on the other side, with my leg resting over the top of his. His fingertips have been aimlessly tracing the inside of my knee for the last several minutes and both boys have my unspoken permission to touch me however they please.

Even with so many questioning eyes on us.

I legit don't give a shit.

I've been aware of the onlookers all night. Sandwiched between two of the hottest guys on campus, with both their subtle touches making it clear there's more than friendship between us is guaranteed to draw unsolicited attention. I'm sure the guys have noticed it, too, but they *always* function on the highest level of 'who gives a fuck', so it's no surprise they haven't reacted. But people are definitely wondering how I fit into their world, how they fit into mine, and the truth would shock the shit out of them if they really knew. Knew how deep the connection runs, knew how equally twisted, addictive, and beautifully imperfect it's evolved into. But in truth, I don't really care who understands and who doesn't.

These two... and Tate... are what I need.

"Enzo just texted. Pizza's here," Fletcher says as he rushes toward the house. The announcement prompts about half the crowd to flood in the same direction.

But the guys never move. They've gone out of their way to make sure I know I'm protected, but that also means they haven't left my side, or enjoyed the party, all night. While I'm more than content having them close, I feel like a piece of shit for hogging them, the hosts of the party.

"Ok, that's it," I announce. "You guys cannot sit here all night, babysitting me. Go mingle, speak to your friends, do... *something*," I add with a laugh. "I'll be fine. Promise."

Ash's thumb smooths over a small patch of my inner thigh. His eyes flash toward mine.

"The party's more for them than us," he reasons. "Besides, we see these assholes all the time."

I laugh again. "And you see *me* almost just as much."

He's quiet, and I think one last nudge will get him on his feet. And, hopefully, Vince will follow.

"At least go grab some pizza before it's gone."

His expression shifts and it looks like he's considering it. Food and sex are always good motivators for guys.

"Fine," Ash finally caves, pushing up from his spot on the lounger. "Want anything?"

Before giving an answer, I stare at him, his towering height. He yawns, pushing his hand beneath his shirt, slowly rubbing his stomach while he stretches, and I glimpse a sliver of his inked torso in the process.

"No, I'm good. There's something I need to take care of anyway,"

I answer in a daze. All because, now, my eyes have slipped lower, to the noticeable imprint at the front of Ash's sweats.

"We'll go, but don't get into any trouble while we're gone," Vince teases. My eyes dart to him as he slides out from where half his body rested behind mine to stand.

"Thanks to Ash's little gift, I think I'm good." I smile, patting the front of Vince's hoodie I've claimed as my own. Inside the pocket, I've stashed the knife.

Ash smiles, too, and I don't miss how pride flashes in his eyes, knowing he's the reason I'm currently armed with a weapon.

"Good girl," he says with a wink. "Be right back."

His eyes linger on me until I nod, then they're gone, walking side by side. Tall and broad, like gods among men.

There's still a smile on my lips as I reach for my phone, but it fades as I begin to tap out a text. It's to my group, letting them know that I'll need more time before we resume our meetings. Between the scare at the rink, and now this shit with my mother, I'm not sure I'm quite in the right headspace to be of any help to them. They're used to the positive, supportive version of me. Not this broken shell of who I was even a few weeks ago.

So, I hit send, and won't even try to read their responses until morning. I'm not sure I can handle knowing they're disappointed in me for letting them down.

When I lift my eyes from the screen, I focus on the water for a moment. Noting how it's void of bodies, pool floaties, and beer cans tonight. Not because these guys have suddenly grown up and toned down their parties, but because fall is in full swing. The leaves are beginning to turn, and warm summer nights are a thing of the past. Hence the reason I topped my shorts with Vince's hoodie instead of a t-shirt.

My eyes drift again, this time above the water to where a crowd clearly not interested in pizza still lingers on the other side of the pool. And much to my dismay, I lock eyes with the one person on the premises I hoped to avoid tonight.

Fucking Micah.

He's already watching me when I notice him, which means he's probably been doing that for a while now. There are girls seated at either side of him, one clearly hoping he notices her tits, but I don't think he even knows she's there. He's reared back in a chair, emptiness in his eyes, locked in on me like I'm the only other person here.

"Fucking creeper," I whisper to myself, forcing my gaze away from his. But, of course, I inevitably glance in his direction again. It's impossible not to know that I know he's there.

I hate that there's still a connection, hate that when I look at him—wearing a t-shirt with their team's logo in the center, ripped jeans, hair wrangled into a knot at the back of his head—I only see him naked.

Every pussy-drenching, detailed inch of him.

And this dickhead has the audacity to watch me? Staring without shame, knowing he's been in the wind for weeks?

If it was so easy to forget me then, *forget me* now, *asshole.*

Before I can stop myself, I take out my phone again, but this time it's to type out the bitchiest message I possibly can to him, intent on sending it, but then I come to my senses. No. He doesn't deserve to hear from me. Not even if I was only texting hateful, angry words.

So, managing to keep my dignity intact, I shove my phone into the pocket of the borrowed hoodie, and stand from the lounger, heading inside. The volume in the house is ten times louder than outside, and there are bodies everywhere, packed into the kitchen and game room. I swear these boys have a sixth sense when it comes to me, because I lock eyes with Ash on my way to the steps. Curious where I'm headed, he arches a brow, prompting me to mouth the word, "Bathroom." He nods and seems to relax as I continue toward the hallway.

It's quieter in this portion of the house. There's a bathroom nearby that I could use, but with all the traffic that's passed through the house tonight, I'm pretty sure it's wrecked. So, the one upstairs is a far more appealing option.

I call for the elevator, and it isn't until I'm standing there, alone, that I start getting creeped out. Dim, recessed lighting above casts strange, spotty shadows along the edges of the corridor. And, of course, the elevator's taking forever.

"Come on."

I press the button again, knowing that won't make it get here any faster, but I do it anyway. To ease my nerves, I fondle the knife in the pocket of my hoodie, brushing my thumb back and forth over the lever that will spring the blade forth should I need it. But just in the nick of time, the elevator doors part, and I rush inside, pressing the button to close the doors quickly. They're mere inches apart, and I've just breathed a sigh of relief when an arm slices between them.

A muscular, tattooed arm with veins protruding beneath lightly tanned skin.

Unfortunately, I'd recognize that ink anywhere. Despite having tried to forget it these past couple weeks. The doors open wide again, and there he stands.

Master avoider, fuckboy extraordinaire.

The elusive Micah Locke.

Chapter 22

Stevie

I get the full view of him as he stands outside the elevator and, damn him… he's still hot as sin, and his hair is part of the problem. I've never seen it this way—pulled back in a knot, exposing a freshly trimmed undercut. With it away from his face, the angles of his jaw and the thickness of his neck are more apparent. If there was a picture beside the word "man" in the dictionary, it would be of Micah.

His t-shirt fits in this perfect way that makes me hate him even more—snug around his shoulders, biceps, and chest, and just fitted enough around his abs that I'm able to see the tapering of his waist into his jeans. Even knowing he's a world-class asshole, I can't talk myself out of acknowledging that he's somehow even hotter now than when we last talked.

He steps in, his height and broad shoulders making it impossible to slip out past him if I were to try. Especially seeing as how I'm about ninety percent sure he trapped me here on purpose and would only grab me before I could make a clean exit.

So, I'm powerless, watching as the doors slide closed behind him.

"Why the fuck are you here, Micah? You've done an excellent job of ignoring me, and I'm perfectly fine with keeping to that trend." I roll my eyes toward the ceiling. But there's no escaping him there, either. Being inside a stainless-steel box means we may as well be surrounded by mirrors.

"I—."

His voice trails off after uttering that one syllable and it's nearly laughable that after all this time, that's the best he could come up with.

"Listen, why don't you do us both a favor and just… go."

There's an unexpected strain to my voice. I wasn't prepared for this—seeing him, *talking* to him. I suppose, in my mind, I was resigned to believe that the last time we spoke was exactly that.

The last time.

"I was hoping we… could talk," he finally says.

"No wonder you couldn't get your words out," I scoff. "Are you fucking kidding me? You're ready to talk because *you* think it's time."

I know Tate and I have already cleared the air, but it's hard not to be triggered, remembering how he put me through something similar.

"Bird, please just… listen for a second."

For the first time tonight, I regret coming here. It's now super clear that I should've found some seedy, twenty-dollar a night motel to hole up. Just until I could sort my shit out.

Anything to avoid this moment.

Reaching around Micah, I press the button to open the doors, but frustration flares within him, and I retreat when he slams his fist into the button panel, effectively jamming the entire system. I guess as much when the doors remain closed, and we don't move.

My eyes are locked on him, not daring to blink. Yes, I've seen him go dark, I've seen him unhinged, but this feels different.

He steps closer, consuming the space between us as he stares into me, likely noting how a spike of adrenaline has me breathing heavier. Only now, with him within arm's reach, do I recognize the dilation in his eyes, the slight tinge of redness in them. Whatever cologne he's wearing masked the smell of weed at first, but now that I'm suspicious of him, I catch the hint of it.

"You're high," I accuse, attempting to step aside when I assume he'll cage me in, but I'm too slow. He rushes in and his reaction time is better than mine, which could be because I'm a little high, too. His palms slam the wall at either side of my head. The sound rings in my ears and I wince, thinking of the knife in my hoodie as my heart races.

I peer up, meeting his gaze. His eyes are unearthly dark, more sinister than usual. It takes a moment to remember to breathe, so I draw air slowly, hoping he doesn't see how rattled I am.

"What do you want from me, Micah? What do you honestly expect at this point?"

There's this pained look in his eyes when I ask, and then they fall closed, blocking me out from whatever he's thinking or feeling. He's motionless and we're silent, breathing one another's air with mere inches between us.

It's weird having him so close, close enough to touch, because I was certain it would never be like this again. Especially not with the anger I feel toward him, the pure undiluted rage that has me gripping the knife now.

I'm just beginning to think he'll never speak when his eyes open and his lips finally part. I shouldn't be intrigued, shouldn't be curious what answer he'll come up with, but I am.

"I'm just... I'm..."

He trails off again and I'm shaking in frustration.

"You what? What the fuck are you trying to say?" Emotion hits me like a tidal wave, making it impossible to hold back everything I've kept inside. "Do you have any idea how fucked up you are? Any idea how it felt for you to disappear after we..."

Now *I'm* the one who can't speak, can't face the truth of what happened.

"I can't do this. Let me go."

I attempt to duck beneath his arm, but his body crashes into mine, locking me against the wall. Every breath I take presses my chest to his, and I hate this, being so close to him, *wanting* him and hating him equally.

"I can't," he rasps, the harsh edges of his deep voice rousing goosebumps on my limbs.

"You can't what?"

He presses into me, resting his forehead against mine. "You told me to let you go, but… I can't."

My stupid heart doubles in speed. "Well, you sure have a funny way of showing it."

His chest swells with a deep surge of air, and I turn my face from his when he cups the back of my neck, the warmth of his touch contrasting the chill on my skin.

"Look at me," he beckons, so softly he sounds like someone else. Someone sane, someone with a soul.

But it works because my eyes find his, and I'm shocked by how they've softened.

He strokes the tendon in my throat with his thumb, and I believe he's focused on my racing pulse. But then his lips part, stealing my attention.

"I screwed up," he says, "and I'm so fucking sorry."

My brain isn't immediately sure how to process his words. Mostly because the tone they're spoken in is still too tame to be the Micah I'm used to—the brute, the alpha. My next thought is to assume this is a manipulation tactic, a means of getting something from me that he wants. Sex maybe. But if he simply wanted someone to fuck, the girls beside the pool with him would've been more than willing. Especially since I'm certain he knows I'm not an easy target at the moment. Not with the mile-thick wall I've recently built to protect my heart from him.

His intentions are difficult to pin down, but when my heart begins to soften, my head screams a resounding *'FUCK no'*.

"You think *you* have regrets?" I ask. "Try being the girl who gave her virginity to a guy who promptly forgot she even exists. *That's* what regret fucking looks like."

"I didn't forget you existed," he says, but I can't listen to this anymore.

I duck to slip beneath his arm again, but one word halts me.

"Tuesday."

I'm motionless, confused. "What *about* Tuesday?"

His hand finds its way to my neck again, sliding up my nape, and I feel myself relaxing into his touch. Because I'm weak and he still affects me. More than I wish he did.

"That's the day you colored your hair," he says, twisting a few strands around his fingers, eyeing the purple tint.

At first, I'm startled that he'd know that, but then it dawns on me. "You only know because Ash told you."

Micah holds my gaze, shaking his head. "Honestly, I haven't spoken to *any* of the guys much lately," he confesses.

His eyes are deceiving, nearly convincing me he's telling the truth, but then I remember who I'm talking to.

"Whatever. Feel free to blow smoke up my ass all you want, but I'll never believe another word you say," I promise.

But when I step aside, he grips my arm this time. My gaze lifts to meet his and I'm locked in his stare.

"Stop acting like you don't know."

My head spins. He's full of riddles today, and I don't have time for it. "Don't know what, Micah?"

"That I'm fucking insane for you."

His words sound angry and strained. Like they're tearing their way out of him one syllable at a time.

"You're in my head. Every second of every day. I wouldn't be able to pry you out of there with a fucking screwdriver," he adds.

He leans into me again, and this time, I feel him—solid inches pressing against my hip.

"I know what day you changed your hair because I watch you. All the time," he admits.

My head tilts back so I can meet his gaze, look into his eyes. "Why?"

He exhales, and I feel his heat across my lips. "Because you're my fucking obsession."

And there it is again. My traitorous heart, giving him a reaction he doesn't deserve, one he hasn't earned. But when his mouth nears mine and he places a cautious kiss against it, I know I'm not really in control. He is, whether I like it or not.

His tongue moves into my mouth, and he feels like taking a breath of air after having been held underwater just long enough to think I'd drown. Then suddenly, here he is, giving me what I craved, breathing life into those parts of me I forced to die. The parts of me that wanted him back in my world even though he's been the source of my pain.

He sucks my lips, and it feels like I'll fall to pieces right in his hands. He lowers just enough to grab my legs, then pulls them up to encircle his waist. I didn't realize until now how much I missed the feel of him between my thighs, but my sense of it is overwhelming now. The kiss has me dazed, only vaguely aware as he undoes his belt buckle. It isn't until I hear his zipper being tugged down and feel him lowering his jeans that I come to my senses.

"Wait," I mumble against his mouth, but he breathes into the kiss, reaching between my legs. I gasp when he grips the leg of my shorts to pull them aside and out of the way. He grips his cock, aligning it with my center.

"I said *wait!*" He stops this time. Partly because I spoke the words louder, and partly because of the cool steel now pressed to his neck.

You could hear a pin drop inside the elevator, and I note how he's not even the least bit rattled by having a knife being held against his throat.

"You disappeared when I really, *really* fucking needed you," I choke out, holding his gaze as tears stream down my cheeks. "I've had a very fucked up day and I'm not in the mood to just forgive and forget and pretend everything's okay, Micah."

He doesn't move, only stares into me, letting my words sink in. I half expect him to deflect, but he doesn't do that. Instead, he absorbs it all, acknowledges my pain in a way I didn't see coming.

He swallows and I'm fixated on his throat where I've just broken skin. A thin stream of red trickles toward his collar when he leans into the blade like a psychopath, ignoring the pain, the danger. I fight the urge to remove the knife because I'm desperate for him to know this isn't a game.

"You hurt me," I warn him, but he comes closer.

His lips press to mine, putting more pressure on the knife. "Then, hurt me back," he whispers.

I gasp when he squeezes my fingers tighter around the handle, as if making me promise not to move it, making me promise not to spare him.

When he reaches for his cock and barely gives me the tip, I'm wild for him, completely feral, arching away from the wall. I thrust my hips toward him, inviting him into my heat, but he keeps me waiting.

"There's something I want to know first. Before I give you everything," he rasps.

My response is to gently bite his lower lip, feeling completely ravenous as he presses in just a little more.

"Tell me which of my brothers you've fucked since me," he says against my lips, making my heart skip a beat wondering if he honestly wants that answer, wants that image in his head.

As if he's just heard my thoughts and senses my hesitation, he beckons with a softly spoken, "Tell me."

My eyes roll back when he gives me one more inch, and then eases out again. It's enough that I might literally lose my mind if he keeps teasing me.

"Tate," I finally breathe, giving in.

He smirks against my mouth, and I nip at his lip again.

"Bird... you fucked your brother?" he asks with this sexy, throaty laugh that drives me even wilder for him.

"*Stepbrother.*"

He laughs at that, too, licking my bottom lip before giving me his tongue for a moment.

"Spin it however you want," he says. "Or... you can just admit what we both already know about you."

He gives me the tip again, and I'm on fire.

"Which is?"

"You're filthy," he breathes. "And I fucking love that shit."

His hips drive forward, and he powers into my core, stretching me around his hot cock. I gasp in a mix of surprise and relief, listening to the heavy sigh that leaves him.

"Shit, you feel like a fucking dream," he groans.

It's on the tip of my tongue to tell him that I missed this, missed *him,* but I keep it in.

"How did he feel inside you?"

The question takes me back to the night with Tate, remembering how he fucked me quietly, so our parents didn't catch on.

"It was nice," I say, realizing I'm uncomfortable sharing details.

Micah pushes into me deeper, making it hard to breathe.

"Nice? I've seen how you two look at each other, Bird. You're holding back."

He isn't wrong, but I don't know how to talk about *Tate* while my legs are wrapped around *Micah.* Except, I'm the only one who seems to feel weird about that.

"Try again," he beckons.

"It was... incredible. We fucked in his old bed, quietly because our parents were in the next room."

Micah's breath deepens, and I realize this is what he wanted. "Did he use a condom?"

He rocks into me, and the blade at his throat slips, breaking new skin. "No."

His lips move to my jaw, so his breathy words go straight to my head. "Did you make him pull out?"

I squirm and his hands move down from my waist to my hips. "No."

His chest presses mine when he draws in air, then his hands lower to my ass, squeezing tight.

"So, you let him come inside you?" he asks. "You let your step-brother fill this sweet, tight pussy with his cum?"

My chest heaves. I struggle between finding words to answer his question, and not wanting to finish too quickly.

"Yes," I answer. "I wanted it. Wanted to feel *everything.*"

He's clearly getting off on the mental images I've painted. It's like, with each answered question, he gets harder inside me, throbbing as tension mounts within him. He kisses my neck just beneath my ear, and when he does, the slick warmth of his blood drips down the knife handle and onto my hand.

"Now you," I say, panting against the corner of his mouth. "Tell me who you've fucked."

I cry out the next second because he thrusts into me with a hard, punishing blow.

"What the fuck did you just say to me?" he growls.

"I—"

Before I can finish my answer, he pulls out of me, and then drives deep like before.

"Say it again," he commands, speaking sternly.

I hesitate, because I made my way to his lips and had to kiss him first.

"I said I want to know who you've fucked."

I pay for it again, feeling a throb deep in my core when he shoves into me with reckless abandon.

"Shit!" I cry out, tilting my head back when I can't take anymore.

"Did I hurt you?"

I nod before words leave my mouth. "Yes."

"Good," he smirks. "I want you to remember that pain every time that thought crosses your mind. Understood?"

I'm only coherent enough to nod as his pace quickens and his mass fills me, stretching me to the hilt.

"There *was* no one else, and there *will be* no one else," he says, breathing against the side of my face as I take him deep. "You're ours now, Bird. Even when shit's fucked up between us. Even when we go dark, and it feels like it's over, you're *still* ours. Never forget that."

I don't answer. I *can't* answer. Because I'm swimming in this twisted promise, drowning in the deeper meaning that's just taken me under. If I'm honest, there was no need to even touch the topic of other girls, because I somehow knew it was an impossibility. Knew he hadn't been with anyone else despite the few times my imagination wandered. But maybe, on some level, I just wanted to hear him admit it.

Admit that I'm the only one.

I clench around him and my addiction to this feeling is still alive and well. An orgasm hums inside me before coming into full bloom at the exact moment Micah reaches his limit. His fingers dig into my flesh, squeezing my ass as he lifts me higher and pumps into me, letting his eyes drift closed as his head tilts back. I watch him, staring as I come on his dick, taking his release as it surges into my core.

I still feel him emptying inside me when he lowers his gaze to mine, locks me in his stare, and says more with that look than he's ever admitted out loud.

My grip eases and the knife clatters to the floor. We kiss slow and deep, and I want him to know I feel those unspoken words.

"I forgive you," I answer, holding his gaze. "But if you leave me again, I *will* kill you, Micah."

A quiet laugh leaves him, but it fades quickly, giving way to a more serious look as he stares into me.

"I can't promise I'll never go dark again. It's in my nature," he admits. "But you have my word, the next time it happens… I'll take you with me. If that's what you really want."

A slow smile curves my mouth, and I take his lips, breathing my answer against them. "That's what I want. Because *you're* what I want."

He doesn't speak, taking in what I've just said, and then with his cock softening inside me, we kiss, and my fate is sealed.

Wherever Micah goes, I will follow.

Even if that means following him into utter darkness.

Chapter 23

Stevie

Well, one thing's for sure. Micah Locke gives zero fucks.

The looks on the faces of the couple we're approaching as we walk the halls of The Den are priceless, and I can't blame them.

Blood stains half the collar of Micah's t-shirt, and I've likely ruined Vince's hoodie with the few red splotches on the chest and sleeve. My right palm is sticky with more of Micah's blood, and yet we're hand-in-hand, strolling slowly as if we *don't* look like a pair of serial killers.

I barely make eye contact with the girl, but Micah acknowledges the guy as we pass with a casual, "What's up?"

I can hear their whispers behind us, but Micah's already unlocking and opening his door, completely unaware. We step inside and the space brightens when he flips the light switch. He moves to a laundry basket in the corner while I wander slowly, thinking how it's been way too long since I've been here. It's a bit of a mess, but that lines up with the chaos that's been his life lately, so no judgement. Based on what the others have said, he's been a shell of a human lately, which reminds me. There's still so much to discuss, so much to gain clarity on.

I gasp at the feel of his hands on my waist. Then, I'm spun to face him. I'm still not quite steady on my feet when Micah kisses me in the most carefree, lighthearted way. I don't think he's *ever* kissed me this way, but... I love it.

We separate, and I'm grateful to see fresh towels tucked beneath his arm. After our elevator encounter, a little soap and water doesn't sound like a half bad idea.

"Ready?" he asks.

I arch a brow. "You're... coming with me?"

My confusion seems to amuse him. "Shower's big enough for two, so, yeah. If you're cool with it."

I look him over—that face I've missed, that *body* I've missed—and it's a no-brainer.

"Of course," I say with a nod.

He likes my answer, making that crystal clear when he comes in for another kiss. We're on our way to the bathroom when I remember two who are likely very worried that I haven't come back down yet. So, I shoot Vince and Ash a quick text to let them know I'm with Micah, and then set my phone and the knife aside before leaving the room.

We don't linger in the bathroom long. After Micah locks us in, he removes Vince's sweatshirt off my torso, and then the tank top I wore underneath it. He moves to my shorts next, before taking off my bra and panties. Then, once I'm completely naked, I stare in silent awe as he undresses. Shit, watching him get naked is performance art.

Every damn second of it.

He holds my hand while I step into the shower, then he closes the curtain behind us. My hand goes to his neck, seeing the two deep wounds I left there.

"Do you have a first-aid kit? I'll bandage you up when we're done," I offer, but he's already shaking his head.

"No."

A laugh slips. "No? Micah, people will think someone tried to murder you. People will think *I* tried to murder you."

He smiles and my body melts against his when he draws me close.

"My girl marked me and I'm not covering it. Who gives a fuck what anyone else thinks about it?"

And with that, I suppose his answer is final.

He releases me to squeeze bodywash into his palm, then rubs both hands together, lathering up. I wasn't expecting to be pampered and bathed tonight, but that's exactly the treatment I'm being given.

Micah's touch is softer than a man of his stature ought to be capable of, but it makes it all the sweeter that he's so gentle with me. He washes me from head to toe, and somehow manages to avoid making me feel sexualized. There's only tenderness as he goes over my skin. Nothing else.

When he's done with *me*, he washes himself, and then he steps out to grab both towels. On our way back to his room, he holds my hand just like before, and I can't believe this is the same person. The same guy who recently made me feel so insignificant, only to now make me feel like I'm his entire world.

Back in his room, we don't bother with clothes. Not that I have any of my own to change into. We climb beneath the comforter and get as close as two can get—his chest to my back, my ass pressed so close to his cock there isn't an ounce of space between us. A solid, heavy arm drapes across my waist, and I smile at the feel of his legs behind mine. His large, firm thighs are like two tree trunks. Beside him, I feel comfortable. And most of all, I feel safe.

"Sure you don't want to go back down to the party?" I ask.

His hand rests flat against my stomach, and I exhale into his touch.

"Nope. Tonight, all I want is this bed and you. Just like this."

I smile against his pillow, noting that it smells like him, another subtle reminder of how much I've missed him. But the fact that he was away long enough to *be* missed steals my thoughts, drawing me back to the long list of unanswered questions.

My fingertips trail his forearm, moving over the light dusting of hair there as I think.

"Where were you?" I ask, feeling his chest shift against my shoulder blades.

"I've been right here," he says, but he doesn't understand the question.

"I mean, I know you were still around, but... in your mind, where'd you go? What kept you away from me?"

He's quiet this time, and I wait patiently, knowing his response might not be easy to get out.

"I was trying to cope," he admits, releasing a long, steady breath. The hand resting on my stomach moves to my hip, smoothing his palm down my skin. "You know about my sister, what I told you at the cabin."

I nod, letting him know I haven't forgotten.

"Well, that night we found you, seeing you lying on the cement like that, not knowing whether you were alive or..."

His words trail off, and I hadn't expected the emotion that bled through his voice. It's enough that my *own* emotions are heightened now.

"Seeing you like that reminded me of how I couldn't protect Loren either, and I felt like I failed again," he admits. "If I'd been there, if I'd gone to make sure you were safe, you would've been at home, sleeping soundly in your bed that night."

I hear it in his voice, the moment he starts slipping away, so I turn to face him, thinking that if I can just hold his gaze, I can keep him in the present. He stares at me through the darkness, and I feel his racing heart when I place my hand over it.

"What happened to me was not your fault."

His heart slows. His breathing deepens.

"And what happened to Loren wasn't your fault either." Now, he's completely still, and I lift his hand to my heart, too. "I'm here."

My words linger, and we lie there, breathing one another's air for several seconds before he pulls my hand up from his chest to kiss it.

"You didn't lose me, Micah."

His kiss moves from my hand to my mouth. "And I'm so fucking grateful for that," he says, gripping my hair as he finally breaks his silence.

Our lips move together, and the anger fades. It took so long to build up the rage I held toward him, and now, just like that, it's gone.

My face warms when he holds it, staring into my eyes.

"Earlier, when we were in the elevator, you said you had a rough day," he rasps, pushing his thumb across my lips. "Tell me whose world I need to fuck up to make it right."

A laugh slips out, and I lean into his palm. With the whirlwind that swept me up this past hour, I'd nearly forgotten my personal drama. Not that I longed to remember it or anything. But now, it's right in my face, plaguing my head *and* my heart just like before.

The smile he'd brought to my face is nearly gone as everything comes rushing back, and my gaze flits to Micah's mouth when I let out a breath.

"I—it's my mom."

His expression intensifies. "Is she okay?"

I nod. "She's fine, but… I'm not sure *we're* fine. We might not be for a while, actually. Or maybe not ever."

Micah's quiet, and I recall him mentioning how strained things are between him and his parents. We have that in common it seems.

"Tell me what happened." His voice is low and gentle. He's attentive in a way I've never seen from him. If I didn't already know I could tell him anything, I'd know it now.

So, I wrangle in all the scattered details, all the half-truths and broken promises, until I have something close to a complete story.

"Things between us were already strained because she's been hiding something from me. But then, while we were cake tasting today, I got a phone call from my dad. He flat out confirmed it. But until today, I had no idea Mom's secret was so monumental. So… life changing."

Micah's eyes narrow with concern, and I breathe deep.

"The trip I took to Cypress Pointe wasn't just some random trip," I admit. "I went there following a lead, a clue my sister left. At the time, I thought it was linked to her assault, but… I was wrong."

I pause because the weight on my chest feels like it'll crush me. I also hesitate because I feel the sting of tears in my eyes and don't want to cry anymore. I've done enough of that already.

"She lied," I finally force out. "My dad *isn't* my dad, which means the man she allowed to emotionally and verbally abuse me my whole life was only a stand-in. And a shitty one at that."

The laugh that leaves me is dark and fleeting.

"And he told you all of this today? Over the phone?" Micah asks.

I hear my *dad's* voice in my head, the harshness of it. Not only did he tell me over the phone, there wasn't an ounce of remorse in his tone as he spoke. It's left me wondering if he was relieved to deliver the news about Dusty, relieved to finally have the burden of being my father off his chest.

I snap out of it and nod. "Yeah."

Micah gathers me into his arms, squeezing me as I rest my forehead against his chest. "Shit. What an asshole."

He doesn't even know the half of it.

We lie there, me fighting back tears, him likely taking in everything I've just revealed. His rhythmic breathing relaxes me, though, which is why my problems just seem to fade to black as I feel myself dozing. My boys have that effect on me and it's no wonder why, lately, I feel like I can't breathe without them.

"We'll go get your things from the house. Tate can let us in while no one's home. You don't even have to be there."

His words have me wide awake again, and I peer up at him. "But I can't go back to the house with Dahlia. Not after what I did."

Not without me knowing if she played a part in my attack.

I don't say that part out loud, but the look on Micah's face has me so confused the thought leaves me just as swiftly as it came.

"You won't be staying at your moms. And you won't be going back to that shithole to live in the basement, either," he says, the words leaving his mouth with a sharp edge. "You'll stay here. With us."

I feel my brow gather, feel the confusion in my expression. "I'm not quite sure what to say to that."

He laughs, then kisses me. Three pecks on my lips, then one in the center of my forehead.

"Say that you understand, because that's the only answer I'll accept."

I let that sink in, that he'd willingly give up his space, his privacy, his freedom to make room for me.

"But don't you need to talk this over with the others?"

He's shaking his head before I can even finish the question. "I know they'll say yes, because they already have."

Now, I'm even more confused. "But you haven't had time to discuss it."

"Maybe not today," he says. "But you staying with us was the topic of conversation quite often after you... after your..."

He stops short of mentioning what happened, and I don't make him continue. I don't need to.

"No one pushed because we didn't want to get in the way when your mom stepped in. Besides, it was decided that it might be best if you weren't around while I was... while I—"

I interrupt him with a kiss. He doesn't have to explain. All that matters is that we reached this point. How we got here is of very little concern to me right now.

"Yes," I say, breathing against his mouth. "I'll stay."

I don't expect the smile that curves his lips half a second before they're on mine again, but if Micah wanted me to know he's sorry, if he wanted me to grasp the full scope of his feelings for me, then... mission accomplished.

I hear him.

Loud and clear.

Chapter 24

Stevie

All eyes are on us, and rightfully so.

Between the angry gashes to the side of Micah's neck, and me sporting one of his t-shirts and a pair of too-big basketball shorts that fall mid-calf, I'd stare at us, too.

Someone's made breakfast—eggs, toast, bacon, and there's fresh fruit. Yet, the mad rush toward the makeshift buffet has completely halted now that we've entered the room.

Micah strides in like nothing's amiss, of course. Meanwhile, I'm certain my face is bright red as I try to not make eye contact with anyone. He stops in the middle of the kitchen and looks around at everyone, not even the least bit uncomfortable as he clutches my hand in his.

"Since I seem to have everyone's undivided attention, now seems like the perfect time to make an announcement," he says, the commanding depth of his voice drawing them all in.

To our right, I spot Vince and Ash and they gravitate this way, because it's just like that when we're in the same room. We're a unit and can't help but to behave as such.

"As of last night," Micah says, "There's been a new development.

Stevie's going to be hanging out here for as long as she needs to, which means she's to be treated like a guest. After breakfast, I expect this place to get cleaned from top to bottom, and I also expect it to stay that way."

You could hear a pin drop as they all listen in.

"The rules are simple and there are only three of them, so there's no way you assholes can fuck this up. Rule number one, don't look at her. Rule number two, don't speak to her unless she's spoken to you first. Rule number three is imperative, for your own safety and well-being," he adds. "Do not... fucking... touch her. Not under any circumstances. Not ever."

Next, he aims a very pointed glare toward Enzo, who responds by putting his hands in the air, signaling his surrender. Remembering how he and I managed to get under the guys' skin pretty deep in the recent past, I hold in a smile.

"If I see or hear of anyone other than myself, Vince, Ash, or Tate coming within three feet of her, I think I've made it *abundantly* clear that I will not hesitate to fuck you up."

The heat of embarrassment creeps up my spine and my face warms even more.

"Does everyone understand?"

Every member of the brotherhood either sounds off or nods, letting Micah know his words of warning haven't fallen on deaf ears. He seems pleased by this when he smiles.

"Good. Now, let's eat."

Chatter around the room picks up again, and the dash toward the food resumes. Micah's eyes flit over my shoulder before he leans in.

"It's official," he says, his grin broadening, but then his fingers slip from mine just as a strong set of tattooed arms encircle my waist. A second later, a kiss warms the side of my neck.

I melt into Ash as he brings me closer, smelling of shampoo and mint.

"Well, I'll be damned," he says into my ear, amusement in his tone. "You fixed him."

I smile a bit hearing his assessment of Micah.

"We're good now."

He nods, his chin moving against the side of my hair. "And you're staying," he says.

"I am."

Gentle flutters bloom in the pit of my stomach when it dawns on me that he didn't ask, but rather made a statement. And it also hits me that he seems incredibly content at the idea of me sticking around, which means Micah was right.

They *all* want me here.

Mid-thought, Ash grips my chin, tilting my head back so he can reach my lips, and then his tongue is in my mouth. I didn't expect the boys to be so open about sharing me, but I suppose the cat's out of the bag now. It only makes it clearer when Ash backs off as Vince walks up.

I'm used to my quiet storm being laidback, more subtle than the others, but that isn't the case this morning. A high-pitched yelp leaves me when he takes my waist, hoisting me up to the countertop with such ease I feel weightless. Then, with a smile set on his face, Vince settles between my knees while his brothers move about the kitchen like we're merely decoration.

"Welcome to The Den," he rasps, and just as my lips curve into a smile, he takes them, and I can't help but feel dizzy, overwhelmed by all the attention and excitement over having me here.

He tastes like fresh watermelon. I suck the remnants of the sweet juice from his lips and tongue, aware of how wet I've become just since coming down for breakfast. Increasingly so, as Vince's hands slip beneath my shorts, resting on my hips while he pushes his tongue deeper.

It's never far from mind that, soon, I'll have him completely. But right now, as we've all but forgotten there are others in the room, it's all I can think about.

"Oh, shit. What'd we do now," I hear someone say, but don't pull away from Vince until a moment later. When I hear Tate's voice.

"Good morning. Listen up," he calls out.

Vince places one last soft kiss to the corner of my mouth before I lose his focus to Tate. Conversation dies down and eventually, there's complete silence.

"Thank you," Tate says, seeming to have just now noticed that I'm here. The only girl in a houseful of rowdy boys. It takes him a moment to gather his thoughts before speaking again. "There was another complaint."

"You've gotta be shitting me."

"Who the fuck is pulling this shit?"

"Fuck!"

These are the collective responses from the brotherhood, along with a lot of grumbling and sighing in frustration.

"I know, it sucks, but this is what we're facing," Tate adds.

Micah steps up. "Was it the party?"

"More like what happened *at* the party. Or at least what someone falsely reported," Tate clarifies. "Someone claims there was drug use. Not just weed. Hard stuff."

The room fills with the sound of the guys' collectively complaining again, but Tate raises his hand to quiet them when one asks a question.

"So what now? Are they shutting us down?"

"We won't let that happen," Ash speaks up. "For now, we've just gotta keep our noses clean and keep our ears to the ground. Maybe we can find out who's doing this shit and end it once and for all."

"We already *know* who's behind it," Micah seethes, but when Tate shoots him a look, he falls silent. That doesn't stop him from simmering in his own anger.

"Ash is right," Tate says. "We keep walking a straight line. We know you guys have cut way back on partying, and when you *do* party, you've scaled back on size, but we'll have to scale back even more."

"Aw, come on! Are you shitting me?" someone complains from the other side of the room.

"Unfortunately, no. I'm not shitting you," Tate sighs. "This is where we are and the only thing we can do is not get into more trouble while we're appealing the violation. The quickest way to ruin those odds is to fuck things up even more, so... consider this your warning."

The group, still mumbling under their breath, disburses and my guys gather in a huddle around where Vince placed me on the counter. When I lock eyes with Tate, I'm not immediately sure how he'll be around me, but when he approaches and then squeezes me in a hug, my heart skips a beat.

We've all come so far, and my boys have come so far with their feelings, I sometimes forget things were ever so bad.

"Whitlock has to pay for this shit," Micah bites out.

"*If* he's really to blame," Tate cuts in as he backs out of my personal space. Not that he isn't always welcome there.

Micah rolls his eyes, clearly not feeling Tate's laidback approach, but that's why they're all good for each other. They balance one another out when it matters. Tate's more passive where they're more fire and brimstone.

"I'm handling it. I've already put in the request for the appeal, so there's nothing to do now but wait."

The others don't hide their discontentment with Tate's conclusion, but I think they know it's for the best. If they're being targeted, if their brotherhood is truly under attack, I have a feeling the guilty party will indeed hang themselves.

All the Savages have to do is give them enough rope.

Stevie

Thank God for afternoon shifts. I'm not sure my heart could take another night alone in the rink.

Not after last time.

I've never been more grateful for the noise, the chaos. Even when a group of pre-pubescent boys fly past, giggling as one dares to slap my ass.

"Come here, you little shits!" I speed up just to scare them. It'd be nice to trip the assholes-in-training, but Kip might frown at being hit with a lawsuit. They're also lucky I have cramps from hell at the moment.

When the four realize I'm gaining on them and could easily catch up and beat their asses, their smiles turn to looks of panic. That's all I wanted, to see the look of sheer terror on their faces, now I'm satisfied.

I slow my pace again, relaxing as I make a few more rotations around the rink. The last twenty-four hours have felt so surreal. From discovering Dusty's true identity, to reconciling with Micah, and then being invited to stay at The Den indefinitely. Needless to say, my emotions are all over the place, but it was more than nice waking up in Micah's bed this morning, feeling his warmth, hearing his soft breathing behind me while I lie there. Things are still far from being right with the world, but at least one piece has fallen into place.

My boys are all with me again.

My thoughts shift to them, remembering that they're currently at Mom's and Rob's collecting my things. Tate offered to escort them over while our parents are out of the house handling wedding stuff. And this morning, I gave them the key to my old spot in the basement to grab what was left over there. Which means I'll finally have all my things in one place, and that by this evening, I'll officially be rooming with the guys.

It isn't lost on me how my heart rate just increased at the thought of it. I mean, yeah, part of it is because I'm genuinely looking forward to seeing more of them. But the other part is that I'm aware of having just put all my eggs in one basket. Moving in, although temporarily, could bring up issues and discomforts people often avoid by having their own spaces to retreat to. But under their roof, on their turf, that space no longer exists.

And with how volatile things have been between me and Micah especially, the risk is at the front of my mind, for sure.

My thoughts are interrupted when I notice a familiar face. One that has me smiling back as Maddox waves. I skate off the rink and onto the carpet just as Kip is passing by with a clipboard.

"Hey, mind if I take a short break?"

He glances down at the inventory sheet I imagine he'd been busy completing before I stopped him with the question.

His eyes soften and he looks me over, much in the way he has since my recent return to work.

"No problem, kiddo. Take fifteen."

He smiles warmly and walks off, and I make my way over to Maddox. I find him seated at a booth, a white paper bag on the table in front of him.

I lower into the booth and nod toward it. "What's that?"

He arches a brow. "I come bearing gifts."

I watch as he pulls two lidded cups from the bag and my smile grows. "You brought ice cream? Brave move, considering you couldn't have known I'd convince Kip to let me break early. And let's not forget his strict *'no outside food'* policy."

Maddox shrugs, handing me a spoon. "I've been coming here since we were kids. If Kip were gonna throw me out for *anything* it would've been the prank I pulled in the boys' bathroom back in middle school."

I recall the incident and don't disagree.

Maddox digs in, and I frown at him, remembering the disgusting flavor he's never deviated from.

"I will never understand why you buy that shit." My face turns up, staring at the two off-putting gray scoops in his cup.

He laughs. "I came by to check in and *this* is what you want to harass me about?"

I glare as he spoons more into his mouth. "If it helps you come to your senses, then yes. I'll absolutely harass you until you make better choices."

He smiles a bit and it's warm. He's like a favorite blanket or coming home and smelling your mom's cooking. Maddox is familiar, comforting in the midst of the chaos.

"Thanks for coming."

His eyes find mine and he nods. "Felt like we were drifting, so I figured I'd stop by. Silly me thought that with you being injured, you'd be easier to keep tabs on, but I haven't heard back from you the last couple days."

There's an awkward pause because the reason I've been missing is that I've been with the guys.

"I stopped by the house last night. Your mom said you hadn't been there the night before, and she wasn't expecting you back for a bit."

That woman talks entirely too much for her own good. And, of course, I'm not going back there. Not after the shit she pulled.

"Yeah, we got into a fight. I had to leave." I stop there, hoping he doesn't press, but I feel his eyes on me.

"You went back to the university housing?" he asks, and I keep my gaze trained on my ice cream.

"Not exactly."

He's quiet as his wheels turn.

"So, where have you been staying?"

Heat creeps up my back and perspiration has hair sticking to the back of my neck. "I've... been staying at The Den."

He stops eating and just aimlessly pokes his spoon into the one scoop he has left.

"Are you, like... involved with them? *All* of them?"

I think he means to mask it, but I hear the heavy judgment in his tone as he questions my choices.

"Let's not do this. I've had enough of falling out with people I care about lately. Please," I add, hoping he drops it.

"We're friends," he says. "We can't talk about shit like this?"

There's this air of cynicism that has me pulling back.

"I'm just curious how it works. Because that night I found you with them in the supply room, it looked like you—"

"Maddox, stop."

I don't yell, but I'm stern, wanting him to know this is off limits for us. Yes, partly because I'm not a fan of talking about the fact that I now have a sex life, but also because I know how he feels about me. I'd never want to rub my circumstances with the guys in his face. No more than I intended to on the night he's just mentioned.

Our eyes are locked, and I know he doesn't want to drop it. However, he seems to realize that I'm not going any further with this.

"Fine. We'll drop it."

I force the rest of my ice cream down and decide our visit should probably end here, before one of us says something we'll regret. But when I shift to stand from the booth, Maddox's hand lands on mine.

"Don't be upset," he says. "I guess I was just... a little insulted."

His admission has me settling back into my seat as I study him. "Insulted?"

He nods, then takes a breath, gathering his thoughts. "It's just that I've offered my space to you probably a million times. I've even offered to move off-campus so we can find a spot big enough for both of us. And yet, for some crazy reason, you're more comfortable with a group of dickheads you barely know than me."

I'm quiet, having a viable answer to give, but knowing it'd hurt him if I said it out loud. It wouldn't help him to know I think being in such close quarters would be a grave mistake. Wouldn't help him to know that I'm concerned his feelings for me would deepen. Wouldn't help him to know things would become increasingly awkward because… I'll never feel about *him* like he feels about *me.*

It might just be that I'm hormonal and an emotional mess right now, but I feel tears stinging my eyes. He seems to notice them, too, and squeezes my hand.

"Okay, I'm dropping it," he says quietly, sitting back when he finally releases my hand. "What happened between you and your mom?"

I blink a bit to dispel the tears, then find my words.

"I finally found out why my sister was in Cypress Pointe, finally figured out who Dusty is."

Maddox's brow gathers.

"He's my father," I reveal. "So, I couldn't stay in that house another night. Not knowing she'd happily let me continue living a lie just so she didn't have to live up to the truth."

He looks as floored as I felt hearing the news myself.

"Shit."

"Tell me about it," I say with a quiet laugh.

"You think Mel figured it all out?"

I shrug. "Well, based on my mother's lack of a response when I asked that very question, and also considering that stupid look on her face, I'm guessing the answer is yes."

"Shit," he says again, sitting straighter in his seat. "So, what's next? Do you plan to contact him? Do you think he knows about you?"

I take a breath. "These are all excellent questions, but for now, I think my next move will be to reach out to my father—or whoever the hell he is to me now—to gain clarity now that I'm calm. Well… calm-*ish.*"

We fall into silence again while Maddox processes the news. "If you need me, for *anything*," he adds. "Just call me, Stevie."

I peer up and into his eyes, seeing the sincerity in them, and I nod. "I know. And I appreciate you."

He reaches across the table again and takes my hand. This time, he doesn't quickly let go, and I welcome it. Because as strong as I want to be, as strong as I *pretend* to be... I can use all the comfort and support I can get at the moment.

Micah

Vince: Where the fuck did you go? We've still got boxes to unload.

I shove my phone into the pocket of my hoodie and settle against the brick wall outside the weight room. I tried putting the bad thoughts wandering through my head to rest, but I can't.

While collecting Bird's things, Vince thought I was stable enough to tell me about an incident that took place at the rink a few nights ago. Little does he know, I'm stable about everything *but* Bird right now. I already feel like I failed her, so I'll be damned if I let anything else happen to her on our watch.

Vince sends another text that I only read partially before shoving my phone into my hoodie. Enzo walks up. Kid looks shifty as hell, glancing over his shoulder like this is a drug deal.

"Dude, loosen the fuck up. You're gonna make people think we're doing something illegal."

He shoots me a knowing look. "Who knows? The night's still young," he grumbles.

"Alright, let's make this quick. I need you to tail someone."

He's scowling before I even finish. "No. *Fuck that.*"

When my stare darkens, his does, too. How soon I've forgotten that he's one of the most stubborn dickheads I've ever met.

Aside from *us* that is.

"It wasn't a request."

"And I'm not your pledge anymore. I'm in the frat now, so we're equals."

A laugh slips out hearing that he honestly believes this. "Like hell we are. You're the shit on the bottom of my shoe, motherfucker. And the sooner you remember your place in this system, the easier things will be for all of us. Now, unless you want me to put in a call to have all your shit tossed in the pool before you get home, I suggest you shut the fuck up and listen."

He scowls, hating that I have this power over him, but we both know I have him by the balls.

"Who?" he sighs.

"Leo Whitlock."

"From Elmcrest? No fucking way."

"Again, did I say something that made you think you had a choice?"

He glares. "Why?"

"That doesn't concern you."

He laughs but it fades quickly. "So, you want me to stalk the captain of our rival team, without even knowing the reason?" He comes close, stepping into my personal space, holding my gaze. "No. Fucking. Way. Whatever this is, do your own dirty work."

He takes a step away, but doesn't get very far, because I yank him back by his sleeve, then grab his collar before spinning him around to the bricks. My jaw is tight, and I feel myself getting ready to lose it, but then I remember he isn't the enemy. He's defiant and frustrating as hell, but a member of the brotherhood nonetheless.

Slowly, as I come to my senses, I release him and take a step back.

"I shouldn't have done that."

"And I shouldn't have come here."

He moves to step around me, but I move with him, blocking his way, but not touching him this time.

"Hang on. I came at this the wrong way."

He breathes deep, cocking his head as he stares.

"You're right. You're not a pledge anymore. And while no one would *ever* call you my equal, you're certainly not the shit on the bottom of my shoe."

He scoffs, shaking his head.

"I'm not demanding that you do this as my pledge, but what I *am* doing, is asking you to take this on because at the end of the day, no matter how deeply you get under my skin on occasion... we're still brothers. And for what it's worth, I chose you because I trust you."

He continues to stare, impossible to read.

"I'll consider it, but I need to know why."

And there's that defiance I loathe so much.

A breath leaves me when I lower my gaze to the sidewalk, knowing I can't tell him everything, but also knowing I'll have to tell him *something*. So, I weigh my words before speaking.

"I think he's responsible for hurting a friend."

Enzo's eyes narrow. "You mean Stevie?"

When he says her name, an image of him with his tongue jammed down her throat at that party flashes inside my head, and I want his blood on my hands again. But letting the rage in will get us nowhere, so I nod.

"Yes, Stevie. Will you do it?"

He considers it for a moment. "Yeah."

"And will you be discrete?"

He nods, and I don't miss that he seems to be taking this seriously. "Yeah, I will."

There's the slightest sense of relief that fills me now that it's settled.

"I'll need to know everywhere he goes, everyone he sees, everything. Lucky for us, Elmcrest's practices are held at the same time as ours, so he'll be busy when we are, but other than that, I need you to eat, sleep, and breathe Whitlock until you have something solid to report."

There's something he wants to ask, but can't seem to spit it out.

"What?" I grumble, sounding less than friendly, and even less interested.

"It's just that, I'm putting myself out there, possibly putting myself at risk. So, I'm just wondering… what's in it for me?"

Most people would assume he's after money, but we're more alike than either of us would like to admit. Which is why I give the only answer he's interested in, the only one I'd want to hear if I were in his shoes.

He's motionless when I place my hand on his shoulder and look him square in his eyes.

"You do this, and you'll have our respect. And when it's done… there won't be a thing you could ask of us that we wouldn't break our necks to do. You have my word on that."

I have no idea what this kid has been through, no idea what he's seen, but from one displaced soul to another, I see him.

"I'll do it," he agrees, and once we shake on it, it's as good as done.

Chapter 26

Stevie

Ten minutes.

That's how long I've been sitting in the parking lot of The Den, how long I've stared at the blank screen of my phone, working up the nerve to dial my father's number. My mom and Mel were too concerned about my feelings to be honest, but if there's one thing this man doesn't fear, it's hurting my feelings.

"Fuck it."

My fingers move across the screen, and I pull up his contact, then let it ring, feeling my heart race as the seconds tick past.

"Yeah, hello?"

I breathe deep before speaking. "Hey. It's me."

"I know. Your number came up."

"Right." I feel vulnerable, and more emotional than usual, but this can't be put off because Mother Nature chose today to rear her ugly head.

"So, what's up?" He asks that like our last conversation didn't uproot my entire life, my entire past, my childhood. But that isn't really surprising.

"Our last conversation ended abruptly, and I have questions."

He sighs into the receiver. "Stevie, this'll have to wait. I have dinner on the stove and—"

"Can't you just... This is my fucking *life!*" I shout, knowing I should've held back but something wouldn't let me. Not when I'm feeling so broken. So raw.

He's silent and, for a moment, I think he's disconnected our call.

"You'll have to be quick about it. I've got guests," he says in a slightly less irritated tone.

It's not exactly kindness, but I'll take it, knowing it's the best he has to offer.

"I need to know for sure that Mel knew about Dusty. I need to hear you say that she knew who he was."

There's a long sigh that comes first, then he confirms. "She knew."

"How do you know for sure? She talked to you about it."

"She... something like that."

My brow tenses. "What does *that* mean?"

"It means that she came to me looking for answers. Just like you did, because your mother didn't have the balls to tell the truth."

I have so many thoughts, so many feelings, but I hold them in for fear of making him shut down if this turns into a screaming match.

"How'd the conversation go when she came to you?"

"Stevie, I don't have time for—"

"Just answer this one question and I'll leave you alone. I swear."

He's quiet, likely thinking of what a sweet deal that is.

"She stopped by, acting all irate and emotional, getting on my case about how she thinks I mistreat you or some bullshit like that. So, when she got louder, telling me what an asshole I am, I... told her the truth. That it's not in me to pretend to be the dad to some kid my bitch of an ex had with some no-name loser from her hometown."

My heart's racing as it plays out in my head—Mel coming to him for answers, then going to Mom, hoping to be told none of it was true, only to be forced into silence because my family is apparently a fucking circus.

"If you hated pretending so much, why not just tell me? Why cover for her?" I swipe at a tear, awaiting his answer.

"Shit, Stevie, I don't know," he admits. "In the beginning I stayed silent because it's what we agreed to after she told me and the dust settled. But later, it just seemed like a moot point. You knowing doesn't change anything, doesn't *fix* anything."

"How can you say that?"

He likely hears in my tone that I'm sobbing by this point, but I don't care anymore.

"What would have been different?"

"Maybe I would've gone to meet him? Or maybe I wouldn't have, but the point is, it would've been my choice. Not yours. Not Mom's. Mine."

He sighs again, like this conversation is merely an inconvenience.

"How could you do this to Mel? How could *either* of you do this to her? Putting this on her on top of everything else?"

"You think you know so fucking much, but you don't know a damn thing."

"Then, tell me! All I've *wanted* are answers!"

"Then maybe you should've been there for her," he snaps. "If you had, if you hadn't been so caught up in your own world, maybe you would've known the shit she was going through."

A chill runs down my back when his words stab me right in the gut, twisting like a knife.

I swallow deep, brushing more tears aside. "What didn't I know?"

"Fuck, Stevie. What's the point of all this? She's gone. No one mourns that more than I do."

"I need to know."

Pots clang in his background, and I imagine him at the stove. "Let's just say she had some deeper shit going on than anyone else knew."

"Like what?" I force out, bracing myself.

"Damn it," he grumbles to himself, but after a moment of silence, he blurts it out. Whether to free himself or to hurt me. "She was pregnant. About three months along. But I took her to take care of it a couple months before she... before..."

I hear the emotion in his voice, but I ignore it because I'm doing math. Two months before she was assaulted means it would've had nothing to do with that. It means she would've been pregnant by whoever she was seeing. Someone who, for all I know, could still be the same man who assaulted her.

"You're lying. It doesn't make sense. Why would she come to you, of all people, to help her through this?"

He scoffs before answering. "Because despite what you might think, I was a good father. I was the kind of father a daughter knew she could come to with a problem."

"You don't know shit about being a father," I hiss. "I can count on one hand the amount of times you've said anything even *remotely* comforting in my entire lifetime."

He chuckles to himself. "Well, that's the thing, Stevie. Your opinion of my parenting doesn't exactly count, now does it? Because I'm not... your... fucking... father."

It feels like the knife he'd so callously wounded me with before was just snatched out, leaving me to bleed out while he likely smirks on the other end of the line.

There were more things I could've asked, more he could've given clarity on, but I've had all I can take. So, I end the call and vow that this is the absolute last time I'll ever let this asshole break my heart.

Because this will be the last time I'll ever reach out to him for anything.

Ever.

Chapter 27

Stevie

The moment I walk through the door, there they are, posted in the study where they were obviously waiting for me to get in from work. No doubt, they were watching the clock, noting that I'm twenty minutes late getting in. But no one questions me because it's likely they can tell I'm about to burst into tears.

For this reason, I don't even stop to speak as I rush toward the stairs, praying I can hold it all in until I can make it to a bedroom.

I come to Micah's door first and peek inside to see if they've stored my things in there, but it's free of the bags and boxes I expect. So, I head to Ash's room next and find everything stacked neatly to one side. Closing the door behind me, I sniff back tears and just want to find a towel and a change of clothes, so I can get in bed and forget this day ever happened.

However, the knob twists behind me. I knew this would happen. There was no way I could slip in looking as distraught as I imagine I look, and the guys wouldn't follow me to check in. Glancing over my shoulder, it seems Ash is representing the group tonight.

"Tell me what happened?" he says softly, causing more emotion to swell in my chest. Especially after being spoken to so harshly, so *coldly*, just a moment ago.

I can't speak right away, fearing I won't be able to stop the tears once I finally let them flow, so I only shake my head. The safest way I can share my headspace with Ash.

Letting him know I'm not okay.

It's enough. He understands and crosses the room, drawing me into his arms. As my cheek settles against his chest, those tears I've been battling win the fight, and I begin to sob uncontrollably.

"Did someone hurt you?"

The question is asked far less sweetly than when he spoke a moment ago, and I don't miss the change in his tone. His body is stiff and rigid as he awaits my answer, and it isn't until I shake my head and let him know no one caused me *physical* harm that he relaxes, pulling me deeper into him.

His thumb smooths up and down my arm while he lets me cry all over his t-shirt, likely smearing it with mascara and lipstick, but Ash isn't one to care about shit like that. *None* of them are really. I'm learning of their fierce loyalty and it's for this reason that I begin to speak when I honestly hadn't planned to.

"Everything's just so incredibly fucked up," I whisper.

He brings his hand to the back of my hair, but doesn't speak. He only listens.

"I called my dad today, because I know he's the only place I can get answers, but... fuck. I should've just left well enough alone."

I'm bombarded with flashbacks of our conversation a moment ago, remembering how highly he spoke of Mel—despite her drama and shortcomings. His love for her always was and always will be unconditional. Just like she deserved. But it served as a reminder, pointing out that I never stood a chance of receiving his love. Him holding it back from me was never about my fuckups or my issues. It all came down to one simple fact, one he so happily pointed out at the end of our talk.

I'm not his daughter.

And there was no level of "perfection" I could've achieved that would've changed that.

I realize my tears are likely unwarranted. That man doesn't deserve them, so I try to sniffle them away again.

"Sorry," I whisper, pulling away from Ash's chest a little. "This isn't like me. My period started before my shift ended, and I'm just... kind of all over the place." I pause, realizing what I just shared with him, and embarrassment immediately sets in. "You... probably didn't want to know that."

"Shit like that doesn't rattle me. I'm not most guys," he says, and his tone is always so sincere. Whether he's promising to rip your heart out or sew it together, I always believe him.

"I just need to shower and go to bed." I peer up at him. "Can you let the others know I'm okay, but just need some time?"

There's warmth in his eyes I've seen there a lot lately. He nods. "Sure."

I step up on my tiptoes and only intend to peck his lips *once,* but it turns into three before I let him go. He steps out and my search for a towel and clothes continues for a moment before I find what I'm looking for, then I head to the bathroom.

I'm fighting tears the whole time I undress, while I adjust the water temperature, and as I climb in and heat from the shower rains down on me. I hear my father's words echoing inside my head on repeat, and it hits me that I keep calling him that, my father, when not only does he not *deserve* that, but... he doesn't even *want* that.

More tears fall and I'm done fighting it, done pretending this whole thing isn't bigger than me, and I just let it win. I let the entire weight of it come crashing down on me simply because I'm too tired to withstand it.

The sound of the bathroom door opening sobers me quickly, though. Especially seeing as how I vividly remember locking it behind me.

"Um... someone's in here," I call out, wishing there was something I could cover myself with. I'm a second from screaming, calling out for the guys, when a voice quickly changes my plans.

"It's just me," Ash says, closing the door behind him.

My head spins, wondering what he's doing here, but through the thin shower curtain, I make out his silhouette, see him pulling his t-shirt over his head. Then, lowering his jeans and underwear.

What the hell is he doing?

I'm still speechless when he pulls the curtain back and steps in, water soaking half his body as his eyes stay fixed on mine. We don't exchange words as his mouth slowly covers mine. One of his massive hands settles at my waist, but the other cups and squeezes my breast, his thumb brushing over my wet nipple.

I know what this feels like, know what it seems like he wants, but maybe he's forgotten that I'm not exactly in any position to give it to him.

My hands go to his chest when I pull back, but were still mere inches from one another.

"Wait," I breathe against his lips. "I can't. Remember?"

The exact words won't leave my mouth, but I'm hoping he gets the hint, remembering that I overshared about being on my cycle. But when he leans in, the warmth of his breath dancing over my earlobe, down the side of my neck, he has my full attention.

"I remember, and I don't care," he rasps. "I want you."

His words leave me lightheaded, melting against him when the kiss resumes and he proves to me he seriously gives zero fucks when the hand holding my breast smooths down my stomach, and then wedges between my thighs.

He pushes into me with two fingers, and my breathing deepens. Somehow, he sensed that this was exactly what I needed.

The closeness.

The attention.

Him.

His fingers push into me again and a sharp breath leaves my nostrils.

"Relax," he croons. "You're tense and there's no need to be."

He cranes his head toward my neck, then latches his mouth to my throat. Just having him here, touching me, focused on me, I feel today's wounds beginning to heal. And as he pushes in again, I slowly relax like he instructed, and the world is beginning to fall away from us.

My pussy stretches around his large fingers, and I'm breathless, wanting so much more of him. I want him to fuck me, but I'm also not sure I want my first time with him to be like... *this*. With me hyper aware of my situation, the blood. While he said he doesn't mind it, I still don't know what his limits are.

His fingers slide out of me and I'm anxious, wondering what comes next when his hand massages my hip, seemingly enjoying the softness he finds there. With them, they seem to only see my curves as a blessing, which makes me see them as less of a curse.

I gasp when he quickly lifts me, and my legs naturally lock around his waist. The tip of his erect cock teases my opening, and that spike of anxiety is back, making me overthink things to the point that I clam up, consider asking him to leave.

But when his lips graze my ear, I promptly reconsider. "Tell me I can finally fuck you." I feel a smile curving his mouth when he speaks, and I'm weak for him.

"I... don't you... want a condom?" I nearly remind him of my situation again, but can't say the words, feeling embarrassed.

He breathes deep. Almost like he's inhaling the scent of my neck, identifying his prey.

"Why the hell would I not want to feel *all* of you, Bird? When I'm inside you, I want everything. Want to *feel*... everything."

My head tilts, opening my neck where he breathes against it. And going against my own sense of logic, I nod.

"No, I need you to say it. Tell me I can have you," he growls, the tip of his dick nudging me, making me crave this part of him I've not yet experienced.

My lips part, and I hesitate before finally liberating myself by saying those words. "You can fuck me. I *need* you to fuck me."

Ash's chest moves with a brief chuckle, then he grips me tighter. "Good girl."

The next moment, I'm barely given a second to breathe, because his hot, thick length slides into me. He's not gentle about it, which I quickly realize I enjoy. His hips power back and forth, and I throb around him.

"You're so fucking tight on my cock," he groans, his forehead pressing against mine as we breathe one another's air. It's why I notice when his head shifts, and his gaze lowers to watch his cock disappear inside me.

Over and over and over again.

"Fuuuck," he groans again, watching with this intensity that can only be described as primal. Seeing him enjoy the sight of our bodies collide leaves me panting.

The colorful pictures covering his skin seem darker beneath the water. I admire every inch of him, also noting that his scars are more visible now, too. My hand is drawn to them, feeling the puffy, ridged skin raised beneath my palm. He doesn't shy away this time, letting me explore his marred skin. I don't know why I want to touch them, but knowing his outward scars match those that I carry on the inside makes me feel like we're one in the same. Two broken souls who found one another in the dark, syphoning each other's pain as we fuck.

"Harder," I pant, realizing the anxiety has finally left and all I feel is pleasure.

Ash does as I've asked, pushing into me harder, deeper, faster.

"From now on, this is my time," he says, pausing his words to kiss me while he slams in again. "Whenever you bleed, your pussy belongs to me and only me. Is that understood?"

I hear him loud and clear—the possessiveness he's never expressed before. I nod, but he quickly corrects me.

"Use your words, Bird," he warns. "Do you understand me?"

His pace quickens again and I'm starting to come. "Yes," I whimper. "I understand."

He captures my lips, slowly twisting his tongue inside my mouth as he fucks me hard and fast, and I can't hold it anymore. I intend to muffle my moans with his mouth, but he pulls away for that very reason, wanting everyone to hear me lose control, wanting everyone to know he's fucking me, and that I'm enjoying the hell out of it.

A labored cry leaves my mouth as my nails bite into his back. I savor the feel of his huge cock brutalizing me, feeling the muscles covering his shoulder blades go rigid against my palms as he slams in one more time. Then, half a second later, a surge of hot cum pumps into my core.

"This is my time, Bird." he reminds me, his voice strained as he empties inside my pussy, and I nod again. "Promise me you won't forget that shit."

"Yours," I whisper back.

Water pelts the tile under our feet and we're still, breathing loudly as we get our bearings. A kiss is pressed to my lips as Ash lowers my feet to the ground again, and when he reaches for a bottle of body wash to lather his hands, I realize he intends to wash me, much like Micah did the day before.

These boys, *my* boys, are everything I didn't know I needed—four who came out of nowhere, taking care of me in ways I never imagined I would be. And yet, here they are.

Ash finishes, and I quickly wash my hair while he soaps *himself* up this time. We rinse clean together and he's considerate about me needing time to take care of personal things. But before he leaves to give me privacy, he kisses me again, letting me know this might not have only been what *I* needed, but maybe he needed it too.

"I'll make you some tea and meet you in my room when you're done."

Holding in the huge smile I want to flash, I nod. "Okay. Thank you."

He pauses at the counter to grab his towel, then he's gone, and I'm left to realize something. Something that honestly terrifies me the more true and real it feels.

I, the girl who swore she'd never get too deep—might be in trouble.

Because as much as I hate the idea of it, I might just be falling for them.

I step into Ash's room—fully clothed, my hair in a high bun—he's waiting just like he promised. He points to the nightstand and, sure enough, there's tea.

A smile breaks free. "Who knew frat boys keep tea around the house?" I tease.

"We didn't, actually," he confesses. "I Googled things you should have handy when a chick moves in to make her feel more at home, and tea was on the list, so…"

My smile broadens. One, because of his less than eloquent wording. Two, because I find it incredibly sweet that he even thought to do a search.

I sit on the edge of his bed and take the mug in my hands, swirling the spoon as I blow steam off the surface. Ash watches me from his desk chair. His stare's so intense, he's hard to look at.

"I'm all for being sensitive to your needs. All for you having space and privacy," he says, "but I'm gonna need you to talk to me, Bird."

I shift my gaze from him, feeling the pain of today echoing in my bones.

His tone is softer this time when he speaks, but he's still firm. "Tell me what happened."

I bring the spoon to my lips to sip, and I give myself until I lower it again to answer.

"My sister was pregnant and aborted it before the assault. All without me seeing a single sign," I admit, lowering my gaze to the floor while I let that sink in. How many red flags I missed, how many silent cries for help I missed.

"That's not on you," he says, but we disagree on this point. "When people want something to stay hidden, they make damn sure it stays hidden. She probably just couldn't talk about it."

"Yeah, well, she sure as shit talked to our dad about it. Well… *her* dad," I say, correcting myself again. "He's the one who took her to the clinic, and he's probably also the one who took care of her afterward."

A pang of jealousy hits me square in the chest, and I try to dismiss it, because it's completely irrational to have such thoughts, but... I imagine if the tables were turned. Imagine it was *me* who needed a father if I found myself in Mel's shoes. There's not a doubt in my mind that I would've faced that shit alone, and it kills me knowing how different things were for her than they were for me.

I've apparently stared into space too long, because Ash is on his way over. I set my mug aside and he drops down beside me, resting his arm around my shoulders.

"Our family's shit isn't *our* shit," he says. "Besides, we all have each other now, which is how we get through."

My heart squeezes, and I feel emotional again but fight it. All I want is family. All I've *ever* wanted is family. So, hearing him say it, I'm overwhelmed.

But his words trigger another thought. Something I hadn't shared with him yet. Only Micah.

"Speaking of family, I found out he's not even my real dad. My mom cheated before he married her, but they stayed together."

I feel Ash's eyes on me. "You know who the guy is?"

I nod. "Yep. I even met him once. He has no idea who I am, but that doesn't mean he doesn't know he has a daughter out there somewhere."

My heart races, knowing I've got a tough decision ahead. Part of me wants to go to him, tell him I'm here and that I'm open to getting to know him. But the other part of me wonders if he'd rather have nothing to do with me. I'm not sure I could handle being rejected by *two* fathers.

"I vote you at least give him a chance."

Those words coming from Ash are unexpected. I'd expect that, considering what he's been through, he'd be the first one to say *'fuck this guy'*, but I was wrong.

"Yeah?"

He smiles. "Yeah. I mean, he deserves a chance, too, right? Worst case, he tells you to fuck off, and you both go back to pretending the other doesn't exist. Best case… you find out he's a good guy. Someone worth keeping in your life."

I look away, staring at the wall while I think. He made that all sound so easy, and maybe he's right and it *is* that easy.

"Okay," I say, smiling as I meet his gaze again. "I guess I'm headed back to Cypress Pointe soon."

He smiles back, and I think he's about to speak, but then his phone goes off. It's just a text, so he pauses to read it, but his expression slips quickly. The soft, gentle look he'd just cast on me fades to a sinister scowl.

"Is… everything okay?" I ask, reaching for my tea, taking a sip before I set it aside again.

He blinks, holding his eyes closed for a long moment before answering. "My uh… my grandmother's dead."

He mentions it so casually, but I'm not surprised, knowing their relationship was a complicated one.

My hand settles on his back and I'm the one comforting *him* now.

"When's the funeral? I can come with you if you need me to."

He finally meets my gaze, smiling a little, but it doesn't quite reach his eyes. "It won't be until late next week. My uncle said they're holding off for a bit so family can get in from out of town. But I wouldn't expect you to be there," he says.

I frown. "You don't have to *expect* it, but I wouldn't want you there alone, facing all those *people* alone."

He's quiet, lost in thought. "I actually… I don't think I'll go either."

"You're sure?"

He nods. "Yeah. Besides, the funeral's right before our first game, and I need my head to be clear. I can't let the team down by losing focus."

I don't say anything, letting him process it all.

"I think she loved me as much as she could, but… it wasn't enough. I deserved to be protected and looked after, and she failed me. So, I won't bother."

He won't bother…

The sting of sadness in his eyes is contagious. Because now, I feel it too. I squeeze the back of his neck gently, and he leans to the side for a kiss.

"I appreciate you offering."

I nod and lay my head on his shoulder.

I was right about us, about our broken souls. But as we sit in the silence, aiding one another's pain, I realize that life hurts a little less with them around.

And I'll take that.

Any day of the week.

Chapter 28

Stevie

I stupidly thought that waiting a few days for *Aunt Flow* to leave town would make a difference, but I'm still just as nervous and emotional as if I'd left the morning after my talk with Ash. He helped me realize reaching out to Dusty is probably for the best—even if I fear all that awaits me on the other side of this is heartbreak—but I'm still on edge.

I would've been halfway to Cypress Point by now, had it not been for this pitstop. I've hardly slept the past four nights, anticipating this trip. And it was during that sleeplessness that I came to a conclusion. While my dad may no longer be an option for acquiring information, he was never my *only* option.

The constant ringing of the phone and nonstop chatter have my nerves on edge while I wait for Frank to finish up at his desk. He knows I'm here, but part of me thinks making me sit here forever is his way of punishing me for showing up at the station unannounced.

Frank stands from his seat, and I perk up. The scowl on his face likely means I'm right. My presence here is unwanted.

"You couldn't have called first?" he asks, foregoing a proper greeting.

"This won't take long. I need a favor. Possibly a small one."

He eyes me, likely not believing that for even a second. "What is it?"

I breathe deep, finding the nerve to ask. "I need to see Nora. Is there someone at her facility you can talk to and make that happen?"

He scoffs and, for a moment, I think he might actually walk away.

"Frank, please. I think she can fill in pieces of the puzzle no one else can. I'm desperate," I add, wondering if my desperation will even make a difference to him. He is my father's best friend after all. Birds of a feather...

"Listen, kid, I already told you. The facility has strict policy when it comes to outside contact. Why are you so adamant about this anyway?"

I wrangle in my emotions, knowing he'd never understand the depth of my loss. "Because I still have questions about what went on with my sister, and I have a feeling Nora might have similar ones. So, it's possible we can help each other."

"Help each other do what?" he sighs, not bothering to hide his irritation.

I stare him straight in the eyes and take a chance being honest with him.

"Help each other heal."

He stares at me a while, and I have a feeling that just hit him where it counts. Right in the heart. Nora's had a tough life, which is why he took her in, which is why he vowed to protect her. So, if he doesn't care enough to help *me,* maybe he cares enough to help *her.*

"I heard you got in touch with your dad."

I'm not sure what that has to do with anything, but I nod, answering him anyway.

"How'd it go?"

I scoff at the question. "Haven't you heard? I'm not his kid and he couldn't be happier now that the cat's out of the bag. So, it went about as well as you'd expect."

He goes quiet on me again, and if I'm not mistaken, there's sympathy in that look he's giving me.

"I... didn't know."

A dark laugh leaves me. "I guess he's better at keeping secrets than I realized."

My eyes burn a bit, and I know what that means, making it twice as urgent that I get out of here before the waterworks start.

"I'll see what I can do."

Franks words have me meeting his gaze again, questioning whether I just heard him correctly.

"Really?"

He nods. "Really. I might be able to convince one of the administrators to bend the rules, but no promises."

"That's... I'll take it," I beam, feeling the immediate shift in my mood at the thought of things possibly going my way for once.

Frank stays stone-faced, but that trace of sympathy is still present. "Give me a second to make the call."

I nod, smiling for the first time today as he walks away, pressing his cell to his ear. I'm on my feet, too, pacing because it's all I can do to keep calm, glancing toward him every few seconds to see if he's finished. When he finally tucks his phone away and walks back in my direction, my feet *and* my breath stop.

"They'll get us in," he says with a sigh, and I fight the urge to hug him. "But we have to wait a couple weeks. Nora's at a critical point in her treatment. They won't compromise that, and neither will I, so there's no workaround. This is the best anyone can do."

I'm impatient, anxious to possibly have light shed on some of the mysteries my sister left me to sort out, but I know not to push. Two weeks is better than never.

"Understood," I say with a nod, holding Franks gaze as I say more. "And... thank you."

He offers a reserved smile as I move toward the door, counting down the days until I can talk to Nora face-to-face.

Counting down the days until I might finally have the answers to my questions.

Two weeks.

Chapter 29

Stevie

Timing my visit with the diner closing seemed like the best course of action, seeing as how I'm showing up to Dusty's place completely unannounced.

And to drop such big news on him at that.

I'm panting with fear and anticipation as my engine continues to run. I don't quite have the nerve to go in yet, so I just sit there, observing.

There's Scarlett—a girl I once just believed to be nothing more than a kind human who did her small part to look after my sister. But now, I know she's more than that. To me, anyway.

She's family.

I squirm in my seat at the thought of it, at the thought of there being a whole other side to my life that I didn't even know existed. There are so many unknowns. So many factors I couldn't possibly account for while sitting here on the outside looking in.

With a sigh, I kill the engine and clutch my keys, still watching. Scarlett stops at a booth where a group of girls sit. She's laughing with them. I gather from their body language and familiarity that they're friends. One, a blonde, shares the same warm smile as Scarlett. Actually, their features are too similar for them not to be related. She mentioned having a sister, and at first, I'm wondering if this is her. But when the girl swats Scarlett on the ass for stealing a fry as she seals her to-go box, I'm certain of it.

I smile a bit, remembering moments like this with Mel. Sometimes, it feels like I dreamed them, dreamed *her*, but that's all I have left.

Fading memories.

The girls stand from the booth and Scarlett removes her apron before heading to the kitchen. I study her sister and friends. There are four of them—the blonde who could be Scarlett's twin if there weren't clearly a few years between them, another girl with light-brown skin and curly hair, one a few shades darker with long braids stretching down to her waist, and another with wild, curly hair I find intensely beautiful.

They're *all* beautiful.

All so different, but with how close they seem, I get the sense that they consider themselves sisters.

Scarlett reemerges from the kitchen and rejoins the others. I follow them with my eyes as they file out to a black car, watching as they immediately lower the top despite the slightly chilled weather. It's sporty, something so expensive I can't even begin to guess the make or model of it, but as they speed out of the lot, heading to some unknown place, they're laughing so loudly I can even hear it from inside my car.

My gaze shifts back to the diner, and I peer through the window, counting heads. There are only two patrons left and one waitress. If I intend to get inside before they lock the door, I'd better go now.

The trek to the front entrance is a slow one, because if I'm being honest, I'm scared shitless. Armed with nothing but the pieced together story I've been told, I pull the door to me and step inside.

"Evening, sweetheart." The waitress smiles and the crow's feet beside her eyes deepen. "We're closing up in a few, but if you already know what you want, I can get your order in quickly before you sit."

It takes everything in me not to glance toward the kitchen again. "Just a chocolate milkshake, please."

Her smile broadens. "Sure thing. Have a seat wherever you'd like."

She leaves, headed to the other side of the counter, and I find a booth. The same one I sat in the last time I visited, actually. My heart beats wildly, and I can't fight it anymore. My eyes dart toward the small cutout where orders are passed from the kitchen to the dining room, and I see him.

Dusty.

He wipes his brow with the back of his arm, hard at work, completely unaware of how his life is about to shift in a very short while. Seeing him working peacefully, I almost feel guilty for potentially shitting all over his good day. But then it hits me. Maybe it doesn't have to be that way. Maybe... this *won't* be the worst thing that's ever happened to him.

I swallow deeply, smiling when the waitress places a napkin in front of me, and then sets my drink on top of it.

"Can I get you anything else?"

I tear my eyes away from Dusty to answer. "No, I'm all set. Thank you."

She sets the bill down next. "I'll take this up whenever you're ready. No rush."

I nod as she walks away, leaving me to sweat and come up with a hundred ways this can go bad as I sip. Minutes tick past, and I know time's running out. But in the midst of my internal freak out, Dusty looks up, notices me, and I can't freaking breathe.

He smiles, and then awareness fills his eyes as he seems to recognize my face from the last time I stopped in. He waves and my throat feels tight. Like if I try to force another ounce of my shake down, I'll choke on it. Remembering to be human, I respond with a stiff wave back, and then I drop my eyes to the table again, unable to look at him for even a second longer. It twists my insides, makes me regret coming here, makes me regret—

"Fancy seeing *you* here again," a deep voice says, and only now do I realize Dusty's come out from behind the wall to speak.

Breathing wildly, I force myself to peer up and meet his blue gaze. I mean to speak, but I can only stare at him, searching for myself in his features, some sign that this is real. But I find nothing. His hair—dark blond—is nothing like mine, and my eyes are about as brown as eyes can get. And I've inherited my mother's natural tan, as compared to Dusty's pale skin, made red from the heat of the stove and deep fryer in the back.

Maybe I'm wrong.

Maybe this is a mistake.

He arches a brow when I get so caught up in my thoughts I forget to speak.

"Is... everything okay?"

I close my eyes, leaving them shut a moment longer while I gather myself. Then, when I open them again, I smile and pretend to be normal.

"Sorry, it was just a long drive. I suppose I'm more tired than I realized."

He smiles and it's the warmest smile I think I've ever seen in my life, causing me to remember how fondly Scarlett spoke of him before.

"If there's anything I know about, it's having long days," he teases. "What brings you to town *this* time, Stephanie? We're a pretty good distance from where you live, if I'm not mistaken."

Hearing him call me that, reminds me that I hadn't been honest with him or Scarlett before. And now, my mouth gapes while I think of *another* lie. "I—yeah. Just visiting a friend. Thought I'd stop in for a shake before heading back out."

"Well, tell you what. I usually only discount visitors their *first* time stopping in, but I like you," he says with a grin. "This one's on the house, too."

I smile back, and I hate how my heart tugs, wanting to keep this same tone when our conversation shifts, but I'm doubtful.

"Thank you. I promise to start paying in the very near future."

He laughs and places a hand on my shoulder as he shifts to walk away. "Third time's a charm."

His hand slips off me and within half a second, I'm staring at his back, watching him head toward the kitchen again, and I panic. What if this is as close as I'll get? What if I miss my opportunity?

A desperate, "Wait," leaves me and his steps halt.

He arches a brow when he meets my gaze again, doubling back. My shoulders heave like they did before, wording and re-wording what I'll say.

He's been kind not to mention what a mess I was last time, prompting him to follow me out into the alley to make sure I was okay, but this might've been an easier conversation if he *had* brought that up.

"You asked why I'm here," I blurt out.

His large, muscular arms fold over his chest and that look turns even more curious. "I did. Is something wrong?"

I'm not sure how to answer that.

"Yes and no."

He holds my gaze a moment longer, then glances toward the waitress. "Glenda, all orders are out. Think you can handle locking up? I'll shut everything else down in a bit."

"Easy-peasy," Glenda answers, then Dusty's attention is focused on me again.

"Would you like to chat someplace else?" he asks, and I nod.

"Yeah, I think that's a good idea."

He nods, and I don't miss the concern in his eyes. "My office is just through the kitchen."

I stand, abandoning my milkshake when I follow him through the swinging door behind the counter, and then through the kitchen. We pass through a set of double doors beside a rack holding bags of hotdog and hamburger buns, and then step into a well-lit hallway. Keys jingle as he unlocks the door to what I believe to be his office, and then a moment later, we step inside, and he closes us off from the rest of the world.

It's quiet in his space. Too quiet. So much that I not only feel my heart beating inside my throat, I hear it.

"Get comfortable," he says sweetly, gesturing toward the small couch beneath the sole window. He drops down into a chair behind his desk, his eyes staying fixed on me.

Shit… it's my turn to talk.

"I… this…"

Stammering only makes me more nervous, so I pause to organize my words.

"The last time I was here, none of us had any clue why my sister came all this way."

His brow knits with concern. "Right, I remember. Have you figured something out?"

Swallowing the lump in my throat, I nod. "I have, and… it's more complicated than I thought."

Dusty's expression softens and he points at the clock above his head. "Well, the diner's officially closed now, so I've got all the time in the world to listen," he says. "It's been bugging me since that night, wondering if there was something my niece and I missed when she came in. Something that could've, I don't know, *helped* her."

I swallow again, this time fighting emotion as I imagine how distraught Mel must've been that night.

"She came in to see you," I clarify. "I think she needed to know you were a real person, needed to know for herself that you existed."

The creases in his brow deepen when he frowns. "I don't understand."

"That makes two of us," I chuckle, dabbing the corner of my eye with my knuckle when I begin to tear up.

My gaze falls to my lap, choosing to focus on my hands while I say the rest.

"Well, for starters, my name isn't Stephanie. It's Stevie Heron. My mother's name is Valeria Heron, but back in the day, you probably would've known her by her maiden name… Ruiz."

I peer up at him now, needing to see if any of this rings a bell. For a moment, he's in a daze, but then awareness fills his eyes before he meets my gaze again.

"Val Ruiz is your mother? I had no idea you were... I—"

His words trail off there.

"I believe my sister knew she didn't have much time left, and I think she wanted me to have this. I think she wanted me to have... *you,*" I correct.

Dusty's quiet, and I question whether I should've edited my phrasing. The last thing I want is for him to think I'm planning to be any kind of a burden on him, an intrusion into his life, but before I can jump in to clarify, he stands and walks over. I don't know what to think when he drops down beside me on the couch, and then stares at me so intently, I can't move.

"You're... are you saying you're... *mine?*"

His words hit me, making my chest feel tight with the weight of them.

When I nod, there's no stopping the tears. I've completely lost control. But without much time to think through his actions, Dusty's arm encircles my shoulders.

"Why the hell wouldn't she tell me?" he asks, but I get the sense he's talking more to himself than me. Still, I give him the answer I was given.

"That winter you two were involved, I'm not sure if you know this, but she was with someone. Someone she later married," I clarify.

"Shit," he grumbles. "I had my suspicions, but never had the nerve to just... come out and ask her. We'd been on again, off again for years, popping in and out of one another's lives for as long as I can remember. She was just that girl I couldn't ever really shake, you know. So, even though we knew we would never work long-term, we just couldn't seem to stay away from one another."

I stay silent, listening as he fills in more of the blanks.

"But the winter you're speaking of, she was... different," he says. "She was kind of drawn into herself, didn't want to go out much. The only time we really spent together was when she'd pop up at my place, damn-near in tears. But whenever I'd ask her to tell me what was wrong, she'd say it was nothing and just avoided the conversation altogether. And I guess I was just so happy to have her back for a while, I didn't question it."

"She left because of her family, right? At least, that's the story I was told."

Dusty nods. "You could say the Ruizes here in Cypress Pointe are a bit... ruthless," he says. "And I don't know much about your mom *now*, but back then, she was sort of an innocent soul. She couldn't stomach the family's way of life, so she did what she thought she had to do—applied for college out of state, then never looked back."

"Except when she came back to you."

Dusty sighs when our eyes lock, and he smiles a bit. "Yeah, I guess you could say that."

He hasn't mentioned it, but I get the sense there's a chance I might not have been conceived in chaos, but... in love. If anyone knows my mother can be hard to handle, it's me, but maybe Dusty knows something about that, too.

He's still watching me, studying my features like I'd done to him a short time ago. I get uneasy, wondering if it will throw him off that we look nothing alike.

"I know when you see me, all you see is my mom, so if you want, we can take a DNA test. I did some research last night, and if—"

"Stevie," he says, quieting me. "That's not why I was staring at you."

My stomach is in knots despite him being nothing but kind, nothing but gentle with me.

"Then... what is it?"

He smiles and I'm not sure what to think. "I just... you're kind of a welcomed surprise. That's all."

He leaves me speechless. Completely. For so long, I've been resigned to believe I'd never know what fatherly love feels like, resigned to believe that what I've gotten so far is the best it would ever get, but seeing the warmth and softness in his eyes, I'm hopeful.

Maybe I got that wrong.

I swipe more tears and pull myself together. "Do you have other children? Are you married?"

He shakes his head. "Nope, neither. Mostly, I just look after my nieces and nephew, but I suppose I don't do much of that anymore, now that they're grown."

He stares at me a moment and there's sadness in his eyes now.

"Which... I suppose you are too."

I see it, him doing a calculation I've been afraid to do myself, counting all the time that's passed with neither of us knowing the other existed.

All the missed birthdays.

Prom.

The good things.

The *bad* things.

... Everything.

"Shit, I can't believe... I can't believe she..."

He stops there, but I know the *she* he speaks of is my mother. I also know what he can't seem to grasp is why she wouldn't have told him about me.

His eyes water, which has *mine* watering again.

"I missed everything," he says softly. "I'm sorry about that."

The apology draws a quiet laugh from me. "There's nothing to apologize for. You didn't even know I existed."

"No, but a dad should be there to protect his kid. Especially his daughter," he adds. "And God only knows what sorts of things you've faced that I should've been there to shield you from. And I need you to know I would've done that."

I nod, unable to speak because the tears won't stop.

"You couldn't possibly know this about me, but I'm not the kind of man who wouldn't be around."

Even without really knowing him, I wouldn't doubt that for a second. If nothing else, hearing how Scarlett spoke about him, I know he's very much a protector. He pulls his arm from around my shoulder and stands, but only to grab a box of tissue for us both. The last thing

RACHEL JONAS & NIKKI THORNE

I expected to see today is a man of his size and stature crying, but here we are, shedding tears side-by-side.

"Does your mom know you're here?"

I shake my head. "No, but she knows I figured it out. We haven't talked much since then, actually."

He's quiet, staring at the tile beneath our feet.

"I'm trying not to be pissed at her. I mean, I'm sure she had her reasons for not reaching out, but… shit. A simple letter would've sufficed," he says. "Even if she needed me to be damn-near invisible in *her* world, so she didn't lose her guy, I would've done whatever it took, Stevie. Whatever it fucking took to be a father to you."

He holds my gaze, and again, there isn't a doubt in my mind that he's being real with me. I nod, letting him know I believe him.

He stands again and takes his phone from the desk. "If you're okay with me reaching out to you, I'd like to get your number," he says.

My heart flutters and he has no earthly idea how *much* I'm okay with that.

"Of course. You can call me whenever you want."

I scroll to where I saved his number a little while back, shooting him a text letting him know it's me.

He's quiet for a moment while he locks it in. "And if you're comfortable calling *me*, I'd love that," he says. "I'm talking day or night, every single day. As often as you dial me, I'll answer."

I laugh when his eyes widen, making sure I hear him and know he means it. "Yes, sir."

He smiles behind his gold-toned beard, and I can't describe this feeling. It's like, for the first time in… maybe ever… I belong somewhere. Maybe he's been that missing piece for me, that intangible *thing* my soul has been crying out for since forever.

He takes a breath. "Would you be okay with me hugging you?"

I'm already nodding before he even finishes. "I'd like that, actually."

I stand and he doesn't hesitate to bring me in, holding me against his burly chest, making me feel small and safe.

Like a girl *should* feel in her father's arms.

My eyes fall closed and I'm in no rush to let go. Not with all the catching up we have to do.

"I know I missed a lot," he says, squeezing me tighter, "but that just means we get to make up for lost time."

He kisses the top of my hair and then lets go when a thought hits him.

"Did you drive here?" he asks, reaching for his wallet.

"I did, but—"

"Then let me give you gas money. It's the least I can do after you came all this way."

"You don't have to do that. I have a job and money, so—"

"Please. I need you to keep it," he cuts in, holding my gaze. "I take care of my family, Stevie. And if I'd been in the picture, you wouldn't have wanted for anything. So, please, let me do this."

I see the sincerity in his eyes, see that he does in fact need this. So, I give in. "Thank you."

He nods, then my hand warms when he takes it. "I've missed so, *so* much already. But I swear to you, if you'll let me, I'll be there for whatever amazing thing you do next. And the thing after that. And the thing after that."

A laugh leaves me, and he smiles. "I'd like that. Very much."

For the first time in my entire life, I don't feel fatherless, unwanted. And as Dusty squeezes my hand tighter, I believe he's just as excited to have me in *his* life as I am to have him in mine.

And I must say, a girl could definitely get used to this.

Chapter 30

Vince

Stevie: Heading home from Cypress Pointe in a sec, but I have an idea.

I smile at the message and hit pause on the game footage I've zoned out on for the last hour, making a quick note before responding. The puck just slipped past the goalie, confirming his weakness—he lags when shots come in from his left. I grab my phone again.

Vince: You have my attention, but first, how'd it go? The drive down, meeting your dad, all of it.

She was adamant that we let her do this alone, but we definitely fought her on it. It was Micah who suggested that we trail her in the truck against her will, but Ash quickly shot him down. What she set out to do today was huge, and if us staying out of the way made things easier, then we owed her that.

Stevie: It went surprisingly well. I'll tell you all about it later, though. Back to my idea.

I smile, wondering what has her so excited.

Vince: I'm listening.

Stevie: We haven't set a date for our livestream. So, I was thinking maybe we could just, I don't know, go for it.

I arch a brow, reading and re-reading her text.

Vince: When?

It takes her a sec to respond this time.

Stevie: Like… maybe tonight?

I stare at the phone, focusing on the word *'tonight'*.

My eyes slam shut, fighting the thought that enters my head next. On some level, I hate myself. Hate the way I am. Hate that I'm damaged. Most guys on the verge of fucking the girl they're into would have racing hearts just at the promise of getting laid in the couple hours. But here I am, feeling like mine might leap out of my throat, sweating bullets, all because I'm a broken piece of shit.

I want this. More than *anything* I want this, but I'm riddled with this irrational fear that I can't trust my own fucking body. Mostly because I still wake up panting from nightmares on occasion, remembering what was done to me, and in the moment, feeling just as powerless as I did back then. Who's to say I won't get triggered in the middle of the livestream and embarrass us both?

When I asked Bird to join me, I was riding high on the moment, imagining what it would feel like to finally have her, to finally break free from the prison one twisted woman locked me inside of when I was a kid. It doesn't matter that the bars and chains only exist inside my head. It's enough.

It's always been enough.

Maggie—the predator who made a habit of supplying my mother with drugs, so she could violate me while Mom was high—is the reason I began to stream three years ago. Not many people can say that their abuser inspired them, but she was definitely that for me. An inspiration. For so many years, the fucked up things that went on with my body were on someone else's terms. *Her* terms. So, I decided to flip that shit on its head.

I perform on my own time, and it's on me to decide how far things will go while I'm live. Performing for my followers helped me reclaim a sense of power I'd lost so young I wasn't even aware it existed. Maggie stole that from me. Temporarily at least. But now, with Bird, I intend to restore the balance once and for all.

I take so long to answer that she thinks I'm not interested.

Stevie: I mean, I know it's short notice, so it's cool if you want to wait. Plus, there might not be time to notify your followers. Sorry, that was probably really pushy lol.

My hands are shaking when I start typing back.

Vince: No, I want this.

I stare at my wording, knowing I held back, so I try again.

Vince: I want you.

I let out a deep breath to calm myself because those words are true. However this goes tonight, even if I make a complete ass of myself on camera, there will be nothing to regret because... I'll be with her.

Somehow, in the middle of thinking this might be a total fucking disaster, I smile. It comes on when I envision her, beautiful and gentle, brave in ways I could only ever dream about.

Stevie: Then it's settled. I'll meet you in a couple hours.

Vince: Ok, but not here. A hotel. I'll text you the info.

Stevie: Perfect. See you soon.

I set the phone down and it's not lost on me that my heart's still racing. The last time we spoke was before she left for Cypress Pointe. I walked her to her car, kissed her against the door before opening it, but I had no clue at the time that our night would end like this. I'm guessing that, with things going well with meeting her bio dad, she's in a good mood, still riding the high.

I could sit here analyzing for hours, but I should be hauling ass to get to the hotel before she does.

I need to pack a few things, then get Ash's keys. After the other night, when Bird confirmed she was down to do this, I did some shopping online, thinking ahead. We'll *both* need to hide our identities. That means more than hiding our faces. We're both branded, and she's got a tattoo someone could easily recognize. So, I took measures to prevent that.

A quick glance around my room confirms that I have everything I need, including the dark duffle bag that holds my camera equipment. I hit the light, lock up, and then head downstairs.

Ash is leaning over the edge of the pool table. With one fast thrust, he pushes the stick between his fingers and the cueball knocks into the eight ball, sinking it cleanly into the corner pocket.

"Shit!" Fletcher roars in frustration, right before sliding a fifty into Ash's palm.

"We can run it back," Ash offers, smirking as he pockets the cash. "Double or nothing?"

Fletcher considers it, and then maybe realizes he can't afford to lose again. "Not tonight."

Ash, in the middle of laughing at Fletcher's misfortune, notices me standing here. Micah looks up from his phone, a ribbon of smoke dancing from the end of the cigarette between his fingers.

"Hey, I need the truck."

Without giving it much thought, Ash reaches into his back pocket, but then pauses. He flashes a look from the bags I'm clutching in my hand, to the one on my back, and then the one hanging from my shoulder.

His eyes narrow.

"Skipping town?" he jokes.

"Funny. The keys?"

As if they weren't already curious what my plans are, they're interest is definitely piqued now. I knew there would be questions, but I failed to think of a credible lie before now. Not one that would hold up. Besides, when Bird doesn't come back tonight some measure of the truth would come out anyway.

I stand there, not saying a word as another group gathers around the pool table, setting up for a new game.

My eyes flash toward them, the need for privacy becoming apparent. "I'll tell you, but not here. Too many eyes and ears."

Micah's brow arches, then he stands to follow me and Ash out onto the front steps. We're alone out here, but the words are still stuck in my throat. We give each other a hard time about shit sometimes, but I can't take that. Not right now. Not from them.

Man the fuck up and spit it out.

Breathing deep, I force myself to speak. "I'll be back in the morning. Way before the funeral," I add, remembering that Ash's grandmother's service is scheduled for noon.

His head cocks to one side. "Okay, but... where the fuck are you going?"

He seems completely unaffected by the mention of his grandmother's arrangements. In fact, he laughs a bit when he asks that question, but when my expression doesn't change, his smile fades.

"Are you in trouble or something?"

Frustration sets in. Not with them, but with myself. I'm on my way to meet up with a girl who makes me feel shit I've never felt before, and I'm apparently giving a vibe that something's wrong.

What if Bird picks up on that?

What if she thinks it's her?

"I'm going to a hotel," I force out, and then clarify. "I'm meeting *Bird* at a hotel."

At first, they don't give much. They don't speak, their expressions stay mellow and even. But then Micah's eyes widen a bit as it sinks in. It's followed up by a half smirk that has me wishing I could walk away, but don't have the keys yet.

"Well, well, well," he says. "Is tonight the night?"

I don't answer, which is apparently all the answer these two need.

"Damn, seriously?" Ash chimes in, slapping his hand to my arm. "And you were gonna leave without saying anything?"

"Obviously not. I needed the keys."

He rolls his eyes. "I mean without telling us *why* you're leaving."

Again, I don't answer because the last thing I want to do is have this conversation, make a bigger deal out of it than it needs to be.

"Keys."

He hesitates a bit, holding the keys over my hand a moment before he drops them into my palm. But the moment he releases them, I turn to head down the sidewalk toward the truck.

"Hang on."

My steps halt when Micah calls out, but I don't turn to face them.

"I know you don't need pointers and shit like that, but... if you need to talk about the *other* stuff later, just... call."

I hear his words, the sincerity in them as we all silently acknowledge the shit I went through, so I cast a look at him over my shoulder. No words leave my mouth, but when I nod, that's enough.

This isn't the kind of thing the guys can walk me through. Tonight, whatever happens, even with the cameras on... it'll just be me and Bird.

Chapter 31

Stevie

Here I was thinking I'd pull up to some seedy motel when I put the address into the GPS. But leave it to Vince to leave me speechless.

My eyes lift to the enormous chandelier as I walk underneath it, the soles of my sneakers squeaking across the marble tile. On my way to the elevator, I pass a nicely dressed couple. A form-fitting red dress hugs her athletic frame, and a pair of strappy heels lace up her toned calves. The guy she's with wears a crimson tie that matches the dress, and his tailored suit fits him to a tee. They're the embodiment of what this hotel screams.

Expensive.

Their laughter trails behind me when I pass, pressing the button beside the elevator. The room number Vince texted cycles through my thoughts, and I recite it over and over again, trying to quell my nerves. For several reasons.

Being someone's first.

Helping him navigate waters I'm not all that familiar with myself.

And there's the whole… being on camera thing I keep trying to pretend isn't real. In my head, I'll pretend it's just the two of us. At least, I *hope* I'm able to make myself believe that.

I climb into the elevator and press *'five'*, breathing deep as the doors close me in. This is it. The point of no return.

The bell dings and now I'm staring down a long, brightly lit hallway. And as I step off, it's hard to ignore how my hands are shaking. I'm of two minds. One where I'm nervous as hell about this, dreading the exposure. But the *other* side of me wants this so badly I can taste it.

That side of me is the reason I texted him so boldly.

The reason I bit my lip when he sent the address to this hotel.

The reason I'm completely wet at the thought of being the first girl who will ever have the pleasure of feeling Vince's cock inside her.

I lift my hand to knock, but notice the door isn't completely latched. He must've known I was close by. I'm not sure what to expect when I walk in, but I'm not expecting the scene he's laid out. The camera is perched on its tripod, angled at the bed with an armchair in view as well. Plastic crinkles beneath my feet when I step in further, closing and locking the door behind me. It's a clear tarp covering the carpet, which makes my heart leap, wondering what he has in mind.

My gaze shifts to the bathroom when I hear the sound of running water coming from the shower. With a few minutes to myself, I drop down onto the giant bed, falling back to stare at the ceiling. My eyes flit to the camera again and if my head is going to be in the game, I need to own my shit.

I've come so far with my body image issues. Too far to be so in my head about being seen. Too far to be so in my head about being seen with *Vince.*

With his perfection on display so close to my body, I can't help but to wonder if people will judge. I can practically hear them now, realizing that the girl their beloved obsession has chosen to invite onscreen isn't a stick figure. I mean, if it were *me* watching, that's what I'd expect. But then a thought hits me.

It doesn't matter what anyone thinks, what anyone expects. What matters is that Vince and I have a connection. One so strong that it brought us here tonight, preparing to express ourselves in the most carnal and satisfying way known to man.

And woman.

The sound of the bathroom door opening has me sitting upright again, straightening my t-shirt half a second before Vince steps around the corner, meeting my gaze as he stands there.

Soaking wet from the waist up, wearing nothing but a white, fluffy towel from the waist down.

I was completely right calling him perfect, because damn...

I finally tear my eyes away from his body and look into his eyes. And when I do, he's smiling a little.

"How was the drive?"

I shrug, swallowing my anxiety back down when it rears its ugly head again. "Not too bad. It gave me time to process everything that happened today."

He seems pleased to see that I'm in such a good headspace, but no one's happier about that than me.

"Good. I want to hear all about it when you're ready. Maybe over breakfast in the morning."

My heart skips a beat hearing him speak those words, reminding me that there will be more than just sex. We'll be spending an entire night together and waking up together. It won't be the first time we've had a sleepover, but it *will* be the first time we've done so after having sex.

And sex... changes things. At least that's been my experience with the others. And now, I'll get to have that with Vince, too.

"Mind if I shower?" I ask, nodding toward the small backpack I set down near my feet. Thanks to my *mother's* lifelong paranoia becoming *my* paranoia, I'm accustomed to traveling with a few things. So, I packed a small bag that went with me to Cypress Pointe. Just on the off chance that I had car trouble.

"It's all yours," he says. "And no rush. I didn't post that we'd be streaming at a specific time, so... whenever we're ready."

He smiles, trying his best to be confident, but I see through the façade. Maybe because he's told me his story, and I know what a big step this is for him. So, when I stand, I don't simply walk past him, I stop so we're toe-to-toe, gazing up as he towers over me, staring into his beautiful green eyes. And when I press my palms to the sides of his jaw, he cranes his head lower, until our lips meet.

His tongue explores my mouth, and I want him to feel that it's just me. Whatever I can do to make this comfortable for him, I'll do it.

"Be right back."

I feel his eyes trailing me as I walk away, and I note that my emotions have suddenly shifted.

Are there nerves? Yes, of course.

But more than that… there's desire.

And soon, that desire will turn into satisfaction.

Vince

Everything's laid out when she steps out of the bathroom, and when I turn to look at her, I can't even blink. Long, purple-tinted hair falls over her shoulders, covering the straps of the black bra obstructing my view of her tits. The thin chain of a gold necklace rests in her cleavage, and I fixate there, imagining my mouth tracing every inch of her skin.

Every.

Damn.

Inch.

I find myself wondering if she has any idea how beautiful she is, but then it hits me that this would probably be a great time to tell her instead of just thinking it.

"You look… fucking amazing."

"Thank you." She smiles shyly and that innocent look has my dick hardening already.

Her eyes dart from the bed to the dresser, and finally to the camera.

"So, what's the plan?" she asks, sighing a little. Which could mean she's nervous, too. Although, for much different reasons, I'm sure.

"I should probably explain the tarps first," I say with a laugh, which draws one out of her, too.

"Oh, you mean you're not planning to kill and dismember me?"

My gaze shifts to the jars on the dresser. "It's to protect everything from *this*. Neon, edible body paint."

Bird arches a brow as she comes closer to investigate. "Hmm..." she says, picking up a jar to check out the label.

"Hot pink is strawberry. Yellow is vanilla, and Blue is chocolate."

After my explanation, she continues studying the words on the container, but the only thing I'm focused on now is her. Because she smells vaguely familiar, and it only takes a couple seconds to realize she used my shower gel. I left it on the ledge of the tub, so she must've helped herself to it. It's different on her than it is on me. Softer. I breathe her in again, realizing something else.

It's a fucking turn-on that she smells like me, that something of mine touched her skin. Every-fucking-where.

She glances up and catches me staring, but I don't turn away, don't pretend it was a coincidence that our eyes locked. Her full lips part with a breath and knowing where this is headed, I'm suddenly impatient, feeling bolder, so I hold on to that.

"What are we doing with it?" She lifts the pink jar into the air when asking, but then laughs when she seems to realize the answer is sort of self-explanatory.

Although, I'm still certain she's missed at least *some* of the point.

"Let me show you."

I take her arm and turn her until the left side of her body is angled toward me. I grab the paint from her hand, setting the lid aside before dipping the tip of my finger into the jar. Goosebumps texture her torso as I slowly slide my hand across it. She shudders a bit and my awareness of her is through the roof. It's like I hear every breath she takes, see even the slightest reaction to my touch. I coat my fingers in more paint before smoothing it over the puffy, S-shaped scar on her hip, and then look it over, ensuring that it's no longer legible.

Bird takes a breath, holding my gaze as the tension in the room soars. If things heat up like this from a simple touch, I can only imagine where the night is headed.

"Now you," she says tearing her eyes away to focus.

I turn my back toward her and there's rustling behind me as she chooses which of the three paints she'll use. Then, the next thing I feel is sticky wetness being slathered over my brand. She chose the blue one, chocolate. The scent gives it away without needing to see the label.

"There, it's all covered," she says. "Should I do more?"

"I figured we'd just cover ourselves completely," I explain. "That way, it won't be so obvious that we only did it to hide markings."

She nods, understanding, but then her gaze shifts toward the bed. And when her eyes narrow, I realize she's just noticed the bedding. I stripped the comforter off while she showered, tossing it into the closet, so it's out of the way. What covers the bed *now,* instead of the expensive, high thread-count sheets housekeeping placed over the mattress, is a dark, fitted play sheet. The rubbery texture will keep whatever mess we make to a minimum.

"It's so we don't have to be careful with the paint," I explain, and she arches a brow.

"You seriously thought of everything, didn't you?"

I shrug, wondering if it's too much, wondering if she thinks it's weird that I started planning for this in advance. But when she smiles, and then stretches up on her toes to kiss me, it's clear I'm over-thinking it.

She pulls away and a second later she's holding the jar of straw-berry paint. I stare as she plunges her finger inside it, and then locks eyes with me. In fact, she doesn't even blink as she sucks the pink coloring off her finger, giving it a taste before we go any further.

"Hmm, it's sweeter than I thought it would be. I like it," she smiles, using her tongue to swipe at a small speck in the corner of her mouth. "May I?" she asks, eyeing my chest before her eyes flit up toward mine again.

I'm so entranced by her, I can only nod, and then watch as she smears pink paint all over my pecs and torso. I expect her to move on to another section of skin, but instead, her full, soft lips are on my chest, her tongue flat against my nipple as she teases me in that insanely hot way that sends every ounce of blood in my body straight to my dick. She knows she's being a little shit, making me want her more than I already do. The devious smirk curving her mouth tells me so.

She pulls away, and I grab the blue jar. Her eyes are locked on mine when I lower to my knees, lifting her thigh to my shoulder. Her breaths come in shallow bursts when I trace the inside of her thigh with my finger, painting a thin line there before dragging my tongue over her perfect, smooth skin. From the inside of her knee, to just short of tasting her pussy. And when her fingers instinctively brush over the top of my head, I know she'd like that.

Now, I find myself wondering... does she know she'll be my first for that, too?

Impatience gets the best of me and I'm back on my feet, wanting to move things along more quickly. She lifts her arms and spins as needed while I cover her skin with a little of each of the colors, camouflage style. When I get to her face, I smile while I paint.

"What the hell are you doing?" she laughs.

I shrug, not answering until I'm done. "It's possible I just gave you devil horns."

Her laugh grows louder. "Fuck you."

"That's the plan."

We lock eyes for a second and she pokes her finger into my ribs. "Smart-ass."

"If it makes you feel better, I'll put a heart on your cheek to balance it out."

"Gee, thanks."

She holds still while I add more designs to her face. Enough that when I turn on the black light, no one will recognize her. Slowly, I'm beginning to feel the nervousness wear off. I don't know if it's just from being here with her, feeling her energy, or if it's because the longer I'm in her presence the more fucking her becomes a need. One I don't think I've ever felt this strongly in my entire life.

For her.

For anyone.

We switch rolls, and she paints me next. Her hands glide over my skin and that need for her only grows. So much that waiting becomes painful. She giggles in this way that sounds far too innocent when she paints a star around my eye.

"There," she says, leaning back to admire her work. "Now you look like Paul Stanley."

"Who the fuck is that?"

The question seems to offend her. "Who the fuck is that?" she repeats. "Only the frontman for Kiss, and a fucking legend in his own right."

"Heard of them, but couldn't tell you a single one of their songs."

Again, it looks like I've insulted her personally by my lack of pop-culture knowledge tonight.

"You're lucky you're fucking hot," she says with an eye roll and my dick pulses. I mean, it full-on jumps hearing her say that shit. I haven't even had her yet, and I'm already positive her pussy will send me on a bender, taking her as often as she'll let me.

I'm quiet while she finishes, purposely spending a ridiculously long time placing pink handprints all over my torso, and then she's done.

She looks me over again, like an artist would stare at their canvas.

"Seems like a shame to cover you up," she says, "but I suppose it's for the best."

She's doing it again, flirting. It has this wicked effect on me, making my cock tingle and my balls tense. It's a cause for real concern that if I can't even take her shit-talking without nearly blowing my load, what the fuck will happen when I'm inside her?

As if she's just heard my thoughts, she flashes this smirk that makes it impossible not to pull her to me, smashing her body against mine.

"Wait," she giggles. "The paint's not dry. You'll smear it."

"Who gives a shit about the paint?" The words are muffled against her lips when I steal a kiss. And the way she bites and sucks mine has me needing more of her.

Immediately.

"Bed. Now," I growl, and surprise flashes in her eyes. She doesn't question the abruptness out loud, instead doing as she's told, crawling onto the mattress, still clothed in her bra and panties.

I make quick work of turning off the lamps and flipping on the blacklights instead. The room illuminates with a deep, eerie shade of purple, and the paint that covers our skin glows brightly. I take note of how it stands out, darkening Bird's features in comparison, making her unrecognizable even to me.

Good.

Now we get to enjoy the moment in peace without worrying about being recognized. We can just... fuck.

At the last minute, I remember to carry the paint jars over to the nightstand just in case we need more. I double back to the foot of the bed where the camera's set up. After turning it on, I adjust the settings a bit until they're perfect. Through the camera's lens, I can't take my eyes off Bird. She's completely fucking perfect, and also completely unaware that she even has this power over me, over my brothers. She shoots me this look when she realizes she's being watched, and I've done all the waiting I care to do tonight. I send out a quick update to my followers that we're about to go live, and then set my phone aside.

"We'll be online in ten seconds," I inform her.

My heart's racing, and when I move to the side of the bed to get closer to Bird, the way her tits heave in the glow of the dark lighting, I can guess hers is, too.

The sound of my phone lighting up with comments means there are now hundreds of eyes on us, eyes on this beautiful girl I'm more than ready to give everything to. She rests on her shins, her knees pressed into the mattress, and as badly as I want to touch her, I'm admittedly having a momentary lapse in nerve. I'm inside my head again, spinning myself into a web of shitty memories and insecurities I never speak about.

But then Bird's hand lands on my chest, and she looks up at me in this way that makes me wonder if she senses it. Senses that I'm spiraling. But the feel of heat moving through her palm and warming my skin, brings me back. It's just us again. Even knowing we have an audience probably larger than any I've ever garnered on my own.

She takes a breath. "Ready?"

Her voice is soft and low, too quiet for the camera to have picked it up. So, when I nod, it's the only indication there's any sort of conversation between us.

Bird's eyes leave me, lowering to my towel as she slowly undoes it, making a show of exposing me to our audience. By the time she lets it fall to the floor, I'm already rock-hard and dreaming about how it'll feel to be inside her. My eyes are glued to her, focused intently when she reaches behind her back and undoes her bra. I'm hypnotized, watching as the weight of her full tits settle when she removes the black lace, tossing it aside. Tight, pink nipples have my mouth watering, imagining the feel of them against my tongue, sucking them until she's pooling between her legs.

She grips my cock and a sharp breath hisses between my teeth. She finds my eyes again while stroking me, and I remember the way her mouth felt on me, the way she made me forget my own boundaries as she swallowed my cum like it's a fucking endangered resource.

She seems to read my mind again and holds my gaze as she leans forward, until her soft, full lips are around my cock, slurping me into her hot, silky mouth in skilled rhythm.

"Shit. You're killing me," I warn, already feeling my balls tighten, anticipating the moment I get to explode inside her.

Her hands grip the backs of my thighs as she hunches forward, drawing me into her mouth again, deep, faster now as my breathing deepens. It's like the more I react, the more she gives.

She hums a soft moan onto my shaft when my fingers wind into her hair, letting her know what she's doing to me, letting her know her touch is the only touch I'll allow...

Letting her know it's the only touch I crave.

In fact, she's all I think about when I film now, because I know that out there somewhere, she's always watching.

But tonight, she's here in the flesh.

The head of my cock tingles when she twists her tongue around it, teasing the ever-loving fuck out of me. But two can play that game.

A surprised gasp leaves her mouth when I take her shoulders and force her back onto the bed, until her tits point skyward, and the soles of her feet press into the mattress. Her knees are drawn, and she stares as I slowly push them apart. My focus is singular when she spreads her legs even wider for me, and the scent of her makes my mouth water. So much that I don't bother removing her panties, in favor of yanking them to the side so rough the sound of a stitch or two ripping fills the air.

Bird places a hand on my head, and I lower my mouth to her pussy, entranced by the softness of it against my lips. She's so turned on, the outside glistens with her wetness. I taste her, lapping my tongue up one of her pussy lips, and then the other, taking in this new flavor I'm instantly addicted to. Because it's her—in her rawest, most carnal form.

She gasps when I taste her again, bolder this time because I feel like I could literally fucking *devour* this girl. I pull her lips apart with my fingers and taste her clit this time, noting that it's swollen, and so tender that she whimpers when I flatten my tongue against it a second time. Her reaction is fucking everything to me right now, and I need more. I need to know I'm making her feel so damn good she's out of her head.

"Vince," she whimpers, lifting her hips off the bed to grind against my face when I suck her clit into my mouth. It swells even more against my tongue, and I suck harder, feeling her wetness soaking my chin.

She needs relief, needs to be filled, and without any thought about my hangups or nerves, I leave her writhing on the sheet for only a few seconds as I climb the length of her torso. Now, it's no longer my tongue she feels against her. It's the tip of my dick, pressing between her lower lips, teasing her opening as I process—that this is happening, that I get to have this with her—and then… I push deeper, feeling the heat of her wet channel welcoming me inside her.

"Ho-ly fucking shit," I groan, unable to move for a few seconds, because if I do, I'll come and ruin everything.

I'd fucking die if it were over that fast, if it ended without her being satisfied, without me getting to savor this.

She squirms beneath me, and I know she needs this, needs me to please her, so I force myself to settle, sliding into her deeper, feeling the tight squeeze of her slick pussy around me. If something exists on this planet that feels better than what I'm experiencing, that shit's gotta be illegal, locked away in a vault beneath the damn ocean.

Fuck… I don't even know what I'm talking about at this point. My head's spinning and it feels like I'm losing my shit.

"You feel fucking amazing," I whisper, craning my neck lower so I can kiss her. Just once before I lift my weight off her, rocking into her over and over again.

Her eyes fall closed as she pants and moans, turning her face into my forearm as she grips it, kissing and tonguing my skin while I watch her like a man obsessed. Hell, maybe I *am* fucking obsessed.

With the feel of her.

With how she draws all the pain and bad shit away.

Or maybe just obsessed with *her* in general.

All of her.

"I'm about to come," she whimpers, and I thank my lucky fucking stars, because I won't be able to hold it much longer either.

She gets wetter by the second, and she thrusts up, matching my pace, adding to the already insane friction. My phone's going wild, and I'd nearly forgotten we're recording until now. I can only imagine the things people are saying as they watch us, but I don't really give a fuck about anything right now but this.

Her.

"Right there," she cries out, and the sound of her voice has my dick throbbing inside her, pulsing as pressure builds in my balls while they pummel the softness of her ass.

When she grips my arm again and tension spreads across her

brow, the moan that leaves her mouth afterward means I didn't fuck this up. It means I pleasured her and made my girl come... and now I can stop holding it in.

My pelvis slams into her, and I love that her body's soft where mine is hard and rigid. I grind my hips, circling into her, reveling in how I feel her on every inch of me, and then I lose myself, shocked by how much more powerful it is releasing into her *pussy,* instead of her mouth, or my own hand.

This...

This feels... right.

My cum fills her to the brim, squelching out of her opening as I continue to pound into it, wanting to make this intense feeling last as long as humanly possible. It feels like my heart will actually beat out of my chest, but I don't think I'd even care if it did. If the exchange for the pleasure her body just brought to me is death, I'd come inside her and then gladly go into the light, because... shit.

My body stills and we're breathing loud and erratic. She hasn't opened her eyes yet, but I want her to. Or maybe I *need* her to. I don't know why, but I'm almost desperate for that level of connection now that it's over. Only, it feels too vulnerable to admit that out loud. So, instead of using words, I brush my thumb down her jaw, and it has the intended affect. She opens her eyes.

Her brown irises are fixed on me and there's this strange sense of relief that starts in my head, and then it travels down my body until it reaches my chest, my *heart.* Bird smiles at me warmly as I soften inside her, and when she grips the back of my neck, she barely has to pull me down to kiss her, because I was already lowering to take her lips. Her tongue lazily wanders into my mouth, and I suck it soft and slow, just like I'd done to her clit.

The notifications are streaming in at a near constant rate. Finally, my followers got what they wanted, but more than that... I finally got what *I* wanted.

This perfect girl who came out of nowhere and is somehow everything I need her to be.

This girl who's undeniably and irrevocably... mine.

Chapter 32

Stevie

Tate: Good morning, beautiful.

I've barely got one eye open as I read Tate's text. Vince and I were up half the night putting the room back in its regular state, then we showered again to clean off all the body paint. Needless to say, my body's protesting as I blink and attempt to focus.

Stevie: Good morning, Mr. Ford.

I smile after hitting send, then I pull the blanket up my shoulder to lock in me and Vince's body heat beneath it. Neither of us bothered with clothes after the shower, so while it was nice to roll over in the middle of the night and feel his bare skin against mine, I wouldn't hate to have on a pair of flannel pajamas right now.

Tate: Damn. Mr. Ford. I like that.

I laugh quietly, being careful not to wake Vince.

Stevie: Did you text me at 8:00 a.m. just to flirt?

Tate: Well, it's not the only reason. I'm also wondering if you're going to the guys' first game tomorrow.

Stevie: Of course. You?

Tate: I am, and I'd like it if you rode out to Richton with me. I know you've got a car now, but it seems like a waste for both of us to drive.

I smile at the subtle sense of chivalry.

Stevie: I'd like that.

Tate: Good. Did you already book a room?

I have to laugh at his question. Well, mostly at my lack of preparedness.

Stevie: Nope, figured I'd just crash with the guys when we got there.

Tate: Then you would've been sorely disappointed. Coach has strict rules for when they're on the road. The night before the game, they have curfew, and all the coaches keep a close watch on them.

Stevie: Shit. I had no idea. Guess I would've been spending the night in my car then.

Tate: Maybe. But now you have options. Sleep in the cramped car with the gearshift jabbing into your thigh, or crash with me.

I smile as I type my response.

Stevie: Thanks for the invite. I'm in. For the ride and the room.

Tate: Perfect, I'll text once I know what time I'm leaving tonight.

I set my phone aside just as Vince stirs, and I can't fight the grin that takes over when his solid arm slinks across my midsection. He lifts his hand to cup my breast, and I've come to learn that this is his thing. The last night we spent together, he fell asleep in this very position—with his dick to my ass, palming my boob.

He kisses the back of my shoulder, then nestles in closer.

"Sleep okay?" he rasps groggily.

"Like a baby. You?"

"More like a bear." He laughs a little, and I enjoy the sound of it, curling deeper into his side.

"That would explain the snoring," I tease.

"Fucking lies. I'm the most dignified sleeper you know."

I arch a brow. "Like hell you are. You woke me up twice, actually."

He chuffs another short laugh. "No shit?"

"No shit. You sounded like a foghorn," I lie, pulling this entire story out of my ass. If he *did* snore, I wouldn't know anything about it because, thanks to our late-night activities, I went to sleep thoroughly exhausted.

Vince is quiet, and I'm holding in a laugh, but when it slips out, I'm caught.

"I knew you were lying," he accuses, drawing the ugliest laugh known to man from my throat when he digs his fingers into my side, tickling me.

"Okay! I give! I lied! You're the most dignified sleeper we *both* know!" I yell out. He eventually stops, but when I try to wriggle from his grasp, he only pulls me closer.

"Don't ever fucking lie to me again," he warns, the playful growl of his voice proving to be more of a turn on than a threat.

"Yes, sir."

He places a kiss on the back of my shoulder, and then much to my disappointment, he leaves me in bed and heads to the bathroom. I lie there, staring at the ceiling while he flushes and then turns on the faucet. He takes a while, and I assume he brushes his teeth after washing his hands. And judging by the scent of mouthwash on his breath when he returns, I know I'm right.

He's in bed again, and when I push back the covers, intending to stand and pay the mouthwash a visit *myself,* a thick arm encircles my waist. My back slams against Vince's wall-like chest and he buries a kiss in my neck, making me cry out for mercy. All while laughing too hard to be taken seriously.

"Did I say you could fucking leave me?"

His words vibrate against my neck and, for a moment, I forget I'm supposed to be struggling against him.

"Okay, you win. But if I hear *one* joke about morning breath, that'll be your ass, Vince."

"Fair enough." He loosens his grip, but the closeness between us stays intact.

Lying beside him, I think about our night. Our incredible, plea-sure-filled night. It was perfect. *He* was perfect. It was liberating in so many ways, including the fact that I—Stevie Heron—had sex on a live stream. Body image issues be damned, I guess, because I hardly even thought about stretch marks or cellulite while I was with Vince. And if I'm being honest, it's been like that with my guys for a while now. I know that when they look at me, all they *see* is me.

Not my flaws and imperfections.

Me.

"Tell me how things went yesterday," he says, redirecting my thoughts. "I want to hear all about your visit with your dad."

His statement has me smiling for a different reason now, at the thought of Dusty and how incredible it felt to finally have answers. To finally solve one of my sister's puzzles.

"It was… everything I could've wanted it to be. He was open and receptive to what I had to say, and believe it or not, he never once rejected the idea that what I was telling him was true. And considering what my *'dad'* before has been like, speaking to Dusty was a welcomed surprise."

"Sounds like everything was perfect," he says. "Any plans to meet up again soon? Or is it too early to tell?"

I shrug. "We didn't, like, set a date or anything, but I know I'll see him again. Soon if *he* has anything to do with it," I add with a laugh. "He was actually really excited about getting to know me better, and needless to say, I'd like that, too."

It seems crazy to say this, but just that short meeting with Dusty yesterday has already begun to fill the void in my heart. It's nowhere near restored, but I can tell the edges of the wound are starting to heal.

"He's lucky to have you," Vince says, and I smile against the pillow.

"I don't know much about him yet, but I get the feeling I'm lucky to have him, too."

The high from yesterday has yet to wear off, especially seeing as how it ended so well—being here with Vince, having more fun than I even imagined we would. Which reminds me…

"We crashed pretty quickly after cleaning up, but… I wanted to say that last night was incredible. *You* were incredible."

He's quiet, and I hope he knows I'm not just saying this to stroke his ego, but if I hadn't known beforehand that last night was his first time, I would've never guessed. He was skilled, knew exactly what to do and how to do it. I didn't expect things to go so smoothly, but the entire evening was, in a word, perfection.

"I'm not sure if *'thank you'* is the right response, but... thank you," he says. I hear the amusement in his voice, and it makes me smile.

"It's the right response."

"Good."

I expected him to say more, but he pauses, maybe finding the right words.

"And... the other thing... that was okay, too?"

At first, I'm unsure what he means, but then I recall what he did to me *before* we fucked. I remember it, every sensation his tongue brought to my pussy, and I feel myself getting wet again.

"Was that the first time you went down on someone?"

He breathes deep before answering. "Was it that obvious?" He laughs a little to hide that he's nervous how I'll answer. But when I reach behind me, placing my hand on his thigh, I hope there's no need for nerves around me.

"Every single thing about last night was perfect. Even if I *wanted* to give you pointers, I couldn't. You completely blew my mind."

His body relaxes then, settling against me like before. I could lie like this with him all day, but one thing we did talk about before we drifted off was that he needs to get the truck back early this morning. On top of all three of them having a plane to catch tonight before tomorrow's game, Ash is attending his grandmother's funeral. So, while we have a little time, we can't return it too late. And speaking of the funeral, I've come to learn that I wasn't the only one Ash turned down when asking to accompany him to the service. He declined the guys' offers as well, stating that this is something he needs to do on his own. So, although we'd like to be there for him, we've all agreed to respect his wishes.

As bad an idea as it may be.

"We got a lot of feedback last night," he says, causing me to focus. "I didn't read any of the comments, but if you're interested, we can check them out together."

I freeze, failing to give an immediate response. If there's any place a person can expect to find the God's honest truth regarding how society sees them, it's in any comment section anywhere. So, to say that the idea stresses me a little would be an understatement.

But considering how brave he was to experience his first time on camera, I'm determined to be just as strong as he was.

"Sure."

My words prompt him to put space between us just long enough to reach toward the nightstand for his phone, and when he does, I slip out of bed before he can stop me.

"Be back in a sec," I say, flashing a triumphant grin, rushing off to the bathroom to finally brush my teeth. When I finish and return, he glares at me playfully, but clearly isn't holding a grudge when I slip back into my spot—with my back warm to his chest. He has his phone and holds it around my shoulder so we can both see the screen.

Anonymous: ($70 tip pledged) "Lucky fucking girl."

Anonymous: ($65 tip pledged) "Agreed, but they're BOTH pretty lucky if you ask me."

Vince's chest moves when he laughs at that. "I'm definitely the lucky one," he says, and I can't fight the smile his compliment draws out of me.

Anonymous: ($120 tip pledged) "OMG is anyone else still in disbelief that this is really about to happen?"

Anonymous: ($50 tip pledged) "Shit... look at the ass on him. Forget bouncing a quarter off it. I want to bounce my FACE off it!"

We both laugh reading that one, and it's strange reading his comments from this side of things. Not just as a fan, but also as a guest star.

Anonymous: ($80) "I love our boy's solo acts, but it takes things to a whole new level seeing this Mystery Girl's lips wrapped around his dick. Why am I jealous in real life right now?!?!"

Anonymous: ($75) "Does anyone know if this chick has her own *channel? I'd love to check out her vids. You know… for research purposes."*

Vince chuckles again. "Looks like you've got a few fans."

I smile a bit, but squirm at the thought of putting myself out there like he does. It's one thing popping in for a cameo, and another to be that vulnerable and open all the time.

"I feel like I should say something, put it out there just in case you decide to livestream in the future."

A laugh slips, anticipating what he'll say. "This should be good."

He's already close, but he moves his mouth to my ear, making sure I hear him loud and clear.

"The only person you can ever film any one-on-one footage with… is me," he says. "Am I clear?"

My smile broadens, especially when he kisses a trail down the rim of my ear to my neck.

"Depends."

"On what?" he asks.

I glance at him from over my shoulder. "How you intend to punish me if I disobey."

He grins when I tease him a bit, and then I regret it because he tickles me again. Our naked bodies writhe against one another beneath the covers, and the mood shifts from playful and innocent to hot and erotic in the blink of an eye.

"Such a fucking smart-ass." He buries his face into the side of my neck, and then kisses me there. My entire body goes still, feeling the residual lust still lingering with us both.

"Is it bad that I already can't wait to fuck you again?" His kiss moves to my shoulder, and I'm entranced by the feel of his lips, his hand slowly pushing down my torso. He stops just beneath my navel, and I want him to keep going, want him to touch me *everywhere.*

"Then why wait?" I ask. "What's stopping you from fucking me *now*?"

He chuckles against my skin. "But what about the time? We've got to get back for Ash."

My eyes flit to the clock. "We've got thirty minutes. We can do *plenty* with thirty minutes."

My words have his heart thundering against my back, giving away how badly he wants to give in. This won't take long, especially considering how ready I am. I scoot my hips back, brushing against his hard dick, and I amend my statement.

How ready we *both* are.

"No cameras this time. No one watching. Just us," I remind him, sweetening the pot.

He's completely silent while he thinks, and then the words, "Fuck it," fly from his mouth as a smile curves mine.

Instead of waiting for him to act, I take the lead this time, turning onto my side before flipping him onto his back. It's convenient that we're both naked already, so there's no time wasted undressing. And he's already so hard, causing the sheet to tent a good nine inches off his body. I push the covers aside and toss my thigh over his waist, climbing on top of him.

His length rests against my ass while we kiss, my body covering his, the warmth of his chest against my sensitive nipples. He palms my ass, squeezing tight as my tongue explores his mouth. His hips lift, creating just enough friction between us that I grow tired of waiting. I need him inside me as quickly as possible. The urgency becomes clear when I abruptly tear my mouth from his, repositioning myself so that his dick is perfectly aligned with my core.

This will be a first for me, being on top, but I can't think of anyone better to experiment with than Vince. Whereas I feared it might feel like the blind leading the blind, it's been nothing like that.

It's been more like... the curious leading the curious, and so far, that's served us well.

"Fuuuuck," he groans, squeezing my waist to the point of it being painful when I lower onto him, taking him in slowly. It's such a tight fit, and he fills me completely, stretching me in that way I've grown to obsess over.

The sound of my wetness is the only sound in the room as I lift off him halfway, only to swirl my hips back down, inciting another of his delicious groans. Then, his eyes drift closed. I stare at his chest, watching the way it moves with his labored breathing, the way his stomach twitches when he flinches and squeezes my waist like before. I settle into a comfortable rhythm, and I have his eyes again. They're focused on my tits as they bounce with every thrust of my hips, bringing us *both* to the edge.

My fingers dig into his chest where I brace them for support, quickening my pace a little more because he feels so fucking good inside me.

So. Fucking. Good.

"Slow down," he pants, and while I've heard his request, I can't grant it. Because I've beat him to the punch.

"Shit," I cry out, squeezing his chest as I come. My movements aren't nearly as graceful as they were a moment ago, because it becomes less about rhythm and pace, and becomes more about grinding down on him as my pussy throbs and pulses around his cock.

I feel his eyes on me, but I'm too far gone to meet his gaze. Not even when he slips a hand between us and swirls two fingers around my clit. As the intense feeling spreads from my core to my swollen bud, I soak his dick *and his* fingers.

I'm nearly done when his entire body tenses and he loses his breath, exploding between my legs, giving me his cum, and I realize I have an unhealthy obsession with getting him off. There's something about being the only girl to bring him pleasure like this. It's so powerful that... I want it to *always* be like this. Where no one's allowed to be this close, no one's allowed to touch him like this but me.

Feeling ownership over this beautiful specimen I've now taken *twice* in the last twelve hours, I ride him until he's done, until he's gone soft inside me and we're both spent and satisfied. I lean in, kissing him again, and if I have one takeaway from this experience with him, it's simple.

If the statement, "practice makes perfect" is true, I intend to singlehandedly turn Vincent Ricci into a fucking pro.

Chapter 33

Ash

Everything feels… off.

Me in a suit.

Me in a suit heading to a funeral.

Me in a suit heading to the funeral of a woman who never once lifted a finger to protect me.

Suddenly feeling uncomfortable, I loosen my tie with the hand not holding the steering wheel. Loosening it isn't enough, so I snatch it off completely, and then toss it to the passenger seat.

God only knows what sort of shitshow awaits me once I get there. Half the family hates me, and the other half pities me, but none of them really know me. I've always just been poor, little troubled Ashton. The one no one ever really wanted, but no one quite had the heart to leave in the wind.

But I sure wish they had.

Maybe if I'd been raised by a family who actually *wanted* a kid, instead of one who just kept me out of obligation, things might've been different. I might not've had my first concussion at age seven, might not've spent two consecutive summers nursing a broken arm back to health. And most of all, my head might not be so fucked up.

Before I fully know what my plan is, I hit a U-turn and swing back in the opposite direction. I blow through the light at the intersection with a visual in my head. It's of the house I grew up in. I flash through every single room under that roof and can recall having experienced pain in every one of them. No, it was never my grandmother who did the beating or the tossing around, but she was there, standing in the shadows doing absolutely nothing.

My tires screech when I whip into the driveway, remembering the last time I was here. Then, it'd been my grandfather's face I lit into, today... well, today it'll be everything else.

I climb out and pull off my suit jacket, tossing it across the center console before slamming the door shut. On my way around the tailgate, I grab my baseball bat and head toward the back of the house. No one ever thinks to lock the doors to this hellhole, but after today, they might reconsider that habit.

The place wreaks of stale cigar smoke and filth, like usual. I close the door behind me and look around, feeling my pulse race with the possibilities. A smile crosses my face, thinking about the looks that'll be on Uncle Lewis' and my grandfather's faces when they walk in. The way their jaws will drop when they see how I've chosen to pay my respects *instead* of showing up for some bullshit ceremony. The place is sure to be filled with people lying through their teeth about what a good woman my grandmother was.

She was *not* a good woman.

She was a piece of shit enabler who deserves to rot in hell.

Holding that thought, the bat's in the air, and I swing, smashing it into the face of the hutch against the far wall of the kitchen. The sound of the glass shattering, and then raining down on the floor is like fucking music. I swing again, this time aiming for the empty cookie jar on the edge of the table, and before all the pieces settle, I've already destroyed the ceramic plates decorating the walls, before heading to the living room.

I loosen the top button on my shirt now that I've broken a sweat. Then, I set the bat on the edge of the sofa to roll both my sleeves, too.

I pick it up again and try to decide what will be next, which is a moot point because *all* of it is next.

"Fuck you!" The words fly from my mouth as I slam the bat down onto the coffee table, ignoring how the dog's going crazy, barking in the basement while I make my way through the house, destroying everything I lay eyes on.

The end tables, the stereo, framed pictures lining the mantle and hanging on the walls—memories that deserve to be forgotten, destroyed. Tossing the bat to the floor, I have a new idea as I race toward the laundry room. Finding a full bottle of bleach underneath the washtub, I head back to the living room while removing the cap. The sound of liquid spattering the sofa, and then the loveseat and recliner is intoxicating. Slowly the color begins to fade from every-where the liquid soaks into it, effectively ruining the entire set.

Staring at the couch, I remember one incident in particular. One where my grandfather held me down, burying my face in the cushion while he whaled on me with a thick, leather belt. He thought all the flailing around was because of the pain, not realizing I couldn't breathe. Not until I blacked out, anyway. When I came to, he'd rolled me onto the floor to recover, while he sipped a beer and watched the news. His only words to me as I opened my eyes were, "You weak son of a bitch."

I swing at the wall, but not with the bat. It's my fist this time. And as my knuckles smash through the cheap wallpaper and drywall, I feel the rage seeping deeper—beyond my flesh, to my bones.

I take the steps by two and storm upstairs with a plan. One that has me ridding the closet in the main bedroom of my grandfather's clothes, tossing them onto the bed. I empty his drawers, too, tossing all his t-shirts, socks, and underwear into the heap. I should feel ashamed as I unzip my pants and free my dick, acting on sheer impulse as I begin taking a piss all over his things, making sure I get everything, and even the pillows and mattress where they're exposed. I want this asshole to walk in and feel like it'd be easier to burn this bitch down than to try putting it all back together.

As I finish up and refasten my pants, I finally feel like my work here is done. Or at least I *thought* I was done, right up until I start down the steps. I'm not sure what comes over me, but I take out the final traces of frustration on the railing, slamming my foot against it until it loosens, and then breaks free from the wall and the post at the foot of the stairs. The entire banister topples over, landing in the front foyer and the hallway leading to the bathroom.

A plume of wood dust settles in the dim sunlight passing through the window above the entry way, and *now* I think I'm done.

I step over the debris and carnage on my way to the back door, retracing my steps when I remember my bat, and then I let myself out. A smile crosses my face as a dark thought enters my mind. Today already feels like a win, but it'd be even sweeter if that old bastard walks in this afternoon and has a damn heart attack, keels right over on his bed. It would serve his ass right to die on a bed covered in piss.

I walk the length of the driveway, making my way to the truck. I check my watch now that I've calmed down, and there's still plenty of time to stop off for a bite to eat before heading home to pack and make tonight's flight.

Suddenly my head's clear and I'm more than ready for tomorrow's game.

It's gonna be a great fucking weekend.

Chapter 34

Stevie

We had a plan—head out early to meet the boys' plane in Richton for tomorrow's game. It was a *solid* plan, but not so solid that we prepared for *this*.

Small droplets of rain are starting to pelt the windshield as Tate and I sit on the edge of a dirt road in the middle of nowhere, watching smoke billow from underneath my hood.

At the last minute, I suggested that we take my car to Richton instead of his. Sure, his is fancy and quite a bit newer than mine, but mine has more space. A whole lot of good that's doing us *now,* though, as it also becomes clear there's another difference between the two vehicles.

Tate's isn't a lemon.

"There was a mechanic's shop back a couple miles. I'll walk it since this is my fault."

My offer draws this look out of Tate. It's giving *'over my dead fucking body'* vibes, which my mind also interprets as *'hot as fucking sin'* vibes. I suppress a smile because I need to be taken seriously. Because the *offer* was serious.

"No way in hell I'm letting you walk alone out here. It's getting dark, neither of us has any phone reception, and if that huge, dark cloud rolling in is any indication, we're in for a storm soon."

"Yeah, but—"

"It isn't happening," he cuts in, doing that broody, macho thing the other guys have pulled on more than one occasion. It's as if they think they're entitled to having the last word.

He reaches into the backseat for the hoodie he tossed back there when we first set out on the road a few hours ago. Then, he pats his pocket for his wallet. But the second I see him reach for the handle, I reach for mine.

"What are you doing?"

"Walking with you," I say in a matter-of-fact tone. "If you're going, I'm going."

He frowns and it's clear he still doesn't like the idea of it.

"What would you prefer?" I ask. "To leave me here in the dark for at least an hour while you're gone? Anyone could stop and walk up to the car while I'm alone. So, it's safer if I go, too."

There's frustration in his expression, but I can see my words hit the mark. He's caving right before my eyes.

"Fine. Zip your hoodie and don't leave your wallet."

I smile, having gotten my way.

We set out and the first ten minutes into our walk are okay. A little light drizzle never hurt anyone. But the full-on torrential downpour that follows is ungodly. I can barely see from all the water blowing into my face and eyes when the wind kicks up. We're soaked, walking side by side on the edge of the now muddy road, and the shop is still nowhere in sight.

"Watch your step," Tate warns, reaching out to steady me, but he's too late.

My foot dips into a pothole, and I go down in a flash. My hands and knees are filthy, and there's cold mud filling my shoe, soaking my sock. I'm breathless, in shock that this just happened, but the sound of quiet laughter to my right has me peering up, squinting to see Tate trying to hold back.

"You're not gonna even ask if I'm okay?"

The question makes him laugh even harder, but he's now taking my arm, helping me up.

I crack a smile because he's now laughing uncontrollably as he takes in the site of me. But it shuts him up when I fling remnants of mud from my hand to the front of his hoodie.

"There. Now, we match," I say with a grin, no longer bothered by the unprecedented rainfall. I mean, it's not like it can get any worse.

"Oh, we're twins?" he asks, a devious grin on his face as he steps toward me.

Watching his every move, I back up, waiting for him to lunge at me. So, when he does, I quickly hustle to the left and he slips, nearly going down completely, but his athleticism saves him. Instead, he lowers one hand to the mud and manages to catch himself, and then he catches *me* right after. While he could take advantage and toss me down to get revenge, he brings me against his chest and kisses me instead.

The chill of October rain covers us both, wetting our faces and mouths as we savor one another's lips. He warms me a little, lending me a bit of his heat until he lowers me again. My guard is down, so I'm not expecting this to be a trap, but it is. As he holds me to his chest, he smears his hand down the side of my face, covering it with the mud he scooped up when he nearly fell.

"You motherfu—."

He lets go and takes off running before I can even get the whole word out. But I'm right behind him, slipping and sliding over the road, disillusioned in thinking I can actually catch him. Which is why, when I finally *do* get my arms around him, I'm certain it's only because he *wanted* to be caught.

I hold him from behind, which actually shields me from the rain, so I stay there, my forehead resting on his back, arms cinched around his waist while one of his hands rests on top of mine. We walk like this the rest of the way actually, and when we reach the mechanic's shop, I'm marginally less cold and wet than I would've been. Thanks to my human shield.

"Shit."

I peer around Tate when he mumbles the word.

"They're closed?"

"Looks like it."

Which means we just made this trek for nothing. And it also means we've got no car, no place to stay, and we'll also likely miss the guys' game tomorrow.

Shit is right.

He pulls out his phone, checking to see if we're still out of range, and when he lets out a heavy sigh and tucks his phone away again, I can guess that we are.

I look around, spotting the small, single-wide trailer just behind the shop. When I point, Tate's gaze follows.

"Maybe we can knock, see if they'll let us use their phone?"

"Actually, those might be the shop owners," he suggests, and he might be right. These are the only two structures we've seen for miles.

We walk the short distance to the front door, pulling the rickety screen open before knocking. I'm hopeful someone's home since there are a few lights on, but that hope turns into relief when I hear footsteps.

I stand a bit straighter but can't do anything about my appearance. I'm wet and dirty, but it is what it is. Tate reaches for my hand and holds it as the door swings open. On the other side of the threshold, a guy stares back. He looks to be around sixty or so, but with the obvious dye job to his hair, it's clear he wants us to think he's younger than that.

"Can I help you?" He casts a suspicious look toward Tate and I, eyeing our clothes.

"Yeah, sorry to bother you, but our car overheated up the road a couple miles. We were hoping a mechanic could help, but the shop is closed. Is it yours?"

The guy cranes his neck a bit, as if to make sure we're alone. Then, he nods. "It is."

Tate breathes a sigh of relief. "Is there any way we could get a tow and maybe have you take a look at it tonight? I'll pay extra since it's after hours."

The man waves him off. "I wouldn't charge extra, but the trouble is I don't have access to a tow truck. And I won't until morning."

I see that small inkling of hope drain from Tate's shoulders.

"Damn it." He thinks for a second. "Then would you mind if we use your phone? And if you have a phonebook, maybe we can find another shop. We're kind of in a hurry."

The man's already shaking his head before Tate finishes speaking. "No can do. I mean, not that I mind you using my phone, but you won't find another mechanic around here. I'm the only one for miles, and none of them will send a truck out this far with it being so close to closing time."

"Terry, who is it? Dinner's on the table."

We now know his name is Terry, and we also know his dinner is getting cold.

"We didn't mean to bother you. Enjoy your evening, sir," Tate says, turning to head back down the steps, but before we make it to the bottom, a second shadow darkens the doorway.

"You folks need some help?"

I peer over my shoulder and find a short, thin woman standing beside Terry. I can assume the voice we heard before belongs to her.

"Uh, we did, but I think we're just kind of screwed for tonight," Tate says, flashing a polite smile as he blinks rainwater off his lashes.

"Their car broke down up the road, and I just explained to them that we won't have a truck until morning," Terry says.

The woman frowns. "Then, why didn't you invite them in?" She doesn't seem to realize she's half Terry's size when she shoves him aside, widening the door. "You're just in time for dinner."

She offers a warm smile, and I glance at Tate before removing my dirty shoes and socks, and then stepping inside. He trails me and, in my head, I'm already listing the *numerous* slasher movies that have started with this exact same scenario. I'm not fooled by the charming living room set with a doily placed over the back of the sofa, or the collectible tea sets in the curio cabinet. These people could seriously be having *last night's* visitors for dinner this evening.

"I'm Lizzie, by the way."

I glance at Tate again when the woman introduces herself. Lizzie, as in… Lizzie Borden?

I shake the thought from my head, choosing *not* to believe this woman is the infamous axe murderer reincarnate, but rather that she's just a kind woman who brought us in out of the rain.

Happy thoughts, Stevie.

"We're Tate and Stevie," Tate says.

"Should be easy enough to remember." She stops at the counter, but with the place being so small, we still have a full visual of her from the middle of the living room. She's grabbing two extra bowls from the cabinet, and then makes her way over to the stove. "Terry, why don't you get these nice people a couple towels to clean up with while I finish up here."

With a small sigh, Terry does as he's asked, passing Tate and I on his way to a small closet in the hallway, where he retrieves washcloths and towels that he then hands to us.

"Bathroom's the first door on the left. Can't miss it," he says, offering a faint smile.

I glance toward Tate for reassurance, not feeling super comfortable going *anywhere* in this house without him, but he nods, letting me know he thinks it's safe. So, off I go.

Behind the closed door, I turn on the water, then do a quick sweep of the bathroom. It's clean and organized, but there's nothing that says a murderer can't be tidy. There's nothing that indicates these people are weirdos, though, so I relax a little, deciding to do what I came in here to do in the first place, wash my hands and face.

Thick mud rinses down the drain, and I wipe the few droplets of water I left on the sink before going back out to join the others. I nod silently at Tate to let him know things seem cool, and then he heads into the bathroom to do the same. While I wait, I watch in silence, listening to the offbeat banter between Terry and Lizzie, who have resorted to debating whether the new mark on Terry's hand is just a new liver spot or something more concerning. Which is why I *also* know he'll be heading to the doctor first thing Monday morning.

Well, I can at least say they're relatively normal.

Tate reemerges and I'm grateful he's back. And just in time, too.

"Have a seat. Lucky for you, I made plenty," Lizzie says with a smile.

"Best beef stew for miles," Terry comments, dropping down before his own bowl at the head of the table.

Tate has my hand again, leading me behind him as we approach the kitchen. We sit side-by-side, and Lizzie places two portions in front of us, a slice of bread on top. She comes back with spoons and napkins, then drops down into the seat across from me.

"If you two need a place to lay your heads for the night, you're welcome to stay," she offers.

"We got rid of the spare bed just last week. Our son bought it off us, but the couch is just as comfortable," Terry adds, drawing a laugh out of Lizzie.

"He should know. I've made him sleep there on too many occasions to count."

Terry rolls his eyes, likely remembering a few of those instances.

Tate tries the stew, and I'm apprehensive, probably just being overly cautious. But when he nods, letting Lizzie know Terry was right to pay her such a high compliment, I dig in because I'm starving. Within five minutes, I'm staring at the bottom of my bowl.

"Can I get you more, dear?" Lizzie asks.

"No, but thank you. I'm stuffed."

She nods, and then gets up to clear the table. "Well, the offer still stands. If you'd like to crash here for the night, you're more than welcome."

Tate looks at me, and when I shrug, he turns to Lizzie again. "Thank you. We'd appreciate that."

A smile stretches her cheeks as she begins rinsing dishes in the sink. "I mean, provided you two are married, of course." After speaking, she lifts her gaze to the cross hung above the sink. "We can't very well condone sin taking place under our roof."

I slide Tate a look, but he's already looking at me.

"You *are* married, aren't you?"

Tate and I simultaneously hide our left hands underneath the table, which Terry at least notices.

"Uh… yes, ma'am. For a year now," Tate answers, and I hold in a smile. Noticing how Terry's eyes have suddenly fixated on me, I nod a few times, going along with Tate's lie.

Lizzie smiles. "How nice. The first five years are always the toughest, then you find your groove and it's smooth sailing from there."

I catch Terry rolling his eyes, and I wonder if it only became smooth sailing for Lizzie.

"Something tells me there will be no tough days with this one," Tate says, smiling at me just enough to make my stomach flutter. The thought crosses my mind, envisioning what it would be like spending forever with him.

"Yeah, well, just live long enough," Lizzie teases, and then turns off the sink before placing the dishes on the rack to dry. She faces us again. "I'll grab blankets and a couple pillows from the storage trunk. And I think we might have a couple pieces of clothing that should fit you both. At least until you get the chance to toss your things in the wash."

"That would be great," I chime in. It's a miracle she even tolerated us sitting at her table with how dirty our clothes are, still sporting remnants of mud from our fight earlier. The rain did its part to wash *some* of it away, but we could still use a little help.

"Then it's settled," she smiles. "Terry and I like to turn in early, so if you two don't mind keeping it down, we'll get along famously."

"Oh, right. Of course," Tate replies. "We're pretty out of it ourselves after being on the road all day."

"First thing in the morning, I'll get on having your vehicle towed in, so I can take a look at it and get you two back on the road. Sound good?" Terry asks.

"Sounds perfect. And again, thank you both so much for your kindness."

Smiling at Tate's polite words, our hosts head down a narrow hall-way, and Tate and I make our way over to the sofa. I shoot the guys a quick text to explain the strange turn our evening has taken, then set my phone aside, hoping it eventually goes through. By the time we sit, Lizzie returns with the promised blankets, pillows, and changes of clothes. She smiles sweetly, tells us goodnight, and then proceeds to turn off the lights after locking up.

The moment we're alone again, we sort through the neatly folded pile of clothes Lizzie brought, and I do a quick sniff test. The hint of lavender eases my mind.

"All good. They're clean."

Smiling, Tate arches a brow, then proceeds to whisper. "Did you honestly think that sweet old lady would bring us clothes from their hamper?" he asks, slipping out of his hoodie and t-shirt, and then out of his jeans.

I admire him for a moment, loving the way his boxer briefs hug his toned thighs and the impressive bulge in the front. But before I can get caught, I turn away.

"Sweet is relative," I finally shoot back. "Haven't you ever heard the saying *'you get more with sugar than you do with shit?'* Of course, she'd be sweet. That's how they lure you in, how they get you to let your guard down."

"They?"

I nod. "Serial killers."

He shakes his head again, laughing as he steps into a pair of plaid pajama pants that match the night shirt I'm guessing is meant for me. I pull off the damp clothing we walked here in, and put on the night shirt, holding it out from my body as I take in the sight of us.

"Dressed like this, we really *do* look like a married couple, don't we?" As soon as the words leave my mouth, I regret saying them, knowing that could've sounded a bit creepy. I don't *actually* think matching clothes are an indication of marriage, I just…

Tate pauses while spreading one of the blankets over the couch, then turns to face me. He smiles, seeing what I've put on, and it's safe to say he didn't take my words the wrong way.

"Well, if that were true, I'd be a lucky man," he says, and then casually turns back to finish setting up our bed for the night. I'm grateful he's no longer staring, grateful for the darkness. If it weren't for that, he'd see how his words made me blush.

He finishes, and then gestures toward the couch. "Which side do you want?"

I tilt my head a few times before deciding. "I'll take the inside, you take the outside."

He stares, quirking a brow at my answer.

"Oh, I thought you were going to take one end and I'd take the other, but—"

"Right. That'd probably be more comfortable than both of us smashed together on one end. I just thought—"

"Stevie," he cuts in, quieting me as he flashes that subtly sexy smirk that should be illegal. "I like your idea better."

My face warms again, and I find myself thinking wicked thoughts. Thoughts that would have poor sweet Lizzie clutching her pearls.

I settle onto the couch, getting as close to the back cushion as possible. Then, Tate clicks the TV off and slides in behind me. We're silent as we lie there, my body comfortably wedged between his chest and the back of the sofa. I feel completely safe, even in this town I've never heard of, under the roof of people I've never met.

Because I'm with *him.*

I'm just starting to relax, closing my eyes when Tate sighs, and the heat of his breath moves across my ear. The feel of it makes me stir a bit, as my skin awakens with goosebumps. I squirm, creating just enough friction between us to have my thoughts wandering into unholy territory. And at the feel of his cock hardening behind me, I'm guessing that did it for him, too.

"Sorry," I say softly, hoping he knows I wasn't trying to get him aroused.

"You're fine."

I'm starting to think tonight might be unbearable. Especially as I begin to fantasize about our last time together. Lying like this, I should've known sleep would be the last thing on either of our minds. There's this unnervingly high level of heat that's always smoldering between us, and I suppose I forgot to account for that before suggesting this arrangement.

"We're officially newlyweds now, right?" Tate rasps, drawing a smile from me.

"That's the word around town," I tease.

His chest moves with a soft laugh. "Then, I've got an idea."

"And I'm interested in hearing it."

He inches closer, and his erection persists against my ass, making my nipples harden into stones against the fabric of my night shirt.

"Lizzie said they turn in early, so I'm thinking the second we hear silence coming from that back bedroom, we... *celebrate*."

With those words, his hand leaves my thigh, gathering the fabric of my gown. And when he cups my pussy, I suck in a breath through my teeth. It seems sneaking around, fucking at the most inopportune times, in the most inopportune places, is Tate's thing. So, being the tease that I am, I push my hips back, needing to feel him more. I don't stop until I draw a groan from him, and with three simple words, I let him know I'm game.

"Yes, Mr. Ford."

Chapter 35

Stevie

Terry and Lizzie clunk around their room for what feels like forever, having one final spat that apparently couldn't be put off until morning. We're growing impatient waiting for them to finally settle down for the night, so we find creative ways to entertain ourselves.

Which includes Tate sliding his hand inside my panties.

His fingers separate my lips, and then tease my clit. I'm already slippery, feeling my heart race just at the thought of having his dick inside me again. His lips are hot against my neck when he kisses me there, sucking and then teasing his tongue in a circle, matching the rhythm of how he swirls my clit.

"I can't wait to fuck you," he whispers, and my eyes drift closed, remembering that night in his old bed, with our parents on the other side of the wall. We had every reason to stop, every reason not to cross that boundary, but our bodies tend to overpower our morals. When I'm close to him, I want to be closer.

He pushes his fingers deep and lets out a breath, realizing how wet I am. "You're so fucking ready for me."

And I am. Completely. So much that I listen harder, checking for noise coming from Lizzie and Terry's bedroom. It seems they've gone quiet, so I listen a few seconds longer and the silence seems consistent.

"I think they're asleep," I whisper, and that seems good enough for Tate.

There's movement behind me as he reaches into the slit of his pajama pants, freeing his dick. Then, he lifts my leg, directing me to prop my foot on the back of the couch while he tugs my panties out of the way. A quivering breath leaves me when I feel his tip prodding between my lips when he guides himself there, and then with one confident push, he's inside me, rocking his pelvis against my ass while we pant, breathing as quietly as we can while every nerve in my body comes to life.

My gown gathers in Tate's hand when he pushes it up my body until he finds my breast. He squeezes and doesn't let go, resting his chin in the crook of my neck while he pumps his hips—slow and powerful, reaching deep inside me with every motion.

"I've missed this," he breathes. "I don't care who thinks it's wrong. I will *never* stop fucking you."

My pussy floods and the sound of my wetness fills the room. Tate pistons his hips harder and faster, and neither of us cares much about how the couch squeaks beneath us. I'm so close to coming. The tension in his body as he holds me from behind hints that he is, too.

He teases me a little, only giving me the tip while I writhe against him, silently begging him to go deeper. And then he does, plunging all the way inside me as the couch groans beneath us even louder now.

I can only imagine what these poor people must think of us if the sound carries back to their bedroom, but I honestly don't give a fuck. Or at least I didn't... until the bedroom door swings open and one of our hosts comes trudging down the hall.

I drop my foot from the back of the couch and draw it back beneath the blanket. Tate is perfectly still behind me, still balls deep in my pussy as someone crosses through the living room and into the kitchen.

Through my closed lids, I'm aware of a faint light filling the space when the switch clicks. We're frozen, both trying to steady our breaths, so we don't give ourselves away, but... he's still so hard inside me. I'm losing my shit, waiting, wishing whoever's wandered out and ruined our session would go back to bed.

A cabinet creaks, a glass slides across the shelf, then the sink turns on. And with that sound, Tate shifts behind me, sliding his dick in with one slow, delicious push.

I suppress a moan, but it's harder the second time. My heart's racing, knowing we could easily get caught any second, but I can't tell him to stop. Not when he feels so good inside me.

Whoever's at the sink drinks loudly as Tate draws his hips back, and then slowly feeds me his length again, and that's all I can take. Right there, with someone maybe ten feet away, I'm coming.

My breaths deepen, and I nearly draw blood when my teeth clamp down on my lip, but Tate's relentless, pulling out and driving in again, with that same deliberately slow pace that proved to be my undoing. My nipples harden against his palm as he continues holding my breast beneath the cover, and I push my hips back toward him.

A silent whimper claws its way up my throat as I clench around him. Then, a moment later, the kitchen light clicks off again, and whoever had come in at the perfectly wrong time, leaves just as I begin to descend from my orgasm.

Tate's body goes still for a moment, and I lean away, exposing more of my neck as he places a kiss there.

"Good girl," he whispers, and I know he likes that I'm learning to keep quiet.

He doesn't even wait until the one who crashed our party is back in the bedroom before thrusting in again, quickly picking up speed as my pussy squeezes around him. His pelvis slams my ass and the moment the bedroom door closes, he grunts behind me, filling me with liquid heat.

The couch goes quiet and so do we, lying perfectly still as our breath steadies. Tate's hand that once cupped my chest moves to my chin, forcing me to turn and kiss him over my shoulder. I suck his tongue, feeling him soften inside me. The angle is awkward and stretching my neck in this way causes a twinge of pain, but those things are hardly a concern.

"That was close." I smile into another kiss before Tate lets me go. "You like playing dangerous, I see."

I expect him to laugh, but he's silent, which draws my eyes back toward him.

"Maybe a little *too* dangerous."

My curiosity piques. So much that I turn over and face him. "What do you mean?"

Through the darkness, his eyes wander a bit, and the feeling of having my question being avoided sets my nerves on edge.

"What am I missing?"

He finally meets my gaze. "The last time we were together, my dad... he saw me climbing down from your window in the middle of the night."

My stomach rolls, and I immediately feel sick, and seeing me spiral, Tate takes my face in both hands.

"He probably thinks I'm terrible. Probably thinks *we're* terrible." A million thoughts race through my head and as much as I don't care to think of my mother right now, I can't stop myself from wondering if she knows, too. "Oh, God."

I bury my face in my hands, but Tate pulls them down, forcing me to look into his eyes.

"I threw him off our scent. He has no idea," Tate assures me, and it takes a moment for my head to catch up and actually believe him.

But my next thought isn't so black and white, isn't so clean cut. In the very recent past, Tate wasn't sure about this, wasn't sure about *us,* all because of what he feared our being together could mean for our parents. And while neither of us wants to stand in the way of their happiness, Tate had taken a considerably stronger stance on the situation than I did. Which is why, now, after hearing about what Rob saw, I'm admittedly a little scared.

"Are you... Does this mean you're gonna check out on me again?" I force the question from my lips before I lose the nerve to ask it.

Tate's brow gathers and he looks deeper into my eyes now. "Stevie, I'm not going anywhere. I'm in this. All the way. No matter what."

I study what I can see of his features in the darkness, and something about the sincerity in his eyes comforts me, lets me know there's nothing to worry about this time. So, I kiss him, letting him know I'm choosing to trust his promise.

"I need to clean up. Be right back."

He steals one more kiss before letting me go, offering his hand as I climb over him and stumble to my feet.

It's a dark, clunky walk to the bathroom, but I make it and rinse off a bit before rejoining Tate on the couch. He wraps me in his arms, holding me as his breathing slows. I yawn once and close my eyes, only opening them again when he speaks.

"Goodnight, Mrs. Ford," he teases, and I can't fight the laugh that leaves me. One so loud there's no way Lizzie and Terry don't hear it.

His chest moves when he chuckles, too, and then starts to drift for real this time. Lying there, on the brink of sleep *myself,* I recap our day. At first, this night all felt like one incredibly long string of disasters, but as I lie here with him, wearing the goofiest pair of matching plaid pajamas known to man, I couldn't have dreamed up a more perfect night if I tried.

So, maybe disasters aren't disasters at all.

Maybe they're fate showing us that, on occasion, good things come to us in ways we'd never see coming. The lesson of the day is a simple one for me.

Expect the unexpected, and no matter what... keep your heart open.

Chapter 36

Stevie

Our morning flew by in a blur.

First, my car was towed to the shop where Terry sorted out what the issue was. Busted radiator fan. So, while he worked on replacing it, Lizzie let Tate and I shower and change once we had access to our luggage. Then, in just enough time to make it to the guys' game, we set out on the road again.

It was around the halfway mark of our trip that I got an interesting text.

Frank: If you're still interested in seeing Nora, my connection at the facility says they can get us in tomorrow. It's a one-shot deal, so are you in or out?

Stevie: Definitely in.

Frank: Meet me at the station around noon. I'll drive.

I've gone over what I'll say to Nora a hundred times, and now that I've got less than twenty-four hours until seeing her, I'm wondering if I even know enough to ask the *right* questions. But it's now or never, and like Frank said, this is a onetime shot.

Tate and I make the drive to the arena and, seeing as how it's almost time for the game to start, it's no surprise it's completely packed. So packed that the only parking spaces left are on the furthest side of the lot. In addition to the hundreds of cars and trucks, there are even nearly a dozen charter buses, too, painting a picture of the kind of mass chaos that awaits us on the other side of the arena doors.

It would've been nice to at least speak to the guys before the game —beyond the texts I sent this morning—but at this point, Tate and I are lucky we made it here at *all*. There was one hiccup after another, but we pushed through it to be supportive.

We make our way inside with the last of the stragglers. The decked out crowd is just about an even fifty-fifty split between our boys and their opponents. Some brought signs with messages for their favorite players, some have jersey numbers painted on their faces like me. Although, I'm sure I'm the only person with *three* numbers painted on her cheeks and neck. But overall, even just walking up, the fandom for *both* teams is clear. Here's hoping Bradwyn pulls out a win, even if I'm mostly rooting for only three players.

Tate and I slide into our seats and the arena is jammed packed, as expected. Our burgundy, Bradwyn U t-shirts make us fit in perfectly with this section of the crowd. We're down near the floor, almost right behind the glass, and my heart's already racing from excitement.

"Is it weird that I'm a little nervous?" I lean in to ask.

Tate smiles. "Don't be. As a former King, I can confidently say we've got this in the bag tonight."

"That's a pretty steep claim you're making."

Still smiling, he shrugs. "I mean, everyone has to live with a loss every now and then, but tonight won't likely be one of them."

"Why? Does the other team suck that bad?"

"They don't suck, but it's rare that they beat us. *Extremely* rare," he adds.

"Do you miss it sometimes?"

He gives my question some thought. "I do, but I never had plans to go pro or anything. Hockey started off being the thing that gave me direction when I didn't really have any, then it turned into a brother-hood, and now it's a core memory for me. I wouldn't be who I am today if it weren't for hockey. I think we all have that thing that anchored us."

Hearing him mention this, I think of my body positivity group, how that space is the anchor for so many. I've had to step away while I manage my *own* emotions, fearing what might happen if I pile on the baggage of others, but maybe it's time. Maybe I'm nearly ready.

The lights dim, and the crowd's practically buzzing with anticipation, but the arena fills with an odd, lingering silence. But then a loud voice booms from the speakers and the room livens up once more.

"Ladies and gents, we're honored to welcome you to tonight's exciting matchup! Please focus your attention center ice as we present to you the starting lineup of our very own Ravens, and their formidable opponents, the Kings."

My eyes are drawn to a now brightly lit tunnel across the ice when a spotlight shifts that way. The once silent crowd suddenly explodes into cheers and applause, and Tate and I are on our feet, too.

One at a time, the players file out of the tunnel, their bodies rigid with intense focus and confidence. Their blades etch thin lines in the ice, and goosebumps enliven my skin. I don't think I realized until this very moment how much I've looked forward to seeing Vince, Micah, and Ash in action. Once the Ravens have all taken to the ice, standing on one side of the blue line, I listen intently as the names of the Kings are given next.

All three of my guys are called out first, and I scream at the top of my lungs. Laughing, Tate shoots me a surprised look, maybe not realizing I had it in me.

"Let's go! You've got this, boys!"

The Kings stand posted on the other side of the line, staring down their opponents. Even from here, I can see the tension, and it doesn't subside during the National Anthem. I find myself wishing I were inside the guys' heads, feeding off the adrenaline and determination.

Both sides get into position, and when the ref drops the puck, signaling the start of the game, it's like the noise of the crowd takes on a life of its own. I can hardly hear myself think over the sound of it, and I'm screaming right along with them, knowing I'll likely be hoarse by the end of the game.

My entire body vibrates with excitement, intently focused on every pass, every shoulder check, every goal that carries the Kings closer to a win. Tate was right, there isn't anything to worry about. While the Ravens are indeed worthy opponents, our boys are far more skilled. Their footwork, their precision. It's like watching living art.

I'm on the edge of my seat, watching as Ash slices through the Ravens' defense and makes a goal that seemed like such a longshot. It's so impressive that a guy seated a row behind us jumps out of his chair so fast that he dumps his bucket of popcorn on the head of the kid sitting a couple seats down from me. The moment ends with an apology and a few laughs, and then everyone's right back in the game.

Tate and I are on our feet with the rest of the crowd. Micah meets the Raven's center in the circle, and they're glaring at one another until the puck falls between them. Micah's quick, gaining possession of the puck, and from there, everything moves so fast. My heart races to match the pacing, and I don't realize I'm smiling as I watch until my cheeks begin to hurt from the strain.

"Yeah! Keep that up!" Tate yells, and it feels like I haven't blinked since the game began. I imagined how it would be, seeing them on the ice, but no amount of imagination could've prepared me for this.

My emotions sway with the rhythm of the game. I'm elated and cheering when we have possession of the puck, then I'm on pins and needles when we don't, despite being up a point. And by the time the period ends, and intermission begins, I'm in desperate need of a break.

"I'm gonna go grab snacks. Want anything?" Tate asks.

"I'll take a bottled water and popcorn. Need help?"

He shakes his head. "Nah, I can manage."

"Then, I'm gonna run to the bathroom. Meet you back here in a few."

He's off in one direction, and I head in another, following the signs to the restroom area. I find it pretty quickly, and while I didn't really need to use it, I do need the short breather.

I listen to chatter about the game and the weather going on around me as I turn on the sink. Dampening a paper towel, I dab it over my eyes, but I'm careful not to smudge the guys' numbers. The water is cool and calming, bringing me back down from the high of the first period.

I lower the paper towel back underneath the flow to wet it a bit more, but when I shift to touch it to my eyes, I stop dead in my tracks. Because I'm staring at the last person I expected to see standing over my shoulder, wearing the annoying red t-shirt of her sorority.

Fucking Dahlia.

I don't speak. Actually, if it weren't for the fact that we made eye contact, I wouldn't have acknowledged her at all.

"Look who it is," she croons. "My old roomie. How have things been?"

She has to be putting on this act for those around us, because we both know she doesn't really care what my answer would be.

"Fuck off, Dahlia."

My crass response has a mom glaring at me as she covers her daughter's ears, and then promptly escorts her out of the restroom.

"Looks like you're healing up nicely after you're little... incident," Dahlia points out, lowering her voice on that last word.

I turn off the sink, glaring at her in the mirror's reflection. "Speaking of healing, it looks like the swelling in your face is finally going down from when I beat your ass."

Now, there are a few more eyes and ears paying attention, and I'm not nearly as embarrassed as I probably should be. And from the looks of things, that was just enough to get under Dahlia's skin. She steps closer, pure hatred in her eyes as she speaks.

"Careful, bitch. Wouldn't want anything *else* to happen to you."

She starts toward the door, and I call out after her. "That an admission of guilt?"

She smiles. "Nope. Simply a warning from one friend to another," she says. "And if I were you, I'd stop with the pranks. You don't want to see how far I can take things."

My brow tenses. "What the fuck are you talking about?"

She rolls her eyes in annoyance. "Sure, play innocent. I don't give a fuck. Just know that you and your boy toys don't scare me."

"Wait."

"Fuck you, Stevie," she says as I begin trailing her to the door.

With my eyes glued to the back of her head, she exits the bathroom and I'm fuming. The excitement and joy I'd felt just a moment ago is completely sullied now.

Thanks to *this* bitch.

What fucking pranks is she talking about?

It doesn't sit well with me that she just walked out like that, giving zero clarity as to what she's even talking about. I'm pissed because she can never just... cooperate. I'm not really sure what I'll say or do to get answers out of her, but lucky for her, she's gone, disappeared into thin air. So, when I spot Tate, I go to *him* instead, stepping up to the concession stand just as the cashier hands him our food and drinks.

His eyes light up with surprise when he sees me, but the look quickly fades as we step away from the counter with our snacks in hand.

"You okay? Did something happen?"

Okay, so maybe I'm not hiding my frustration as well as I thought I was.

"I'm good," I sigh. "Just ran into my old roommate in the bathroom."

Right away, his head is on the swivel, searching the area for someone who might look suspicious. None of us have ruled her out for having had a hand in what happened to me, but there isn't a whole lot we can do about it here.

We walk to our seats again in silence. Me, because I'm furious and filled with unshed frustration. Him, because he's letting me be in my feelings, I guess. But when we're sitting, and he tosses a piece of popcorn against the side of my face just to make me laugh, it works.

"Keep it up and I'll divorce you," I tease, reminding him of the lie we had to live the night before.

"Good thing I had you sign that prenup."

I throw a *handful* of popcorn at him. "Asshole!" I whisper, but he's laughing so hard he probably didn't even hear me. All of a sudden, it's like nothing was ever wrong, like I hadn't just seen my nemesis in the bathroom.

The game restarts and the second period is just as fast-paced as the first. Our boys are still up a point, but that changes in the last few seconds when the Ravens tie it up. This time, we stay seated during intermission, and when the final period begins, there's a strange vibe in the arena. Both sides are hopeful, but both sides also have a healthy sense of pessimism because someone has to lose.

"Thought you said this was a sure thing."

Tate shrugs. "Well, that was before I saw they made a few adjustments to their roster. They picked up a few guys from Clifton Heights. *Good* players."

I settle back in my seat when he's done whispering, and I'm a bundle of nerves, watching the minutes wind down on the clock.

The Kings gain possession again with twenty seconds left on the clock, and Vince has the puck. The other team is on his ass, trying to get in his way *and* in his head, but he's sharp, calculated.

I stand to my feet, unable to stay in my chair as I watch the swift, skillful movements of his skates, holding my breath as he nears the goal. Another defender closes in on him, but Vince isn't fazed. The crowd waits, holding their breath, but then there's an eruption of cheers and screams as Vince swipes his stick toward the puck, and slices it in past the goalie just as time runs out. There's intense emotion on the ice and here in the stands, as fans of both teams process the outcome of the game.

Tate sweeps me into a hug and my feet leave the ground for a second.

"They fucking did it!"

"Told you they would."

I let him have this one, even though there was a moment in there that he wasn't so sure.

"Can we talk to them?" I ask. "We didn't get to see them before the game and they're leaving straight from here to catch their plane."

Tate looks for an opening in the crowd. "If we're fast, we might be able to catch them at the tunnel."

It's not a guarantee, but I'll take it, desperate to at least lay eyes on them before they're gone. I shoulder check a couple people to get through, but it's worth the dirty looks and name calling. Because there they are.

My boys.

I'm not even sure they'll see or hear me with all the chaos, but Ash is pretty close.

"Looking good, seventeen!" I call out.

He glances around at first, trying to find me, and when he does, his smile is infectious. He nudges Micah and Vince to get their attention, too. And now, all three giants are coming this way.

Ash makes it to me first, and I imagine that the triumphant glow I find in his eyes is there after every win. I thought they'd just come close enough to maybe touch my hand, but when Ash, steps up, hanging onto the rail, he kisses me in front of everyone.

The scent of sweat and hard work might be a turnoff to some, but not me. That shit's like a fucking drug to me right now. I'm still reeling when he releases me, and I'm painfully aware of everyone close enough to have witnessed the act is currently staring. And that attention only grows when Vince steps up next, holding the rail with one hand and pressing his helmet to my lower back as he pulls me close. The flavor of his Chapstick lingers on my lips when he hops down, and then winks at me before continuing to the locker room.

Micah makes it to me last and my heart's still thundering. It's no surprise when he steps up, too, and by now I'm sure the crowd has drawn their own conclusion about my closeness to the King's star players, but when Micah shoves his tongue down my throat, gripping my ass with one hand as he sucks my lips, I imagine they've given up trying to guess.

Our eyes lock when he pulls away.

"You were amazing out there. Good game."

He smirks, and I swear my entire circulatory system malfunctions.

"We had to pull out a win for our girl, didn't we?" That question leaves him, and he bites his lip in this teasing way before climbing down. Meanwhile, that phrase is still ringing inside my head.

Our girl.

I back away from the railing now that they're gone, and Tate's hand slips into mine. We make our way toward the exit, moving at a snail's pace with the rest of the crowd when I spot Dahlia. She'd been seated just above the tunnel, which I hadn't noticed until now, but that definitely means she saw me with the guys. My connection to them has always been a sore spot with her, so I'm sure that display just pissed her off even more.

Which is why I decide to add fuel to the fire and flip her not one, but two middle fingers. Because, seriously, with how big a bitch she is, she totally deserves a double fuck you.

But as soon as I turn away from her, it's like she no longer exists. Tonight was perfect in every way imaginable, and I'm not about to let Dahlia ruin that.

Not in a million years.

Chapter 37

Ash

Calls from my uncle and grandfather are easy to ignore. Even when they called in fifteen-minute rotations the entire time I was out of town for the game.

But a call from the cops?

Yeah, not so easy to ignore.

I've been sitting with this detective for almost half an hour, and he still hasn't managed to back me into a corner.

Not for lack of trying, though.

"Your grandfather told us you play for Bradwyn's hockey team. Is that right?"

Bored with this conversation already, I nod. "Yes, sir."

"You guys had your first game last night, didn't you?"

Again, I nod. "Yes, sir."

"So? How'd it go? Did you win?"

I take a breath and let it out slowly. "Yes, sir."

"My brother played in high school years ago. He hoped to play for Bradwyn, but didn't make the cut," he shares.

"Pity."

He glares, knowing I'm being a smart-ass. When he glances down at his paperwork again, I assume he's getting back on topic.

"This report says that you outright vandalized your grandfather's place—broke personal effects, bleached the furniture, urinated on his clothing and his bed. All while the man was burying his wife?"

There's judgement in this guy's tone, but I don't let it sway me.

"Someone did these things, yes. But it wasn't me."

We lock eyes and he doesn't blink. "Hm. Wasn't you. Interesting."

"It is. But it isn't so hard to believe, considering my grandfather is a man with a lot of enemies."

"Is that so?"

"It is."

"Is there anyone in particular you think we need to take a look at?"

A laugh slips out when he asks. "Sure, start with every co-worker he's ever had, half the girls at the strip club over on Clover, my grand-mother's entire side of the family, and every cashier, bank teller, and customer service rep he's ever had contact with."

The detective lowers his pen, realizing I'm not likely to be of any help to him. So, he sips his coffee instead, staring me down. My gaze drifts out the window and that's when I spot someone I never expected to see walking into the front entrance of the station.

Bird.

My brow tenses for a second before I catch myself and straighten my expression. For some reason, I don't want this cop knowing Bird's somehow connected to me.

"Am I done here?"

He stares me down a few seconds longer, then lifts his hands in defeat. "For now, but keep your phone handy in case we have more questions."

"Will do," I say casually as I stand, keeping my eyes trained on Bird as I make my way back toward the door that leads to the waiting room.

I pull it and it doesn't budge.

"Step back. I need to buzz you out," an officer behind the counter informs me, so I do as he says and wait for the buzz before rushing out to the waiting area.

Bird looks up when my steps make a small commotion. She's clearly just as shocked to see me as I am to see her.

"What are you doing here?" she says.

"I was going to ask you the same thing."

Her lips purse together, and she glances around, as if she doesn't want the few people holding down chairs around us to overhear.

"Outside," she says in a quiet voice, motioning for me to follow.

She doesn't speak again until we're out on the sidewalk. "It's about my sister," she says. "I think I might be able to get answers."

I open my mouth to speak, but stop when a tall, burly guy walks past, eyeing Bird.

"I'll be in the car. Don't make me wait," he says, glaring at her before flashing a dark look toward me, too.

"Be there in one sec," Bird answers, and my mouth opens again. This time to ask this guy who the fuck he thinks he's talking to, but Bird places her hands on my chest. "Don't. He's helping me," she says.

"You're getting in the car with this asshole?" My gaze flashes toward his dark sedan, and I memorize the license plate.

"I have to. He's taking me to see his niece. She's a friend of my sister," she explains, but her eyes slam shut when she corrects herself. "*Was* a friend of my sister. Anyway, she's in a facility and today's the only day we're able to get in and... I just... I need you to trust me, and I need you to let me go."

I hold her gaze, remembering how it felt to find her on the cement in that abandoned warehouse. It's enough that I can't in good conscience let her leave with this dickhead unattended. But because she's so adamant, and because she's in such a rush, I don't press.

So, when I nod, she stretches up on her feet to kiss my cheek, and I let her walk off. She doesn't have to know I've got my own plan.

Stevie

Ash doesn't even try to hide that he's following us. He hasn't bothered to hang back or let cars get between him and us. He's blatant with his pursuit and all I can do is shake my head as I watch him pull into the parking lot of Nora's facility right behind me and Frank, and then park a few spots over.

I shoot him a look as we walk inside, and sure enough, his cocky ass smiles and waves.

So much for letting me do this on my own, I guess.

We get buzzed into the facility, and then Frank stops at the counter. He gives the attendant our names, then tells her who we're here to visit, and we're handed two visitor's passes and told to have a seat in the waiting room.

I can still see Ash's truck, see his inked arm hanging out the open window while he stares right back at me like the stalker he is. But I can't be mad at him. What happened to me affected us all, so when I think of it like that, having him follow me is... kind of sweet.

Kind of.

"That your guy?"

My gaze shifts to Frank when he asks. I blink a few times, not quite knowing what to say.

"You could call him that."

"Hm," he grumbles. "Does he escort you *everywhere* or is today a special occasion?"

My gaze shifts toward Ash, but I don't answer because Frank's clearly just being a smart-ass.

"Your dad met him?" he asks.

The question prompts an eye roll. One so fierce it leaves me dizzy. "We already went over this, remember? He isn't my dad."

Frank shrugs with a sigh. "We did, but... I'm sure he didn't just cut you off cold turkey."

I glare at him, wondering if he's blind. Or maybe it's just that they're such good friends he refuses to see the truth.

That the man formerly known as my father, is a real asshole.

"Trust me, he definitely cut me off," I finally say, and Frank goes quiet. Maybe because he's coming to grips with the same ugly truth that I've had to face.

He witnessed my father's cruelty and mistreatment, so he must've known this would put the final nail in the coffin.

For better or worse.

"I'm sorry to hear it's played out like this, kid."

"Yeah, well *I'm* not. It's best this way."

Frank sits in silence and I'm okay with that. Pity isn't what I need from him. All he owed me was bringing me here, and now his work is done.

"Right this way," a nurse says, offering a smile as she gestures toward a long hallway to the left of the reception area. Frank grips the arms of his seat to stand when I turn to him.

"Would you mind if I talk to her alone first?"

He holds my gaze, as if he's surprised I have the nerve to ask for yet another favor.

"Please. There are things we need to discuss regarding my sister, and I don't know if she'll talk freely in front of *me,* let alone in front of *you,* so…"

Frank puffs a sigh, and then that hardened look on his face softens.

"Make it quick," he says. "And let her know I'm out here waiting to see her."

I nod. "Of course."

I stand and leave before he has a chance to change his mind, and the entire walk back, I'm going over what I'll say, what I'll ask. And by the time the nurse and I push through a set of locked double-doors, and I lay eyes on Nora, I've at least got some semblance of direction.

"Thank you," I say, smiling at the nurse as she exits the room. And now, it's just Nora and me.

The space is cold and sterile, white painted walls, white tile with green flecks in it, a lone telephone on the far wall, and a sea of empty, round tables. Well, empty except for the one right in front of me where Nora sits staring, looking like she's seen a ghost.

"Well, shit! If *this* isn't a surprise!"

She smiles, the piercing in her lip glinting in the pale, fluorescent light.

"Hey. You look good," I say, thinking she looks a lot healthier than she did the last time I saw her. Which also happens to be the time we fought.

She's cropped her blond hair into a pixie cut, and there are more tattoos and piercings than I remember. But even without the heavy makeup I'm used to seeing her in, she's pretty.

"To what do I owe this pleasure?" she croons, a devious grin set on her lips. Watching me lower into the seat across from hers, she draws her feet up onto her chair and hugs her knees.

"Frank brought me. He's out in the waiting room."

Her head tilts and curiosity fills her eyes. "Interesting."

Her eye contact is intense, but I keep talking. "How have you been? Have they been treating you okay in here?"

She shrugs and her expression matches the nonchalant gesture. "It is what it is," she says. "What about you? They treating you okay out *there*?"

I shrug like she'd just done. "Most days. Others, I… honestly feel like Mel took me with her when she left."

The smug grin set on Nora's face fades then, but she's still staring.

A question pops into my head, one that was a bit further down on my mental list, but I'd like to ask it now.

"Sorry if this is too forward, and you don't have to answer if you don't want to, but… how'd you end up in here? Last I heard, you'd gotten yourself clean?"

She breathes deep and for the first time since I arrived, her gaze leaves me in favor of staring out the window. For a moment, I think she'll pass on answering.

"I *was* clean. For several months, actually. But… you'd be surprised the lengths someone would go just to quiet their own thoughts," she says, and then adds, "especially after what happened."

"You mean after Mel's death?"

She doesn't answer, just continues staring out the window at other residents walking around the courtyard. I know I need to get her talking again, before she shuts down and this conversation is dead in the water.

"Is it guilt? Is there something you need to get off your chest?"

Her eyes flit back toward me, and she arches a brow. "What is this? You think you're my therapist or something?"

"Not at all. I'm just someone who loved Mel, too. And I'm also someone who carries guilt, wishing I'd done things differently. Wishing I'd done *more*, so... I just thought you might be carrying some of that, too."

She's quiet again, but it's a contemplative silence, so I don't push.

"My one and only regret is that I'm a fool. One who's eternally and unwaveringly loyal," she says. "So, when your sister asked me to keep my mouth shut and pretend it never happened, I stupidly kept my mouth shut and pretended it never happened. But then... that shit just started getting to me, you know? Especially when the memories started coming back."

"What memories?"

Nora blinks at me, and I get the sense she isn't sure she should keep talking, but I need her to keep talking.

"Please, Nora."

Her breathing deepens as she stares, thinking. "At first, the flashes came and went. Then, they turned into nightmares, and then *waking* nightmares. It went on like that until I finally pieced it all together, and that's when I started making my rounds."

My brow tenses. "What does that mean? Making rounds?"

She looks out the window again. "First, I visited Tory the day of Mel's funeral. Then, you, which I'm sure you remember didn't end so well."

I think back on that day she approached me, got in my face, talking trash about my sister while those wounds were still too fresh for me to cope. So, instead of asking what brought on the barrage of insults and name calling aimed at Mel, I reacted by throwing a punch. And then another, and another, until someone pulled me off her, and the cops were called.

"What are you saying?" I ask. "What was behind that?"

She's starting to fidget, which means her nerves have kicked in. "I was desperate," she admits. "Desperate for answers. I just couldn't fathom that your sister took the answer with her to her grave. Without telling a single soul."

"Took *what* to her grave? I don't understand."

My heart's beating wildly and I'm now, literally, on the edge of my seat, waiting for an answer. Waiting for *something*. And when Nora meets my gaze again, tears welling in her eyes, I hold my breath as she answers.

"The name of the person who assaulted us that night."

And now, my heart's stopped beating altogether, trying to comprehend what I'm hearing. Trying to rearrange the few pieces of the story I *thought* I knew, but... I'm so, *so* confused.

"Maybe talking about this will help me cope, so I can finally stop doing this shit to myself," she scoffs, lowering her gaze to the floor.

"You were assaulted, too? By the same person? On the same night?" My voice is thin and quiet, still trying to process what I've heard.

Nora's chest rises when she draws in a deep breath. "Mel had been so paranoid near the end," she says. "She confided in me that she thought someone was following her. Like, everywhere. Being honest, I didn't really believe her, but I never said that out loud because *she* believed it. But then that night, when we were chased through the woods... I guess you could say I became a believer."

She pauses and fishes a box of cigarettes from her pocket, and I wait while she lights up, puffing a thick plume of smoke from her mouth. Her whole body is shaking now, and I realize in this moment that my hands are trembling, too.

"We'd gone to our usual spot to smoke. Which, like I said, was out in the middle of the woods. We heard a couple sticks break, like someone was walking up, but I didn't think much of it. Mel did, though. I was cool just ignoring it and finishing my joint, but she grabbed my hand and made me run with her. So, we ran," she says. "At first, I was just doing it to appease her, but then I turned and... I saw it, too."

"Saw what?"

She barely gets the cigarette to her mouth this time with how she's trembling. "All I could make out was a shadow—tall, fast. And I remember thinking in that moment, *'Holy shit! She wasn't making it up!'* So, we ran faster, but it wasn't enough. It wasn't enough," she repeats, letting her eyes fall closed. "The next thing I remember is being grabbed from behind. Whoever he was, he was strong, and he was prepared."

She needs another break, and I don't push.

"He was choking me, and yelling out for Mel with a play-by-play, taunting her, saying he'd kill me if she didn't show herself. So, using me, he lured her back out into the open," Nora says, and more tears fall. "I wish she'd just taken off, forgotten about me. Because what he did to us was just as bad as death."

Before I can think twice about it, I reach across the table and touch Nora's hand, the contact stops the shaking a little, but she doesn't look at me. She just stares at our linked hands.

"The last thing I remember is a white cloth going over my mouth. Whatever was on it didn't put me all the way out, probably because my tolerance to most substances is high, but I came close. I could see, but I couldn't move. It felt like my entire body was weighed down, pinning me to the soil. He went to Mel then, once I was incapacitated. He was on her and all I could see was his back, but I heard her. Heard her screaming out, heard her ask why he was doing this."

"And you never saw his face?"

She shakes her head. "No. Never. When he was done with Mel, he put her out using the same shit he gave *me*, and then he came back to me. But I couldn't move, I couldn't turn my head to see him. I could just... *feel* him."

She recoils then, pulling her hand free from mine as if human contact is too much for her right now. So, I settle back into my seat, giving her space.

"That asshole just left us there. So, once Mel and I were both conscious and semi-capable, we ran. And when we got close to home, she stopped and made me promise to keep it a secret. And stupid me agreed to that shit because I loved her and didn't want to somehow make this worse for her."

She pauses, and the shaking starts again.

"It wasn't the first time that had happened to me, but until then, I don't think Mel realized the world was such an ugly place. And I guess, on some level, I believed that being silent with her would maybe help her pretend it didn't happen. And if I could somehow shield her from what that night really did to us, how it *changed* us, then I was willing to do that. For *her*," she adds. "But then I became less content as I saw how that night hollowed her out, made her a shell of who she was before, so I started thinking we needed to take a different approach, and if *she* didn't have it in her to go to the cops, then *I* would do it, but she wouldn't give me a name. Then... she was gone, and that answer went with her."

I'm shocked into silence, having to bring myself back to the present and out of a memory that was never mine as I try to envision that night.

"Do you remember anything? Even if it seems small," I add.

"The guy who was following her, it was more than that." Nora sighs while she thinks. "I just wish I hadn't blown that shit off. I just thought she was being paranoid, but I should've listened."

"What else did she tell you?"

"She said there was a car following her. Like, it'd pop up in random places where she was hanging out, she was getting calls from a blocked number, and when she'd pick up, there was no one there. She even said she'd see the guy's silhouette, this dark figure lurking in the shadows. Once, she even ran from it, and she swore he chased her until she made it to a friend's house."

My heart's pounding, partly because I'm imagining the fear my sister must have felt, thinking no one would believe her. But it's also pounding because... these are all experiences I've recently had, too.

"Did she describe the car?"

Nora shakes her head. "Nope. Hell, I'm not even sure it was a car. Could've been a truck or a van for all I know. All that stood out was that she was terrified. The look she'd get when she'd tell me these things... that shit still haunts me in my dreams."

She zones out, and I stare at her, seeing that she genuinely loved my sister. And also seeing how Mel's death has impacted far more lives than I realized.

"I think there's something you should have. Wait here."

My eyes follow Nora when she stands, taking quick strides out of the room. My head reels while she's gone, trying to reestablish how I viewed things. And I'm also more convinced now than ever that whoever was stalking my sister has a new target.

Me.

My eyes flit toward the door when Nora returns, carrying a small shoebox she's decorated with cut-out flowers and skulls drawn with marker. She places it on the table, then slides it across to me.

"These are letters I wrote to Mel. Letters I *still* write to Mel, but the recent ones are more like therapy," she adds. "They're kind of like a diary of our friendship—the shit we got into, the things we talked about. If it will help you find whatever answers you're looking for, I want you to have it. Maybe it'll do you more good than it's done me."

With that, she lowers back into the chair, and when her gaze slips out the window again, I know she's said all she can for today. And I respect that boundary.

Standing from my seat, it feels like one burden has been lifted, only to be replaced by another. And if I'm being honest with myself, I've never felt more like giving up than I do right now.

Chapter 38

Stevie

This helps. Being held while I manage the myriad of emotions today has brought with it.

Micah's solid arms have been my only comfort as my mind's own visions of what Nora and Mel went through plague me. In the past, I've tried to imagine where Mel was assaulted. Tried to imagine what the circumstances were. And now that I've talked to Nora, and I know firsthand the events that led up to that night… it's like trying to process the tragedy all over again.

"I'm here if you want to talk about it," Micah says quietly.

I can only nod, because words escape me at the moment. I don't know how to put into words that my sister was being stalked and didn't think she could tell her own family about it. I don't know how to put into words that she purposely didn't give up the name of her assailant. I don't know how to put into words that I'm now concerned that the same person who was after *her*… is now after *me*.

I rode back with Ash this afternoon, so Frank wouldn't have to rush his visit with Nora. I didn't have much to say then either. I simply sat in silence, clutching the box of letters Nora passed along to me before I left.

The same box that sits on Micah's desk that I can't tear my eyes away from *now,* even though I can't bring myself to read what's inside.

Not yet.

"I'm guessing you found out a few things about your sister that you weren't ready to hear," Micah says, and his words send a tear racing down my cheek, toward his pillow.

Again, I nod.

"I have no idea what this feels like for you, but I do know the pain gets easier to bear," he says. "It's not like that every day. Some days are shit and you feel it all over, in your bones, but... there are days you actually feel like the sun hits your skin. Even if only for a few hours."

More tears spill from my eyes, thinking of how he's spiraled recently, thinking of how seeing me broken and beaten sent him down a dark road. I'm guessing those were some of the days he's speaking of. The ones where the sun is nowhere in sight and all you have are clouds.

My hand lands on his arm, stroking his skin as my lips part.

"I've had these... really, *really* dark thoughts," I admit. "At first, I wanted whoever did this to her to spend the rest of his life in prison, rotting in jail, but I know the law doesn't work that way. He'd only be charged for the assault, even though he's directly the cause of why she's not here anymore."

My jaw tenses at the thought of it, this asshole walking free after a few years. In the big scheme of things, that's little more than a slap on the wrist. A slap on the wrist for costing me *everything.*

"I... want him dead."

It feels awful letting those words leave my mouth. But it also feels like a weight's been lifted off me.

"I know it's wrong to wish death on another human being, but in this case, and in cases *like* this case... death feels fair. A life for a life."

He's quiet after I speak, and for the fraction of a second, I think I've said too much.

"No one who's felt a loss that deep, at the hand of someone else, would find any fault with this."

I breathe deep, and I don't know why I questioned whether this was a safe space to speak freely. None of my guys have a judgmental bone in their body. On any given day, in any given situation, they support me.

Even when *'supporting me'* consists of condoning my dark, murderous thoughts.

"Talk to me about something else. About *anything* else," I say, letting my eyes close when Micah breathes against my neck, sending a wave of comfort through my body. Every movement, his warmth, are reminders that I'm not alone and don't ever have to be again.

"Since you want to change the subject, I guess now's as good a time as any to bring this up."

"Tell me," I say, suddenly intrigued as a weak smile breaks free.

"I'm sure Ash and Vince will probably try to kill me for this, but... I want you in my jersey tomorrow," he says. "It's our first home game and I'd like to see my girl in the stands wearing my number."

My smile grows and I'm grateful he's burned away some of the sadness.

"Seriously?"

"Seriously," he says, placing a kiss to my shoulder right after. "What do you say?"

"I say... yes. But if Vince and Ash ask, tell them I put up a fight."

He chuckles and his chest moves against my back. "Deal."

I stroke his arm and he's quiet now. I realize he's starting to doze when his breathing deepens, and my gaze shifts to Nora's box again. I'm still not sure I'm ready to look inside it, but curiosity is killing me.

Within ten minutes, Micah's in a deep sleep, and I carefully lift his arm from around me. He doesn't stir while I slip out of bed and turn on the light at his desk. I sit, holding the box between my hands.

"Fuck it."

I set the lid aside and take out a letter. It feels heavy as I balance it on my fingertips. Heavier than the sheets of paper sealed inside. I look it over, wondering if there are dates or numbers on the envelopes that might tell me where to start, but they're all blank with one word hand-printed on the outside.

My sister's name.

Mel.

So, I start with this one, opening the seal as I hold my breath. I scan the beginning. Nora states how she's starting to think writing the letters is pointless, knowing she'll never send them. Knowing Mel is no longer around to receive them even if she did. But she says she can't stop ripping sheets of paper from her notebook and writing out her feelings.

She moves on to talk about an incident where she and Mel are hanging out behind Teller Mall—a shopping center that's been shut down and abandoned for at least three years. They got high and just hung out, but Nora got brave. Her eyes locked with Mel's, and she went for it.

She kissed her.

According to Nora, things got weird in the seconds that followed, because Mel kissed her back, but it left Nora feeling like Mel only reciprocated because she didn't want to hurt her feelings. And even though she recalls that as one of the most embarrassing experiences of her life, it brought them closer because Mel never made her feel like an idiot for misreading the signs, never made her feel ashamed for being who she was. Nora cites this as the first time she'd experienced unconditional love from another human being.

Somehow, I'm smiling and wiping tears at the same time. I love that Mel responded that way. What could've ruined their friendship or broken Nora's heart turned into an opportunity for Mel to show Nora what real love looks and feels like.

Even if the romantic aspect of it was only ever one-sided.

I pull out another letter, smiling at the funny story Nora recalls. It's one where she and Mel were feeling adventurous, I guess. They walked out onto a golf course, flirted with a group of old guys, and then stole their golf cart while the guys chased them down.

It does my heart good to imagine Mel smiling, having fun. Nora has a bad rep, and yeah, a lot of what gets spread around is true, but without a doubt she loved my sister. And what's more is she showed Mel how to be free and have fun. Even if the fun sometimes got them into trouble.

I open another letter and unfold it with less care this time. I'd opened the others with fear and hesitation, concerned what I might find inside, but I'm starting to loosen up, realizing these are mostly just a collection of pranks and fond memories. At least, that's what I thought until scrolling to the second paragraph of the new letter.

My lips move as I read Nora's words, depicting an incident where she and Mel got into an argument. She recalls it being mild and short lived, but it stuck with her enough that it made it into this archive.

Context clues make it clear that this incident took place before the assault. The disagreement started when Nora admitted to Mel that, out of concern, she mentioned to the school counselor, Carroll, that Mel thought she was being stalked. Mel blew up at her, which Nora seemed to think was completely irrational when all she wanted to do was help.

But as I skim the remaining details about the fight and how a carefully worded apology from Nora brought the whole thing to an end, I'm questioning whether I might've just found a new lead. Or at least a new avenue to explore.

Tory mentioned that Mel confided in her that she'd been seeing the school counselor, and now Nora mentions that she *also* had spoken with the counselor, Carroll. The name is unfamiliar, which means she wasn't working there when I attended, but that might work to my advantage.

I've got a new plan. And as I cut off the light and slip back into bed with Micah, I know what I'll do next.

First chance I get, I'll visit the high school and attempt to talk to Carroll. She may not be able to help, but one thing's for sure.

She couldn't possibly set me back further than I already am.

Chapter 39

Stevie

"Let's go boys!"

I lower my hands from around my mouth when I'm done screaming, but I'm still on my feet. One of the opposing team's players is in
Micah's face, and Micah gives it right back to him, backing the guy
down as they stand chest-to-chest, yelling.

I focus on the guy's name embossed on the back of his jersey—
Whitlock. We've never met, but I definitely know of him. The first
time I heard that name was at the cabin with the guys. Micah
explained to Tate that he initially targeted me because he thought I
was somehow connected to this guy, but this is honestly the first time
I've ever laid eyes on him.

Vince finally wrangles Micah in, but my nerves are completely
frazzled. This game is far more nerve wracking than the last. Both
because it's the Kings' first home game, and also because they're
playing their rivals—Elmcrest, with this Whitlock guy clearly leading
the pack.

If Tate were here, he'd give me the scoop on why Whitlock and
Micah seem to be at each other's throats, but alas, I'm here alone.
With papers to grade, Tate had to sit this one out, unfortunately. And

to make things worse, I spotted Dahlia seated with her sorority sisters a little while ago.

At the last game, when we spoke, she mentioned something I still haven't quite been able to sort out. Something about pranks she seems to think I'm behind, but my best guess is this is actually the doing of someone *else* she managed to piss off.

In other words, it could be anyone.

Literally.

The hairs on the back of my neck stand up, and I swear someone's watching me. Unable to help myself, I peer over my shoulder again, thinking it's Dahlia, but I'm wrong. She's laughing with a girl from her group, not even paying attention to me. However, as I start to turn, my eyes connect with a guy seated one row behind.

His dark, stylish hair and trimmed beard are the first thing I notice, and then it's his eyes. They're vaguely familiar, but I can't quite place them. He's young-ish, maybe in his late thirties or early forties, and he's wearing a gray and burgundy Kings hoodie with his jeans. So, we're at least on the same side, but I don't know him, which makes his intense stare even weirder.

My heart races, remembering what Nora shared about my sister having a stalker, and at this point, everyone's a suspect. Especially creepy guys who sit right behind me, smiling like a, well… creeper.

I force my eyes forward again, but still feel him watching. So, of course, *my* nosey ass has to check again to see if it's him. And it's definitely him. Feeling on edge, my lips part, and I'm about to ask him what the fuck he's staring at, but before I get the chance…

"I'm sorry for staring," he says. "It's just… I think we're here rooting for the same person."

He lifts his hand and points at my shirt.

"Your jersey. It's my son's."

Well… shit.

My demeanor changes immediately, and I'm sure my face is quite red, too.

"Name's Nate," he says, introducing himself. "Micah might've mentioned me, but then again, maybe not."

He laughs with the joke, but I recall Micah hinting more than once how things with his parents are strained. So, maybe it's not so much a joke after all.

He extends his hand, and I shake it. "Wow, nice meeting you. Micah didn't tell me you'd be here."

"Yeah, he didn't know. Figured I'd let it be a surprise," Nate says, still eyeing me like I'm some sort of mythological creature. "Forgive me for staring. It's just that… Micah hadn't brought up that he's seeing someone."

"Oh… well, it's relatively new, so I'm not surprised you didn't know."

He nods, a friendly smile still curving his lips. And now it makes sense why there was an heir of familiarity about him. Micah's eyes are *his* eyes, but instead of the dark, mysterious brown I'm used to staring into, Nate's are ice blue, contrasting his otherwise dark features.

"I didn't catch your name."

I snap out of the daze that's been brought on by shock. "Oh, sorry. I'm Stevie."

"Well, great! Now we're not strangers anymore." He finishes speaking and points at the seat beside me. "Mind if I join you?"

I glance at the chair, and then back at him. "No not at all."

He gathers his jacket off the armrest, and his drink from the cupholder, then gracefully steps over the back of the seat. He's tall with long limbs just like Micah, so that's something else he inherited from his father. And as Nate settles in beside me, I'm calculating just how awkward this night could get.

Over the next ten minutes, he's mostly quiet, but we do discuss the game from time to time. But when Whitlock shoulder checks Micah, slamming him into the glass enclosure, Nate and I are both on our feet.

"I fucking hate this guy," he grumbles, and I side-eye him, smiling a little.

There's more of him in Micah than I realized.

"This asshole still thinks he's big shit, I see."

301

"Still? You know Whitlock?"

Nate nods. "Unfortunately. He's from the same town as us, so with him having been as involved in hockey as Mic was over the years, we've crossed paths a lot. Not to mention, his father's work and mine intersects a bit, so I've had to deal with *that* asshole for years, too."

"What sort of work do you do?" I ask, still keeping my eyes on the ice while Vince, again, cools Micah down.

"I'm a firefighter."

I'm shocked I've never heard this, seeing as how that's such a cool job, but he and Micah must really not be close. I'm only now realizing how little he's spoken about him.

"Oh. Sounds cool."

Nate shrugs, continuing to eye Whitlock. "It has its perks, and definitely its risks."

"I bet." I nod toward the ice, switching back to our original topic. "So, these two have always had it out for each other? Or is the beef between them recent?"

Nate shakes his head. "It's always been like this. For whatever reason, my son and Leo Whitlock are like oil and water. Even the one or two times they played on the same team, it was still very clear that they hated each other."

"I've met people like that. People whose very existence just... rubs me the wrong way." My immediate thought is of Dahlia, but I resist the urge to turn and glare at her.

"Yeah, I think we all have someone like that. My ex is one of them," Nate jokes as the game moves forward and we lower into our seats.

We're barely settled in when Micah slices through the defense with such quick and precise movements on his skates, it's like he never takes them off and just lives in them day and night. A couple others from the opposing team try to stop him, try to steal the puck, but both fail, and Micah pushes the puck into the net for a goal.

Nate and I shoot out of our seats again, both shouting at the same time while the rest of the crowd goes wild, too. My eyes are glued to Micah, which is why I don't miss when he points at me, and then puts his hand over his heart. As if to say... that was for me.

I match his gesture, placing a hand over my heart as well, feeling how wildly it beats for him. Whitlock catches Micah, then follows his line of sight right to me, but I ignore him, not allowing that smug look on his face to kill the moment.

I'm blushing. No, I can't see the redness spreading over my face, but I feel the heat of it. And when Nate glances over and begins to smile, I'm certain of it.

"And... how long did you say you two have been a thing?"

"I... well... it's only been a couple months," I stammer, which makes Nate's smile broaden.

"Only a couple months and he's already this into you?" Nate chuffs a quiet laugh, shaking his head. "I must say, I've never known my kid to fall for a girl, but he has very clearly fallen for *you*."

His words make my heart skip a beat. In fact, it's drumming beneath my palm where my hand still covers it.

I don't speak again as we lower into our seats. I'm still processing Nate's words as Micah and Whitlock meet center ice for another face-off. Micah's back is to me, but I have an unobstructed view of Whitlock. So, when he flashes a look my way before staring straight ahead again, I don't miss it. Nor do I miss when he smirks, and then mouths something to Micah.

The next thing I know, Micah stands tall, straightening his posture as his voice carries off the ice. I can't make out his words, but his tone is loud and angry. He's on Whitlock again, standing chest to chest as he bumps him hard, but Whitlock gives it right back to him, and Nate and I slowly rise out of our seats, watching it unfold.

There's an argument, and several tense moments while teammates from both sides try to separate them, but it proves to be futile when both guys' pull off their helmets and gloves, then toss them aside. My hands are pressed to my mouth as I helplessly watch things escalate.

"Don't do it, Micah," I whisper to myself, but my words are in vain because he throws a punch and it lands, connecting with Whitlock's jaw.

What happens next is all a blur, a frenzy. It's hard to tell who's fighting and who isn't at this point, but Micah and Whitlock are definitely going at it, exchanging blows. The refs attempt to make their way into the chaos to break it up, but things have gotten out of hand way too quickly.

It takes several seconds for Vince and Ash to pull Micah back while a couple of Whitlock's teammates do the same on their end. But these two are far from calm. Micah's thrashing his arms, trying to break free and finish what he started, hurling a string of insults and foul language at Whitlock, but I'm at least grateful they were able to separate them.

"Next time, save that energy for the play, Locke!" his coach yells out, but Micah doesn't react to being scolded. He seems to have a one-track mind at the moment.

As both guys are hauled off to their respective penalty boxes, Micah rages and has a full meltdown. At first, he tries to hold it in, but then his stick slams the glass as he loses control.

"Should we go down there and, I don't know... do something?"

Nate's eyes are filled with concern, but he shakes his head. "We can't get to him, and with him fired up like that, he wouldn't listen even if we could. You've just gotta let him ride it out."

I've never seen him like this, which leaves me to wonder what the fuck Whitlock said that got Micah so fired up? And why did he look at me like that before he said it?

I'm on edge for the rest of the game, watching as our boys narrowly pull out a win. Tension is still insanely high, so when the teams disburse and head toward the locker rooms, I'm on my feet, headed that way, too.

"It was nice meeting you," I say, turning to Nate in a rush as I start toward the end of the aisle.

"Nice meeting you, too. Maybe we'll catch each other at the next one."

I offer a polite smile and wave, but the moment I turn and head toward the floor, the smile fades. My only thought is to get to Micah and make sure he's okay. Even when the game ended, he was still very visibly upset, and... I'm concerned. Having just seen him fight his way out of the darkness, he's susceptible to succumbing again, falling right back into the same abyss.

So, while I know these things happen, especially in hockey, I still need to know for myself that he's okay.

I reach the locker room and stand outside the doors, pacing. One-by-one, players exit the room, wearing street clothes instead of uniforms now. But there's no sign of Vince, Ash, or Micah.

My nerves are shot as I walk the same short path, glancing up every time the door unlatches, until finally, I can't take anymore. A guy exits, and I grab the knob, glancing both ways before entering a space I'm positive I shouldn't enter, but I'm already inside.

Sounds echo and a blended aroma of sweat and body spray hits my nose. I follow the sound of heated conversation when I recognize the voices, but when I round the corner and stop between two rows of lockers, they fall silent, shocked to see me standing here.

I assumed *my* guys were the only ones still lingering, but I was wrong. Fletcher and Enzo stuck around, too. They all have towels tied around their waists, but only the two I *haven't* seen naked seem shy about it.

My gaze shifts to Micah and I'm filled with concern. His face is as red as a beet, and he's pacing, shoulders heaving as he brims over with unshed rage. Hence the reason his fists are clenched at his sides.

"What happened out there?" I ask, hearing how timid I sound.

Micah doesn't answer, and I'm reminded again that whatever Whitlock said was likely about me. God only knows what sort of lies he's told Micah. All I know is the look on his face is enough that I'm regretting coming in here. What if it's *me* he's angry with? What if—

The thought is erased from my head because Micah's rushing toward me. I'm frozen in place, unsure what's happening or whether I should run or stand in place. I brace myself, fully thinking he's rushing me to yell or cuss me out because of whatever false words were spoken to him during the game, but I'm wrong again.

Instead, hot lips are on mine, and my back is now pressed to a set of lockers. Micah presses against me, his pelvis locked against mine as he grows harder, behaving like there's no one here but us. He reaches behind me and cups my ass, squeezing so hard through my jeans that he nearly lifts me off the ground with the force. I'm not really sure what to do with the others still present.

Micah tears his lips away, but only long enough to issue a brief warning.

"Either leave or watch. I don't give a fuck."

With that, he pulls his towel off, dropping it to the ground before Vince and Ash have a chance to escort the others to another area to change. I step out of my slides, listening to their echoing steps. Next, there's the sound of them putting on their clothes and shoes while Micah removes mine. My jeans, my underwear. I'm still dressed from the waist up, and I note that he smiles when he sees me in his jersey.

But the important part is… he smiled.

Which means whatever darkness had overtaken him on the ice seems to be fading.

I grip his shoulders, still damp from the shower. He lifts me off the ground and my legs cinch around his waist. I'm breathless, panting into our kiss as he reaches between us, aligns himself, and then pushes into me.

The door finally closes, which means we're alone now, and Micah stops holding back, rearing back and slamming into me with brute force. Over and over again. My teeth bite down on his lip, and he smiles again when I accidentally break skin. Either he doesn't *feel* pain, or he enjoys it.

I'm startled out of a daze when I hear footsteps. Footsteps I'm not sure Micah hears. But when a figure darkens the end of the aisleway, and then comes into view, my heart skips a beat.

"Oh, for fuck's sake, Micah. Geez…"

His coach's steps are already headed in the opposite direction as he retreats back to his office, I assume. Micah lets out a quiet laugh, never missing a beat, never losing rhythm.

"Should we stop? Won't he report you?"

Micah's hips don't slow as he continues to plough deep into my pussy, hitting this spot that has my eyes threatening to close.

"Maybe," he answers. "But it'll most likely just cost me extra practice time this week. Either way, you're fucking worth it."

His words—words that make it clear I'm the most important thing right now—have me smiling into our kiss when his tongue plunges into my mouth.

He pummels that spot again and I'm coming, my back slamming the locker as he fucks me harder and with reckless abandon. He slides into me a few more times before squeezing my ass tight again as he empties inside me.

"Fuuuck," he groans, and I grind my hips into him, driving the friction between us through the roof.

The high has barely subsided when his mouth crashes against mine again.

"How the fuck do you do that?"

"Do what?" I breathe, stealing another kiss.

"I can be having a totally shitty day, and then the minute you come around, it's like it all just... disappears," he says, drawing a smile out of me.

I don't know what led up to the fight, and at this point, I don't even care anymore. But I get the sense that he knows I'm here if he needs me.

Just like I'll always be.

Chapter 40

Micah

My phone's been blowing up with texts from the team since we pulled out of the lot. They're badgering us about not coming to tonight's dinner. I'm just about to shove my phone back in my pocket and watch the road as Ash drives, when a *new* text pops up. This one isn't from the guys.

Dad: You played your ass off tonight. I'm proud of you, son.

I take a breath, only now giving any thought to seeing my father seated in the stands. Beside Bird, no less.

Micah: Thanks.

Dad: Don't let that asshole, Whitlock, get to you. He just knows you're a superior player. Always have been. Always will be.

I don't answer, hearing Leo's words echo inside my head. He's got this way of getting to me. Mostly because he knows my secrets, knows what a fuck up I am, so he plays on that shit whenever he can.

Dad: I had the chance to meet your girlfriend. The one you forgot to mention. She seems great.

His words have me glancing into the backseat to have a look at Bird, dozing on Vince's shoulder as Ash's truck rocks her to sleep. I smile, knowing that our fuck session in the locker room is likely the reason she can't keep her eyes open.

Micah: It's pretty new, but glad you like her.

Dad: When you're ready, I'd love to take you two out to grab a bite to eat. It'd be nice to share a meal, nice to talk.

I stare at his message, imagining it, sitting at a table with him, watching as he pretends to be father of the year. No thanks.

Micah: Maybe. I'll let you know.

With that, I put my phone away, ignoring the notification that comes through next, because I have zero intention of taking him up on this offer.

My head hits the seat, and I let my eyes close. Tonight was a bittersweet victory. I loved seeing Whitlock eat shit when his team lost, but I'm also pissed at myself for letting him get under my skin. He's a shit-talker and always has been.

"You've gotta be fucking kidding me."

Even before opening my eyes, I see the glow of blue and red lights brightening the interior of the truck. I turn to glance over my shoulder as Bird and Vince do the same, watching as a cop car pulls close to the bumper. Ash takes his foot off the gas and pulls off to the shoulder as we roll to a stop. He kills the engine, and we all dig our IDs out of our wallets, knowing the routine.

Ash's window lowers and the officer flashes a bright light in on us.

"Evening, folks. License and registration, please."

Ash collects everyone's IDs and hands them over. "Is it okay if I grab the registration from the glove box?"

The officer nods. "Go ahead," he says, watching Ash like a hawk while he grabs the small piece of paper out and hands it to him. "Any idea why I pulled you kids over?"

Ash shrugs. "I wasn't speeding. Are one of my brake lights out?"

"No, we actually got an anonymous call from a young lady who's certain there are drugs and alcohol in this vehicle. Is there anything you need to tell me?"

"What the fuck?" Vince grumbles from the backseat. Just low enough that the cop doesn't hear it.

"Listen, we're no saints," Ash explains, "but the truck is clean and so are we. We haven't even had time to get into anything. We had a game tonight and just pulled out from the arena."

The officer arches a brow. "You boys play hockey?"

Ash nods. "Yes, sir."

"For what school?"

"Bradwyn University."

A proud smile has his face lighting up. "That's my alma mater," he says. "Who'd you guys play tonight?"

"Elmcrest," Ash answers.

"Did you kick their asses?"

Ash smirks. "Yes, sir."

Still smiling, the officer glances down, looking over our IDs again. "I'm gonna let you kids take off. Sounds like a prank to me. Probably those Elmcrest dickheads."

No one will argue with him on that.

"Thank you, officer. We're just heading home," Ash promises.

"Well, for your sake *and* mine, don't party too hard."

He leaves us then, allowing us to start the engine, and then slowly pull back onto the road. At first no one speaks, and I can imagine their wheels are turning just like mine are. But it's Vince who speaks up first.

"That cop was right. This wreaks of Whitlock."

"Abso-fucking-lutely," Ash chimes in, but I don't think they're considering all the facts.

"Maybe. But he said the tip was called in by a woman."

They fall silent again, because, yes, it's possible Leo put one of his puck bunnies up to making the call, but I have a more practical theory.

One that has me circling back to a chick who might have a chip on her shoulder that needs knocking off.

"She's asleep?"

Vince nods, answering my question. "For about twenty minutes now. What's up?"

My eyes dart to the door of the study when Ash walks in, and then a moment later, Enzo joins us, too. It's clear from Vince's expression he's confused by the new addition.

"Now that we're all here, Ash and Vince, I'll bring you two up to speed. I've had Enzo following Whitlock."

Ash's gaze narrows. "Has Whitlock done something you haven't told us about? Do you suspect he had something to do with what happened to Bird?"

I take a breath, not feeling the need to fill him in on what caused the fight. Nor do I think he'd understand that most of what I'm driven by is based on a hunch, so I don't answer in quite the way he's hoping.

"I have reason to believe that. Yes."

He nods and his expression gives nothing away. "And... you didn't think to tell us about this sooner? You didn't think that maybe we could help in some way?"

My gaze shifts to the ground, and I know they won't get why I've mostly dealt with this solo, but my head was so fucked up before now. I wasn't sure what was paranoid delusions and what was real. For a while, nearly *everyone* was a suspect. But after tonight, after Whitlock opened his smart-ass mouth, I'm starting to think I've been looking in the right direction all along.

"I know you're probably both pissed, but I'm letting you in on things now. I can't take back how I handled things before, but at least I'm not hiding anything moving forward."

Vince nudges Ash with his elbow, and Ash breaks his gaze, ending the stare-down he initiated between us.

"Enzo, I'm interested in hearing what you've found."

He sighs. "Well, I haven't reported anything, because I haven't really caught much. With class and practice, I don't exactly watch him around the clock, but for the most part, he seems pretty normal."

Frustration creeps up my spine and feels like it has a chokehold on me.

"Have you seen him go anywhere near Birds work? Seen him anywhere near her mom's house? He'd likely still think she's staying there."

Enzo shakes his head. "No. Nothing suspicious like that. He mostly does his own thing—parties a little, goes to bars on the weekend, hangs out with his teammates, with girls."

My head tilts. "Have any of the girls you've seen him with looked familiar?"

He shrugs, and I give him uninterrupted time to think. "Some of them," he says. "A few have been chicks I've seen pop in and out of the parties. Sorority girls and shit like that."

My heart's racing as a few pieces start to fall together. "What about Dahlia? Is she one of the girls?"

Enzo looks confused for a second, and I'm already reaching for my phone. I go to her sorority's website, and it doesn't take long to pull up photos from this year. All the new pledges have profiles up, so I zoom in on Dahlia's and turn the screen to Enzo.

"Her. Is this one of the girls you've seen him with?"

It doesn't even take a full second for awareness to fill his expression. "This is the one your girl fought at The Hunt, right?"

I give a stiff nod. "It is."

"Yeah, they hang out," he says, causing my pulse to race even more. "She's been to his house a few times, but I have no clue what happens once she gets inside. For all I know, they're just fucking and it's all innocent."

I'm already shaking my head before he's even finished speaking. "Nah, not with these two. Nothing's ever fucking innocent." My gaze shifts to Ash. "I need your keys."

His brow creases with confusion, but before he has the chance to ask what I'm thinking, I'm on my feet and headed toward the door.

"Where the fuck are you going? It's the middle of the night," Vince points out.

"Come with me or don't, but I'm leaving either way."

"What about Bird?" he asks next.

"Text Tate. Tell him we have an emergency and to get here to look after her as soon as he can," I answer, already trudging down the sidewalk, but he's right. Bird's safety is everything right now. "Is your door locked?"

I stop long enough to meet Vince's gaze, and my feet aren't moving again until he nods to confirm. Then, I'm back on my mission.

"What the fuck did Whitlock say to you out on the ice tonight? Is that what has you so fired up?"

Ash's question settles into my thoughts, and I recall the words that made it impossible not to fire my fists on that asshole. I couldn't shake them then, and sure as shit can't shake them now.

"He told me I need to keep an eye on my girl," I tell them. "He said there are threats all around, and I don't even realize it. And with that call to the cops, and now finding out he and Dahlia have been hanging out... I know what I have to do next."

We climb into the truck, and Ash asks one final question as I start the engine. "So, what's the plan?

I throw the truck into reverse, and then meet his gaze. "It's simple. Whatever it takes, whatever it costs... I'm ending this shit. Tonight."

They think I'm insane, and I get it.

After all, I'm the reason we have a terrified girl tied up in the backseat. And in the bed of the truck... supplies.

She hasn't stopped whimpering, trying to speak through the gag in her mouth, but she can scream and cry all she wants. Where we're taking her, no one will hear her anyway.

I feel Ash's eyes on me as I turn off from the main road, but I don't look at him. Mostly, because I don't feel like being judged by someone I consider to be closer to me than my own family. He and Vince both. Speaking of Vince, I peer up into the rearview mirror at him. He's staring off to his right, likely watching Dahlia writhe on the seat. He's not on board with this, and I get it, but...

We've gotta do what we've gotta do.

The truck lurches to a stop and Dahlia gasps. I turn after putting the car in park, taking in the sight of her tear-streaked face. Mascara slides down to the gag, staining the top of it black.

She looks fucking pathetic, which has me smirking.

This should be fun.

"Grab her. I'll get the supplies from the back."

Both Vince and Ash hesitate, but eventually exit the truck in silence. Dahlia squirms as one takes her feet and the other grabs her beneath her arms.

"Where are we taking her?"

I glance up when Vince asks, then nod in the direction I'd like them to stand her up. "Against that tree."

They do as I ask, then I'm on my way over with the rope.

"No, please," she mumbles. There's more, but that's all I can make out through the fabric.

I ignore her plea, knowing she doesn't deserve mercy. Another whimper leaves her when I tie the last rope extra tight, scraping her wrists against the rough tree bark. Then, I finally relieve her of the gag before stepping back.

"What the fuck do you think you're doing?" she sobs.

"What do you mean? We're taking you for a drive. This is just a little pitstop," I answer, smiling when her eyes slip to the ground beside me. Realizing I've got a canister of gasoline sitting there, her gaze floods with terror when she looks up again.

"You're insane!"

I shrug. "When it comes to Stevie, you're abso-fucking-lutely right. Too bad you didn't realize that shit sooner."

There's hatred in her stare. "Why are you doing this? I haven't even *touched* that bitch."

I step closer, gripping her face. "Watch... your fucking... mouth," I warn, and when she sees the sheer, unadulterated crazy behind my eyes, she seems to regret speaking out.

"I'm just confused," she says, sounding far more docile this time. "I haven't done anything to her. I've only seen her, like, twice since she moved out."

"Maybe. But that sure as shit doesn't make you innocent." I let go of her face, taking a few steps back. "What's your business with Leo Whitlock?"

The question has her eyes widening with shock.

"I'm guessing you didn't realize we knew about that."

"It's nothing. We just hang out sometimes. You know, like… hooking up."

She's lying through her fucking teeth, and it doesn't sit well with me. Her breaths are audible now, as she watches me reach toward the gas.

"Wait!"

I pause and straighten again. Maybe she'll finally have something interesting to say.

"What do you want to know? I already told you I haven't had anything to do with Stevie in weeks!"

"Was that you who put in that bullshit call to the cops tonight?"

My question has her eyes slamming closed. "Yes, but—"

"And all the calls to the IFC, reporting our parties, trying to get our frat shut down. Was that you, too?"

"Leo said that if—"

"Leo said what?" I ask. "That if you helped him take us down, he'd teach Stevie a lesson?"

I grab the pack of cigarettes from my pocket while she stammers, and then I light up, staring at her boring-ass face, counting every breath she takes.

"That was the plan, but…"

"But what?" I step closer.

She doesn't answer right away, because she's eyeing me as I stoop down to grab the canister, and then remove the cap. When she doesn't speak, it's just as well, I've got more to say anyway.

"So, let me take a guess at what happened," I begin, pacing as I piece it all together. "Leo knows Stevie's close to us, so when someone blabbed about her kicking your ass, he sought you out, said you two could work together to fuck shit up? That sound about right?"

She rolls her eyes as more tears start to fall. "Yes, but... we only got to *my* end of the bargain," she says. "Yes, I've been making the calls to report your frat, and yes, I called the cops tonight, but that's it! I was supposed to be thinking of what I wanted him to do to her while I finished working on his list."

"List?"

"There was a list of things he wanted me to do to piss you guys off, and when I finished with that, he said he'd make good on our deal and do whatever I asked him to do to Stevie. But the attack had nothing to do with us!"

"So, I'm supposed to believe that two days after you two got into that fight, she's attacked, and that had nothing to do with you whatsoever?"

"I know it's all super hard to believe, but I swear to you! It's just one big coincidence," she explains, but my patience is wearing thin. She realizes this when I lift the canister higher, and then pour it over her head, dousing her from head to toe in gasoline.

"Wait! Stop!" she pleads. "I pulled the plug on my plan because of the threats! I was just following through on my promise to Leo because he said he'd expose me for what I'd done to your frat if I didn't. And we both know my life would've become a living hell if that happened."

She's rambling, but I only heard one part of her entire rant.

"What threats?"

She's panting and isn't answering quickly enough. I take the cigarette from between my lips, eyeing it, imagining how quickly she'd go up in flames if I were to just... drop it.

"Let me explain!"

My eyes slowly shift back to her, but the cigarette's still burning between my fingers. "I'm listening."

"That shit you guys pulled, it... it got to me," she admits. "I was all in to destroy Stevie, even *after* her attack. I didn't give a shit that someone got to her before we did. She was still going to pay."

"Speed this up, or I swear you'll have these entire woods smelling like fresh barbecue," I warn, and her eyes shift to the glowing end of my cigarette again.

"Your plan worked. If you meant to creep me out and make me back down, mission accomplished," she adds. "The phone calls, the pictures taken of me while I was out. And you freaked out my entire house leaving that dead cat on the front porch, but like I said, it worked. I changed my mind after that, thinking I'd *avoid* shit like this, but... fuck! What else do I have to say to convince you?"

I glance toward the guys, and I'm not surprised by the look of confusion on their faces. Because none of what she just described had anything to do with us.

"When did this all start?" I ask.

Dahlia's quietly racking her brain. "Shit, I don't know. Within days of Stevie's attack?"

I move in closer to Vince and Ash. "Thoughts?"

They're both eyeing Dahlia, seemingly less concerned with whether I'm insane for doing all this. Likely because, had I not, had I just let Whitlock's shit slide, we wouldn't have found out about any of this.

"Please, you have to believe me. Yes, I *wanted* to hurt Stevie, or... shit, I don't know... *scare* her. But—"

"Enough. You're useless."

"Wait! What if... what if I can give you info that might matter to you? What if... I can help you in some way?"

My eyes narrow, knowing she's most likely bluffing. But nonetheless, I'm intrigued.

"Talk."

She swallows and then blinks as droplets of gasoline fall from her lashes. "I just know that... Whitlock has something on you. Something that will ruin your life if it gets out. He didn't tell me any details, but... if I were you... I wouldn't push."

I stare at her, feeling like my heart will beat out of my chest.

"She talking about what I *think* she's talking about?" Ash has stepped closer to ask this question just barely louder than a whisper.

I don't respond, because we *both* know the answer to his question is yes.

"Cut her free," I say through gritted teeth, still itching to toss my cigarette at her soaked shirt.

Vince works a knife against her ropes, and once she's loose, I hear *three* sets of feet fall in step behind me. When I stop and turn, meeting her gaze, there's confusion in my eyes.

"Where the fuck do you think you're going?"

Dahlia seems puzzled. "I... I thought we were done here."

"We are. But did you think that meant we were giving you a ride?"

"We're in the middle of nowhere," she scoffs. "I have no idea where I am and you made me leave my phone when you came to the house, remember?"

I shrug, turning forward as I start walking again. "Not my problem. And if I hear that you've spoken a single word about this to anyone, *especially* Whitlock... you'll be hearing from us again. And the next time we come for you, it won't be to ask questions."

And with that statement, I finally hear her steps halt behind us. I load what's left of the gasoline into the back, and we all climb in, staring as Dahlia stands there like a lost dog. The idea of her being stuck out here for hours until she finds a way home brings a smile to my face.

Taking this chance on her brought a few things into perspective. One, we now know she can be eliminated from the list of suspects for Bird's attack. Two, she's also clued us in that someone else might be pulling the strings, someone we maybe haven't even considered yet. And lastly, we've been made aware that Whitlock is still up to his usual ways.

If Dahlia does decide to go back and blab to him, I hope he realizes one thing.

That I'm coming for his ass next.

Chapter 41

Stevie

It's quiet. Too quiet. I startle awake, pushing my hand over to Vince's side of the bed.

Empty.

There's a bit of noise floating up from the first floor, but that's always the case. So, I'm guessing he wasn't tired and stepped out for a bit. But without his body and his heat to keep me company, I'm not all that tired now, either.

I stare at the ceiling, thinking I'll eventually doze, but it's no use. I'm wide awake. The screen of my phone glows when I check the time—just past midnight.

With a sigh, and half a mind to haul Vince back up here just to cuddle with me, I climb out of bed and wander over to his closet, the most recent place I've stashed Nora's letters. I've only gone through half so far, pacing myself so I don't get overwhelmed. But I began this journey into her world with my sister thinking it'd be too much, but honestly? I've only found comfort in her words, seeing Mel through someone else's eyes.

Someone else who loved her.

I click the flashlight icon on my phone, then set it down with the light shining toward the ceiling. It's enough to illuminate the small space where I've settled in, nestled into a corner of Vince's room with my back to the wall. I take out an envelope but don't open it right away. Instead, I smile, tracing the shaded in hearts Nora colored all over with a pink pen.

Popping my finger beneath the flap, I carefully break the seal and then pull the letter free. The penmanship is now familiar, and I've even learned the difference between when Nora wrote angry, and when she wrote with love. This one is the latter.

Another profession of her love for Mel, and with how deeply she felt for her, I'm shocked she was able to hold back. Aside from the one misguided kiss, I've seen no further evidence that she acted on her feelings. Especially as I'm reading about an incident where Mel confided in Nora about her secret boyfriend.

Nora starts out by stating what we *all* say when the person we love loves someone else, that more than anything, she wanted Mel to be happy. And if he was the one who made her happy, then she was fine with that.

Meanwhile, we're never truly fine with it.

But Nora tried, and this letter makes it clear.

My brow furrows when she mentions Mel's tin. Apparently, my sister actually showed it to her, shared the contents, because Nora goes on a rant, complaining about how Mel kept all those keepsakes to commemorate her outings with this mystery guy, but didn't have any such collection of memories dedicated to their friendship. I smile again, wondering how she kept her composure while Mel poured through every item, gushing about whatever date it represented.

I read on and the handwriting turns stiff, rigid, the way it looks when she's writing angry. She's pissed that Mel won't give up this guy's name. She has a feeling it's someone she knows, but can't confirm because Mel played it so close to the cuff with this one. I've said it before, but if my sister didn't want a secret to get out, it would never get out.

I skim to the end of Nora's letter, then replace it in the envelope, and then into the box before setting it aside. My sister's tin is stored in a large box in the corner of the closet, so I crawl over and pull it out into the light. The pale-yellow facing with blue butterflies catches my eye, and I pull it from underneath a stack of t-shirts before sitting flat again.

It's always difficult opening it, because I know Mel was the last to touch it, and because I know these contents were some of her most prized possessions. So, when I pop the top off, I hold my breath, thumbing through the seemingly random items I've only ever looked at twice before.

I stop when I get to the napkin from Dusty's diner, reading Scarlett's name and phone number printed on the back. I feel a sense of peace, knowing that I've at least solved *this* mystery, but I'd love it if I could solve them all. Or at least if I could figure out who Mel's mystery guy is. With how close they seemed to be, he might at least know who she thought was following her.

Or… hell… he could *be* the person who was following her.

A chill races down my spine, and I place the lid back on the tin, but don't close it all the way. On top of the other items sits the receipt from an ice cream date, but I thought I saw something I hadn't noticed before. So, I reopen the container and examine the small slip of paper more closely. And when I do, my heart stops cold in my chest.

Because there it is.

Plain as day.

The smoking gun I'd been looking for all along.

Two scoops of vanilla and two scoops of licorice.

As long as I've lived, I've only known one person on this planet who eats licorice ice cream, and that person… is Maddox.

———

I've never driven so fast in my life. I've never taken *stairs* so fast in my life. But you'd be surprised what you'll do when you're pissed and on a mission.

My fist slams Maddox's door. I don't care that it's the middle of the night, or that I'm probably waking his roommate or even the entire dorm. All that matters to me is that he opens up and gives me some fucking answers.

"Maddox! Bring your ass out here *right* now."

I pound on his door again and it flies open mid-knock. He's standing there, shirtless with a terrible case of bedhead while he rubs his eyes and squints into the brightly lit hallway.

"What the hell, Stevie?"

"What the hell is right," I hiss. In my haste to get over here, I somehow had the presence of mind to grab the receipt, so when words escape me, I dig it out of the pocket of my jeans.

He stares as I flash the incriminating evidence in his face. And I note the exact moment that he's suddenly more awake and keenly aware of having been caught.

"How could you do this to me? You were fucking my sister behind my back?"

"Stevie, it—"

I recoil from his touch when he reaches for me.

"It wasn't like that."

My head cocks to one side. "Oh, so you *weren't* fucking her?"

He sighs, lowering his head in frustration, but how the hell can *he* be frustrated right now? A fresh wave of anger washes over me when something I hadn't thought of until now is suddenly stuck in my head. It's the little tidbit of information Mel's dad shared with me. That she'd been pregnant by whoever she was seeing near the end, but aborted it.

I now know that shithead was the guy I *thought* I could trust. My best friend.

A tear slips down my cheek, and I swipe it away angrily.

"We need to talk," he says, and I couldn't agree more. "But not here."

He peers over his shoulder, into his dark room, and then meets my gaze again. "Give me two minutes to change, and then we'll go somewhere private. And I promise, I'll explain everything."

I stare at him, and for the first time since *ever,* I'm not even sure who he is, not sure I can trust him. This discovery has turned our entire world on its head.

He seems to notice the skepticism in my eyes, and his soften.

"Stevie, I'm still me," he says. "You can trust me."

I hear him, but don't readily believe him. However, I can't pass on this opportunity to *finally* have answers. So, when he disappears inside his room for a moment, and then rejoins me in the hallway, I follow him out of the building, and into his truck, headed God-knows-where in the middle of the night.

I've made up my mind to do this, because I wouldn't be able to live with myself otherwise, knowing I didn't do every possible thing I could to get justice for my sister.

Even if, sometimes, that pursuit leads me straight into chaos.

Or worse… right over the edge of a cliff.

Thank you so much for reading COLD AS ICE! If you'd like to let others know of what you thought of book two in the series, simply visit https://amzn.to/3PhNxGr

GRAB THE NEXT BOOK
Get more of Stevie and her boys.
https://amzn.to/464GF6a

BONUS CONTENT
Click to download a bonus scene, plus much more!

https://mailchi.mp/c87e1fcdb81d/3y84du269s

PATREON
I post chapters live as I write!
Get access to new content months early.
https://www.patreon.com/racheljonas

CONNECTED WORLDS
Explore more books in this world to see how it ties together.
https://www.racheljonasauthor.com/connected-worlds

A NOTE FROM THE AUTHOR

Thank you so much for reading **Cold As Ice,** *Savage Kings of Bradwyn U, Book 2.*

If you have enjoyed entering the world of Bradwyn U, show other readers by leaving a review!

Just visit: Cold As Ice
https://amzn.to/3PhNxGr

Join my readers' group for more news The Shifter Lounge
https://www.facebook.com/groups/141633853243521

and my Newsletter today!
https://us14.list-manage.com/subscribe?u=
73f44054c9dda516cc713aea7&id=ad3ee37cf1

SAVAGE KINGS OF
Bradwyn
U

Love ARCs, random giveaways, and fun bookish conversation? Come
hang out in my Facebook group for readers,
THE SHIFTER LOUNGE!
Can't wait to chat with you :)
https://www.facebook.com/groups/141633853243521

For all feedback and inquiries, email me at author.racheljonas@
gmail.com